The
Alphabet Woods

A Novel

Jenny Poelman

ISBN: 978-1-960146-26-7 (hard cover)
       978-1-960146-27-4 (soft cover)

Edited by: Erika Nein

Published by WARREN Publishing
Charlotte, NC
www.warrenpublishing.net
Printed in the United States

For Ken, my True North.
And for Lindsay, Danica, and Courtney,
my South, West, and East.

Chapter 1

ABRASIONS

Wain. Early March

"Hungry, retard?" Callahan said, not looking at Wain, just standing there, slightly bent, staring into the open fridge, the light spilling out onto his still-damp hair, illuminating the quarter-sized bald spot he tried to cover and the black widow spider tattoo on his calf. Wain could see Mudflap Girl's inked legs peeking out from under the towel around Callahan's neck. *Wain's* towel. His CartWheels towel.

Why wasn't Cal at work? Wain never would have come in the kitchen if he'd known, because the scariest version of his mother's boyfriend was out today. There were others: the Cal who barely tolerated or simply ignored him; the jovial, pretentious Cal (only if other people were around and he wanted to impress them with his fakey fathering skills); but worst by far was the nightmarish monster who appeared with a fourth or fifth drink in hand, looking for ways to torment and terrify.

"Well?" Still not looking. "Do I have to remind you of your manners?"

Wain remained frozen, still as a trapped rabbit. All he could manage was a whisper. "No."

"No, *what*?" Turning slowly, Callahan fixed his penetrating ice-blue eyes on Wain. They were as hard and glittery as the marbles in the counting jar in Wain's first-grade classroom, as terrifying as a massive hand wrapped around his neck, strangling him, stealing his voice.

Carefully, Wain set his CartWheels backpack on a chair and forced the words out. "No, sir," he replied, his voice catching in his throat. It wasn't true. He was home a little early from school and was, as usual, very hungry when he ran through the front door, anticipating a warm hug and a "hey there, honey!" from Callahan's housekeeper, Mrs. Titus.

"No, sir, what? How many times do we have to go *over this*?" Callahan crossed the room and twisted Wain's collar, yanking him upward. "No, sir, *what*?" he said again, emphasizing each word with a vigorous jerk, his contorted face inches from Wain's. Little flecks of spittle flew from his mouth, and he smelled of beer and the skinny cigars he smoked when he was on a binge. "And speak up. No pansy voices in this house."

Wain twisted sideways and raised his hands to his throat, attempting to loosen the fabric cutting into his neck. "No, sir, I'm not hungry," he choked out, in the futile hope that it was the right answer. But he knew that whether he was hungry or not had nothing to do with it. Whatever he said would be wrong. The fuse was already lit and burning, closer and closer to the explosion.

★★★

On the very day Callahan was hired as general manager at the Sojourner Hotel three years prior, he had zeroed in on Wain's beautiful ambitious mama, Angela, who managed the accounts; and in no time at all, she was swept irrevocably downstream in the flash flood of her sophisticated new boss's charm offensive.

"But your *angelic* name is boring," Callahan announced one night at dinner, and she agreed. They made a list of ideas, and then and there, after discarding several options, they settled on Lyric.

"You're gonna love it there, baby. Cal's got a pool," the newly christened Lyric had told Wain when they moved from their apartment to become fresh residents in Callahan's imposing, roomy home in Goldendale Heights, an upscale neighborhood on what she called the rich side of Brookings, Florida. "And now Cal's your new daddy; obviously no one else is doing it."

When it started, Wain had been just under four years old, bright and optimistic as a puppy, still untarnished or cowed by the abrasions to come. "You break my stuff; I break yours," Callahan said in a deceptively calm drawl one afternoon when Wain had accidentally tipped over his cup of milk, which knocked an expensive ashtray from the kitchen table where it shattered on the tiled floor. Placing his martini deliberately on the counter, Callahan lunged forward and snatched Green Kippy from Wain's lap, then flipped open his pocketknife and methodically slashed Wain's very best friend into clumps and slivers. The only witness to the attack, a hysterical little boy, was then commanded to clean up the shredded green chenille and fluffs of white innards, the comforting black button eyes and snubby embroidered nose.

Cradling Green Kippy's remains on a sterile yellow dustpan, Wain was propelled by the back of his collar to the garage where Callahan held the lid open on a wheeled garbage bin, laughing drunkenly as Wain stood on tiptoe watching his short years of trust and security and confidence slide with a final insignificant swish into the dank interior. That was the same day Callahan had added offhandedly, "By the way, baggage, you're not gonna call her *mama* anymore."

When Lyric got home later, she had briefly gone looking for the stuffed dog, but Callahan told her to give it up, that Wain was too big for baby toys anyway; and his mother tucked him in that night acting as though Green Kippy never existed.

From there, it escalated quickly. "Hungry, Wain?" Callahan had asked, way back then, in the kitchen as he was today, with a tray of snacks and drinks waiting on the table. No one else was home.

"Yeah!" Wain answered, reaching for a chip, wary but willing to move past the loss of Green Kippy, excited to share a snack with the man his mama said was his new daddy.

With snake-strike speed, Callahan backhanded Wain across his face—violently enough to throw the stunned little boy to the floor, hard enough to leave a dark V-shaped bruise on his right cheek from the oversized emerald-and-gold ring Cal never took off. (Later, Cal told Lyric that Wain had tripped and hit his face on the corner of the coffee table when they were playing catch. Wain hadn't said a word when his mama scolded him for being clumsy.)

"*Sir*," Callahan had said furiously, twisting his fingers into Wain's hair, enunciating each word with beer breath and a hard upward yank, "you will *always*, in every circumstance, call me *sir*. Got that?"

Trying desperately to stifle his sobs, Wain nodded.

"Say it! YES, SIR. Look at me! Stop your baby bawling. Stop being such a pansy. As long as you're in *my* house, your mama's-boy days are over. Now, we're going to start over. Are. You. Hungry?" And there the seeds of the Hungry Retard Games had germinated and grown into the unthinkable, terrifying suffocation of today.

★★★

Now, almost exactly three years later, Wain stared despairingly at Callahan, feeling like he was going to throw up. "I'm not hungry. Sir," he added quickly.

"Uh-huh. Liar. You just get home from school and you're not hungry? Don't give me that. Admit it. You're hungry. *Admit it.*" Callahan let go of Wain's shirt and flicked his ear, hard, then placed his hand squarely on the boy's chest, shoving him backward. Wain stumbled but caught his balance by grabbing the chair. He kept his head down, breathing shallowly, desperate not to show even a hint of fear.

He could hear Mrs. Titus vacuuming in the living room. Maybe if Wain wished strongly enough, she would pick up the radar beams of his thoughts. *Stop and come in here, come in here, come in here.* But the vacuum cleaner droned on. Not that it would have made any difference. Mrs. Titus was intimidated by Callahan too. Every vacuum line on the carpets had to be perfect, not a speck of dust on the furniture, nothing out of place.

"So, slackwit, guess what." Callahan tossed the words over his shoulder as he strode back to the refrigerator, then turned to stare once more at Wain. "*Look at me.* Your teacher called your mother today. Somebody in this room isn't keeping up with his class. And news flash! It ain't me. You and me, pansy, we need to do some *homework* because you obviously have learned *nothing.*" His icy tone matched his eyes. "But maybe you'd rather have me take away that disgustingly infantile backpack instead." He indicated the chair where Wain had placed his red-and-gray CartWheels backpack. Wain dropped his eyes again, so Callahan couldn't see the panic that rose instantly at the thought of losing his backpack.

"Knew it. Pansy, pansy, pansy," Callahan said in a smug, singsong voice. "Let's see …." He made a smacking noise and dug into the back of the refrigerator. "What is our pansy boy hungry for today? Oooh, what have we here? Is that an ice-cold Biggars Root Beer?" He held up a green-and-white can. "How about this—and this bag of Cheddy Chipsters? Aren't these your favorites? *Why* haven't you eaten them?" He put a finger to his nose and looked theatrically at the ceiling, as if thinking.

Biggars Root Beer and Wain's favorite Cheddy Chipsters, the ones in the yellow-and-red bag—Lyric had bought both treats months ago for a reward Wain had no hope of earning, so they'd sat unconsumed on his designated food shelf, within reach but as inaccessible as if they were behind bars. Wain knew better than to try; he'd learned his lesson when he'd once taken a box of crackers from the pantry without permission. As punishment Cal had forced Wain to curl under the bottom shelf in the pitch-dark pantry for over an hour, confused and terrified, his pinched muscles burning, tamping down the panicked fear he'd suffocate. Lyric, exasperated, said nothing in his defense. After Wain emerged stiffly from the pantry, she sent him to bed without dinner, telling him to leave Callahan's things be and if he was going to be a thief, he deserved what he got. Since then, Wain had been locked in the pantry for various made-up infractions many times, but never for taking food without permission.

From across the kitchen, Callahan pointed with the can of Biggars. "Sit."

Wain sat gingerly on the edge of the nearest chair and put his hands in his lap, between his thighs, trying not to shiver, while Callahan made a show of it, pouring the chips into a clear glass bowl, grabbing a frosty mug from the freezer. He added one more bottle of beer, then arranged it all on a white wooden tray on the table in front of Wain, making obnoxious smacking noises.

"Beer: check. Chips: check. Root beer: check. Frosty mug: check. We're ready!" He said it jovially, as if they were a couple of best buds about to have snacks in front of the TV, watch the game, shoot the bull. "Let's get going on your homework. What's Wain gonna read today?" He opened a drawer in the kitchen desk and took out a thin box, which he also laid on the tray. "I've got the retard cards." He chuckled, ugly and low.

The vacuuming stopped, and Wain heard Mrs. Titus's solid tread as she carried the vacuum up the stairs. Then the noise started up again, farther away. She was working in the bedrooms. His heart sank. His radar beams hadn't worked.

Callahan picked up the tray and pointed with his chin. "Move it. Get that door for me." Wain's ear still stung, but he didn't dare rub it. Callahan would call that being a baby, a pansy, and maybe smack him harder, give him something to cry about. He picked up his backpack and slung it on his shoulder, feeling the reassuring *thunk* of the cars inside.

"Leave that," Callahan said sharply, "unless you want me to Green Kippy it. You can't go anywhere without your security blanket, can you, Linus? You're pathetic. Your *mama*," he said the word in a whiny, high-pitched voice, "thinks so too. You know that, don't you?"

Mutely, Wain slid open the spotless glass door, held it while Callahan walked through, and then stepped out and pushed it back with two fingers, careful not to shut it too hard or touch the glass. Though it was just early March, the afternoon sun was very warm.

Eyes fixed on the spider tattoo, Wain followed Callahan to a table and chairs shaded by an awning between the pool and the house.

Callahan set the tray next to five empty beer bottles, a pack of thin cigars, a lighter, a black ceramic ashtray, and his cell phone, which he glanced at; then as he started typing, he said irritably, "Go get your trunks on. Move it. Time for a swim—or maybe not. Depends on how stu-stu-stupid you are today."

In the bathhouse Wain put on his blue trunks with the pink sharks, then sat trembling, hands clenching the edge of the chair cushion. Callahan popped a chip into his mouth, crunching loudly as he poured root beer into the mug, then took a long drink and delicately dabbed foam off his upper lip with Wain's towel. "Mmmmm! Great root beer and chips. Too bad only people who can *read* are allowed to eat them. But it may be your lucky day. Let's see if you can earn a chip." He set three Cheddy Chipster pieces in a line on the table, then pulled three large cards out of the box he'd taken from the drawer. Leaning back in his chair, Callahan fanned them out, chose one, and held it up. "What's this one? Read it. Five seconds."

Hopeless and panicked, Wain studied the card. There was a big squiggle and a little one just like it, but he saw nothing he could identify.

"Five ... four ... three ... two ... one." Callahan stood up and kicked Wain's chair onto its side, dumping him onto the concrete, then pointed at the card. "*K. K* is for kick. Put that chair back where it belongs. Next time, *you'll* get the kick." He ate one of the three chips he'd laid out, then took another slug of root beer and held up a second card. "Hurry it up. What's this one? I'll give you a hint. *Yank.*"

As Wain picked himself up and righted the chair, he stole a glance up toward the house. Mrs. Titus stood on the master-bedroom balcony with a throw rug in her hand, staring in disbelief. Her dark, shocked eyes met Wain's, instantly understanding his fear and desperation.

Callahan followed Wain's gaze and, without a word, strode into the house.

"That nosy old biddy is gone," he said when he returned. "Get over by the edge of the pool. I need to decide if today's the day I'm going to drown you for good. Wouldn't your mama be sad about that! Better hope you don't choose *D*!" Laughing, he lifted the box of cards in the air like a lit torch and snapped the cap off his sixth beer. "Let the Retard Games begin!"

Chapter 2

MAMA

Lyric pushed open the door to Wain's bedroom and stood silently above his mattress, her familiar scent of perfume and cigarettes mingling with the enticing aromas wafting up the stairs from the kitchen. Wain lay with his back to her, clutching his backpack. He hadn't eaten since lunch at school.

She tucked her hair behind her ears and leaned down. "Hey, baby. How was school today? Did you recognize any letters?"

Wain turned to face her. "I got *x* and little *i*."

Lyric raised her eyebrows disbelievingly. "Without help?"

"No," he admitted reluctantly. "Um, my teacher helped me."

Lyric slapped her thigh. "Ugh! Seriously, Wain? Your teacher has to help you recognize little *i*? It's a simple straight line with a dot over it! I'm *super* tired of dealing with this embarrassment! You knew all your letters in preschool! How are you *dumber* at almost seven than you were at four? Every other kid in your class can read!" She ticked her fingers. "*A. B. C.* How hard is that?" Snatching Wain's backpack from his hands, she shoved it at his face, her navy-blue painted nail tapping insistently on the letter *C* in *CartWheels*. "What's this?"

A deafening, freezing wind screamed through Wain's brain. He knew his mama hated that he couldn't read, but he was locked up inside, like in his nightmares when he saw Callahan coming and tried his hardest to get away, but couldn't make his legs move; he was mired in mud, paralyzed, unable to escape the monster with glaring blue eyes advancing toward him, hand raised, holding up a flash card, saying coldly, "*C* stands for *cut*, retard," ready to press the edge of his pocketknife just so against Wain's arm, or yank on his hair, or hover a lit cigar over Wain's leg, just high enough that its burning tip wouldn't touch the skin if Wain didn't move a muscle. Twenty-six punishments, one for each letter. Wain turned and buried his face in his pillow.

"You're ridiculous," Lyric snapped. She dropped the backpack with an emphatic *thunk* onto the mattress and stood up. "Cal said you didn't earn your snacks, but he still let you go for a swim." She was that bright, glittery, edgy mama she became when she talked about Callahan.

A swim? Cal had pushed Wain into the pool and held him underwater until Wain's lungs almost burst. *D for "dunk."* Wain turned over to face her. "Mama?"

"*Mom*. You're not a baby." Cal's favorite grunge music drifted up the stairs, causing Lyric to glance at her watch and move toward the open door. "I've been up here long enough. Cal is waiting on me for dinner. I hope you thanked him in your nicest way for helping you today."

"Where's my real dad?"

Lyric paused, then turned and said snappishly, "In Texas. You know that. And as far as him being your *real dad*," she sketched air quote marks with her fingers on the last two words, "well, you do look exactly like him, but that's where it ends. So we are *very* lucky that Cal stepped in. You need to try harder to obey. Ugh. No wonder Cal gets impatient with you!"

She clicked out the light and started to leave the room, then stopped in the doorway and said in a more agreeable tone, "Oh, just so you know, I'm still looking for the Black Diamond CartWheel." She'd flipped the switch back to kind mama, rarer all the time. "I know it's the only thing you want for your birthday, so you have two months to start reading, or no Black Diamond for you. Got that?"

Feeling an unfamiliar surge of hope, Wain ignored the last part of her words and said excitedly, "Black Diamond is the hardest one to find! Rico doesn't have it either."

"John Cart has made a gazillion dollars off those little cars," Lyric said petulantly, fiddling with a chandelier earring. "Some people have all the luck. There's gonna come a time that Cal and me will be rich like that."

"Lyric! What's keeping you?" Downstairs, Callahan was getting impatient.

"Coming, Cal!" Lyric called in a lilting voice. She stared dispassionately at her son. "Say your prayers. Pray you start reading if you want that car, and come to think of it, maybe you better start praying you can keep the ones you have. Babies who can't read don't own CartWheels." She smoothed her hair and adjusted her shirt, then pulled the bedroom door shut behind her.

Wain could hear her fading words as she descended the steps: "Wain and I were just talking about how lucky we are to have you."

"Give me a break. I doubt it's unanimous," Wain heard Callahan retort with a harsh laugh. He didn't hear his mother's reply. He slid his hand into his backpack and pressed it onto the solid comfort of his cars, hidden safely inside in their secret place. He was so hungry. He prayed he could keep his cars. He prayed he wouldn't dream.

Chapter 3

PIKE HOUSE

Key. Early May

"I still can't believe you're doing this." Iris removed a stack of plates from a box and crossed the kitchen, slapping them onto a cupboard shelf unnecessarily forcefully, Key thought. Iris hadn't bothered to ask which cupboard would be best, and as a matter of fact, Key would not have chosen that one, but it was easier to switch the dishes around later than to deal with an offended Iris by implying she'd gotten it wrong.

"Why?" Key asked mildly as she transferred a bottle of ketchup from a cooler to the refrigerator, which was brand-new but looked vintage: white, with rounded corners, a horizontal pull handle, and a pullout freezer compartment on the bottom. It fit perfectly into this older home, and she was ridiculously proud of it.

Iris continued clattering the dishes. "Oh, please, Key. You know it won't be the same as living at Sage Pointe. No friends or neighbors for miles, no golf courses that I saw, and you know the book club won't drive all the way out here. Plus, I didn't see anything in York that remotely resembled a coffee shop."

"It's *Troy*," Key replied flatly, well aware Iris was using her phony ignorance act to telegraph her disdain.

"Troy. Whatever." Iris settled onto a nearby chair and perched her glasses on her nose. Rustling in her purse, she pulled out lip gloss and her cell phone, which she glanced at briefly and thumped onto the table, saying irritably, "Not to mention, cell service is terrible out here." Using the toaster as a mirror, she slicked up her lips. "So isolated! It took me over an hour to get here from Porterville, on those two-lane roads. It's *wrong* for you, Key, especially now."

Key hadn't planned for Iris to be there. That morning, as she had joyfully motored south from Porterville to Troy, Iris's call interrupted Key's sing-along to Queen's "I Want to Break Free." When Key answered, Iris told her she was on her way, coming to help for the day. Key had laughed at the irony. *Me too, Freddie Mercury, me too.*

"Hey," Key said now, "I'm not technically *in* Troy. I'm four miles past it, on the edge of civilization. I'll try to get word to you of my well-being now and then when the traveling tinker comes through and can take my ciphered missive." She laughed. Iris did not.

Key sighed and swiped an invisible smudge off a jar of salsa with the hem of her T-shirt. "Iris, literally no one is going to miss my golf game. I'll try to keep up with the book club. I've got a booster coming for better cell service and a landline for internet and TV. I did see a cute café in Troy called Chix on Broadway. They have a sign with three dancing chickens and a neon Espresso sign." She stopped herself. She was babbling. So often in her conversations with Iris over the decade of their friendship, Key felt relegated to a weirdly juvenile status, required to defend any decision not sanctioned by Iris herself. Taking a last pleased look at the tidy arrangement of condiments, she closed the fridge and tucked the bag of ice into the freezer, then leaned against the counter and smiled at her friend. "Fortunately, I don't have to have all the answers right this minute. One day at a time."

Iris waved her hand around the kitchen. "You think that moving here is going to fix things. A new fridge, a little spit and polish on a … a *worn-out* place. But the truth is, you can't run from your problems.

You know I'm a firm believer in facing things head-on, and you are running, Key. You're running."

Key lifted her hands, palms up, shrugging. "I don't see it as running. What was keeping me in my Sage Pointe house? I lived in basically three rooms of eleven. I'm fifty-seven years old. My life lately has been both cataclysmic *and* catatonic. I *need* a change."

Iris stubbornly refused to back down. "But *this*?" she argued, gesturing around the kitchen. "Why not one of those new condos in downtown Porterville? Where you'd actually *have* a life? What can possibly attract you to a … a *backwoods* bohemian redneck area like this?"

Key took a quiet deep breath, blew it out surreptitiously, and ignored her. If Iris refused to understand, no amount of explaining would clarify. She sliced open another box with a steak knife. "Yay! French press! I'll clear a space. I think we've earned a cup of coffee."

★★★

Key had not given one moment's thought to the idea of moving until one early February day three months prior, when, desperate for distractions, she had left her house on another of her spur-of-the-moment bird-photographing expeditions. There was some Freudian explanation, she was sure, for her envious fascination with their feathery freewheeling independence. She had driven for an hour, then trekked around a remote nature preserve for two hours, scouring leafless trees and needled pines with her binoculars for her dream find, the excellently camouflaged eastern screech owl. No luck.

She'd continued south and, outside the small town of Troy (Pop. 5557), turned her Jeep down Pike Road, ignoring a Dead End sign. Moments later, she saw another sign: For Sale by Owner, staked into the ground beside an ancient, dented-up mailbox. Stopping in the middle of the road, Key took one look and fell instantly in love with the subject of the sign: a square, light-gray cottage sitting as confidently as a hat on a queen's head, dominating a slight rise to the west. Set fifty yards back from the road on what looked to be about two acres, the house had an effortless, piquant charm that added to the landscape in the way some houses do, as though it had been welcomed like another jewel in the necklace of trees and shrubs and several large boulders scattered about. It had a whitewashed brick foundation, dark-gray shutters and roof, and a raised porch with three broad redbrick steps that led to a dark-gray door. A real white picket fence framed the sizeable front yard, but it was the porch swing that sealed the deal; Key had always dreamed of having a porch swing. She put the Jeep in reverse, then turned onto the gravel driveway, counting six gracious loblolly pine trees marching to the right along its slight curve. Their rough gray-blue bark and elegant, sweeping branches issued a homespun welcome as she hopped out and knocked on the door. No one was home.

Walk away, she told herself. *You're being whimsical, Key, not practical. Walk away.*

Instead, she had wandered the property, convinced step-by-step this was going to be her next home. The curtains were drawn, so she couldn't see in, but she could tell the cottage had at least two bedrooms, possibly three. Positioned to the north of the house was a sturdy shed with double doors, perfect for storing the lawn mower and whatever of Jeff's tools she decided to keep. Best of all, behind the house was a lush, grassy expanse with an overgrown path sloping easily down to a dry creek bed; and beyond that, acres of trees. A line of four huge oaks guarded the meadow like giant muscled sentinels, silhouetted against the faded late-winter blue of the sky. Key spotted movement between the leathery brown leaves that still clung to their branches and raised her camera in time to capture images of the magnificent red-shouldered hawk that rose crying from one of them. *A bird paradise.*

A clothesline strung between two solid-metal T-shaped posts told another simple, folksy story, emphasized by three ancient wooden clothespins that perched like vintage sparrows on one of the strands. (Clotheslines, even in the backyard, weren't allowed in Sage Pointe.) In the course of the eleven moves Jeff's job with Whitmore Bank had required over the decades of their marriage, Key had toured dozens and dozens of houses; if there was anything she had learned, it was what kind of house constituted a home. And this one was perfect. Just perfect.

Her heart racing, Key tapped the number on the sign into her cell phone, then headed back the way she'd come. She stopped just outside Troy, in the parking lot of Connie V's Fuel Mart and spoke with the daughter of the man who had lived there for decades and recently passed away. The sign had been put up just that day, the woman said; she could meet Key there the next afternoon. It felt meant to be. Key could hardly sleep that night.

The following morning, before she drove back to the house, Key met Iris for coffee at Java U. "It's the craziest thing I've ever done, but I just *know*," she said, scrolling excitedly through the pictures on her camera, hardly believing she'd taken such a huge impulsive step.

Iris merely sipped her sophomore-sized caramel chai latte and listened. When Key finished, she narrowed her eyes and commented, "Well. I don't know what to say. This is the most animated I've seen you in years. Maybe ever."

"Considering everything I've dealt with lately, that's not saying much," Key replied with a laugh.

Iris nodded seriously. "Exactly, Key. You've had far too much trauma recently to make a life-changing decision like this! And you know what they say: don't get emotionally involved with a house before you buy it! Best to wait. I can't go with you today to look at it."

"It's too late for that!" Key laughed. "My heart is already invested! You don't need to come, Iris! I'm much too excited to wait."

She bought the house that day. Despite needing updates and a new roof, Pike House (she already called it that in her mind) brimmed with robust personality. Solid and full of light, it had a generously sized living room and kitchen, three bedrooms, and one bath, with space for another once she did some remodeling. She could see potential everywhere. Most importantly, it was as welcoming as Grandma at the front door.

Now, three intensely busy months later, making her first cup of coffee in the new-to-her kitchen, Key sent a silent prayer of thanks for the bird-hunting foray that had led her to this moment. She hadn't minded the home in Sage Pointe, but it had been Jeff's choice, not hers; and as always, she had deferred to his wishes.

Iris took off her glasses and snapped her handbag shut. "You're lucky your Sage Pointe house sold as quickly as it did."

Key nodded, slowly pouring steaming water into the French press. "I know. But even if it hadn't sold right away, I still would have bought this place."

"You would still have bought this place?" Iris repeated. "Not to be nosy, but you've said nothing about the financial piece of it, to me anyway. Has the insurance payment come through? Is that how you're doing this? With insurance money?"

"It came through quite a while ago." Key left it at that, hoping Iris would get the hint.

"*Really?*" Iris replied, a bit waspishly, "So it's all settled? Including death and dismemberment?"

A familiar prickle of irritation brought color to Key's cheeks as she finished the coffee prep. Iris had always played fast and loose with the boundaries of her privacy, but this was pushing it. However, she merely said, "Yes. It's all settled," and handed Iris a mug of coffee, a section of paper towel for a napkin, and a spoon. "We can talk in the living room."

Iris stirred cream into her cup, then crossed to the living room and sank onto a navy-blue sectional, kicking off her flats and tucking her feet up under her. "This sofa is … attractive. Is it new?"

Key settled across from her into an upholstered off-white leather rocker. "No. It was in our master-suite sitting room for years. So was this chair. They fit better here than anything from the main rooms at Sage Pointe."

Iris nodded. "I wondered. It looks *just* a little dated. The fireplace is … um, homey."

Key beamed. "I know! It burns real wood! I'll need to get a smallish chain saw. I plan to check out some antique stores for accent pieces. I want to create a truly inviting place that reflects *my* tastes. I can't wait to hang sheets on the clothesline. Mow the lawn. Or 'cut the grass,' as they say here."

Iris stared at her disbelievingly. "You're not serious. You moved all this way to hang sheets and *mow a lawn*?"

Key laughed. "Not *only* that, of course, Iris! But I do love to mow the lawn. Jeff was annoyed that I even wanted to. He felt it was out of place for either of us to do it when everyone around us used lawn services. I think he worried that they might think we couldn't afford to have our lawn cared for."

Iris kept her eyes on a fly buzzing frantically from window to window. "And this bothered you why?" she asked.

Such a typically Iris response. Key regarded her thoughtfully. "Why should our choices ever be dictated by worry about what others might think? But, Iris, it's about far more than a lawn or a clothesline! It's about having a life filled with what's important to *me*, with what brings me joy. I've been"—she hesitated, searched for the right words—"cut adrift. Stagnant. Paralyzed. I can feel myself coming a tiny bit more alive here in this wide-open space. It's already been wonderful for my soul."

Iris kept her eyes averted and didn't reply. Except for the insistent buzzing of the fly, the room fell silent.

Key closed her eyes for a moment and took a deep breath. Her emotions the past fifteen months had been colored almost exclusively by a mixed palette of unrelenting, throbbing angry reds and heavy, oppressive gray blues, keeping her tied in knots and torn apart, lethargic all day and sleepless all night. In her grief support group, she'd gained helpful insights into navigating the pitfalls of the painful, unfamiliar path her life had taken. But she had not been completely honest with the group about the scope of her anger and grief, so how could they honestly help? Counseling with Dr. Dwyer had lasted for two sessions before the suggestion arose that she consider taking antidepressants. Key thanked the woman, told her she needed more time to process her thoughts on her own without medical intervention, and never went back. Difficult as it was, she believed facing her uninhibited feelings and raw emotions head-on was essential to healing. And she wanted, very much, to heal.

Now that she'd chosen to move away from Sage Pointe, she was beginning to grasp how desperately she'd longed for a place where she could fully relax and negotiate the complex memories that emerged like uninvited, unsettled specters in every room of the house she'd left behind. Watching the steam rise from her cup, she smiled to herself. Was that a bit of mental fog dissipating in a tiny ray of hope? She already *did* feel distinctively different here, as though these homey, protective walls were the blank slate she would use to write her own story; pages waiting to be filled with adventures yet to come.

Across from her, Iris quickly tapped a text message, then gave an exasperated sigh when the message didn't go through. *That is another issue I need to address,* Key thought. She was at a loss as to how to approach it, but over the past several months, she'd realized she also needed distance from Iris's possessive, overbearing brand of friendship. Well, fifty miles of two-lane road would help.

"You think too much, is what I think." Iris interrupted Key's thoughts. "Okay. So for better or worse, you're here." She set her cup down. "I've got a lot on my plate for the next couple weeks, so I won't be able to come back and help. Let's get this done."

Chapter 4

BIRTHDAY

Wain. Mid-May

The night before his birthday, Wain was in his room lining up his cars on his mattress when he heard shouting.

"Just remember, Lyric, two priors?" Cal bellowed. "I *own* you! Who got you out of some *very* hot water? Who paid the attorney? Who paid the fines?"

"Maybe it's because *I'm* on the front lines, Cal!" Lyric snapped. "*You* owe *me*! You're as much into this as I am! You've never completed your end of the deal! I have to do *everything*!" She almost screamed the last sentence.

"We are going to *stop talking* about this!" Wain heard Callahan yell. "You are literally insane!" He hollered some more and said a really bad word before going into his office and slamming the door.

Wain waited a few moments, then stowed his cars and went to find his mom. She was outside on the pool deck slouched in a lounge chair, knees up, smoking a cigarette, a glass of chardonnay dripping condensation droplets onto the table beside her. Wain thought she looked upset as she tapped quickly on her phone.

He approached her quietly, then asked, "What's the matter, Mom?"

Instantly Lyric sat up straight, dropping her phone facedown onto her lap.

"Wain! I didn't hear you. Come here, baby." Lyric ran a finger under her eyelashes and combined a heavy sigh with the smoke leaving her mouth, then tapped her cigarette out in the ashtray and put her arm lightly around his waist. "Big people stuff. I'm just frustrated about some business that's not going the way it should. Nothing for you to worry about." She let loose of his waist and gave his backpack a little smack, changing the subject. "Remember what I told you! You're to leave this on the kitchen table tomorrow, Wain. You never know what might be in it when we have your pool party tomorrow!"

Because tomorrow was his birthday! And he was going to have a party with just his mama and him and Cal. Wain still wasn't reading, not a single letter, but maybe … "Black Diamond! I have a special slot for it! Want to see?" he asked excitedly, tugging his backpack from his shoulders.

Nice mama vanished. "Seriously? No. We've done it a million times," Lyric replied crossly, picking up her wine. "Not everyone is as into those cars as you are. Go away now. Go!"

Wain leaned over, trying to give her a hug, but Lyric elbowed him back. "Ugh! Stop. You're spilling my wine! Go to bed." She picked up her phone and didn't look at him again. "Leave your backpack on the table. Say your prayers."

The next afternoon, Wain got off the school bus at Peppercorn Avenue and ran toward Callahan's house, distractedly calling goodbye to his friends Mitchell and Rico, his mind full of his birthday celebration. He could hardly wait for his party, to open his backpack and find Black Diamond. Why else would his mama tell him to leave it at home? Maybe she'd even gotten him a cake! Last year on his birthday, she had bought him a single cupcake because she was on a diet and didn't allow sweets in the house.

Mrs. Titus stood outside the front door, watching him run at full speed up the sidewalk. When he reached the top of the steps, she leaned down and wrapped Wain in a hug, her soft arms squishing his face. He squirmed out and looked up at her.

"Did you know today is my birthday?" Wain asked her excitedly. "I'm seven!"

Mrs. Titus shook her head and lifted her eyes to the sky. "Oh, Lord Jesus, give me strength," she said, prayerfully. "Give me strength." With effort, she squatted down and put her hands gently on Wain's upper arms, watching the joy fade from his eyes as she spoke.

"Wain, honey. I've packed you a bag. You're coming home with me."

Chapter 5
PHONE CALL

Key. Mid-May

Exhausted but satisfied, hair still damp from her shower, Key picked up the tray containing her dinner and made her way from the kitchen to the porch swing. Now that the bolts were tightened and she'd added a couple throw pillows, it was her favorite place to sit. The air felt as perfect as a second skin; she was neither hot nor the slightest bit chilled. *North Carolina in May is about as flawless as it gets*, she thought.

Her entire day had been spent in the shed sorting through boxes, reinforcing shelving, installing pegboard, arranging gardening and yard equipment, and organizing Jeff's barely used tools, all of which she'd decided to keep. The back seat of her Jeep was now filled with bags and cartons of unwanted items. She'd find somewhere nearby to consign or donate them.

Over the past two weeks, she had worn out two pairs of rubber gloves, but the gleaming results were worth every moment she'd spent scrubbing Pike House's interior, scraping at least a pint of dried paint off window glass, making minor repairs, and repainting a few extra-grubby walls, even though some of those would be removed in the renovations she had planned.

Her first items on the remodel list were a new roof and a screened deck off the back of the house. She could already see herself relaxing out there under a ceiling fan, admiring the oaks and the expansive view. She'd get contractor recommendations the next time she was at Troy Hardware.

Once she'd tackled the house, for three days she'd concentrated on the front yard—trimming, weeding, spading and hoeing, mixing fertilizer into weary dirt, laying a brick border—sweating more than she had in years and scrubbing her hopelessly grimy fingernails in the shower each night. The pink dogwood in the southeast corner and the peachy azaleas outside the fence had dropped their blooms weeks earlier, their colors replaced by the mounds of perennials in whites, yellows, and purples now dotting the landscape.

How ironic, she thought. *In Sage Pointe, everyone pays for gym memberships and hires landscaping companies.* And here she was toughening up more from a few weeks of hard work than years at the gym had accomplished, all for free. Best of all, whole sections of the days had gone by where, to her relief, her troubled thoughts of Jeff remained in the shadows, barely acknowledged. Now that all the main tasks had been accomplished, she could hardly wait to take a few hours off, to explore the woods and beyond.

Lightning bugs would show up soon, signaling what Key considered true summertime. A noisy, self-important mockingbird darted between the loblolly pines and a fence post; and overhead a thin jet stream melded lazily into a stretchy pink mist of cirrus clouds, reflecting the setting sun. She could feel the day putting itself to bed.

She sipped her iced tea, admiring both the results of her hard work and the colorful layers of the sandwich sitting on the plate on her lap: melted Swiss cheese, mayo, avocado, bacon, lettuce, and tomato stacked between the thick slabs of a buttery grilled ciabatta bun. It sat enticingly beside crisp apple slices and a cup of coleslaw from the tiny deli at the grocery store in Troy.

Just as she was lifting her sandwich to take the first bite, she heard her cell phone ring. *Iris*. Who else would it be? With a tiny groan, Key reluctantly set her plate on the primitive green table she'd moved from the kitchen to the porch and hurried inside. Several missed calls showed on the screen.

"Hi, Iris!"

Reproachfully, Iris exclaimed, "Key! I told Clive that if I didn't get an answer this time, I was getting right into the Lexus and driving out there. *What* are you doing?"

Key's sense of peaceful freedom evaporated a bit. "All is well! I'm on the porch and left my phone in the house. What's up?" She settled back on the swing, smiling widely as a tiny baby bunny, ears twitching, made a tentative, courageous foray into her yard and stopped by a large gray heart-shaped rock Key had recently discovered by the shed door. The rock was a bit of a mystery; she didn't remember seeing it there when she first moved in, but she was too busy to think much about it and had simply admired it, then nestled it among the carpet phlox.

"You'll never guess," Iris burst out. "I had a visitor earlier today. Someone looking for you."

"For *me*?" Key asked, very surprised. "Who was it?" She had no immediate family left, and she and Jeff had relocated so often that for the past decade Key, by her own admission, hadn't put a lot of effort into establishing new friendships. She volunteered for various charities, tended to her part-time job writing greeting-card sentiments for CORE Cards, and came to realize she preferred her own company much of the time anyway. And after this year, except for Iris, even her current crop of acquaintance friends had wilted away, unsure how to handle a situation as delicate as Key's.

Iris crinkled a paper. "A young man. Late twenties, early thirties, maybe? Very good looking I might add. He said his name was Guy Banfield."

"Guy!" Key almost dropped her tea. She set it on the table and switched the phone to speaker. "Guy Banfield? Are you sure?"

"Now how would I know to tell you the name Guy Banfield if he hadn't told me?" Iris's voice filled the space, reasonable but annoyed.

"Who is he, Key? He would give me *no* information, only that he had gone to your old house, and your buyers, the Clements, sent him down to our place because they knew I know you. They're very nice. They—"

"Yes, I met them. I'm glad you like them, Iris. What did Guy want? I can't believe it."

"He asked me for your cell number, which *of course* I would not give him! We agreed I would call and give you his number, and have you call him. Who is he?" Iris asked again.

Key stepped into the house again to grab a pen and paper. "Guy is my only cousin Edie's son. My mother's older sister's daughter's son. So that would make him, um … my second cousin, I think?"

"No." Iris had extensively researched her family's genealogy. "If he's your cousin's child, he's your first cousin once removed. Your second cousin would be your mother's cousin's child."

"You've lost me already!" Key replied, laughing. "So, yes, okay, Guy is my first cousin once removed. His mom was like a sister to me. She and I were very close when we were younger, but our relationship had dwindled into exchanging Christmas cards, which I deeply regret to this day. Sadly, she passed away quite a while ago. I did go to her funeral and saw Guy there. I haven't seen him since. He had this beautiful girl with him." She thought for a moment. "Angela, Angie, something like that."

A heavy sigh wafted into Key's ear. "So back to the topic at hand … the mysterious and handsome Guy wants you to call him," Iris read Key the number. "Oh, one more thing, Key. He asked for you *and* Jeff. I didn't say anything, just told him you'd moved."

"Well, that makes sense. I don't know how he'd know. Thanks, Iris. I very much appreciate you not saying anything." She hung up with Iris and dialed Guy.

Chapter 6

GUY

"Hello, Guy?"

"Key! Is this really you?"

It was wonderful to hear his voice. "Yes! This is the best surprise ever! Where are you?"

"I'm in Porterville, staying at a place called the All Inn. I fly back to Houston tomorrow afternoon, but I wondered if you and Jeff wanted to have breakfast with me? I know it's out of the blue, but I need some … well, I need …"

Some money? Key wondered. What could he possibly need from her?

"Some, I guess I'd say … for lack of a better word, advice," Guy finished.

"Advice!" Key answered, laughing. "Guy, are you sure you've got the right person? Of course I'll drive into Porterville tomorrow! Are you by yourself?"

"Yes, just me."

"I'll be by myself too. Let's see … a couple blocks down the street to the east of your hotel is a great little café called Rooster House. It's got a green metal roof. Does eight work for you?"

"Rooster House, eight o'clock," Guy repeated. "I'll find it. Can't wait to see you, Key!"

Very mysterious, Key thought as they hung up. How old was Guy by now? She did a quick calculation. Thirty-three! It seemed impossible. Maybe he wanted her thoughts on marriage, she thought wryly, taking a buttery, bacony bite. Even after sitting so long, her sandwich tasted wonderful.

Key woke the next morning in plenty of time for the hour-plus drive ahead of her. For the first time in weeks, she scooted hangers along the closet rod, touching clothes she'd had no reason to wear. White capris, a short-sleeved navy-and-white striped tunic top with an anchor design, and dark-brown platform sandals with cork soles provided a surprisingly welcome wardrobe change from the ratty T-shirts, cutoffs, and muddy wellies she'd been wearing for the past few weeks.

She applied a little mascara, pulled her dark-blond hair into a ponytail low on her neck, added a pair of large silver hoop earrings, and briefly studied her reflection. Blue-green eyes in a tanned and much more relaxed (and freckled) face than she remembered seeing in a long time gazed back at her. Grabbing her camera, her purse, and her favorite pair of walking shoes (she knew she'd never last all day in the sandals), she headed to the Jeep, groaning when she opened the back door to put her shoes in and saw the pile of donation items she'd been continually stuffing in there. Well, that was no problem. She would drop them off that afternoon in Porterville.

Entering the crowded, noisy restaurant, Key recognized Guy instantly, seated by the window two booths from the front door, a cup of coffee in his hand, studying the menu. As she paused beside him, he glanced up, looked past her, did a double take, then set down his cup and leapt out of the booth. That smile.

"Key!" He hugged her tightly. "It is so great to see you again!"

Blinking away joyful tears, she hugged him back. "Oh, Guy, you too! I wasn't looking for a short-haired man!" she added with a grin, sliding onto the wooden bench across from him.

Guy laughed and rubbed his neck. "Yeah, lost the man bun, cleaned up a little." With his almost-black hair and his mother's deep-set green eyes and broad smile, Key's first cousin once removed had the kind of effortless good looks that immediately turned heads. He was dressed simply, in a dark-blue T-shirt, khaki shorts, and tan deck shoes.

Key tapped the navy-blue baseball cap sitting on the table. "You're still a Cubs fan, I'm happy to see!"

"Of course! No matter where I live, I take the heat. Now I'm a cub among the astronauts."

"What are you doing now?" Key asked. She couldn't get over how happy she felt, just seeing him across from her. It was like having a lost loved one come to life.

"Oh, I'm still in Houston, with the same company, Citrine Oil. Got my degree online and I'm in management now." The smile hadn't left Guy's face.

"Congratulations!" Key exclaimed. "I'm not surprised." Guy had always been a natural learner, the kind of kid who simply absorbed knowledge. "Do you like it?"

"I love it," he replied. "It's very diverse, a great career path so far, and one that I wouldn't be on if I hadn't started in the oil fields. It's been a good fit."

"Hi, there. Coffee?" A plump, middle-aged waitress in jeans, a red Rooster House logo T-shirt, and a pin that said *Pam* materialized beside the booth and poured Key a cup. "I'll give you a minute to check the menu."

Guy was studying Key, bemused. "Key, you look great! You don't look a bit older than I remember; in fact, you look younger."

"Thanks! I finally acted on my goal to get in shape, and I feel better than I have in decades." She took an appreciative sip of coffee. Dark roast. Rooster House did it right.

"I hope Jeff appreciates your hard work," Guy replied, not looking at her. He made a minuscule adjustment to his watch. "I mean—"

So strange to hear Jeff's name in the present. As though he were ... Key interrupted. "Guy, the woman you talked to last night, my friend Iris, *truly* didn't tell you what's been going on? With me? With Jeff?"

Guy frowned slightly, stealing a glance at her ringless fingers. "To be honest, I didn't give her a chance to say much of anything, just gave her my number when she refused to give me yours, then escaped. So what's up? Divorce? Is that why you moved? And Key, no offense, but if it's divorce, you know I would say it's about time."

He might have cut his hair, but Guy's straightforward nature certainly hadn't changed. Blowing her breath out slowly, regretting the hard turn their conversation was about to take, Key said with a quick nod, "Death, actually. Motorcycle accident."

Guy froze. "*What?* Oh man." He placed his hand for a moment on Key's elbow, his eyes wide and full of concern. "Jeff *died*?"

"Y'all ready to order?" Pam was back, notepad in hand. At her suggestion, they both ordered the Farmer's Market Skillet, a concoction of hash browns, eggs, bacon, and cheese baked in a cast-iron skillet, served with a fluffy biscuit. Judging by the sizzling sounds on tables around them, it was a popular choice.

"Key, a motorcycle wreck? What exactly happened?" Guy asked as Pam refilled their coffees and hurried away. "Is it something you're okay discussing?"

Key nodded. "Oh yes. It was in Miami, a year ago this March. He was in the HOV lane, and a car stalled right in front of him. He rear-ended it going seventy miles an hour and died instantly."

Guy grimaced. "Oh man. Jeff always did love his motorcycles. I'm sorry, Key."

"Thank you. It's been, um, very difficult, but time is helping." She looked down and realized she'd folded her paper napkin into a tiny fat triangle.

"Wow." Guy moved his baseball cap from the table to the seat, then leaned his elbows on the table, holding his coffee. "This is … a lot to take in."

Key felt for him, in the way she'd come to sympathize with anyone who asked about her husband. Over the past fifteen months, most of her conversations about Jeff had awkwardly disintegrated to uncomfortable silences, causing her to feel an inexplicable kind of guilt. No wonder she felt more relaxed at Pike House, where her solitude was not due to the friends who didn't call, where the elephant was out of the room simply because no one else was there to see it.

She said bemusedly, "I know. I'm a *widow*. Such a strange word! Most days, even now, it doesn't seem real."

"How did I not hear about this?" Guy asked, almost to himself.

Key shook her head. "You know, Guy, I had no recent contact information for you, and truly had no idea where you were. I mean, I knew vaguely—oil fields, from our talk at your mom's funeral—and I thought Texas, but it could have been North Dakota or Canada or Bahrain, for all I knew. I'm so sorry that I've lost touch with you since your mom died."

"It's not like I was trying on my end! I've been working all over the place, but Key, you know I would have come to the funeral."

"I know you would have." They watched in silence as outside the window, the driver of a gigantic SUV expertly manipulated his car into an impossibly tiny parallel-parking space. Then Key raised her eyebrows and added with a straight face, "But, Guy, you also know perfectly well that Jeff would never have invited you to his funeral anyway."

Startled, Guy stared at her for a few intense seconds, then burst into huge guffaws. "Key," he said, when he stopped laughing, "have I *ever* told you I'm sorry?"

Key grinned at him. "Nope. Not one single time in twenty-two years!"

Guy sat back and locked his hands behind his head, still smiling widely. "Good. Because I'm really not."

"Come on, Guy," she said, laughing. "You could at least be sorry you ruined Jeff's Thanksgiving."

He frowned. "Hey, no way. He ruined yours. All of ours. Even at that age, I saw it. What a first-class jerk."

Key nodded pensively. "You're absolutely right. But Jeff had this way of making me feel so ... responsible for everything *he* did. I felt like *I* ruined it." She set down her coffee cup and leaned her chin on her fist. Though decades had passed, she still saw it all perfectly.

Key and Jeff had been seated at Thanksgiving dinner at Edie's home in Illinois. Besides Guy, Edie, and Guy's younger sister, Lara, a few other people were around the table. Edie's neighbors, maybe? Key couldn't remember. She did recall how warm the day had been, and that she was wearing a dark-green, sleeveless shift dress that set off her eyes. She felt beautiful.

Jeff had been seated at the end, Key to his left. Guy was across the table, two people down. When it was time for dessert, Edie's famous pumpkin-pecan cheesecake with maple whipped cream, Jeff had loudly asked Edie to make Key's slice extra-small.

"Key's gotta drop the pounds. She doesn't need any more of *this*." Jeff had laughed boisterously, and pinched Key's bare upper arm tightly, moving the skin back and forth.

Mortifying didn't begin to cover it. Cheeks burning, Key yanked her arm away from him, keeping her eyes on the cloth napkin in her lap, willing herself to slide under the table and disappear like a magician's rabbit into a hole in the floor. In their six years of marriage, Jeff had never before humiliated her this way in public, but that day, for reasons she'd never figured out, he'd barely been civil to her and her family. As the entire table sat in stunned silence, unsure how to overwrite Jeff's words or alleviate Key's extreme embarrassment, Guy, eleven years old and smart as a whip, spoke up. "So how much weight do you need to lose, Key?"

"What?" Key, along with the rest of the table, swiveled their heads to now gape at Guy in shock.

But Guy wasn't looking at her. He was glaring at Jeff, his young face scrunched in fury under his mop of dark hair.

"Guy!" Edie, flustered, knowing her son, put her hand up, palm out. "Stop!"

He ignored her. "Looks to me like Key needs to lose, oh, about"— Guy stood up, walked over, and appraised Jeff—"maybe a couple hundred pounds? Yeah, at least. Hey, the sooner the better." Everyone sat like statues as Guy stormed from the room and slammed a door so hard it shook the house.

After another speechless moment, Jeff stood up abruptly, knocking over his chair and declaring furiously, "We're leaving."

The ride back to their hotel with her seething husband was excruciating, a sad prediction of the way Key's relationship with

Edie would ultimately play out. Though it wasn't the last time Jeff or Key ever saw Edie and her children, the effortless camaraderie that had been the hallmark of Key's childhood and Guy's early years was lost. Jeff remained coldly aloof, refusing to even acknowledge Guy, and their visits grew shorter and farther apart until finally they stopped altogether.

And now the adult version of that eleven-year-old was sitting across from her. "My little knight in shining armor," Key said warmly. "I owe you a long-overdue thank-you. How did that comeback pop into your brain? It was classic."

Guy shrugged. "I really don't know. Inspiration by white-hot fury, maybe? I wanted to hurt him like he hurt you. So, Key, tell me genuinely, how are you?"

"I'm doing well, overall. I've come a long, long way since the police first showed up at my door."

"That must have been an unreal shock."

Key nodded. "It's one of those life-changing moments that moves you irrevocably from 'that was then' into 'this is now,' you know? I was working in my home office and had just finished designing a card, superhappy with the result. It was a little picture of a sandwich and the words, 'Want to have LNCH?' on the front, and then inside, 'Because I've been missing U.' It's been one of my contract company's bestsellers."

Guy smiled. "Nice. Very 'you.' No pun intended."

She took a sip of coffee. "When the doorbell rang and I saw two police officers outside, I was a little curious, but never imagined their presence had anything to do with me." A dish shattered loudly in the restaurant kitchen, making them both jump as she continued. "Until they came in and told me what had happened. I remember saying, 'Miami? Are you *sure* it's the correct Jeff North? Because my husband is in Daytona.' But it was Jeff, and it was Miami. I didn't know anything about that part of the trip." It was as far as she wanted to go with that piece of the story.

Guy shook his head. "One instant and everything changes. It's hard to know what to say except I'm truly sorry for all you've been through for the past year, Key."

She smiled. "Thanks. I'd describe myself as walking on a shadowy path where only the next couple steps are illuminated."

"What's your life like now?" Guy asked curiously.

"Well, my new place outside the tiny town of Troy, which I absolutely love, has given me as much change and busywork as I can handle, but better than that, it's been wonderful for my heart. The truth is, Guy, that I had essentially lost myself long before Jeff died. I had become a lonely, disillusioned person who went through my days with very little passion or enthusiasm about life."

Guy frowned, pushing the salt-and-pepper shakers to the middle of the table. "That is so *not* the Key I knew. Jeff did that to you."

She gave him another affectionate smile. Even as a kid, he'd been a loyal friend. "Well, yes and no, Guy. And really, mostly *no*. I take full responsibility for the parts I allowed to happen. In truth, with Jeff's death, I've felt as much anger as I have grief. Most of my adult life was wasted on a man who wasn't crazy about being married to me but didn't care enough to divorce me. What is it they say? Indifference is the opposite of love? Jeff was the very definition of indifferent."

"Key, I would have come. For *you*," Guy said once again, flashing a friendly smile at Pam, who had refilled their coffees.

"Thank you. I brought his ashes back from Florida and somehow got a memorial service pulled together and his ashes interred. I was shocked at how many people shared Jeff's life; people I'd never met. We had grown so far apart." Key absentmindedly moved the salt several inches away from the pepper. "It's crazy, isn't it, how you can live for decades with someone and not *really* know them? People get estranged for one reason or another: maybe marry someone who doesn't like their family, hold grudges, drink too much, fight over money, get too busy, live far away ... and important, meaningful pieces of our lives don't get tended to, so they fade. And parents—especially mothers— are so often the ones who hold the family together. When they're gone, it's so easy to ... I don't know ... get on with it." She moved the salt back beside the pepper. "Not real profound, but it's the truth. And so ironic in this era when we have a thousand ways to stay in touch."

"Funny you should say that," Guy said pensively. "This whole thing about Jeff's death has thrown me completely off, and I am sitting here wondering if it's an answer in and of itself. That it means I shouldn't ask you for the, um, advice."

Exactly the track she had been expecting. By discussing Jeff's death, she had trumped him. "Guy, you surely didn't go to the trouble of coming all the way from Texas to North Carolina to hunt me down and ask about something unimportant!"

"No, it's actually extremely important." He scratched the back of his neck, as though the thought of what he needed to say made him itchy.

"Are you getting married?"

He chuckled. "No, no, nothing like that. I mean, I do have a girlfriend, Jessica. We're semiserious, I guess, but both very busy .... I'm thirty-three. You'd think I'd know whether she's the one. But I don't."

Key nodded, feeling a little embarrassed. She'd just inadvertently given Guy several more reasons to question the decision to marry. "I understand. So, Jessica, not Angie, the really beautiful girlfriend I remember meeting at your mom's funeral."

Guy's eyes widened. "Holy cow. I totally forgot you would have met Angie. This is getting weirder and weirder. Just for the record, Angie doesn't go by Angie anymore; she changed her name a few years ago to Lyric."

Key couldn't help the puzzled laugh that escaped. "*Lyric?* Why?"

"Who knows?" Guy rolled his eyes and shifted a little in the seat. "She always did have this side to her—how would I put it— discontented with the status quo. She believed she deserved more than being 'Angie from California,' and my oil worker's salary definitely didn't make the cut."

"She sounds confused."

Guy gave a short laugh. "That's one way to put it."

"Here you go!" Pam placed wooden cutting boards on the table containing cast-iron skillets that sizzled enticingly next to huge fluffy biscuits.

"This is going to last me the whole day!" Key was sure she was looking at her dinner for that evening too. She sliced the biscuit and put a pat of butter and a squeeze of Rooster House's hot honey on each half.

They caught up on simpler issues as they ate, mostly reminiscing about people they both knew, including Guy's twice-divorced younger sister, Lara, who lived in Chicago and tended bar at an upscale private club. Around them, conversations hummed, low and slow, unhurried, as thick as the humid Southern air. There was lots of laughter. It was one of the things Key loved most about the people of North Carolina: the innate civility, the friendliness and goodness of the people around her, not to mention their wonderful way of talking.

"You know," Key said, as she surveyed the room, "you can't really hear the words, but you can hear the Southern accent in the hum of the conversation."

"Exactly. I hear it in Texas too. But it's a different accent here." Guy, like Key and his mother Edie, had grown up in central Illinois.

"Y'all doin' good?" Pam came by again with the coffee pot.

"No more coffee for me, but I'll need a to-go box, please!" Key told her, then studied her first cousin once removed, who was obviously enjoying his breakfast as much as she was hers. "So, Guy. What is it you want to ask me? I can't promise my advice will be any good, but I can try."

He placed his fork and knife perfectly across the center of his empty plate, then cleared his throat and looked directly at her. "Okay. Well, here it is. Uh, I have a son."

Key pressed her hand to her lips to stop her mouth from dropping open, hastily swallowing the last bit of honey-drenched biscuit. "Guy! You have a *little boy*?" she exclaimed when she could talk.

"Wain Owen Banfield. He's Angie—Lyric's—boy. He lives in central Florida."

"How old is he?" Key asked. She couldn't believe Guy had taken so long to bring the conversation around to something this monumental, but almost simultaneously she realized their entire conversation so far had been about Jeff's death.

Guy thought for a moment too long. "He just turned seven. This month. May 17."

He doesn't know his own son's age instantly? "Just a few days ago," Key replied.

"Yes." Guy cleared his throat. "I'm not proud of what I'm going to tell you, but I want to be very clear with you about everything." He toyed with his fork, putting it down, picking it up, then putting it down again.

"Okay ...?" She still couldn't imagine his need for her advice.

"I haven't actually seen Wain since he was three years old. I tried, for a while. Then Angie—I mean, *Lyric*—met this guy in Florida, Gary Callahan, and flat out told me not to come anymore, that it would confuse Wain if I kept visiting. I was angry at first, of course! What gave her the right to decide that? Wain is a supercute kid, very sweet, but frankly ..." Guy stopped and waved his hand as if to ward off Key's upcoming disapproval. "Key, this is going to sound terrible, but it was almost a relief in a way. She resented every minute I was there, so the visits were tense and uncomfortable and had to be very confusing to Wain."

"That seems unfair. Why would Wain's mom resent you?" Key asked curiously. Did Guy need legal advice? she wondered. But why ask her?

"It *is* unfair. But I didn't fight her. I stopped going. What you said about relationships fading—that's exactly what happened. I got busy, and Lyric and Wain moved in with this Callahan guy, and it all kind of ... faded. I do send a generous child-support check every month, but most days, it's been pretty easy to forget he exists ... as harsh as that sounds." He closed his eyes for a moment and shook his head.

It did sound harsh. "Do you have a picture of Wain?" Key asked.

He glanced up at her with a half smile, half grimace. "Ah, no, I don't. I have some old ones on a cloud somewhere, but I haven't even gotten a picture in probably over two years."

Which most likely means he hasn't asked. Key hoped she was hiding her dismay. "What about social media?"

Guy snorted. "Never in a million years would I be on social media. And my girlfriend, Jess, used to look now and then but never found either Angie *or* Lyric."

"Guy, your mother would have *loved* being a grandma."

He nodded. "Yeah. Yeah, I know. Talk about unfair. But there's more to this story."

Key pointed out the window. "Okay. Let's go for a walk, free up this table for the hungry masses waiting. There's a park with a walking path just down the street."

"Sounds great." Guy picked up the receipt, grabbed his cap, and slid out of the booth. "My treat."

"Thank you, Guy! Let me just swap my shoes and stash my to-go box in my car, and I'll meet you at the corner."

Chapter 7

THE REQUEST

"So tell me what's up with Wain and his mom," Key said as they started for the park. Porterville was waking up. Everyone they met along the way smiled at them or said good morning. Key noticed the women noticing Guy. *Some things never change*, she thought, amused.

Guy walked quickly, paying no attention to other people or to their surroundings. "The short answer: it's a mess. Are you ready for this, Key? Lyric and her boyfriend, Gary Callahan, have been arrested. They're both in jail."

"*What?*" Key jerked her head to gape at him, and Guy unceremoniously yanked her sideways just in time to save her from smacking headlong into a sandwich board menu. "No way! Arrested for what?" Before he could answer, she asked, "Where's Wain?"

"He's staying with the housekeeper, a woman named Mayetta Titus," Guy replied. "She got my number from Lyric and called me. She knew both Lyric and the boyfriend were in jail but had very few other details. A very sweet lady, and you can tell she loves Wain, but of course his staying with her is temporary. Then Lyric called me and said I needed to come get Wain. I could not figure out why she couldn't make bail until she finally admitted that she can't— this is her *third* arrest! I mean, I knew she was *ambitious*—I'd even go further and describe her as greedy—but *criminal?*" He shook his head. "The other two times were lesser types of ID theft, and she was bailed out within hours by this Callahan guy, who, by the way, happens to be her boss as well as her boyfriend. This time, though, the charges are far more serious because they obviously teamed up to steal from the hotel where they both work, and it's a *lot* of money. Apparently, it's been ongoing for at least a couple years."

Key managed to overcome her stunned silence to say, "This is unreal, Guy! Your poor little boy!" They had reached the park.

Guy nodded. "Yeah, it's got to be devastating for him. Lyric was sobbing the whole time we talked; she *never* expected she'd have to stay in jail. I'm truly shocked; up until now, I thought she was a great mom. I never had reason to believe otherwise!"

"Wow," Key said faintly, still at a complete loss for words. She wasn't sure the definition of "great mom" included being a three-time thief, but what did she know? She moved aside for a huffing middle-aged man, then two brightly clad fast-walking women deep in conversation. At any other time, she would have loved sharing the energy of a day at the park with like-minded strangers, but today all she could think about was a confused little boy whose one involved parent was in jail.

Guy reached up and plucked a large leaf from a low-hanging branch. "And as if all this isn't bad enough, the arrests happened on the morning of Wain's seventh birthday. He still doesn't know his mom's in jail. He thinks she's on a trip."

"Oh *no*. This is heartbreaking! When will you see Wain?" Key couldn't believe Guy wasn't in Florida already.

Guy gestured with his leaf to a nearby picnic table. "Could we talk face-to-face?" They sat down across from one another. While he gathered his thoughts, leaning his forearms on the table and staring unseeingly at the leaf, Key studied his watch. It was custom made and looked expensive, with a rim of burnished silver connected to a dark-brown leather strap. An understated logo on the watch face told her more: a thin golden *C* encircling a broader black *O*. Citrine Oil. Edie's son had definitely come up in the world.

Guy began shredding the leaf, sprinkling tiny green confetti on the battered wood tabletop; then, drumming his two ring fingers, he said, "Here's the deal: the hotel owners are throwing the book at them. And given her previous arrests and the severity of this offense, Lyric will probably do significant prison time, possibly several years. Since I never waived my parental rights, I've been given custody of Wain." He paused, looking Key straight in the eyes. "I've come to ask if you will take care of him for me."

Chapter 8

EDIE

If Guy had asked her to store his captive yeti in a cage in her living room, Key could not have been more shocked. She stared at him. "Did I hear you right? You want me to take care of your little boy? Do you want me to move to Texas?"

"Ahhhh, crap." Guy rubbed his chin. "No. The fact is, Key, I'm in the process of moving to the Middle East, to the UAE. It's been in the works for several months."

Since breakfast, Key thought, it seemed her eyes had stayed in perpetual "wide" mode. "Seriously? As in, the United Arab Emirates?"

"Yes. Dubai."

It was impossible to take it all in. Jeff's death, the move to Pike House, and now this lightning bolt of a request. Her life lately had become a series of startling swings into uncharted territory. "Could you, um, take Wain with you?"

"No. I can't take him. It's out of the question." Guy compressed his lips and pushed the leaf confetti into a straight line.

She put her hand over her heart. "But *me*? Surely Wain has other, closer relatives ... what about your sister?"

He barked out a laugh. "Key! You know Lara! She's as immature and scatterbrained as ever, and I'm pretty sure she's gone through all the money Mom left her. I wouldn't trust her to raise a cat. Well, she has two cats," he added, randomly. "But you know Lara."

Key nodded. It sounded like not much had changed there. Lara's irresponsibility had always troubled Edie. "What about Lyric's family?"

Guy shook his head. The confetti morphed into three small piles. "Lyric is estranged from her one sister. They had a falling out before I ever met her. And Lyric's mother is also not an option."

"What's wrong with the grandma?" Key asked, intrigued.

"I doubt she'd appreciate the title," Guy replied. "Lyric's mother lives a very full life in a senior community in California and has never shown an interest in being a grandmother. I know, I know." He held up his hand, adding ruefully, "Said the absentee father who plans to leave the country."

"Excuse me." A young woman in jogging clothes approached, pushing a stroller. "Do you mind if I sit here with you? I need to feed my baby girl." Not waiting for an answer, she extracted her squalling infant, then sat down and immediately raised her shirt.

They stood. "It's all yours," Guy replied, heading back to the path.

"Your baby is darling," Key told her and got a brilliant "yes, I know" smile in return.

Dodging a leash and the energetic black dachshund attached to it, Key caught up to Guy. "Let's walk the loop," she suggested. "And please forgive my bluntness, but why *can't* you turn down this promotion and take Wain to live with you in Texas?"

"It's simply not an option. I'll be based in Dubai on and off for the next three years, but my schedule is never stable. It's not the kind of job that can incorporate a kid." Guy walked quickly, staring straight ahead, his eyes hidden under the shade of his Cubs hat.

"So you'd say your career is on the line?" Key asked, struggling to grasp his thought process.

He glanced at her briefly. "It is, Key. I've worked for *years* to get to this point, and a boatload of people have sunk huge amounts of time and money into my career, expecting me to fulfill my end of the bargain. Because Lyric locked me out of their lives, I honestly never had reason to consider that Wain would ever be a factor. Yes, I allowed it, but she made it very clear that she didn't want me around. I know it's as selfish an act as you've ever seen, but the bottom line is, if I took Wain, I know I'd resent him. I'd resent giving up everything I've worked so hard to achieve."

That's the perfect definition of brutal honesty, Key thought. So typical of Guy. They walked in silence for a few minutes. Finally, she said sympathetically, "It's very complex. And to a large degree, I do understand, Guy." She did. In her experience, forced or resentful relationships created a whole subset of unpleasant issues that oozed into every crevice of life. She tried again. "Let's say you did decide to stay and take Wain in. There's a good chance you'd end up loving your son with all your heart and not minding that you gave up this job."

"It's possible," Guy replied tersely, "but unlikely. I know myself. And Jessica has told me in no uncertain terms that she doesn't want kids. So if I took Wain in, that would be the end of that relationship as well." He groaned and plopped down on a green metal bench, burying his head in his hands. "What a huge, unbelievable mess."

It felt like a good time to let them both gather their thoughts. Key sat next to him and put her hand on his back, feeling the sun's warmth on her capris and Guy's shirt. She was floored by his request; she had absolutely no experience in child-rearing because she had never been able to have children. In that respect, she and Jeff had lived a life very different from most of their friends and family.

In the middle of the loop, oblivious to the fact that they were underscoring the jarring dissonance of Guy's words, a young family had settled themselves onto a large rust-colored blanket for a picnic. While the father nestled a baby boy on his lap, the mother unwrapped a sandwich for the toddler girl sitting next to her. Key watched as the father handed the baby to the mother, saying something. The mother took a long sniff around the legs of the baby's diaper, shook her head no, and kissed his chubby foot before plopping him affectionately onto her outstretched legs. The father laughed and turned to the girl, who offered him a bite of her sandwich. They made it look so easy, so natural.

And beside Key sat a man—her own beloved relative—who didn't want to raise his son. Shouldn't it be instinctual? Key had known mothers *and* fathers who became consumed with their children's well-being, almost to a point where they lost themselves along the way. Jogger Mom back there at the table would probably not unselfconsciously raise her shirt in public, but to feed her child she would. The woman who sniffed the baby's diaper would no doubt have been repulsed by the very same action before she had children. Parenthood volcanically changed people. Most people, anyway.

Guy spoke up. "Where were we in all this?"

"A huge, unbelievable mess is what I believe you said. But you seem to have made up your mind."

Guy stared down at his hands. "I have." He said it quietly. "I know what the happily-ever-after answer is, but I can't see my way clear to letting down a whole bunch of people who've put their faith in me. I can't tell you how much I've missed my mother the past few days. She would have adored Wain." He looked back up at Key, smiling. "She always said you were the little sister she never had."

Dear, dear Edie. Key sat silently, watching the young family, her hand still on Guy's back. "Your mom was so wonderful to me when we were kids," she said, after a bit. "She didn't have to put up with someone seven years younger trailing around after her, but she did, and she never, ever seemed to mind."

Key could see Edie's room perfectly, the two of them sprawled on the double bed, feet hanging off the pink-and-orange-striped comforter, ten-year-old Key absorbing Edie's every word, WLS radio playing Top-40 music, the orange-flowered wallpaper, the white dresser with gold trim, the mirror with the mysterious and ever-expanding dark spot on the top-left corner, the beat-up bulletin board with pictures of heartthrob movie stars torn out of magazines, and curiously, a guide to clouds, left over from an earth-science class Edie had taken in eighth grade. Stratus. Cumulous. Cumulonimbus. Cirrus. "I love clouds," Edie had told Key when she asked, "especially cirrus."

"She taught me how to recognize different cloud types," Key said to Guy. He was watching the young family too. The parents sipped drinks, baby between them, keeping an eagle eye on the little girl, who was chasing something Key couldn't see. Maybe children saw things other people didn't.

He smiled. "Yeah, me too." He scanned the sky, squinting, and pointed. "Cirrus. Right over there." It felt good to laugh.

"What happened, Key?" Guy asked seriously. "My mom loved you so much, and you just sort of melted away. I know she missed you forever."

Key's eyes filled with tears. It was one of her biggest regrets. "I know. It breaks my heart to think of how I hurt her, the time I wasted. But the truth is, your mom and I lost touch mostly because she flat out didn't like Jeff."

"Yeah, well, none of us did," Guy declared bluntly, shrugging his shoulders.

In spite of herself, Key laughed out loud. "Don't sugarcoat it, Guy! Before Jeff and I got married, your gutsy, caring mother invited me to lunch and tried to talk some sense into me. She said I wasn't myself around Jeff and that he didn't value me. Her exact words were, 'You are invisible to him.' So Edie."

"So Edie," Guy repeated, appreciatively. "She was always spot-on in her character assessments. If Mom had met Ang—I mean, Lyric—I have a feeling I'd have seen her differently long before she ghosted me."

Key nodded. "Probably so. And where Jeff was concerned, your mom was a good judge of character. I so regret not trying harder to mend the fences with her before she died. But in all honesty, I knew she'd instantly sense my unhappiness. It was easier to stay away."

Guy regarded her questioningly. "Why'd you stay married to Jeff, if you don't mind my asking?"

"He was …" Key hesitated, then started over. "Jeff lived his life wanting to be perceived in a certain way, and I lived my life trying to meet his standards. He'd freeze me out; I would double down, try harder to please him, and end up feeling rejected and resentful, but with absolutely no idea who I was without him. It was an excruciating, wasteful way to live, and sadly, it has taken his *death* for that to become clear to me." Though it felt wonderful to finally speak so honestly, all the familiar emotions of the past fifteen months rushed to the surface, threatening to overwhelm her. If only she had talked to Edie, really talked to her, long ago. What she wouldn't give for a good long chat right now. She stood up. They couldn't both fall apart here on this bench. "Guy, listen. About Wain …"

"No, Key, stop." He stood, too, and adjusted his cap. "I can't just appear out of nowhere and ask you, especially now that I know everything you've been through, to take on a seven-year-old that you've never met—a kid that in reality, *I* barely know. I don't know what I was thinking."

They started the walk back to the restaurant. "But, Guy, I *don't* think this should be the end of the conversation," Key protested. "It's been a *lot* to take in. I can't say yes *or* no right at this moment. Will you give me a couple days?"

"Of course, Key!" Guy gave her a quick sideways hug. "It's a huge decision, a shocking bolt out of the blue. I appreciate your even thinking about it."

They strolled along, Guy's arm draped easily over her shoulders. "Tell me about Wain. What are seven-year-old boys all about these days?" Key asked.

"To be honest, I have no idea. He's got my dark hair, and his eyes are bluer than mine, come to think of it, more like yours and my mom's. Kind of green blue. Cute kid. He's supersmart, kinda shy, pretty artistic. Way back, Lyric used to send me his little-kid hieroglyphics now and then."

An unthinkable loss for Edie. "What will you do if I decide I can't take him?"

They passed the oil-change garage, where an elderly man in greasy coveralls handed them each a coupon. "Running a special this week. Free wiper blades when you do a full service." He gave Key a friendly wink.

She couldn't help smiling back. "Thank you."

Guy handed Key his coupon. "I don't know. Dubai is nonnegotiable. Boarding school, maybe."

"Boarding school? Seriously?" That possibility had never entered Key's mind.

Guy shrugged. "It's a last resort, of course, but boarding school is an option for thousands of parents, and their kids turn out just fine."

"True," she admitted. As far as she knew, she hadn't ever met anyone who'd gone to boarding school, but of course he was right. "Will you visit him before you go?"

Guy said slowly, "I've considered it, but no. I don't want to show up in his life for a brief second, confuse the heck out of him, then disappear. It wouldn't be fair."

"To you or to him?" Key asked, pushing the "Walk" button.

Guy thought. "To both?" he asked, then added, "But mostly to him."

"I have one last question," Key said, as they crossed the street. "I know how virulently you disliked Jeff … and you had no idea he'd died. You truly would have been okay with him helping to raise your son?"

Guy laughed ruefully. "Believe me, I struggled with that before I came looking for you," he replied. "But, Key, don't sell yourself short. I love you far more than I disliked Jeff! Most of all, I thought how lucky Wain and I would be to have you in our lives."

Again, Key blinked away tears; thankfully, they had reached Rooster House. "Stand right over there by the window," she told Guy. Unlocking the Jeep, she grabbed her red camera, set the timer, and trotted over to stand beside him. The camera blinked and clicked. "Now one of you alone." She photographed him standing next to the Jeep, then gave him a final hug and told him she'd call with a firm answer within two days.

As she headed back to Troy with no noise but the wind and the whine of the Jeep's wide tires on the asphalt, her head felt impossibly crowded. It had been her most bewildering morning in over a year of bewildering mornings, but she was positive of one thing: regardless of how Guy saw it, Key would never have chosen to take on a seven-year-old boy while married to a man as self-centered as Jeff.

It was telling that Guy had not mentioned his father, Harmon, whom Key vaguely remembered as a kind and quiet man, significantly older than Edie. He had died when Guy and Lara were quite young. From across the country, Key had sent a card with a sympathetic note, a spray of flowers, and a donation to hospice. Edie had never remarried, remaining in the small Illinois town where they'd all grown up, working at the bank, pouring her life into her two children and the community. Was Harmon's early death a contributor to Guy's view of his role in Wain's life? It was possible. And if a mother shoves the father out of the picture, and he accepts that and makes a life for himself, is he selfish? Or is he simply being pragmatic? Should Guy have fought harder to have access to his son? Maybe. Probably?

She sighed. She could be lost in this thought maze all day long. "I need a sign, Edie," she said out loud, looking through her windshield at the high cirrus clouds riffling like lines of snowy rickrack across the deep-blue Carolina sky. "A very definite, undeniable sign."

Chapter 9

SOUTHPAWS

A s if the clouds had answered, at that very moment Key heard a little "ding," and the bright-orange low-fuel icon lit up her dashboard. Fifty miles to empty. Well, that was no problem. She was just outside of Troy.

"Argh!" Key said it aloud as she jumped out of the Jeep at Connie V's Fuel Mart and saw the boxes in the back seat. In her shock at Guy's request, she'd completely forgotten to drop off the donation items. "Excuse me?" She leaned around the fuel pump. On the other side, a young blond woman in a red sundress was closing the gas cap on her car.

"Yes, ma'am?"

"Do you know of any secondhand or thrift stores around Troy?"

"Yes, ma'am. There's Shepherd Ministries right here in town and one called SouthPaws—that's Jukey and Mary King's place—just a little ways out on Marshall Road." She gave Key directions. "It's a real popular antiques place. They do consignments and have a produce stand too. Let's see … if you get to the Radiant Love Second Methodist Church, you've gone too far."

"SouthPaws," Key repeated. "Thank you so much!"

SouthPaws had at one time been a country store/gas station, the vintage pumps now long gone. Key pulled the Jeep up beside a portico extending about twelve feet over a cracked concrete pad and stepped out in front of a block building painted dark green, with double glass doors. A blue-and-red neon Open sign shone through one of the gleaming windows, and on a piece of metal above the door, the neat yellow letters outlined in red made her laugh out loud.

SouthPaws

Fruit and Such

Framing the sides of the building were two enormous live-oak trees ringed with artifacts of all ages and kinds. Several yards from the concrete pad sat the produce stand, not yet in business; and on a sunny patch of grass, an ancient yellow Labrador retriever dozed, twitching his ears and tail but never opening his eyes. Awestruck, Key rotated slowly, taking it all in. This hidden treasure was on no antiques corridor she had ever driven.

Near the front door, a vintage iron pump caught her eye. It was rusted in spots but still sporting much of its original red paint. It would be a perfect addition to her rock garden in the front yard. She entered the store, jangling the bells on a piece of old horse harness attached to the door.

"How do. Welcome." From behind the counter, an older man looked up from a crossword-puzzle book and greeted Key with a smile that traveled effortlessly up his face to friendly brown eyes. On a low table behind him and to Key's left stood a huge cage containing a beautiful orange-yellow bird with red-and-green markings on its head and wings. It fluttered onto a swinging bar and imitated the jangling of the door's bells perfectly, followed by a series of chirpy, cheerful *hellos*.

"Hi," she replied, laughing, moving closer so he could hear her over the bird. "I heard you do consignments, and I have had boxes of stuff in the back seat of my car for over a week."

"Sure thing. You caught me at the right time, pretty quiet in here at the moment, except for a certain feathered friend. Let's have a look.

Hush, birdie!" The man lightly tapped the cage, and miraculously, the bird obeyed, bobbing its head.

The man pocketed his glasses, attached his mechanical pencil to his shirt (he was left handed, she noted with a smile—a southpaw), then slid off the stool. He was probably around seventy years old, tall and trim, with once-black hair going silver, wearing jeans, a tucked-in khaki chambray shirt with the sleeves rolled up, and low-top white canvas Converse sneakers. She liked him immediately.

"I'm Orville King Junior, but everyone calls me Jukey." He held the door open, jangling the bells and creating another series of echoes from the bird. Before she could introduce herself, he asked, "You don't by any chance happen to know what a Miley Cyrus dance would be? Five letters, *w* is the second letter."

Key smiled. "I hate to admit I know this. Twerk."

"Beg pardon?"

"*T-W-E-R-K*. Twerk. It's a—in my opinion—very unattractive dance Miley Cyrus popularized." Key opened the back passenger door and picked up a box.

"Here, I'll take that." He set the box on the concrete. He clicked his tongue and said ruminatively, "*Twerk*," then grimaced, as though he were chewing on a bitter bite of food. "Never heard of it. The clues from nowadays leave me shaking my head and feeling my old-man ignorance. You ask me about blues singers, Bible verses, American rivers, movie stars, I will figure it out. But *twerk*? Nope." He leaned down, rummaging through the boxes, setting several items aside. "And I refuse to look it up on the World Wide Web except as a last resort. Seems like that's cheating to me."

"But you asked me," Key pointed out, grinning.

"Oh, now that's a different ball of wax," Jukey replied, pointing a forefinger in the air. "It's human connection, true conversation, not some electrical voodoo that won't take you one step further than what you can type. Unplug that and what have you got? Yet here we are, talking fellow man to fellow man, discussing a crossword-puzzle clue. Brains at work. Voices. The way it should be."

Laughing, Key tugged out more boxes. "I completely agree! Please take whatever you feel is a fit for your store. None of it is very old, and you have some wonderful antiques here."

"Oh, no worries, we sell everything. Just got to wait for the right buyer." Jukey sorted through the tailings of Key's recent past, separating everything into piles, then walked over, opened the door to the store, and stuck his head in. The bells jangled. The bird screeched. "Mary!" he called over the noise, then glanced back at Key. "Mary's my fashion expert. I need to ask if she wants the box of scarves and pocketbooks."

"There's a bag of jewelry there too. So you don't want what's left here?" She pointed to a few remnants.

"No, all that is best taken to Shepherd Ministries. These items here we can most probably sell. I'll explain the terms to you. This lamp have a shade?"

"Oh yes! It's in the far back." She opened the rear door of the Jeep. "And here are a couple more items, if you're interested." Along with the shade, she hauled out a hammered cast-iron candelabra and a small metal end table.

"Yep, sure will take all that too. Are you new to these parts?" Jukey asked.

"Yes, I bought Mr. Grimes's place on Pike Road, about four miles out of Troy."

His eyes lit up. "Oh yes! I know it well. Welcome to the neighborhood. Elvin Grimes was a good friend. My dogs and I used to retrieve birds for him and other members of the hunt club that had stands in the stretch of woods behind the house. Have you been to Dogleg Pond? About a mile and a half in, covers maybe a couple acres."

"A pond?" Key repeated, surprised. "I had no idea! I've been meaning to get out and explore but haven't had a chance yet."

"Mr. G was one of the last of that shooting crew. They don't hunt there now. Most of the land was bought up by the horse farm at the end of the road. You might see the old tree stands still scattered about if the kudzu hasn't hidden them." He pointed to the dog, who still hadn't moved except for opening his eyes and thumping his tail.

"Badger there is fourteen, my last bird dog. Used to train them, but all good things come to an end."

"Is it private land?" Key asked. "I plan to do a different kind of hunting and shooting. I've taken up bird photography."

"The woods are open to the public. All kinds of flora and fauna in there, as well as unused railroad tracks." Jukey placed the box of leftovers back into the Jeep.

"That's exactly what I was hoping!" Key said happily, adding this latest tidbit of information to her ever-growing "pros" column of reasons for moving. "I've heard the trains. I love the sound!"

"Do you now?" Jukey considered her intently. "Those particular tracks near Mr. G's place—now your place—don't go anywhere anymore, but nearby there's still some in use. Love the sound of trains myself. I worked for the railroad a good portion of my life, laying and repairing track."

He propped the door open with a worn triangular piece of wood, and they carried Key's items inside. "Mary!" he called again. Still no answer.

"Now the way this works," Jukey said, pulling out a large old-fashioned ledger, "I will list everything you consign with me, price your items accordingly, and we split it 40/60, you getting the 40 percent. That agreeable to you?"

"Absolutely." Key wouldn't have cared if she had gotten 10 percent. She was just happy to have it out of her car and off her hands.

Jukey pointed with his pencil to the boxes. "After three months I will give anything unsold back to you or donate it to charity."

"Perfect. Please donate anything you don't sell."

Mary still hadn't appeared. While Jukey listed her items in his ledger, Key wandered around the store. It was charmingly organized, full of the flotsam and jetsam of lives lived, each piece with its own story. She picked up a hand-carved wooden bread-making bowl. It was worn clear through, the hole on the bottom patched with a small heart-shaped piece of tin held in place with tiny nails. It would be perfect for her kitchen table. She carried it up front.

Behind the counter, a door slowly opened as a woman backed into the room. When she turned around, Key saw that she carried a tray with two mugs of coffee, a small bowl of apple chunks, and two plates containing slices of apple pie with cheese melted on top.

"Oh, we have company," the woman said, smiling widely. "I see I should have brought another plate."

Jukey turned around, saying affectionately, "Mary! Been calling you, honey! I need you to check this box of fashion items."

"Sorry, Jukey! I had my earbuds in; had to see how my podcast ended. Hello," she said to Key, placing the tray on the counter.

"Hello," Key answered. Mary was so pretty, with hair more gray than black arranged into a low bun. She was average sized and wore jean capris and a white T-shirt, untucked. Her dark skin and brown eyes were set off by silver cross stud earrings. "It has been decades since I've seen a piece of cheese on pie! My father ate it like that!"

Jukey pointed at it with his pencil. "Best pie in the state, right there. Fortune Dairy's sharp cheddar cheese on top—spoil you forever. Anything else tastes like stale cardboard."

Mary raised her eyebrows as she began examining the jewelry and accessories. "Maybe this lady makes a good pie."

Key laughed. "I do love to make pie, but I can tell that mine *would* be stale cardboard in comparison."

Jukey put his arm around Mary's shoulders. "We sell them on Fridays or Saturdays at the stand, or when the mood strikes. Line down the road to buy them starts early in the mornings. This is my better half, Mary. Mary, this is—" He stopped. "We've been talking like old friends, and I've neglected to get your name."

Key smiled. "Key North."

"Y'all have a beautiful name," Mary said. "Would you eat some pie with us? Have coffee or sweet tea?"

"Oh, it's tempting, but no, thank you," Key said. "I ate a huge breakfast in Porterville, and I've taken up so much of your time already. I do want to get this bowl, and could I get a price on the pump out there by the front door as well?"

"Not Key West ... Key North," Jukey said, a grin spreading across his face. "Name like that, you're for sure someone's true north. That's what I call Mary here; she's my true north. When I feel myself getting blown sideways, bothering myself into a lather with what can't be changed, or wondering what's around the bend, she sets my compass straight again. Calm in the storm." He turned around and gently tapped the cage, where the bird was chirping madly. "Petey! Hush, birdie! Hush. You'll get your treats." He picked up a piece of apple, opened the door, and placed his hand inside. "Hop on, Petey Parakeety." A heavenly silence descended as the bird hopped onto Jukey's finger and nibbled the fruit. "He's not a parakeet," Jukey said to Key. "He's a sun conure. We adopted him from a couple who visited SouthPaws one day."

"How does that even happen?" Key asked with a laugh. "Someone just happened to have a bird in their car as they shopped for antiques?"

Jukey chuckled. "No bird in the car. I don't recall how the conversation started, but they told me about Petey. They traveled a lot and couldn't care for him, or maybe they just didn't want to. For some reason I took their number, and Mary and I talked it over and decided to try our hand at bird ownership. Traded him for a pearl ring and an antique ruby peacock brooch. One bird for another. Had him four years now."

"We got the better end of that deal," Mary put in, nodding. "He's brought color and life to our little place here."

"Yep, he's a handful of noise and bossiness, but we wouldn't do without him. Sometimes the best gifts are the ones we never expected. Now, where were we?" Jukey picked up his pencil. "I'll sell you the pump for sixty dollars and the bowl for thirty. How's that sound?"

"Perfect." Key handed him her credit card.

Mary left for a few minutes, then returned with a cheese-topped piece of pie on a paper plate, wrapped in plastic. "Here now, Key North. You take this pie with you and, come dinnertime, eat it warm with a cold glass of milk, and you'll know all is right with the world."

It might take more than a piece of pie. "Oh, thank you, Mary! So you adopted the bird, just like that?"

"Pardon me?" asked Jukey, looking confused.

"Petey." Key pointed to the bird, now perched on Jukey's shoulder, regarding her with assessing, white-ringed ebony eyes. She got the impression Petey hadn't quite decided whether she passed muster. "Did you have to think about it? Did you have reservations?"

Mary laughed. "I surely did. Having a loud, messy bird is a big commitment. They live a long, long time. I could think of a dozen reasons not to take him, but in the end, there was only one fact that mattered. He needed a home. That made it easy. Now we can't imagine SouthPaws without our Petey."

"And I've learned over our thirty-five years of marriage to trust Mary's instincts," Jukey said, smiling at his wife. "Petey's been a big asset in our business, something we never anticipated. People remember our place as the one with the loud, friendly bird. On slow days, we let the kids hold him, and now Petey's got a little fan club on social media too."

"I see all the photos behind you. He seems to love the attention."

"He does that. You spend any time here, Petey will be your friend too." Jukey lowered Petey back into the cage and went out to load the pump into Key's Jeep.

"You never know, do you, what one decision might mean in the long run." Mary came around the counter and walked Key to the door. "Come back anytime and visit us, Key North."

Chapter 10
THE TRUTH

Wain. Late May

It had been five days, and still no word from Mama. Holding an unopened juice box, Wain sat dejectedly on the narrow wooden steps behind Mrs. Titus's house, unaware of the condensation dripping onto his legs or the sharp edge of the doorframe pressing into his back. Mrs. Titus had brought him macaroni and cheese, tortilla chips, and mandarin oranges. "An orange lunch on an orange plate," she had said with a smile that failed to conceal the concern in her kind, dark eyes.

He didn't smile back. The food sat untouched, chips wilting in the humidity. Only pansies cried, Wain knew, and he was dripping tears onto his legs, but he couldn't help it. He didn't want to be a pansy, but he just didn't understand.

School was out now too. "Why aren't you riding the school bus anymore?" his friend Rico had asked the day before, their last day of first grade.

"My mom and Cal are on a trip, so I'm staying with Mrs. Titus." That simple explanation had seemed to satisfy Rico, which made

Wain feel better too, for a moment. His mom and Callahan just needed some space, like Callahan was always saying. "Wain," he would put on his impatient, fake fatherly voice, "give your *mom* and me some time alone. Go to your room for a while." Wain's mom would grimace and flap her hand impatiently—*go on, do as he says*.

But now, again he was filled with worry. Why did they leave on his birthday, the very day of his promised pool party? And *where* was his backpack? When she'd gone to collect more clothes for him before her car broke down, he'd been devastated when a puzzled Mrs. Titus told him she hadn't been able to find it.

He carried his orange meal back inside and spent the rest of the day listlessly watching cartoons. After he'd gotten ready for bed, Mrs. Titus came to his room. "I've got some news for you, honey." She pretended not to see his tear-stained cheeks.

His eyes lit up. "My mama is back?"

With a deep sigh, Mrs. Titus sat down next to him, squeaking the bedsprings. "Oh, Wain, honey, I'm so sorry. No, that's not my news." Wain tried to stop himself, but he slid against her, into the crevice created by her bulk. She put her arm, heavy and soft, around him. "I talked to your daddy, his name is Guy. He told me you're going to live in North Carolina with your cousin."

"My *real* daddy?" Wain asked, confused. "I thought he lived in Texas."

Mrs. Titus nodded vigorously. "Oh yes, he lives in Texas, but he can't take you there; he's busy with work. You'll be living with your daddy's cousin, whose name is Key."

"Key? Is he my age?"

Mrs. Titus offered a few more words of explanation. "Key is a lady, kinda like a grandma. She's your relative, on your daddy's side."

Wain looked down at his bare feet just brushing the floor. It was as though Mrs. Titus had begun speaking a foreign language. "I have to live with an old lady? Why isn't my mama coming back?"

Mrs. Titus sighed again. "Oh, honey, there's no way to doctor up the truth to make it better. Your mama is in jail, Wain. Mr. Cal is there too. They stole a lot of money, and the police took them to jail. She can't get out, honey. She can't get out to come to you."

It was too much to comprehend, too terrible to absorb. "What about my backpack?" was all Wain said.

Chapter 11

NEIGHBORS

Key. Late May

The vivid, emotional relief and gratitude in Guy's voice when Key called him the afternoon after their visit to give an unequivocal yes to his request made her wonder if he was having second thoughts. She had asked yet again if Wain could possibly join him, but Guy's answer had been as firm a no as before. That settled it. She refused to overthink the decision. Edie's grandson would come to live with her, and she was driving to Florida tomorrow to get him.

While she was in her bedroom packing, five sharp knocks sounded at her front door. Surprised, Key dropped her one decent pair of summer pajamas into her overnight bag and hurried through the living room, opening the door to find a tired-looking woman in a sleeveless leopard-print top with an asymmetrical hem, black legging capris, and sturdy but worn two-strap Birkenstock sandals from which shone bright-pink toenails. In her arms was a baby—a little girl, by the looks of the pink onesie and the yellow plastic barrette that clasped her blond hair in a wispy fountain of ponytail. The baby was barefoot and looked too small to walk.

The woman appeared to be in her late thirties, very thin, with light-brown hair in a long side braid secured at the end with a fluffy red scrunchie. Her dark eyes, with striking heavy brows, were accented with blue eye shadow, and her mouth was a fuchsia color Key would never have dared try, but it suited the woman. A necklace of oversized red beads circled her neck, and the baby, sucking on a pacifier, was playing with it. Standing next to the two of them was a young girl.

Wilma and Pebbles Flintstone are at my door! Key couldn't help the smile that spread without permission across her face. "Hi!" she said brightly to the trio, the word sounding simultaneously like a greeting and a question.

"Ma'am," Wilma shifted Pebbles to her other hip and said somberly, "we are the Morgans, your neighbors down Pike Road a ways. These are my daughters Ellen and Dibsy, and I'm Gayle." She put a delicate hand on the girl's head. "We need to talk to you. Well, *Ellen* needs to talk to you." Her voice was smoker husky with a beautifully deep Southern accent. She gently shook the girl's shoulder. "Ellen, look at the lady."

Ellen, as boyish as her mother was feminine, had straight, neck-length, dark-brown hair held back with clips over each ear. Her yellow T-shirt featured writing that, under her tightly crossed arms, Key couldn't read; and she wore worn cutoff jean shorts and beat-up dark-blue high-tops that looked a bit too big. She could have been anywhere between seven and twelve (Key was terrible at guessing children's ages) and remained scowling at the floor, tapping her foot, radiating anxiety.

"Key. My name is Key North. Would you like to sit down out here on the porch?" She especially wanted the little girl to feel more at ease; it was uncomfortable standing there blocking the doorway like she was warding off a stubborn salesman.

"Nice to meet you, Miss Key. No, thank you, we can't stay. Ellen here needs to tell you something, and we need to make amends. Ellen, you tell Miss Key what you've come to say."

Key could not fathom what the woman was talking about. "Amends?"

Ellen kept her arms akimbo but gazed directly up at Key. She had a charming sprinkle of faint freckles across her nose; and her eyes, full of defiant remorse, were a startling deep purply blue, the color of spring iris. "I'm sorry I took your pot." She stared back down at the floor.

"My … pot?" Completely bewildered, all Key could visualize was marijuana. Was it growing in the ditch along the fence? Behind the shed?

Gayle gestured toward a pink flowering plant in a decorative ceramic bowl, sitting on the steps. "Right there. That pot."

"Oh! My petunia! What … where did you …?" If mother and daughter hadn't been so solemn, Key would have burst out laughing. She had been missing that flowerpot for days and had finally concluded that she'd inadvertently left it at the garden center.

"Ellen came by a few days ago to see if you all needed help with anything because we knew this house had new people in it," Gayle said, hoisting the baby with a thin arm.

"It's just me," Key said, finally stepping onto the porch and letting the screen door tick shut. For the first time she saw the red metal wagon in the driveway. Had they walked? From where?

Gayle nodded. "Ellen is very industrious, and that's a good thing, but at times her entrepreneurial heart can lead her a bit astray. She took that pot of flowers from your place here and gave it to me for a late Mother's Day gift." Gayle rolled her eyes slightly, as if this wasn't her first go-round with Ellen's entrepreneurial heart gone astray. "Anyway, Ellen told me she earned it helping feed horses at the Mistic Meadows Horse Barn, down where Pike Road dead-ends. I said something to those two ladies who own it, when we saw them out riding in the meadow that borders our place. They had *no* idea what I was talking about, so I knew something was up, and I made Ellen tell me where she got the flowers. We know this isn't how you'd like to acquaint yourself with new neighbors, but if you can overlook this egregious transgression on Ellen's part, we would like to begin anew."

"Oh, I see." Key couldn't keep the smile from her face. She turned to the girl. "So, Ellen, did you—"

"Ell," the girl said firmly, finally moving from the door. She took a seat on the porch swing and gave it a little push with her toe. "I want to be called Ell. *E-L-L*. I hate Ellen."

"Honey, it's your Grandmama Line's middle name!" Gayle exclaimed. Following her older daughter's lead, she sank into the rocker next to the swing with a sigh of relief and settled Dibsy on her lap.

"Well, I hate it." The arms stayed crossed, the swing swayed faster.

"Wait a second." Key gave a little wave, a conversational traffic cop. She was sure she'd just solved a mystery. She fixed her gaze on Ell. "Did you by any chance leave me a heart-shaped rock?"

Ellen's face brightened. "Yes, ma'am! I found it in the ditch when I was riding my bike over here. It was so heavy in my bike basket that I had trouble steering! I put it by the shed door."

Gayle rescued her braid from a chubby baby fist. "Ellen Louise. A rock is not something you can use to pay. Stealing is stealing. You could have given me the rock instead of stealing a flowerpot! I could have put it in my flower garden."

"You don't *have* a flower garden! That's why I stole the pot!"

Key again sternly told herself not to laugh. "I'll be *right* back, and we will sort this out." Hustling into the kitchen, she dumped a box of butter crackers into a bowl and found a nearly full pint of pimiento cheese in the fridge, then filled cups with ice water and set it all on a wooden tray. At the last minute she added three small paper plates and some leftover cocktail napkins with a golf motif, remnants of a long-ago world that didn't include pot thieves and heart-shaped rocks and little boys with mothers in jail.

Back on the porch, Key distributed the glasses to her guests. Dibsy dropped her pacifier and drank messily from the cup Gayle held, dripping water all over them both, then stuffed a tiny fistful of cracker into her mouth and gnawed away, creating a cascade of crumbs. Key watched, fascinated. Babies. Tiny helpless humans, with the brain they'd been blessed with for life, but able to access it in barely discernible stages. It was startling, really, when she thought about it. All that potential in a human being approximately the weight of a Thanksgiving turkey.

She pulled the white wicker chair toward the group. "Okay, let's iron this out." Smiling, Key said, "My parents named me Katherine Elizabeth Yates, but the day I was born, my father used my initials to give me the nickname *Key*. From that day on, I was never anyone else." She touched Ell lightly on the leg. "So if it's not a problem, I'll call you Ell." She glanced at Gayle, who shrugged agreeably and nodded.

"Yes!" Ell exclaimed, lifting her fist and pulling it triumphantly toward her chest. Key was rewarded with a huge grin. She had a tiny gap between her front teeth; with the freckles and those amazing eyes, the effect was slightly mesmerizing.

Key slapped her hands lightly on the arms of her chair. "Okay, that's settled! As far as the flowers, I'm just happy to know I have such honest and enterprising neighbors. Gayle, I want you to have the petunias, and I'll keep the rock. And, Ell, I can use some help around here now and then, so if it's okay with your mom, just come over and knock on my door! Are we all agreed?" She decided not to mention Wain's upcoming arrival; the whole situation was simply too tenuous to share with new acquaintances.

Mother and daughter both nodded. Ell appeared to have relaxed, but Key sensed a tenseness still in her mother. "Thank you for your understanding, Miss Key," Gayle replied, arranging Dibsy comfortably on her lap and crossing her legs. "Ell will be visiting my parents for the next two weeks, but after that, she'll be happy to lend a hand."

"That sounds fun! How old are you, Ell?" asked Key.

"Nine." The anxious little girl was gone. Ell sat quietly, sipping her water, dipping crackers in pimiento cheese, listening to Key and her mother talk, her eyes and ears not missing a thing. Key saw for the first time that her shirt said CRABBY JOE'S MARINA, with a caricature of a grumpy man in a captain's cap, and the words Charleston, SC.

"Are you from South Carolina?" she asked Gayle, who appeared mystified by the question.

"No, ma'am, I'm from Florida. The Gainesville area. My husband, Lonny, is from here."

That explains her accent, Key thought. "Oh, I was going by the writing on Ell's shirt."

"Thrift-store find," Gayle replied. "Shepherd Ministries in Troy."

"It's a cool retro shirt," Key said to Ell. "Where do you go to school?" She listened as Ell told her about her school in Troy and how she and her fourteen-year-old brother, Cavender, were the only ones on Pike Road who rode the school bus.

"Where, exactly, do you live?" Key asked, hoping they didn't feel like she was interrogating them. It was just so enjoyable to have her first real chat with neighbors on her porch.

Gayle finished giving Dibsy a drink. Little chunks of cracker had floated to the bottom of the glass. Pointing a fuchsia nail out toward the road, she said, "Go a quarter mile past here, turn left down Wildflower Lane. At the bottom of the hill, there's a house where Lonny's mama lives and a double-wide—that's where we live. I help out with Granny Jewel, and Lonny works with his brother Larry at the concrete-block plant." Smoothing Dibsy's hair, Gayle gazed out over the lawn. "We've been here for several months now. We needed a change of scenery, and Lonny was having a hard time getting decent work."

Ell, who had two fingers and her thumb in her glass, intently excavating a piece of ice, piped up. "Because Daddy was in jail in Florida." She crunched her ice loudly, ignoring her mother's resigned look.

"Oh. Jail?" Key asked. What a weird coincidence. For the second time in as many days, she was hearing about someone in a Florida jail.

"Yes, ma'am. Ellen spoke out of turn." Gayle cleared her throat and stared out at the front yard, then sighed and without looking at Key, continued, "Lonny got himself into an unfortunate situation with a friend of his. They chose to steal some equipment from a rental place. He's done his time, two years." She finally met Key's eyes and tilted her head toward her older daughter. "You can see why I am cognizant of Ellen's leanings toward a life of crime."

"Mama! At least I come by my thieving honestly! And it was a flowerpot! Not a compressor!" Ell pushed her feet to make the swing go faster. Key held her breath, hoping it wouldn't hit the railing behind it, but the chains were just short enough to avoid a crash.

"There's no such thing as an honest thief, Ellen Louise!" Gayle replied sharply. "Theft is theft, missy, and you ain't gonna do what your daddy and Mickey done."

"That must have been very difficult," Key said sympathetically, biting her lip. She could tell already that Ell and family were true originals.

"Yes, ma'am." Gayle shifted her arm to support a drowsy Dibsy, unconsciously caressing the baby's chubby leg. "It was. We survived, but I wouldn't wish it on no one. It's real humiliating, and the kids suffer the most. Cav got teased almost every day at school."

In the awkward silence that followed, a sudden thought occurred to Key. "Gayle ..." she hesitated. "We don't have to talk about this if you don't want to, but this conversation could not have come at a better time for me! When you knocked on my door, I was packing for a trip. Tomorrow I'm driving to Florida to visit a woman who happens to be in jail." She nodded as Gayle and Ell both stared at her, eyes wide.

"The thing is," Key continued, "I'm nervous about the meeting, mostly because I've never visited someone in a jail, and I have no idea what to expect. Do you have any pointers on ... how do I put this? Jail-visiting protocol? Like, what do they do at the door? Will I be searched? That kind of thing."

Ell jumped off the swing to retrieve Dibsy's pacifier, which had fallen with a flat little *clunk* onto the porch floor. She gave it a quick swipe on Crabby Joe's face and popped it back into the baby's mouth, then said to Key, "Just be yourself. It's people same as us, except locked up. That's what Mama told me."

Gayle tipped her head. "Yes, honey, I did say that. It's true, for the most part. I've never been to a women's jail, but first thing, you have to be on an approved visitor's list."

"I am, as of today," Key replied.

Gayle warmed to the subject, giving Key a quick rundown of what else to expect, ending with, "And no jewelry or provocative clothing."

"No worries about the clothing," Key said, laughing. "I own nothing that comes close to provocative! I would have worn jewelry, though. Thank you! That's exactly the kind of advice I need!"

"We had to wait a *long* time to see Daddy sometimes," Ell said, slumping her shoulders, pulling on the chain to make the swing go sideways. "But I liked getting a Snickers bar from the vending machines."

"It was easier with Ellen because she was younger, but some days Cav refused to go," Gayle said. "He hated it, hated seeing his daddy there. We were all so happy the day Lonny was released, Cav maybe most of all. And Dibsy here was born nine months after Lonny got out." She grinned, and Key laughed out loud.

"Why is that funny?" Ell asked.

At the mention of her name, Dibsy began to squirm and fuss, causing Gayle to stand up, gracefully ignoring Ell's question. "Baby needs a nap. We appreciate your understanding with the flowers. Thank you, too, for the water and crackers. It was real nice of you."

Key smiled ruefully. "Crackers and water! Sounds like I had *you* in solitary confinement. Would you like a ride home? It looks like it could rain." She pointed to dark thunderheads gathering in the southwest.

Ell jumped up. "Yay! Can we, Mama?"

"You sure you don't mind, Miss Key?" Gayle asked.

"Of course not!" Key led the way to the Jeep and helped Ell lift the wagon into the back.

Wildflower Lane, bordered as Gayle had mentioned by a horse pasture, descended gently to an open space where a tan ranch-style brick house surrounded by trees and an impeccably kept lawn stood off to the left. Key parked in front of an older white double-wide mobile home with red-brick-patterned skirting and gray plastic shutters. Bare wooden steps led to a small landing where a yellow broom leaned against the doorframe and a multicolored braided rug hung over the railing. Everything was tidy but Ell was right. Gayle had no flower garden, just patches of grass. The starkness told a story of a family still struggling to get to their feet.

Ell jumped out of the Jeep and called cheerily to the three people who sat on the porch at the house. "Hey, Granny Jewel! Hey, Uncle Larry! Hey, Auntie Pee!" They waved but didn't get up, watching curiously as Ell placed the flowerpot into the wagon, took a wailing Dibsy from Gayle and put her in too; then, wiry muscles straining, she pulled the jolting wagon across the gravel drive.

Key looked around. Several black-and-white hens pecked here and there in that desultory, dainty, erratic way chickens do, strutting and clucking in a circle of enormous, leathery dead leaves underneath a giant, almost Jurassic-looking magnolia tree. A tire swing on a fraying rope hung from one of its branches.

"You have chickens!" Key said to Gayle delightedly. "Do you sell eggs?"

"Yes, ma'am, that's the plan. We've raised them from incubated eggs. None right now, but them chickens is close. Maybe a couple weeks."

"I'd love to buy eggs from you!" Realizing she'd left her phone at Pike House, Key retrieved a pad and pen from the Jeep and traded numbers with Gayle. "Would you like me to save my egg cartons?"

"That'd be nice. I'll let you know when they start laying." Gayle took the paper with Key's number and started toward the house. "Thank you again for your understanding. And the flower."

"Let's stay in touch! It's been a pleasure and thank *you* for the advice!" Key answered, waving at Ell who was now holding Dibsy, one thin hip jutting out to manage the baby's weight. "Bye, Ell! Have fun with your grandparents! Come see me sometime once you're back!"

Just before she got back into the Jeep, Gayle called from the porch, waving the piece of paper. "Miss Key! One more thing! Don't wear leggings!"

Key turned around. "Pardon?"

"When you visit your friend! Don't wear leggings! It's not allowed."

"Thank you, Gayle! I never would have known that!" As she got in the Jeep, she said to herself, "Make a note: Snickers and egg cartons. And don't wear leggings."

Chapter 12
ROAD TRIP

It was raining and muggy when Key left at four the following morning, but as she drove southeast, the clouds dissipated; and by the time she reached I-95, she had to lower her visor against the intense sunlight strobing through the trees. She was not a tentative driver, but tourists, RV adventurers, NASCAR wannabes, and semi-truck drivers weaved in and out, passing her like she was standing still.

Key loved road trips. The creative portion of her mind welcomed the opportunity to range deeper, free of the urgency of home-based distractions and interruptions. Some of her best card ideas had come while she was driving and listening to music. Today, though, her mind was far from card sentiments. She turned on her "Absolute Faves" music list and let the miles unfold, contemplating once again the extraordinary chain of events that had led to the road she was now traveling. Though they didn't know it, Jukey and Mary's story about adopting Petey the bird had provided Key exactly the perspective she needed to process Guy's request.

What did she know about living with a seven-year-old boy? Exactly nothing. She'd set up a bedroom with just the necessities: a bed, a dresser, and hangers in the closet—but in the flurry of preparation, she hadn't had time to find more than that. Surely Wain's room at his old house would be full of the familiar toys, books, and pictures that would help him feel at home. They would go shopping together for whatever else he needed.

She sighed. Toys and clothes were one thing; Wain's state of mind was something else entirely. Her expectations alternated between a solid confidence that she would succeed at being a stable, loving caretaker, while almost simultaneously experiencing the abject fear that she was hurtling headlong toward a collision with a fractured, angry child who had every right to resent her sudden, uninvited appearance in his life. *Wain has to be feeling angry, depressed, and heartbroken—kind of like me for the past year—but I'm old enough to navigate my emotions. I understand that scars take time to heal.*

As an incredulous Iris had so bluntly put it when Key had shared with her the reason for Guy's visit, "A criminal for a mother and an absentee father. That's a child who's bound to have all kinds of issues! Tell your cousin to take responsibility for his *own* son." Having dispensed her advice, Iris had obviously considered the subject closed, and once Key had made her decision, she had not shared it with Iris.

Her phone rang. *Speak of the devil. Here we go.* Key put it on speaker. "Hi, Iris!"

Iris's voice filled the Jeep's interior. "Hi, Key, it sounds like you're in the car. Are you heading into Porterville, by any chance? If you are, do you want to have lunch before I leave this evening?"

"Are you going somewhere?" Key asked, scrambling to recall whether Iris had mentioned a trip.

"My yearly cruise with my girl posse! This year we're sailing out of New Orleans." Every year Iris and three of her longtime friends from Connecticut took a cruise together.

"Oh right!" Key had completely forgotten. "Iris, I hope you have a wonderful time! When will you be back?"

"June 10," Iris replied. "So ... lunch today?"

"I'm sorry, I can't, Iris. I am driving, but I'm headed to Florida, to get Wain. I'm going to be packing up his things tomorrow and bringing him home with me. I'd love to have you meet him when you get back." She counted twelve seconds before she heard a reply.

"I'm *speechless*," Iris said abruptly. "I thought we agreed it was an outrageous request! I had no idea you were even considering it!"

"The last time we talked, I hadn't reached a decision," Key replied evenly. "But it hasn't been an impetuous one, Iris, believe me. I'm positive I'm doing the right thing. In fact, I'm excited." To the hollow, unbelieving silence that followed, she added, "I hope you have a very fun trip. You always do."

"Yes, I do," Iris answered, the insinuation clear that Key's days of kicking up her heels with any type of posse, girl or otherwise, were over. "Good luck. I strongly suspect you're going to need it."

"Talk to you when you get back, Iris." As she tapped the dashboard screen to hang up, Key took a deep breath, surprisingly energized by her own firm words. There was a time when she would have put far more weight on Iris's opinions, meekly accepting that she herself probably *didn't* know best. She shook her head, realizing her friendship with Iris in many ways mirrored aspects of her marriage. *How did I allow that to happen?*

She sang along to Crosby, Stills & Nash's "Southern Cross" and told herself for the thousandth time that she didn't have to have every jot and tittle planned out. She would simply become Wain's friend. *That's all the planning I need for now.* One minute at a time.

Aside from Iris's call and six hundred miles of Key's own unrelenting introspection, it was a typical drive with the usual stops—gas, lunch, rest areas. She checked in at her downtown-Brookings hotel in early evening, then went for dinner and a walk, relieved to stretch her legs. Finally, fatigued but restless, she fell asleep around midnight. She had one pressing appointment the next morning at nine, then she'd drive to 287 Leon Boulevard to meet her cousin's grandson.

Chapter 13

BARS

Key woke early enough to have coffee and a shower, then pulled her hair into a short braid, removed her diamond stud earrings, applied a little mascara, and dressed in a pair of black-and-white-checked capris, a plain black T-shirt, and white slip-on canvas shoes. At 8:30 a.m. she pulled into the parking lot of the Ann DeLavein Correctional Facility for Women. A little disconcerted, she double-checked the map on the dashboard screen. Was this the right spot? The modest three-story brick structure that currently housed Wain's mother was far less bleak than what she'd been expecting. Maybe there was a fence with a barbwire topper and an exercise yard around back but from her vantage point, it could have been an office building, an industrial facility, or a library. She cut the engine, locked her purse into the center console, and got out.

After checking her lipstick one last time in the passenger-side rearview mirror, Key headed for the entrance carrying only her car key, driver's license, and seven one-dollar bills. She had tried to imagine what it must have been like for Lyric to be taken from her home, read her rights, handcuffed, and then extracted from a police car and taken unwillingly into this very building, knowing that from that day forward, her life would not be the same. Was she frantically worrying about her little boy? Overwhelmed? Regretful? Terrified? Probably all of the above.

Outside the front door, she joined the visitors' queue as it inched along through the double glass doors and down a hallway that opened into a sternly utilitarian waiting area with several dingy, white plastic chairs lined against a melancholic beige wall. When it was her turn to check in, she smiled through the glass that separated her from a large, no-nonsense, middle-aged woman on the other side.

"Hi, I'm here to visit an inmate, Angela Tremain. I have a nine o'clock appointment." Was *appointment* the right word?

The woman tapped computer keys. "Name?"

"Katherine North." She laid her driver's license into the rounded silver tray below the glass. The woman glanced at it, then her, then returned it.

"Okay, you're on the list. You will have an hour to visit with Ms. Tremain. Do you have any belongings you need to put in a locker? Handbag? Coat?" When Key shook her head, the woman said, "Keep everything out of your pockets and wait over there."

Key thanked her, went through the metal detector, and was directed to the visiting area by the officer on the other side, a muscular bald man with a lion's-head tattoo on the back of his left hand. "You'll do your visiting in there," he told her. "Take a seat at any empty table. No talking with other visitors." It was all so rote and emotionless.

Key chose a spot near the vending machines and smiled slightly, thinking of Ell, all the while suppressing an urge to run for the door, far from the industrial smells and the palpable sadness and anxiety that hung like inverted smog over the room. *What am I doing?* Up until just days ago, these people had been no part of her life, and now they would be front and center. It didn't seem real.

To calm her nerves, she took several deep breaths as she studied the room. It was obvious children were regulars here; the far wall featured an incongruously cheerful jungle scene, and in front of it on a low shelf was an assortment of fatigued-looking books and toys.

Every other person waiting seemed to know the drill. Long-suffering partners or grandparents tried to contain children who hopped about excitedly, straining to see if their mothers were coming through the door. At one table a woman laid out paperwork; at another, two restless, unhappy-looking teenagers sat with a weary-looking older man, none of them speaking. It was strange seeing teens without the ubiquitous cell phones. She couldn't help wondering who they were visiting. As the inmates began trickling in, Key almost teared up watching a small girl who was finally able to embrace her overjoyed mother. It was obvious that these visits were regular, indispensable lifelines for so many people, both inside and outside the walls.

"Are you Key North?"

Startled, Key stood quickly, scraping her thigh painfully on the edge of the table.

"Hi! Yes! I'm Key. Angie?" She held out her hand.

"It's *Lyric*." Ignoring Key's proffered hand, Lyric settled onto the bench across from her.

Key quickly sat back down, rubbing her throbbing thigh. "Oh, of course, Lyric. I'm sorry. Yes, I'm Key, Guy's cousin. I remember you from his mother's memorial service." She would never have recognized Lyric, who seemed to have transformed herself as much physically as she had done with her name.

Even so, she was still a knockout. Blue eyes with dark lashes, perfectly arched dark eyebrows, high cheekbones, pale lips, front teeth just a tiny bit prominent. She wore an oversized gray short-sleeved T-shirt and baggy gray sweats, sneakers without ties, and had her bleached-blond hair knotted on her head in a messy bun. An inch of dark roots showed the hair color Key remembered, but that's where it ended. Beautiful as she was, Lyric bore almost no resemblance to the stunningly vibrant Angie who'd accompanied Guy to Edie's funeral.

"Afraid I can't say the same," Lyric said, shrugging. She had just a hint of a lisp.

"Oh no, I wouldn't expect you to remember me!" Key hastily replied. She already felt off-balance. "Would you like a drink or a candy bar or anything?"

Lyric waved a hand in the direction of the vending machine. "A diet whatever. And a pack of cheese crackers. Cal needs to add money to my account."

Grateful for a few seconds to gather her thoughts, Key fed dollar bills into the slot, pressing buttons for Lyric's items and a bottle of water for herself.

"Thanks." Lyric popped the can open and took a long drink.

"You're welcome." Key leaned her elbows on the table. She wished she had a way to take notes; she'd just have to commit everything to memory. "Lyric, we have only one hour to talk, and I want to learn as much as possible about Wain, how I can help him, while, um, while you're in here. What he likes, dislikes, what activities he was in, that kind of thing. Who your little boy is as a person."

Lyric kept her eyes lowered, slowly rotating her soda can. "You haven't seen him yet?"

"No. I just got in last night, and I haven't gone to Mrs. Titus's house yet."

"Okay. Yeah. Well." Lyric took another sip, then wiped her mouth. "As a *person*, he's simple. Likes his cars, likes playing with his friends. Annoys the heck out of Cal and me because he's a *kid*. That type of *person*." She shook her head, rolled her eyes ever so slightly, and took another long swig.

Was she mocking the question? *She can't be.* Key tried a different tactic, something more practical. "Any special foods he likes?"

"He eats what's put in front of him; Cal sees to that. He gets his favorite snacks as a reward for doing what he's told. Biggars Root Beer and Cheddy Chipsters." She gave a short laugh. "Let's just say he doesn't get them very often."

Key unscrewed the cap on her water bottle and took a drink. This certainly wasn't shaping up to be the teary, regretful conversation she'd anticipated. For all the emotion Lyric exhibited, the two of them could have been at a table in a café discussing an evening babysitting gig. "Okay, Cheddy Chipsters ... good to know," she said matter-of-factly, trying to match Lyric's tone, once again averting her eyes from the young mother two tables over whose little daughter clung to her as if she were drowning. "What about bedtimes? Favorite school subjects?"

"He goes to bed at seven, at least to his room, so Cal and I can have *our* free time. And school"—Lyric made a face—"Cal and I cannot figure out what that kid's deal is with school."

A tiny alarm went off in Key's head. *That kid.* "What do you mean?"

"Wain has *literally* dumbed down. He used to be so bright, knew all his letters by age four, before he even started school. I don't know if it's his teachers or what, but he doesn't even recognize letters anymore. Cal has been wonderful, working with him." Paper crinkled as Lyric tore open the package of crackers.

Key took another drink and waited. Was Wain's mother capable of saying anything without dragging Callahan into it?

"We're going to move pretty soon, so Wain will be changing schools anyway," Lyric continued, nibbling just the edge of a cracker. "Cal and I aren't really into the type of neighbors we have. We're looking at our options."

That would probably be on hold for a while. "You said Wain's not reading yet?" Key asked curiously.

"No. He's in the 'remedial' class." Lyric rolled her eyes as she made quote marks with her fingers. "So embarrassing!" She took another drink and added, "Cal says he's just stubborn, and I agree. Wain needs to *snap* out of it."

With difficulty, Key hid her shock. "Um, I've done some volunteer tutoring for elementary-age kids. Maybe I can help Wain."

"Yeah, well, good luck with that," Lyric retorted, resting her chin on her palm, and tapping the top of her soda can with a long fingernail. "It's been one big, annoying headache. Cal has tried everything—flash cards, books, set up a reward system and all. Even goes home early now and then to work with him."

"Oh, okay, how did the reward system work?"

Lyric shrugged and extracted another cracker. "Wain got special treats, extra privileges—that kind of thing. I don't know the particulars. Cal set it all up. Cal is so good to him."

Once again, we invoke the revered criminal, Cal. Key tried another track. "What about television shows? Toys? Hobbies? Do seven-year-olds have hobbies?"

"No TV. Cal set it up as part of the rewards he could earn. Wain never earned them. The closest thing he has to a hobby is his CartWheels collection." Seeing Key's blank look, Lyric waved the cracker around and exclaimed, "You know, the little cars? CartWheels? Oh my gosh, seriously? You've never heard of them? The whole world knows about those! They're his favorite toys; he carries—" She stopped talking midsentence, took another gulp of soda, and said breezily, "Anyway, he loves them."

The remainder of Key's visit was spent eliciting as many details about Wain as she could, but it was as though Lyric viewed her incarceration almost as a type of vacation; soon she'd be home from the Ann DeLavein Resort and Spa, unpacking her bags, rejuvenated and ready to embezzle more money. Callahan's name came up constantly, possessively; Key wondered if Lyric had decided anything for herself since she met the man, and Wain seemed to have been as much a hindrance as anything. Even so, Key was appalled when she asked if she could bring Wain to visit and Lyric emphatically shook her head, lifting an elbow and moving it imperceptibly sideways to point at the heartbroken little girl Key had been watching.

"Yeah, my kid's not gonna be *that* kid," she replied. "No way am I interested in that kind of over-the-top melodrama."

"Time!" the guard at the door called out. The little girl stayed clamped to her weeping mother's arm, fighting the young man who tried to pull her away.

Lyric unfolded herself from the bench and observed the scene dispassionately, then said to Key, "Tell my boy to be good. Cal will be getting me out soon; you can count on it."

Key stood as well. "If you change your mind about a visit …"

Lyric interrupted. "I won't. Like I said, I'll be out soon. Cal will *definitely* see to that." She gave a little laugh. "Then we'll come get Wain." She brushed tiny orange crumbs off the front of her shirt. "Oh yeah, if for some reason he does start school at your place, he's gonna need a new pair of shoes. He needs something new every time we turn around. Thanks for the snacks." She turned and walked toward where the guard was waiting.

Key shook her head. *The woman thanks me for the snacks, but not for taking care of her child?* Lyric was obviously nowhere near allowing the grim reality of her situation to permeate her thoughts. Key wondered how long it had been since she had.

As she emerged into the already-sultry Florida morning, Key felt as though she had been underwater, holding her breath for an entire hour. No intake of fresh air had ever felt so intensely essential. Once in the Jeep, she pulled a notebook from her purse and quickly scribbled as much as she could remember of the conversation. All in all, she thought, as she started the car, her talk with Lyric had been useful, more for the impressions of the woman herself than for the indistinct generalities she'd learned about Wain. The fractured picture emerging was colored more from what *wasn't* said than what was. Something was way off, and Key hoped Mrs. Titus could provide some clarity.

Chapter 14

PACKING UP

Mrs. Titus's boxy ranch house sat on a corner lot at the intersection of Leon Boulevard and Polo Avenue. Key parked along the curb, smiling at the concrete dog and blue-booted gnome that greeted her from a tiny rock garden by the mailbox. Over the front door a sheet of corrugated gray metal attached to two wooden posts formed a small porch, and to her right an older black sedan with a flat rear tire sat under a detached carport. Two large plastic pots filled with red geraniums and ivy flanked the shaded entrance. Everything was immaculate, and the homey cheeriness lifted Key's spirits, especially coming on the heels of where she'd just been.

Before she could raise her hand to knock, the door opened, revealing a plump woman in a colorful floral housedress and white sneakers. Her welcoming, wide smile put Key instantly at ease.

"You must be Wain's cousin! Come in! I'm Mayetta Titus." She held out her hand.

Key shook it with both of hers. "Key North! It is *so* nice to finally meet you, Mrs. Titus!" she said warmly. Stepping from the front door immediately into the living room, she stopped beside a well-used wingback recliner, heart pounding, as Mrs. Titus made her way down a short hallway.

"Oh, please, call me Mayetta," she said over her shoulder, then called out, "Wain, honey, your cousin Key is here!" There was no answer. She lowered her voice and said to Key, "He's been so sorrowful these days. And who can blame him. What that little boy has gone through! He must be outside." She crossed the room and opened the kitchen door. "Wain?"

As Key waited, not moving, barely noticing her surroundings, the surreal, dreamlike feeling again rushed into her every vein. *What am I doing?* Iris was right. She *was* impetuous. She still had time to escape. *Stop it right now*, she told herself sternly. If she felt like this, how must Wain be feeling? She at least had a choice in the matter.

"Wain, this is your cousin, Miss Key, who I told you about." Mrs. Titus had returned to the living room with her hand placed comfortingly on the shoulder of a small barefoot boy in navy gym shorts and a plain light-blue T-shirt.

Key stifled a gasp. It was like walking back a quarter century: the wavy dark-brown hair, her own wide aquamarine eyes staring directly at her through thick dark lashes, the broad mouth, ears that stuck out just a little. Lyric's features showed in Wain's eyebrows and chin, but mostly he was all Guy. The biggest difference, she sensed almost instantly, was a vulnerability in Wain that Guy had never possessed.

Any doubts she'd harbored disappeared like mist in the sun. How had she hesitated for even a minute? How could she have ever considered not taking him? *Oh, Edie*, she thought as she knelt to Wain's level, *he's absolutely your grandson. I'm so sorry you will never meet this little boy.*

She put her arms around his thin shoulders and drew him close. "Hello, Wain," she said kindly. "You can call me Key. I'm really, really happy to meet you." Wain didn't resist, but he didn't respond either. Key let go but stayed kneeling.

"What do you say, honey?" Mrs. Titus said gently.

"Nice to meet you," Wain replied, then looked down at the small car grasped tightly in his left hand.

"Is that a CartWheels car?" Key asked.

Wain glanced at her, surprised. He shook his head.

"His CartWheels cars are still in his backpack, at Mr. Cal's house."
Mrs. Titus pursed her lips. "He's never without that backpack, and
that *one* day I go to look, I can't find it anywhere." She patted Wain's
shoulder. "Honey, you go show Key your bedroom and your things,
and I'll get us some early lunch." She didn't wait for an answer, just got
busy pulling items from the refrigerator.

Key followed Wain down the short hall. On his bed sat a black
garbage bag, not nearly full; when she peeked inside, she saw several
items of clothing, a toothbrush and toothpaste, a pair of worn sneakers,
and a pair of flip-flops. This was all?

Wain stood quietly, watching her. He hadn't said another word.
Key couldn't imagine what he must be thinking. She thought back to
Guy's endless, observant chatter at that age. *That was Guy.* It would be
important to remember Wain wasn't Guy II.

"You just turned seven, didn't you?" she asked Wain.

"Uh-huh." He hurried to correct himself. "I mean, yes, ma'am."

"Mind if I sit down?" He shook his head, so Key perched on the
edge of the bed and put her hands on her thighs. "So." She smiled.
"You're coming to live with me for a while."

"I know. Mrs. Titus told me," Wain replied shyly.

"I live in North Carolina," Key said, pointing vaguely toward what
she thought was probably north. "It takes about ten hours to get to my
house, so we can drive it in a day. Long trip, though." When he didn't
respond, she added, "I drive a Jeep."

Wain looked a tiny bit more interested. "A Jeep? What color is it?"

Cars it would be. "Olive green. Come see; it's parked outside. You
know, when you see another Jeep, you're supposed to wave at the
driver, so on our trip, you've got to help me look for them, okay?"

"Um, okay." He showed no emotion as he led Key out of the room.

Mrs. Titus had set out plates with thick chicken-salad sandwiches,
chips, and carrot sticks next to a pan of fudgy frosted brownies. Key
suddenly realized she was starving. "That looks wonderful, Mayetta!
We'll be right back—we're going to check out the Jeep."

Wain's eyes widened when he peeked inside. Key had stocked up on
snacks and put them in a plastic basket in the back seat. "These are for

you, for the drive home," she told him. "Are there any special foods you like?"

"Not really." He didn't name the favorite snacks Lyric had mentioned.

Back inside, Mrs. Titus had the table set for two. "Wain, honey, if you want to have your lunch and juice outside, you go right ahead." She handed him a plate and a cup. Wain said a quiet "thank you," glanced briefly at Key, and then went out without another word, letting the screen door slap shut behind him. The sound took Key right back to her summer days as a child in Illinois.

"He likes to sit on the back steps," Mrs. Titus explained, placing a tall plastic cup of iced tea in front of Key. "I don't care where he eats, just want him to eat *something*. Key, I hope it's all right that I've taken the liberty of making a plan. After we eat, would you be willing to drive us to Mr. Cal's house? I asked Wain's friend Rico's mama, who lives next door to Mr. Cal, if Wain could play for a bit while you and I gather up his things, maybe have a little talk?"

Key nodded vigorously. "Of course! I'd love to have a chance to talk." She took a bite of sandwich. "Homemade chicken salad! It's so good! Mr. Cal? Is that Gary Callahan?"

Mrs. Titus sat down to Key's right. "Yes, but I never heard anyone call him Gary. And they were always Mr. Cal and Miss Lyric to me. Anyway, I've got so much on my mind about that little boy, I jotted down my thoughts." Digging in her dress pocket, Mrs. Titus produced a folded piece of paper and waved it gently in the air, then tucked it back in.

Key sat forward. Maybe she hadn't been imagining things. "You know, I wondered when I saw the bag on the bed. Surely, he has more than that?"

"Not much more, I'm sorry to say." All through lunch, Mrs. Titus's words tumbled out almost faster than Key could follow. "I've been back to Mr. Cal's house just once to get some of Wain's clothes. Searched all over for his CartWheels backpack, couldn't find it. Then my car broke down, so I took Wain to school on the city bus and never did get a chance to get back to Mr. Cal's house. That little boy's been missing that backpack more than words can say." She narrowed her eyes, looking straight at Key, holding up a stout forefinger. "And, Key, do you know, his mama has called me *one* time? And all she said is, for now Wain's daddy, Guy, is gonna make arrangements. I asked her, 'Do you want me to put Wain on the phone next time you call? He's missing you so bad,' and she told me no! What mama does that?" She shook her head and crunched indignantly on a carrot.

"Lyric told me the same thing about bringing Wain to visit her in jail." Key helped herself to a brownie. It was every bit as delicious as it looked. "Mmm!"

Mrs. Titus's eyes widened. "You talked to Miss Lyric? When?"

"Before I came over here, I stopped by the jail and spent an hour with her." Apparently, no one had told Mayetta much at all.

"You *did*? Mercy! How's she doing? What did she tell you?"

"You know …" Key hesitated, dabbing at her lips with her napkin, not sure how to approach the topic. "I—"

Mrs. Titus broke in. "No, don't tell me. She's *all about* herself and Mr. Cal. No time for her boy."

"Well, yes, Mayetta! To be honest, I was shocked at how seemingly unconcerned she was about Wain."

"Oh, there's no *seem* about it. That's the way it is. She—" Mrs. Titus stopped as the screen door squeaked and Wain entered, setting his cup and plate on the counter. He'd barely touched his food.

With a small groan, Mrs. Titus stood. "Wain, honey, come over here with your plate and take three more *big* bites of your sandwich, please, then you can have a brownie. We've made a plan. This afternoon, Key and I are gonna go pack up your things at Mr. Cal's house while you play with Rico. His mama said you can swim with him this afternoon."

Wain's face lit up. It was the first time Key had seen him animated, and it transformed him. He grabbed the sandwich and obediently took three bites, then said, "Okay! I'll go change." He stopped, dismayed. "But I don't have any swim trunks. They're still at Cal's house."

"We'll bring them over to Rico's," Mrs. Titus assured him. "Let's hop on into Key's Jeep and head over there."

It wasn't quite a hop, but with a little bit of a struggle, Key managed to get Mrs. Titus situated in the front seat. "Never ridden in a Jeep before," she said, arranging herself and gripping her shoulder seatbelt strap with her right hand and a container of brownies for Rico's mother with her left. "How about you, honey?"

Wain merely shook his head and stared out the window. His initial excitement over the Jeep and swimming with Rico had vanished.

After a brief stop to buy plastic bins, they drove to Goldendale Heights, where Rico's mother, Sasha, greeted both Wain and Mrs. Titus with a warm hug, calling after the boys as they ran off, "No swimming until I'm there!" Turning to Key and Mrs. Titus, she said, "Wain can wear a pair of Rico's swim trunks, no need to bring his over." She hesitated, then added, "Our hearts go out to Wain. I was happy to hear from Mayetta that he has family to live with."

"Yes, he'll be living with me in North Carolina for the time being. His biological father, my cousin, has been given custody," Key replied. She couldn't help comparing Sasha's motherly concern with Lyric's antiseptic, emotionless demeanor.

"His bio ... oh! So Lyric and Cal won't be back home anytime soon?" Sasha's eyes were full of questions.

No doubt the arrests would be a topic of neighborhood conversations for years to come. Key merely said, "There's a lot to work out. Thanks again, Sasha."

Callahan's home was imposing: a two-story white stucco structure with a red tile roof. Ornately carved double front doors dominated the arched entrance; on either side bougainvillea in dark-blue pots climbed trellises, spilling bright-pink clouds onto second-floor windowsills. Neglect clung to the property, though—issues that couldn't be explained by the short amount of time Callahan and Lyric had been in jail. The grounds needed weeding and mowing, naturally, but the shrubs were overgrown and spindly, and there were noticeable cracks in the stucco. It all told a story.

Mrs. Titus produced a key and after unlocking it, swung the door open. Key followed her into a two-story foyer where winding stairs led up to a catwalk hallway. Mrs. Titus entered a code on the alarm panel, then sniffed, made a face, and headed for the kitchen, saying, "Oh, that fridge has to have all kinds of nasty food in it."

The house did smell musty and sour, but it was spotless in an almost sinister way. Although they had just walked in, suddenly Key could hardly wait to leave. "Mayetta, unless they're paying you, none of this is your responsibility. Let's just pack up Wain's things." Without waiting for a response, she stepped back out the front door and pulled three nested containers from the Jeep.

"You feel it." She hadn't known Mrs. Titus was right behind her. "You feel the hard things that happened in this house. And the truth of the matter is, Key, *they* aren't paying me! Mr. Cal always had Miss Lyric send my pay from the hotel."

Key frowned. "The hotel paid your salary for cleaning his personal property?"

"Oh mercy." Mrs. Titus grabbed the remaining bin. "You know," she said as they went back inside, "I've got stories to tell." She patted her dress pocket again.

"And I want to hear them! Let's get this done, Mayetta. This place makes my skin crawl."

Mrs. Titus stood with two fingers pressed lightly against her cheek, thinking out loud. "Before I do anything, I'm gonna hunt down that little boy's backpack." She tapped the table. "When I left here the day before they were arrested, Wain had it, just like every day. He laid it right here, said his mama had been telling him to leave it home; she was gonna put a new car in it for his birthday. Those cars and that backpack are his pride and joy; and maybe like a little bit of a security blanket too."

"I'll help you," Key offered. "What does it look like?"

Mrs. Titus manipulated her hands to create an image a little larger than a shoebox. "About this big, red and gray with white trim, with a red car on the front and the word 'CartWheels' in big black letters, wrapped around the whole thing. You just see 'Cart' on the front. And the little black *e*'s in 'Wheels' are shaped like tires."

Key surveyed the spotless house; not a single item was out of place. "Surely something that unique will be easy to find." But it wasn't.

After twenty minutes, she finally left Mrs. Titus to search alone and went to pack up Wain's room, where she saw in horrified dismay that the sterile neatness on exhibit in the rest of the museum-like house did not extend to this depressing space. There was no bed, just a mattress covered with a sheet and a wadded-up gray velour blanket; neither had seen the inside of a washing machine for a long time, if ever. No pillowcase on the grubby pillow; no pictures on the walls; floor devoid of toys. Didn't little boys have all kinds of playthings? A few babyish books were scattered around, which she left; but she did add one called *FireFlyer Wins the Race* to the bin. She opened every drawer and packed every item of clothing, most of which she thought looked too small. In the bathroom she found nothing except a toothbrush, a Mickey Mouse scrub glove, and a nearly empty container of women's bodywash.

As Key was snapping the top on a container of clothing, she heard a shout from downstairs. She ran to see. At the bottom of the steps stood a triumphant Mrs. Titus, who, after searching nearly the entire eerily silent house, had found the backpack stashed in the bottom of an extra-deep kitchen drawer, wrapped in a tea towel and buried under several wadded-up, unused garbage bags. Mystified, Mrs. Titus held it up. "It feels like it's still full of cars. But why would they put it *there*?"

And more importantly, Key thought in consternation as she carried the bin down the steps, *why didn't Lyric tell me about the backpack today, at the jail when we discussed Wain's love of CartWheels?* Had she known it was hidden there? It made Key slightly uneasy, but she decided to give Wain's mother the benefit of the doubt. "Maybe Lyric or Cal hid it so Wain wouldn't see it when he came home on his birthday?" She tucked the backpack, heavier than she expected it to be, into a container. "Let's surprise him with it later."

As Key stacked the full bins on the front steps, she could hear the boys splashing next door. "It sounds like Wain's having a lot of fun. If it's okay with you, Mayetta, maybe we could talk by the pool? I'll run over and tell Sasha we'll be about another half hour." It was warm but sitting outside was preferable to staying in that disquieting house.

When Key returned, cans of soda and cups of ice were waiting on a glass-topped table between two teak chaise lounges. Mrs. Titus opened an oversized green-and-white sun umbrella, then handed Key a beach towel with a design matching the CartWheels backpack. "This is Wain's. He's gonna want it. And he's got swim trunks in the shed there. Blue with pink sharks." Key found them hanging on a hook inside the door and put them with the towel, then sank onto the chaise lounge and took a big gulp of her drink. "Thank you! I didn't realize I was so thirsty. Mayetta, I'm just so curious, even more so now that I've been in the house—how *was* life with Lyric and Callahan and Wain?"

"Oh, mercy. I'm gonna say it was tippy from the get-go. Mr. Cal's *never* been an easy man to work for."

"Tippy?" Key answered, amused. "I've never heard that before."

"Tippy, like you're off-balance. Mr. Cal can be nice one minute and then cold mean the next. You just never know which will show. Especially when he's been drinking." Mrs. Titus lowered herself onto the chaise lounge next to Key's and smoothed her dress over her extended legs, then squinted around, as if she were looking for the more sinister version of Callahan in the shrubbery lining the privacy fence.

Key watched a dragonfly hovering over the turquoise water; she and Mayetta were seated in a beautiful backyard, but it too was beginning to look shabby, and the pool needed a good cleaning. "I know exactly what you mean, Mayetta. Tippy is the perfect description. Did you clean for him before Lyric and Wain moved in?"

"Yes. And before that, I was a maid at the Sojourner, that's the hotel where Mr. Cal was in charge. I never met Miss Lyric there though. The work there became too much, you know, walking those halls all day. So Mr. Cal started me cleaning this house a few times a week. Then Wain and his mama moved in with Mr. Cal ... I don't know ..."—she paused, tapping her lips—"maybe about two, three months after that. Wain was just a little boy—not even four years old. From then on, I've come five days a week, Monday to Friday, noon to six or seven. It varied. Lots of weekends too, when they were gone. Housework, feed Wain dinner, clean up before Mr. Cal and Miss Lyric got home. Mr. Cal wants everything spotless, all the time. Kinda an obsession."

"Yes, that's easy to see," Key replied. "Except ..." She hesitated.

"Except that little boy's room. Mr. Cal didn't allow it. 'I'm not paying you to clean *that* room. Stay out of there, Mayetta.' As if *he* was paying me at all! But I did go in and clean now and then. Washed his bedding when I could. None of that was my biggest worry though."

"What do you mean?" Key asked, dreading the answer.

"Mr. Cal was *always* ragging on that boy. He's the kind who seemed to enjoy knocking down *anything* Wain got happiness from. He's a *joy stealer*." She tipped her head at Key. "Does that make sense?"

This needed to be a face-to-face conversation. Key got up and rotated her chair so that she was looking directly at Mrs. Titus instead of sitting parallel to her, then asked, "Mr. Cal is a joy stealer?"

Mrs. Titus set down her glass and dug in her pocket for the paper she'd shown Key earlier. "Mercy, yes. Mr. Cal found all kind of fault in Wain, ever since almost the first day they moved in." She began to read a list. "Mr. Cal ate his food, threw his toys away for no reason. Mr. Cal flicked his ears." She flicked her own ear. "Like this, but real hard."

"For what?" Key asked, horrified.

Mrs. Titus widened her eyes. "Anything! If Wain didn't push his chair in, he got a flick or a smack. If Wain left a fingerprint on the glass door, he got a smack on the backside of the head. If Wain didn't answer quick enough, he'd get grabbed and shook, hard. You know! Kid things! Oh, that little boy was *terrified* of spilling or breaking something. Anytime that happened, I'd try to get between, mop up in a hurry, fix things before Mr. Cal would see, you know, to protect Wain." Mrs. Titus pulled a crumpled tissue from her other dress pocket and dabbed her eyes. "I did what I could, but I wasn't here all the time, didn't know who to tell, didn't know who would believe me. Mr. Cal just looked real good to the outside world."

This had been Edie's grandson's life. Key was stunned into silence, but she believed Mrs. Titus. She had felt it before they ever opened the front door, felt it when she'd left the jail. No wonder Wain seemed so vulnerable. He had lived nearly half his few years in a house that reeked of contempt and rejection and fear. "Mayetta ... was Wain's mother aware of Gary Callahan's behavior?"

"You met Miss Lyric ... what do you think?" Mrs. Titus replied, sounding uncharacteristically tart. "That woman shuts her eyes to everything about Mr. Cal that isn't pretty." She waved a hand dismissively. "One time I tried to tell her my worries, and she said, all pouty, 'It doesn't concern you. You mind to your cleaning, Mayetta. *That's* what Cal pays you to do.' I think more than once she took Mr. Cal's side over her little boy. Now, what kind of mama would she be if Mr. Cal was out of the picture? I don't know."

"So maybe you'd say she was willfully ignorant?" Key asked. It made sense, considering the conversation she'd had with Lyric.

Mrs. Titus finished her drink, then shook the ice cubes onto the parched soil of a nearby potted palm. "That's a good way to put it. We need to go soon, but, Key, I want you to hear one last important story, from just a couple months ago." She took a deep breath. "I was upstairs cleaning. Didn't know anyone else was home yet. But Wain must have gotten home early. I looked out the window from the master bedroom and saw Mr. Cal and Wain at the table over there. I could tell the man had been drinking, lots of bottles on the table, and he had Wain's towel here wrapped around his big neck. They didn't see me, but I saw Mr. Cal eating Wain's special snacks, nasty as you please." She wagged her finger back and forth. "Not sharing one bite! Wain had his arms wrapped around himself like this." She clutched her sides, arms crossed in front of her. "He was so scared, shivering on that hot day like it was below zero." Mrs. Titus frowned, thinking for a moment. "Then I saw Mr. Cal hold up a card, like a reading card?"

"A flash card?" Key asked, recalling Lyric's words from their visit that morning: "*Cal would spend hours with him, trying to teach him to read. Flash cards ... set up a reward system and all.*"

Mrs. Titus lifted a hand, palm up. "Yes! A flash card. And all of a sudden, that man jumped up and kicked Wain's chair over, and Wain fell!" She jerked her right leg convulsively upward, demonstrating.

"You see, he was *punishing* Wain when he couldn't read the flash cards, and yes, the boy *does* have trouble with reading."

"*What?*" As impossible as the story was to comprehend, Key felt as though the drama was unfolding right in front of her.

Mrs. Titus nodded. "I had to do something! So I came out to the balcony carrying a throw rug like I was gonna shake it, and I stared hard at Mr. Cal." Her dark eyes blazed. "That man needed to know I was there. Needed to know I saw what he did! Oh, my heart was going like a jackhammer! Next thing you know, Mr. Cal came into the house and called me downstairs, walked me to the front door, shut it in my face. I thought for sure he was gonna fire me. But he didn't. And after that, I think because he knew I knew, maybe it got a little better for Wain; at least that was the last time *I* ever saw him do anything to him before they were arrested." Mrs. Titus laced her fingers tightly together and held them to her chest in a gesture of supplication, her anxious brown eyes searching Key's face. "I knew soon as I met you that life is gonna go better for Wain. I pray that little boy finds peace and love and calm at your house. He's *way* overdue."

Key swung her legs off the chaise and leaned toward her. "Mayetta," she said earnestly, "I have never raised a little boy before or, to be perfectly honest, even know much about them. But I can *promise* he will have love and security, and best of all, he'll be far, far from Callahan and his abusive ways. I can't thank you enough for all you've done and the light you've shed on at least a little bit of what it has been like for Wain here. I know his father has *no* idea. You've been the one person Wain could trust."

"I believe the Lord himself put me there. No child deserves what's been happening to Wain. Mm-mm." Mrs. Titus shook her head and gathered up the cans and cups. "We'd best get going."

"Of course." Key picked up Wain's towel and swim trunks and opened the sliding glass door, stepping aside to let Mrs. Titus through. "Mayetta, I'd like to see a picture of Callahan. Are there any around?"

Mrs. Titus began rinsing out the cups. "Mr. Cal doesn't like his picture taken, but there is one in the master bedroom. Upstairs and turn right at the second door."

The framed picture was obviously a selfie. Key picked it up. Callahan and Lyric on a dock, with a boat behind them bearing the name *Knotty Cal*, the ocean glistening silver. They were both wearing sunglasses, Lyric's blond hair lifting in the breeze, Callahan in a plain gray baseball cap pulled low over his forehead, covering most of his sandy-blond hair. Although Lyric was smiling widely, his lips were pressed together. *More like a grimace*, Key thought. In terms of what he looked like, the picture told her next to nothing.

There was still plenty of space in the Jeep once Key loaded the plastic bins containing the shockingly small amount of worldly goods she'd gathered from Wain's room. *No wonder he is attached to that backpack*, she mused. *It must have been the only thing he has been truly allowed to own.* After one more walk-through and double-checking the lock, Key and Mrs. Titus went next door and thanked Rico and Sasha, who hugged Wain again and told him their family would miss him.

Key had asked Mrs. Titus if they could wait to return the backpack until they returned to Leon Boulevard. "Maybe it's crazy," she told Mayetta, "but I think that should happen at your house. I don't want Wain anywhere near this hostile, joyless place when, in the future, he remembers the moment it was returned to him."

"I don't think that's crazy at all, Key. No good memories for Wain at this house. Except maybe Rico next door."

"And you most of all, Mayetta. Even more reason he should associate a good memory with you."

Wain was happy to see his towel but, to both women's surprise, asked nothing about the backpack. After saying goodbye to Rico and Sasha, he climbed into the Jeep and fell asleep almost instantly, the towel wadded up and pressed between his head and the door. Key had planned to take them out to dinner but quickly realized it would be too much for one day. They decided to order pizza instead and drove directly to 287 Leon Boulevard.

Chapter 15

CARTWHEELS

ey grabbed one container from the Jeep while Mrs. Titus checked the mailbox, then unlocked her front door. Wain waited patiently, flip-flops in his hand, towel draped around his shoulders, dried hair pressed against the side of his head where he'd slept on it. His whole body drooped, as though the invisible burden he carried was bowing him down. *Exhaustion, yes,* Key thought, *but more than that.* She recognized sorrow. Hopelessness. It was much sadder when carried by a little boy. She followed him into the house and set the container near the front door. As Wain headed for his bedroom, she spoke up.

"Wain, honey." When he turned around, she said, "Mrs. Titus has something for you. Mayetta, will you open this container, please?"

Smiling broadly, Mrs. Titus set the mail and her keys on a side table, put her arm around Wain's shoulder, and led him to where Key stood. "I think you're gonna like this, honey." She pulled the cover off with a little dramatic flair, swooping her arm downward to point out what sat on top of the clothes Key had packed.

Wain genuinely smiled, a huge, unfiltered grin. Wordlessly he reached in and grabbed the backpack, pressing it close to his chest, then burying his face into it.

"I found it in a far-back kitchen drawer," Mrs. Titus volunteered, digging the well-used tissue out of her dress pocket and wiping her eyes. "Hidden way in the back, under tea towels and whatnot. Don't know who put it there, but it's back to its rightful owner! Everything in there? It felt as heavy as normal to me."

Key, fighting to contain her own emotions, watched as Wain set his backpack on the coffee table and eagerly unzipped it. Inside, it was empty except for a couple of folded papers, which he set aside; then he reached under a gray-and-red fabric CartWheels logo, unzipped yet another zipper, and flipped the canvas back, revealing a collection of several colorful metal cars, each about two or three inches long, arranged neatly in clear plastic mesh sleeves. Wain ran his fingers along the cars; then his face crumpled as he pulled out a black one. "It's *SplishFlash*. Not Black Diamond," he said in an aggrieved whisper, sliding the car immediately back into the sleeve. He dropped his hands to his sides and slammed his back against the couch cushion, fighting to keep from crying.

"Oh, honey, I'm sorry," Mrs. Titus said sympathetically. "I know you were so hoping for the diamond one."

Still looking disappointed, Wain sat forward with a resigned sigh and took out a dark-green-and-yellow car, closing his fist around it. "FireFlyer." He said the name as though he were finally reunited with a long-lost, beloved friend.

Key recognized the name from the book she'd packed. "Whoa. Cool! Where'd you find that second zipper, Wain?" she asked, hoping to distract him from his disappointment.

Mrs. Titus laughed. "I asked him the same thing when he first showed me his CartWheels. You've got no idea he's got a whole car collection in his backpack!"

"It's right here." Wain showed her a zipper hidden cleverly in the seam.

Key sat down on the sofa, leaning her elbows on her thighs. "Genius! What did you call that one in your hand?"

"FireFlyer." It was the most confident he'd sounded so far. His backpack probably *was* a bit of a security blanket, as Mrs. Titus had observed.

"Would you show it to me?" Key asked.

Wain opened his fist, showing her the tiny car on his upturned palm, his fingers still prune-like from playing in the water.

So this is a CartWheel, Key thought. It was a miniature work of art, with a neon trunk and flames painted on the side.

"The back part glows in the dark, and the doors open like wings, like this." Wain showed her.

Key was genuinely intrigued. "Like a firefly! And the flames! Fire! Flying! It's very cool. Are they all this awesome? Is this your favorite?"

"Um, yeah, kinda," Wain answered, then added hastily, "but I like them all the same. I have six—well, seven now 'cause I just got SplishFlash." He said the new car's name grudgingly. "Some are, like, super hard to get."

Mrs. Titus broke in. "Wain, honey, before you get all your cars out, run take a shower and change your clothes. Wash your hair and be sure to rinse it real good. Drop everything outside your door. I'll wash your beach towel and a few other things so they're ready to pack up for your trip tomorrow with Key." After Wain left the room still hugging his backpack, Mrs. Titus explained, "He cleans up himself and washes his own hair, uses the gentle baby shampoo."

Key smiled. "Good to know. I'll get baby shampoo. I love how you treat him!"

Mrs. Titus dropped into the recliner, crossing her ankles, which Key noticed were slightly swollen. "It's just my way, the way I was raised and the way I raised mine. Like I always say, respect them when they're little, they'll respect you when they're big."

Key laughed. "You should trademark that! You let him know what you expect of him, but it never feels angry or punitive. It reminds me of my own parents." She glanced around the room at the many framed photos on the walls and side tables. Mrs. Titus was obviously a very proud mother and grandmother.

"Oh, it's always trial and error with little children, Key! Wain's an easy boy." Mrs. Titus lowered her voice. "Mostly because he doesn't expect promises to be kept, and he's always on guard, afraid of making a mistake. You'd think parent love comes naturally, but it seems to be ever gone from some. Or they lose it real early along the way, and their child becomes a hindrance. That's what I think happened with Miss Lyric."

"But obviously not you!" Key replied. "All these pictures! I would love to hear about your family."

"My kids, oh, they're my life. I've got two. One in Chicago, my girl Tasha. She's got my two grandbabies, Margo and Dellie." Mrs. Titus pointed at a picture of two adorable elementary-age girls on one carousel horse, Tasha, tall and serene, with an arm around each of them. "I don't see them near often enough. Tasha is married to Kwan, a martial-arts instructor."

"They're beautiful. So is Tasha. What about your other child?"

"Isaac." Mrs. Titus picked up a picture of a stocky beaming man on a boat, holding a large fish. "He lives closer, down in Tampa where he drives a cement truck. He's got a serious woman friend now." She smiled widely and held up fingers crossed. "Grandmama has hope." They heard the bathroom door shut and the shower start.

Key had seen no signs that Mrs. Titus lived with anyone, but she didn't want to presume. "It sounds like you and your husband worked very hard to give them a great life. Is your husband still here?"

Mrs. Titus sorted through the mail on the side table, picked up a large postcard depicting a real-estate ad, and fanned herself vigorously, rocking the squeaky recliner. "At least these wastes of paper are good for something. Oh, Sol's been heavenward for a long time now. He was a handyman, had his own business. With a name like Solomon Titus, you know he's got to be honest!"

Key laughed. "Yes. It's very biblical."

"Sure could use his handiness now! Lots around here that needs fixing." Mrs. Titus gestured around the room. "I came home one day, and Sol's van was parked out front. He was never home at that time but told me he didn't feel well and laid down on the couch. I came to bring him a sweet tea—oh, that man loved my sweet tea! And Key, you know, he had gone to glory right there while I was in the kitchen. Heart attack. He was sixty-three. Sleeping peacefully."

"Oh, that must have been such a shock," Key replied sympathetically.

"Miss him to this day. Isaac comes up and helps out when he can. He's gonna come up and work on my car soon. He's real good with motors."

"Mayetta, what will you do now? Now that you don't have the job at Cal's?"

The fanning and rocking continued. "Tasha asked me to come to Chicago for the summer. The girls are out of school, and she and Kwan can use the help. Matter of fact, she's been wanting me to get away from Mr. Cal for a long, long time. But I've been that concerned for Wain, I haven't felt free to make any decisions." Mrs. Titus was still talking in lower tones.

That's how it is with people like Mayetta, Key thought. *They simply do the right thing without obsessively weighing the cost to themselves.* She was a gem. Key dove right in. "Mayetta, I'd love to buy your plane ticket to Chicago. And I have a check from Guy, Wain's father, for the time you've taken care of Wain."

The relief on Mrs. Titus's face was evident, but she merely said, "Wain needed help, and I was there. Can't leave a little boy to blow around like a blade of grass in a hurricane. He's kind of falling into *your* lap too."

Key nodded. "You're right, he is, isn't he? I may need to call you for advice down the road. Maybe I'll keep you on retainer." They laughed, but inside, she felt an unfamiliar sense of shame on Guy's behalf. As painful as it was to consider, Guy's refusal or inability (or whatever it was) to visit or care for his son had certainly compounded Wain's losses. Key added, "Seriously, Mayetta, I want to help you as you've helped Wain. It's small thanks, but it's from my heart."

"You put it that way, I'd be rude to say no. I appreciate it," Mrs. Titus said gratefully. She took a deep breath, as though a worrisome thought had finally evaporated.

"Wonderful! I'll bring you a check tomorrow when I come by to get Wain," Key replied, happy the conversation had transpired so smoothly. She silently resolved that it would cover plane tickets *and* car repairs, along with the generous reimbursement Guy had provided. It was the least they could do.

Key's stomach growled. "How about some dinner?" she asked. "Do you have a favorite pizza place I could order from? My treat."

After they'd had dinner ("more than that little boy has eaten since he's been here"), while Mrs. Titus bustled about, Key sat at the table with Wain, who lined up his cars and proudly showed Key the ingenious detail that accompanied the catchy names.

"What's this one?" Key touched a car with an Asian theme.

"The Martial Star. It's like the kung fu car."

"This one with the dandelion design with a lion's head?"

"DandyLion," Wain replied, lightly tracing the design.

"And this green one with the four-leaf-clover guitar design?"

"ShamRocker. That's my first car. I got it for my birthday when I turned six—no, five."

"It's supercool," Key said, smiling at his enthusiasm. "How about this orange one with the fire on the wheels?" She set it lightly on her palm and held it up to the light, admiring the neon licks of flame on orange tires.

"PyroTire."

"PyroTire! Cool name! Maybe it goes so fast, the tires turn to flames? And here's FireFlyer, and what's this police car with these copper lights on top?"

"CopperTop."

"Oh, that makes sense!" Key replied, laughing. "Love these names! Okay, last one: this black car with—what is this?—'57 Chevy fins and goggles for headlights?"

"SplishFlash. That's the one I got today. It's like, a *boring* one. No one wants it." Wain took it from her and pushed it impatiently back into a mesh sleeve.

Key felt for him. As a child, she'd had birthdays where she'd gotten a lesser or wrong version of the gift she really wanted. She tried to keep the conversation going. "Does it go underwater? You know, because of the goggles?" When he looked at her like she was nuts and shook his head, she said, "These are all very cool. Thanks for showing them to me!" She already felt like *she* was underwater. "Wain," she added, laying her hand gently on his arm. He looked at her questioningly. "I'm so happy you're coming home with me."

He smiled slightly but said nothing, rolling FireFlyer along the edge of the place mat.

"Oh, honey, I'm going to miss you, but you're going to be just fine with Key." Mrs Titus walked over to where Wain was sitting, leaned down, and wrapped her arms around him. "It's mighty good to see all your cars again. I thank the good Lord I could find that backpack. It's like a miracle."

"Thanks for finding it," Wain answered shyly.

After Wain had been tucked into bed with his backpack, Key and Mrs. Titus talked for another hour. Mayetta was a wealth of insight and information; she'd been on the ground floor of Callahan and Lyric's relationship, and even her limited observations gave Key a much fuller picture of Wain's troubling, chaotic life.

As Key gathered her things to head for the Jeep, Mrs. Titus held up the papers Wain had taken out of his backpack. "Oh, Key, look at this! It says notice of foreclosure! All taped up!"

Key took the papers, which were folded in half, writing side out, and secured around three edges with the wide tape that had held them to the door. "Why am I not surprised? Now that I think about it, Lyric mentioned to me that they were planning to move. She must've known this was coming. What a mess."

Mrs. Titus gave a flip of her hand. "Mercy. Seems I would have been out of a job anyhow."

"I doubt it matters now, but I'll take them with me." Key opened the bin and placed the still-folded papers inside, then gave Mrs. Titus a hug and thanked her again.

"Good night, Key. It'll be a new day for that little boy."

After she finally fell asleep, Key dreamed she saw Edie across a wide, fast-flowing bright-orange river, her mouth open in a mute scream, waving frantically, pointing to a tiny rowboat hurtling downstream in the raging current. Key waded out, fighting to stay upright against the rushing water; when she reached the boat, she saw Wain in the bottom, asleep. In the inexplicable way dreams unfold, she splashed easily to shore, pulling the boat by a red dog leash. Then Edie disappeared, but Lyric and Callahan—menacing and angry—waited for Key on the shore. Lyric wore a black T-shirt with white writing that said KNOTTY CAL. Suddenly she (or was it he?) was on top of Key, knocking her down, grabbing for Wain and his backpack. Key fought back for all she was worth and woke herself, yelling, "Get away!" or at least trying to force the words out—it sounded more like a guttural growl. Still shaky, comforting herself that it was just a dream, Key got out of bed and pushed back the curtains. Streaky pink clouds promised a beautiful traveling day. It was time to pick up her new little companion and head home.

It was such a relief to know that man was locked up.

Chapter 16

FIRST HIKE

Key and Wain. Late May

They pulled their backpacks off and sat on the leaf-covered ground, leaning against a long-fallen log. Key said nothing, letting Wain absorb the sounds of the woods, hoping he'd speak first. In the four days since they'd gotten back to Pike House, Wain had answered when spoken to but had not volunteered a single word. He was unfailingly polite, too polite. *Terrified*, she thought. She leaned back, her elbows on the log. "So this is the woods. It's my first time here too. What do you think?"

"It's nice." Wain was looking down, as always, seeming to try his hardest to be invisible.

"Hey! Want to play a little game?" Without thinking, Key gave Wain a light punch on the shoulder, then felt terrible as he flinched and shied away. "Oh, honey, I'm so sorry! I didn't mean to scare you!" *I need to monitor myself*, she thought, shaking her head. Wain had good reason to misread a simple affectionate gesture. "Here's the game. Tell me what sounds you can hear in these woods."

"I hear you talking." He wasn't trying to be funny. In fact, he was shivering, leaning forward, his arms clasped tightly around his knees.

Key laughed. "Touché. Okay. I'll stop talking. We'll sit here, and when you hear something, hold your finger up, like this." She pointed her index finger to the sky. "Ready?"

Wain nodded tensely.

As they sat quietly, Key momentarily shut her eyes. Far overhead, the steady hum of a jet underscored a woodpecker tapping madly, while crows chattered, a hawk screamed; and somewhere out in the carpet of leaves, she heard a critter scuttle quickly past. She opened her eyes to see if Wain had registered any of them, but he hadn't moved a muscle, except that his hands were now firmly grasping the CartWheels backpack on his lap. He was still shivering.

The hawk screamed again. Key held up her finger. "Did you hear that?"

Wain simply shook his head. He seemed to have no idea what she meant.

"That was a hawk. They're big, beautiful birds. Probably hunting for mice out in the open areas. Or maybe another bird is chasing it away. They do that, you know. The littler birds are very brave. They chase away the big hawks and other birds that try to rob their nests." Still no answer. After a moment, Key patted Wain's shoulder. "Okay, let's keep listening, but let's try another game. Tell me what you see." She desperately wanted to unlock any portion of his devastated psyche, help him notice what was around him, give him new eyes. "What's the sun doing right now?"

"The sun?" Confused, Wain gazed up at the patches of deep blue visible between the treetops. "I don't know."

"Look around," Key replied kindly. "What are the sunbeams doing here in these woods? Do you see all these different spots, the shiny areas and shadows? The way the sun makes them sparkle in places?"

"It's ..." Wain swallowed. "Um, I don't know what you want me to say."

Key sat forward, far enough so he could see her face. "Oh, Wain, there's no wrong answer. I'm playing a game with you, kind of like I Spy. Did you ever play that?"

"No." Wain traced the letters on his backpack.

Key plowed on, determined to somehow engage him. "Okay, well, I Spy is a game where I might say, for instance, 'I spy something blue,' and you look around and guess what it might be. Like the blue might be the sky. Or my shorts. Want to try?"

Wain gave a tiny nod, his interest finally piqued. "Okay, but ... I mean, your shorts are actually more like *teal*."

She stifled a laugh. "True! Touché again, buddy!" She surveyed the woods, looking for anything he might be able to guess on the first try. "Okay. I spy ... something ... red. Now you guess what that might be."

Wain's eyes zeroed in immediately to her lap. "Your camera?"

"Yes!" Key held up her hand for a high five and with just a hint of a grin, he lightly slapped it. "Great job! Yes, my red camera. Now it's your turn to spy."

Wain sat up a little straighter and studied his surroundings, still holding tight to his backpack. "Um, I spy something ... gray."

Key could hardly keep from hugging him, but this moment felt as fragile as a fresh butterfly; the wrong touch would kill it. "Gray, huh? My shirt?"

Another tiny hint of a smile. "No." Then fear. "But it can be if you want it to be."

"No, since I was wrong, I have to guess again. Your CartWheels backpack?"

"Uh-huh." Wain patted the gray fabric on his backpack.

Key hugged his stiff shoulders. "You win! I had to guess twice, and you just had to guess once. Good job!"

They kept the game going as they ate the peanut-butter-and-honey sandwiches Key had packed earlier. Wain continued to be fearful of making the wrong guess, but he loved choosing; she was overjoyed that he had relaxed just a little.

"Wow, see that tree over there?" After several I Spy turns, Key tipped her water bottle in the direction of a smallish maple tree with a deep winding scar snaking up its trunk.

Wain nodded. "It's all twisty."

"Let's take a look." She set down her water and picked up her camera, then stood and brushed herself off. "You can leave your things; we'll come back." Wain picked up his backpack anyway and slung it over his shoulder, inexplicably walking just behind her as she strode to the tree. "See this tree trunk, Wain? It'll live for a long time, but it'll never be exactly like the others." As Wain ran his small hands over the deep grooves in the trunk, Key explained, "A big kudzu vine wrapped around it when it was young and changed it forever. But look how tough the tree is. It has scars, but it's going to survive just fine!" Was this analogy over his head? Of course it was. She snapped a photo of him by the tree.

Wain glanced into the woods, frowned slightly, then bent down and stared. To Key's great delight, he spoke. "Those logs over there." He pointed. "It kinda looks like Mudflap Girl's legs."

"Mudflap Girl? Is that a CartWheel?"

Wain regarded her as if she'd gone mad. "No. It's Cal's tattoo. The one on the back of his neck."

Stunned that he'd actually mentioned Callahan, but still not sure what he meant, Key bent down to Wain's level, looking hard; then it dawned on her. "Ohh! Mudflap Girl! The shiny silver girl on semi-truck tire mud flaps." She could see the leg-logs now. "They *do* look like legs! That's the one that's bent, and that's the straight one. Good eyes, kiddo!" She ruffled Wain's hair, unsure how to keep him talking, but dying to find out more. "So Callahan had a Mudflap Girl tattoo on his back?"

Wain nodded. "And a big black-and-red spider on his leg." He clutched his backpack close to his chest and walked quickly back to the log where they'd had lunch.

It was enough. With a much lighter heart than the one she'd brought into the woods, Key gathered their things and shrugged into her backpack. "Want to come back here sometime?"

Wain nodded again. Key gave him a little sideways squeeze. "You're so observant. Your sharp eyes are going to help me find all kinds of birds for my pictures!" She got another faint smile in reply. *Hey*, she thought happily, making sure he walked right beside her, *we've made progress.*

Chapter 17

ADJUSTMENT

Key and Wain. Late May/Early June

As usual, Key was up by five to have coffee and some uninterrupted time with her laptop at the kitchen table. After working steadily on her card designs for two hours, she finally sat back, coffee cup in hand, and let herself consider the achievements and complexities of the past several days.

Their "I Spy" hike had broken the ice in a way that nothing else had; and the awkwardness of living together began to give way to a comfortable routine. They were both on fresh paths, after all; Pike House was almost as new to her as it was to him. Thankfully, Wain was sleeping through the night now and usually joined her around eight, appearing quietly in the kitchen doorway or pushing the screen door open to find her on the porch swing, or already tackling the yard chores. He'd reply with a shy "morning" when she'd say cheerfully, "Good morning, buddy!" He was getting used to her hugs, though he still didn't hug her in return. Now and then she'd catch a glimmer of a smile when she ruffled his hair, but she had yet to hear him laugh.

Somewhat to her surprise, Key genuinely enjoyed Wain's company; and as far as she could tell, it was mutual. She hoped so, anyway. In her eagerness for him to be more comfortable, however, she felt she could easily try too hard to force conversations or interaction, so she let him set the pace as she went about her days as usual, giving him plenty of room to join her for chats if he wanted (he especially loved her stories about when she was his age), explore the yard and grounds, or play with his cars. She'd also discovered he loved watching kids' cooking competitions on TV, so most evenings they'd plop down on the blue sectional and watch one before he went to bed. Bit by bit, she sensed, they were building a friendship, still tenuous but growing more stable. More than anything, she wanted him to know he could trust her.

She poured herself a warm-up. Yes, she was relieved at the easiness with which they'd meshed; but were they simply existing at this moment in the eye of the storm? She had to be realistic. Most likely Wain's compliant personality meant he probably didn't feel completely safe with her yet. After all, his mother, the person he most *needed* to trust, had essentially abandoned him. *What does that do to a child?* Key told herself not to be surprised if Wain had some type of angry fallout down the line; but understanding how that might play out was as elusive as the full picture of his past.

Key had written to Lyric and included a picture of Wain on the front porch, but no mail or calls came in return. *She has my contact information*, Key thought. *She's just choosing not to communicate.* It was completely mystifying.

Guy, too, had seemingly dropped off the face of the earth. Key had left messages twice, but he returned only her second call. He'd been grateful but harried, disconnected from truly engaging in the conversation, as though Wain was a distant relative he vaguely remembered. At one point, Key had heard him say, exasperated, "Jess, will you please *give* me a minute!" He had told Key that his upcoming move was difficult for his girlfriend, and they were trying to work things out, but he wasn't optimistic.

It was obvious that at this point, Wain wasn't a priority for Guy, so she had simply told him all was going well and followed up with a text: two pictures of Wain, one beside a sign at the Florida Visitor Center on their way home and one beside the shed. Guy had texted back: Thanks Key. He's so big! Mom would have loved him! I really appreciate everything.

After that unsatisfying exchange, Key had decided firmly that as much as she loved Guy, he would hear about Wain's abuse at the hands of Callahan only when she determined the time was right. The whole situation was too complex, too fractured to spill onto a father who, Key was deeply disappointed to admit, was showing no inclination whatsoever to become invested in his young son's life. *An incommunicado mother in jail and a father distant in every way.* Edie's grandson had washed up on Key's shore, the lone victim of the storm of his parents' self-absorption. Wain was an orphan in the worst possible sense.

She shifted her thoughts. It did no good to obsess over what she couldn't fix, and thankfully, there were other, more satisfying and uncomplicated changes in the works. She'd hired a builder to design and construct the new deck and replace the roof; and as of this week, Pike House was undergoing the first stage of its transformation. She could tell already that Dawson Plummer ("I go by DP," he'd told her) was meticulous and knowledgeable. He had come highly recommended by George, the gregarious owner of Troy Hardware. Key had been a little shocked at how young DP was—she'd gotten the impression from George that Dawson Plummer was a long-established construction company. When she interviewed the young man, he cleared up her confusion. "I'm Dawson the Third. My daddy started the business and is still doing smaller jobs, but he's closing in on seventy. He doesn't want to throw his back out or fall off a ladder—again—but he never cut corners, and neither will I."

And he hadn't. The deck was going to be a perfect addition to Pike House, stretching across the entire width of the rear, roofed and screened in, with three broad brick steps down to an outside area where, with DP's help, Key had finalized her design for an open patio with an outdoor fireplace and an arbor for shade. Once the work outside was done, DP and his crew would start remodeling inside.

"At least a solid six months' work," DP had told her. "Hope you don't mind living in a mess for a while, Miss Key."

"Best kind of mess," she'd told him.

Chapter 18

BREAKFAST

ey closed her laptop. Her card-idea quota had been met, always a relief. This month's sentiment was *get well*. Over the years she'd worked with CORE Cards, Key had sent hundreds of ideas, about half of which had been used. She was especially happy with one of today's: a small hospital graphic on the front with the words "Glad to hear you're hanging in there" and on the inside "I'm just sorry to hear you're hanging out *there*. Get well soon!" Dorothy, CORE's bubbly, exclamation-point-prone virtual gatekeeper, had emailed her right back; she was up early today. "This is awesome, Key! It'll be a hit!! Have a great day!!!!!"

She had just returned to her chair with fresh coffee when Wain walked into the kitchen, still in his pajamas and carrying his backpack. "Morning, buddy!" she said cheerily as he walked over to where she was sitting. "How's my friend Wain today?" She gave him her usual quick side hug and a kiss on his head; then, not waiting for an answer, she stood up. "Let's get breakfast done early because today you get to plant your flowers!" They had made a trip to Troy Hardware the day before, where Wain had selected a flat of eighteen purple-and-yellow pansies to plant in a small bed she'd created on the south side of the yard.

Wain stood watching as Key pulled a bowl out of the cupboard. On a whim, she turned around. "Hey, buddy, want to help make breakfast this morning?"

Wain's eyes lit up. "I can?" It was his most enthusiastic reaction to any of her suggestions so far.

"Sure! What would you like to make?" Key waved a wooden spoon like a magic wand. "We have pancakes, eggs, oatmeal ... your choice."

"Can I crack a egg?" Wain asked hopefully. "My friend Rico got to crack eggs and so do the kids on the cooking shows."

She tapped the spoon wand twice on the counter like a fairy godmother. "Absolutely. You can crack three! Drag a chair over, and we'll make scrambled eggs with cheese. Sound good?"

"Yeah. And cinnamon toast?" He had never had it before moving in with Key, and he loved it. He set his backpack on the table and pushed a chair over to the sink.

"Yes, cinnamon toast too. Before you climb onto the chair, kiddo, wash your hands, then get the basket of eggs and the cheese from the fridge."

Wain stood on tiptoe to reach the soap, washed his hands, then opened the refrigerator door, and said easily, "I never got to cook at my other house. And I couldn't open the refrigerator."

Key held her breath. It was only the second time he had volunteered any insight into his life with Callahan and Lyric. "Was your refrigerator too hard to open?" she asked. She knew he more than likely meant he wasn't allowed to, but she wanted Wain to tell it his way.

"No, I just couldn't." It was all she was going to get, but it was another small insight.

"Gotcha. Well, here at this house, Wain, if you want juice or a piece of fruit, just ask me first, then you can get it from the fridge. Or a cookie from the pantry. It's your house too! Deal?" She went back to slicing a loaf of French bread.

"Okay," Wain answered, opening the fridge.

"Did you find the eggs?" She purposely didn't turn around; he could do what she asked without her breathing down his neck.

"Yep." He carefully carried the green metal basket, half full of brown eggs, to the counter. "But I can't find the cheese."

Key pointed. "In the lower fridge drawer, on the right side. It's in a bag. No, that's the left side. There you go. Good job."

He set the cheese on the counter, then asked eagerly, "Can I crack a egg now?"

Key laughed. "Yes! Climb up here, and let's get this party started."

"What party?" Wain asked, slightly bewildered.

"Our breakfast party. Let's eat on the porch. What do you think?"

"I think it's fun." He paid close attention as Key broke an egg into the bowl, then perfectly mimicked her actions with the other three.

"Good job! Now mix them up, then we'll pour them into the skillet and cook them slowly, stirring with this big fork. "It's hot, so be careful not to touch the edge." Key stood to the side explaining the steps, telling herself more than once not to take over. He did everything exactly as instructed, and she sensed from his quiet joy at being included that they'd marked another turning point.

They buttered crispy brown toast ovals and sprinkled them with cinnamon and sugar, poured orange juice into plastic mugs and refilled Key's coffee, then carted a loaded tray out to the front porch, where, after Wain ran inside to get his backpack, they sat at the small table and devoured almost everything. Key pointed out the resident mockingbird, the spot where she'd seen the baby bunny, and a lizard on the side of the porch railing.

As they were finishing, DP drove up, parking his dark-blue pickup truck next to the shed. He strode over to where Key and Wain were sitting, buckling his work belt around his hips. He was a big man, over six feet, congenial and polite, with an open, honest face, longish dark-blond hair, deep-set light-brown eyes, and an easy smile. He wore a trucker hat, blue jeans, a plain untucked dark-gray T-shirt, and heavy work boots. Several tattoos peeked out from his shirtsleeves and continued down his arms. Incongruously (Key thought), he had a gold stud in his right ear.

"Mornin'. Looks like y'all got a good start on the day. Hey, little man." He reached over and ruffled Wain's hair. Key watched closely.

She wanted Wain to understand that not every man was Callahan, that in fact, Callahan was an anomaly; but in the time since work had started, Wain had largely avoided both DP and his two friendly workers, brothers named Benito and Miguel. She nearly dropped her fork when Wain spoke up.

"I cracked these eggs," he told DP.

"Did you now, son? You did a dang good job. The eggs look as delicious as my mama's." Still talking to Wain, he nodded toward Key. "Your grandma teach you how to do that?"

"Um, no. I mean, no sir. My cousin." Wain ducked his head. Key could tell he wasn't sure how to communicate who she was to him.

"Well, your cousin knows scrambled eggs. You keep cooking like that, I'll get in line. Miss Key, if you have a moment to come around back before we get started? Just got a couple questions."

Key stood up. "I'll be right there. Run and get dressed, honey," she told Wain. "Put on the same clothes you wore yesterday since we're going to get grubby in the dirt. Brush your teeth too, please."

"Okay." Wain picked up his backpack and with a small smile at DP, disappeared into the house.

DP looked at Key. "Cute kid. Nice he could visit his grandma!"

"It's a little more complicated than that. He's living with me, and I'm actually the egg-making cousin."

"Huh. Really." It was a question, posed as a statement. "How's that?"

"You mean, how does he have an old-lady cousin," she answered with a wide grin, and DP chuckled.

"Well, you're more like a grandma, right?" he asked. "Gotta think there's a 'first or second once removed' type of bird roosting somewhere in the branches of that family tree."

Key laughed. "Oh yes. His grandma and I were cousins. She died before he was born. You know, I was surprised Wain referred to me as a cousin. I didn't realize he understood even that much of our relationship." As they made their way to the back of the house, Key briefly explained the events that had led to Wain's arrival.

DP nodded. "That's a lucky boy to be here with you. So many kids fall through the cracks. I can find an extra piece of wood and a hammer if he ever wants to pound nails. It's the best therapy there is."

"Great idea. I may need to try it myself!"

They went over the crew's plans for the day. The deck was turning out to be more complex than she had anticipated, especially the connection to the existing roof, on which they were also putting new shingles. "Never had a project that didn't present challenges," DP assured her. She'd observed the crew standing back, scribbling with fat pencils on pieces of scrap lumber, discussing solutions in a mix of English and Spanish. They heard Benito and Miguel drive up and park, truck doors slam, the scrape of lumber dragged from the trailer.

"Time for the guys and me to get to it. Today's Benito's birthday. He's thirty-seven. Treinta y siete. I'll check in with you later, Miss Key."

"Thanks, DP! We'll come say happy birthday later. This morning we're going to plant Wain's flower garden."

"Another good therapy." DP smiled. "You have a good day."

Chapter 19

PANSY

fter Key cleaned up the breakfast dishes, she plopped down on the porch swing, swaying gently, watching a white butterfly float as lightly as dandelion fluff onto her purple verbena. The snap of nail guns had begun in back, and she waved as a truck hauling an empty horse trailer rattled by on Pike Road, leaving a thin trail of hay drifting slowly to the ground.

It was another flawless June day. They'd had one good rain since their return from Florida. Perfect weather for the construction crew, but she'd need to turn on the sprinkler after they planted Wain's flowers. Maybe he'd want to run through the sprinkler. Did children run through sprinklers anymore? She sighed. It might be simplistic, and she wondered every day if her intuition was correct, but she was committed to her belief that kindness, patience, and lots of outdoor time were the healing therapies Wain needed at this point. Deep down, there was an uninhibited little boy, she was sure, but he was locked up as securely in his own jail as his mother was in hers.

Then there was the matter of his inability to read. Since Wain had arrived at Pike House, Key read to him every day. Though he mostly sat quietly, he became agitated and shied away when she pointed to letters or words, so she had stopped doing it. Key believed Lyric's assertion that, at one time, Wain knew the letters of the alphabet, but something (or someone?) had destroyed that knowledge. And whatever it was, Key strongly suspected, was related in some way to the flash-card scene between Callahan and Wain that Mrs. Titus had described.

Meanwhile, she would plan activities to keep him engaged and challenged and help him adjust to life with her in North Carolina. Maybe tomorrow they would visit SouthPaws, meet Jukey and Mary and Petey the bird, and check out the children's section of the store. And what about Ell? It was surprising the little girl's entrepreneurial heart hadn't brought her back to Pike House. *Oh yes*, Key remembered, *she went to visit her grandparents*. She'd text Ell's mother, Gayle, in the next couple days to plan a visit; Wain needed friends his age. *He can't simply hang around all day with an old lady, spry though I may be*, she thought with a little laugh. But right now, they'd garden.

"Ready, buddy?" she said to Wain, who had appeared at the screen door wearing yesterday's jeans and T-shirt. He nodded.

"Take your backpack off for a minute. Your shirt is inside out. And backward." Key helped him correct it, then watched as he reached around to scratch the back of his neck. "Is that tag bothering you?" He nodded. "I hate itchy tags too! Come in the house, I'll cut it off." She snipped the tag and handed it to him, saying teasingly, "Toss this annoying thing in the garbage! Feel better?"

He nodded again. "Thanks," he said gratefully, shrugging into his backpack.

"Aw, you're welcome, buddy! Feel free to ask me anytime you need help with things like that, okay?"

As they walked out the gate and across the driveway to the shed, Key said, "You know, I had a great-uncle who wore his shirts inside out when the right side got dirty. He said he got twice the use out of them. Uncle Glen. I haven't thought about him in years! He was a little bit nutty, but in a good way. Guess what he had?"

Wain was listening closely. "What?"

Key held her hand at knee height. "He had a pet about this tall, named Kitty. What do you think Kitty was? A dog or a cat?"

"A big cat!" he exclaimed, completely absorbed in the story.

"Good guess, but nope! Kitty was a brown-and-black hound dog! People were always surprised. My uncle would say, 'Here, Kitty, Kitty!' and a big old dog would come bounding up!"

Wain had a slightly awed half smile on his face. "Was Kitty a boy or a girl?"

"A boy," Key replied, retrieving the wheelbarrow from the side of the shed, "which was also kinda weird, because you know, Kitty is usually a girl's name. But did Uncle Glen care about that? Did Kitty? They did not!"

"Did you play with Kitty?" Wain asked.

"Oh yes! Uncle Glen would bring him to our house, and Kitty and I would hang out together. I would hide treats in the hardest spots, and that dog would always find them because hound dogs have exceptional noses. And I forgot about this until just now, but my uncle lived alone, and he wasn't a very good housekeeper. He'd let Kitty lick his dinner plates to clean them. He said that was a whole lot easier than washing them." She knelt to retie one of Wain's shoes.

"Eww. I wish I could see Kitty. I really like dogs."

"I do too, Wain. Kitty would have loved playing with you! But he died long ago, when I was not much older than you." Key gave his shoe a pat, then stood up.

Wain put his hand on the door handle, then turned around and asked, "Did Kitty get the plates really clean?"

Key laughed. She loved the way his pragmatic seven-year-old mind processed her stories. "Clean enough for Uncle Glen! But, oh, my mother was horrified! My relatives would have long conversations about it. They were a *very* clean family. As you can imagine, we never ate at his house. But we went over there now and then to deliver dinner or holiday treats. I loved hunting through all the junk he had lying around. And having Uncle Glen and Kitty at our house was always fun. Even though they both kinda smelled. Neither one liked baths. But he was such a nice old guy. And you know what I think, Wain?"

"What?" He was still standing by the shed door, listening intently. She wondered if he'd ever had a positive, interactive conversation with any adult besides Mrs. Titus.

"People like that make the world more interesting, don't they? We don't all have to be the same." She picked up two flats of flowers. "Let's load up the wheelbarrow. Your new garden tools are inside on the workbench. Grab your gloves too."

"Can I push it?" Wain asked once everything was collected.

Key hurriedly removed the twenty-five-pound bag of potting soil she'd just thrown in. "Of course! It's heavy, but you're strong. I'll carry this bag and unlatch the gate."

The wheelbarrow was more like a pushcart, with two front tires; it wouldn't tip over, but it was a stretch for Wain's small hands to grasp both handles. Key strode ahead, reluctantly allowing him to struggle across the gravel driveway and then push hard across the grass to the spot she had staked out.

"You did it!" She helped him unload their tools. She wouldn't suggest he take off his backpack. Although the morning was warm already, it was his decision.

Kneeling side by side, they dug, removing rocks, breaking up dirt clumps, spading shallow trenches for the flowers. She was glad to see that Wain wasn't squeamish about bugs or worms; and again, his concentration and ability to follow instructions made his reading obstacles all the more bewildering.

"Ready to plant?" she asked, once the dirt was ready. He nodded. "Okay, bring those pansies over. I love the colors you chose!" As she'd hoped, he had almost immediately removed his backpack; it was lying on the grass nearby.

Wain lifted the flat of flowers from the wheelbarrow and set it next to Key. Intent on her work, she didn't notice when he retrieved his backpack and clutched it close to his chest, then stomped back to where she had begun placing the seedlings on the grass. To her utter shock, he leaned down and knocked them over with one sweeping motion of his free hand, then kicked hard at the flat, scattering the remaining flowers. His voice breaking, he said, "I wish I would have gotten something *else*."

Bewildered and dismayed, Key sat back on her heels, studying his face as he traced the CART on the front of his backpack with a grubby gloved finger. There had to be much more to this. "Something else?" she asked, keeping her voice even.

He sank down next to her and muttered angrily, "I *hate* pansies." She had to strain to hear, but she was sure she'd heard right.

"You hate ..." Key was completely stumped. What had flipped this switch? The happy, relaxed boy who had cracked eggs and eagerly pushed the wheelbarrow was now taking great, heaving breaths, fighting tears. She scooted over and knelt beside him, putting her arm around his shoulders. "Wain, would you be willing to tell me why you hate pansies?" He shook his head.

She gave a little shrug, keeping her tone unforced. "You know you can tell me. I'm not going to get mad. I promise. My guess is that you must have a very good reason to hate pansies."

"Yeah." He sighed, then said tremulously, "That's what he called me. All the time. And sometimes shaked me really hard. And yelled at me and spit on me."

Key blinked and jerked her head back, trying to hide her shock. *What now?* "Wain, you're talking about Gary Callahan? He shook you and spit on you? And called you a pansy?"

"Uh-huh. And retard. And baggage sometimes. I *hate* being a pansy!" He put his hands on the back of his head and buried his face in his bent knees.

"Ohhhh, okay, buddy. I understand. I really do." She scooted closer and put her arm around him. It seemed better not to say anything more right then; companionship with sympathetic silence often soothed in a way that consoling words could not.

Key was all too familiar with grief's private, possessive invasion of the soul, how it clung like lichen to every thought, retreated momentarily, then attacked like a tidal wave, leveling her at the most unexpected moments. Closing her eyes, she saw herself lying listlessly on the sofa in her living room at Sage Pointe one afternoon several months after her husband's death, sipping disinterestedly at an iced coffee and half listening to music. She'd spent most of the day sorting through Jeff's desk, and in a folder in a drawer (not hidden—he knew she never went through his things) she had found several pictures that underscored why he had gone to Miami. *Cannot wait to see you*, she read on the back of one. Later she wondered why seeing the pictures had been such a shock. She already knew from the police that another person—a very attractive, much younger woman from Miami—had died with Jeff in the motorcycle crash, but up until that moment, Key felt she'd been processing this—this *sidebar* of Jeff's death quite well. The photos, however, removed her pain and anger from the abstract and brought it brazenly, with every attached emotion, into her house.

This was the piece she had buried. This was the portion of her story left out of every discussion, every response to others' sympathy. She had not shared it with the grief support group. She hadn't told Guy. And as inexplicable as it was, she felt no desire to expose Jeff, or for that matter, the woman, whose family had been devastated. It was all simply too much. Instead, she'd accepted condolences with thanks and said nothing about her anger or the cause.

Anyone who had gone online for information, however, would have known the whole story; she suspected that was the real reason her friends had such difficulty bringing up Jeff's death. Iris knew, but when Key tried once to discuss it with her, Iris, who had always liked Jeff, simply said, "Why dwell on any part of it? Nothing you can do about it now." It was exactly the way her stoic family had dealt with any type of uncomfortable or too-personal situation, so Key had immediately dropped it. But her buried anger was surfacing, getting harder and harder to control.

Although she'd heard the song hundreds of times, that afternoon the lyrics from Don Henley's song "Everything Is Different Now" flowed into the living room and somehow pierced the debilitating fog clouding Key's brain, illuminating a truth about her life with Jeff that she had never truly faced: she was where she was because of the relationship she'd allowed.

Crying bitterly, she had dropped sideways onto a needlework pillow (later she saw the impression of the fabric on her cheek). It was as much an epiphany as it was a wake; her tears provided an untarnished view of the bleak, exhausting marriage she had tolerated over the years. She wasn't mourning Jeff. She was finally acknowledging her own waste of emotional strength, her endless, futile attempts to be who he wanted, to crack that indifferent shell, make him love her like he seemed to love everything and everyone besides her. She had not required true love; even worse, she had not regarded herself as valuable enough to deserve it.

One by one she'd burned the pictures in a cast-iron skillet out by the pool, then the very next day she left her house and its ghosts and began photographing birds, the hobby that ultimately led her to Pike House, where now the bruised, heartbroken little boy next to her had been reminded in the oddest way of his own terrible loss.

"Wain. I'm so, so sorry." Key said it carefully, patting his shoulder, watching as tears fell from his cheeks onto the grass, clinging like salty dewdrops to the blades; then he fell onto his side away from her, burying his face into his backpack just as she had with the needlework pillow, sobbing brokenly.

Everything familiar to this child has been erased like a cloud in the wind. Key could almost see the shards spilling out, each one etched with a piece of his sorrow. Homesickness. Mama gone. Mrs. Titus gone. Callahan's cruelty. The pervasive fear and deprivation in the one place where Wain should have been safe. Guy's failure as a father. But of them all, Wain's most enormous, confusing loss had to be Lyric's refusal to communicate with him.

Instinct told her not to try and stop his tears. As far as she knew, this was the first time Wain had cried since he'd come to live with her. He had to release his pain somehow. Maybe these tears would be Wain's own tiny beam of light on the path to healing. And to think a flat of pansies had been the trigger.

The nail guns kept popping. Staccato snips of laughter mixed with English-Spanish conversation drifted over the roof. A lone crow flapped overhead screeching, "*Omigawww,*" something Key had only ever heard in North Carolina. Across the yard, she saw DP appear around the corner of the house with a paper in his hand, talking on his phone. He stopped, gave her a little flap of the paper as if to say, "This can wait," and turned back. Key was grateful for his sensitivity.

Wain's sobs eventually dissolved to hiccuping breaths. He flipped onto his side, still using his backpack as a pillow, legs curled up, eyes shut. With his gloved fist, he rubbed the eye she could see, smearing mud down his cheek. There was so much in the few words he had said: *Retard. Baggage. He spit on me.* Fury enveloped her.

Gently smoothing his hair off his grimy forehead, Key said, "Hey, Wain. Remember we were talking about my uncle's dog?" No answer. "Want to hear about my own dog that I loved most in the world?" He still didn't answer, wouldn't look at her, but Key kept talking. "My dog died not very long ago, and I was so, so sad. Her name was ... do you want to guess what it was?"

"Kitty?" Wain asked hoarsely.

"Wow, that's a great guess. Uncle Glen would have loved your guess! But no. Her name was Pansy."

He shifted his head a bit and stared straight ahead, so she could finally see both his eyes. "Pansy?" It came out as a whisper.

"Yep. Pansy." She let it sink in.

"Why would her name be *Pansy*?" He said the name sneeringly, exactly as she imagined Callahan would have used it toward him.

Key lightened her tone; it was easy to do when she thought about the joy that was Pansy. "Well, she was a brown-and-white fuzzy terrier, and she was pretty small, even when she was full grown. But she was tough! Do you know, pansies—these beautiful little flowers right here—are very strong? They can survive in much harsher circumstances than many other flowers. That's why I named her Pansy." She plucked a flower and showed him the petals. "And she had a mark on her side, shaped kinda like this. She kept our yard free of snakes and moles, she chased squirrels like they were her sworn enemies. And try to guess her favorite thing to do."

"I don't know." He sounded exhausted but interested.

"Riding on my husband's motorcycle. She rode in a spot in front of him, in a specially made box. She had a tiny pair of goggles, and as soon as he put those on her, oh, she would jump without any help right up onto the motorcycle. People loved her, kids especially. It was always fun to see." Wain had sat up, rubbing his eyes again, then wiped his face with the hem of his T-shirt.

"How did your dog die?" Wain asked, after a moment.

"In a motorcycle accident," Key said, quietly. "With my husband." She swallowed hard. It was the first time she had ever acknowledged that, yes, quite possibly she was grieving her dog more purely than she was grieving her husband.

"Ohhh." There was a lot in that one tiny response. She sensed that even with all he'd been through, he was offering his sweet, little-boy sympathy, and it touched her deeply.

"Wain, I didn't have a horrible, mean man hurt me and call me names, but I do understand how sad you are because I've been sad too. But there's another, bigger reason I'm telling you about this." It was so hot, but she didn't want him to move. "Wait here. I'll be right back." She hurried into the house and pulled a small wooden box off the top shelf of the closet in her room, then stopped by the kitchen to grab two cold bottles of water and a snack bag of Cheddy Chipsters.

"Here you go, buddy." She loosened the lid of one bottle and handed it to him. "I think we need a break."

Wain took a long drink, leaving the chips unopened on his lap. He pointed at the box lying on the grass next to Key. "What's that?"

"I'll show you in a minute. This is a bit deep, Wain. I mean, it may be hard for you to understand because you're a little kid, but I think today is a good day to talk. You, my darling little boy, have had a very rough time. I know that Gary Callahan treated you terribly; but *it wasn't your fault.*"

Wain twisted his bottle cap, avoiding her eyes. Tears began again to drip, making splotches on his jeans.

"Wain, those names he called you, pansy and retard and other nasty words—he said that to hurt you inside, and when he hit you, or spit on you, he hurt you outside. You didn't do anything to deserve that treatment. He's *not* a good person. He is a bully." Key took a long gulp of water.

Wain frowned. "Bullies are *kids*. We learned about bullies at school."

"Unfortunately, bullies can be any age. Callahan *is* a bully." Key began collecting the scattered pansy seedlings and placing them in the trenches. "Honestly, Wain. If Callahan walked up to that gate right now, you know what I'd do?" She wielded her small spade like a spear.

He stared at her, eyes wide. In this sunlight they were the color of the Caribbean Sea. "What?"

"I'd chase him down the driveway with this shovel!" She was rewarded with a tiny smile. "I'm serious! He had *no* right to treat you the way he did. Wain, I might seem really old to you, but you know what? You can trust me. I'm your friend."

He gave a great, trembling sigh. "Okay. Mrs. Titus is old too, and she was my friend."

Old too. Key hid a smile. "Yes! Mrs. Titus is definitely your friend!" She took off her gloves and tore open Wain's bag of Cheddy Chipsters. "You know, Wain, Callahan used the word *pansy* to make you feel bad, but let's look at it another way. Being a pansy is a sign of strength! Like your courage in facing him day after day. Like my tough little dog. Like these sturdy little flowers. Pansies are strong and brave. Does that make sense?"

"Yeah." Wain fished out a chip with his gloved hand and crunched it. Key had no idea what a seven-year-old was capable of comprehending; he might not be absorbing every word, but there was a lightening of the heaviness from moments before.

"And, Wain, you can ask or tell me anything you want, anytime, okay? I will always listen." She could see him thinking.

"Can I go see my mama?" he asked, hopefully.

Key shook her head and said honestly, "I so wish you could, Wain, but at this point you can't. There's no way to set up a visit." She would gladly have taken him to Florida, but Lyric refused to add Wain to her visitor list.

"Because she's in jail. Mrs. Titus told me. I just wish I could see my mama." He stared at the grimy chip he was holding, fighting tears again.

"I know, Wain. You must miss her so much. I'm so sorry."

Omigawwww!

Exactly, she said silently to the crow, as she dug another small hole by the fence.

Wain foraged in the bag for another chip and said in a different tone altogether, "My mom was gonna get me Black Diamond for my birthday."

Key laughed slightly to herself and took the hint: *time to switch gears.* There was only so much grief any one person could handle. Easier and ultimately healthier, she had learned, to wade in the shallower waters of the practicalities of life. Leave grief out there in the deep for the occasional therapeutic swim.

"Wain, I was planning for us to have a day out tomorrow, so let's go to Porterville and hunt for Black Diamond. Would you like that?" *Oh, please let us find that car tomorrow.* She'd save the SouthPaws visit for another day.

His face brightened. "Yeah! It's *so* super-cool. I'll put it right here." He showed her an empty slot in his backpack, then pointed at the container and asked again, "What's in that box?"

Key picked it up. "This is, um, pansy strength powder. You're going to sprinkle it in the dirt with your flowers." As deep as this conversation had been, she had her limits; cremation was too much to discuss with a little boy. She pried open the top and removed the plastic bag filled with Pansy's ashes. It was surprisingly dense. "Do you know what a symbol is?"

"Kinda like a thing like this?" Wain pointed to the CartWheels logo on his backpack.

She held up a gloved finger. "Yes! Smart boy. The pansies in this garden will be our symbol of overcoming bad memories. How does that sound?"

"Good. Yeah. Can I pour the powder in now?" Wain wiped his nose with his glove and scooted over beside her. She snipped a hole in a bottom corner of the plastic bag with her gardening shears and showed him how to let it flow into the trenches they'd dug together. "Whatever's left over of the ash"—she caught herself—"powder, we'll put in this hole right here by the fence."

Wain held the bag over the dirt, guiding a gray chalky trail along each row. "It's kinda like smoke."

"It sure is." She wrapped her arms around her knees and watched as ashes landed everywhere, drifted, dissolved into a tiny cindery cloud, then disappeared. *Thank you, darling Pansy, for your last and best gift.* The process was messier than she had anticipated, a mixture of tears and runny noses and dirt and ash, but that was perfectly appropriate. Life when lived, truly lived, *was* messy. *Okay, Don Henley and world at large, I'm going to allow this messy love—Wain, Guy, and all.* She felt a spark of shared joy, of holding on, and letting go.

Chapter 20
FELIZ CUMPLEAÑOS

The pansies were finally planted, and the rest of her little dog's ashes poured lovingly into the small hole closer to the fence. Ell's heart-shaped rock was there now too, silver sparkles mingling with purple and yellow. Wain had loved holding the hose, spraying the garden all along the fence, watching the rocks and dirt change color, but when Key suggested he might like to run through the sprinkler, he'd flashed her a bewildered look and said, "No, thanks." Maybe another day. Now Wain was taking a shower, and Key went to find DP.

A blue-striped awning had been set up just outside the work area; under it were two plastic chairs, an upside-down five-gallon bucket, and a cardboard box serving as a table. "Hey, Miss Key." DP holstered his hammer and picked up a clipboard. "Your little boy okay?"

Your little boy. It was the first time she'd heard those particular words, and it made Wain's presence somehow seem more legitimate, more real. "Well, I think so," she replied, "but, honestly, DP, it's hard to tell. I never had children, so I'm flying blind. Today was hopefully a breakthrough. He's had a very rough time, and it's all coming out little by little."

"I will never understand how anyone could harm a child. Makes me want to beat the living sh—, sorry, *tar* out of the guy. From what I can tell, as far as experience—anyone with kids is kinda flying blind, if you get right down to it. My wife, Molly, and I just found out we're expecting a baby. Our first. It's all gonna be new to us too."

"DP, that's wonderful! Congratulations!"

"Thank you, ma'am. We're pretty dang excited, but I think our parents might be more excited, if that's possible." He handed her the clipboard. "I didn't want to interrupt you before, but I need you to sign this invoice for the patio pavers. And Molly's bringing cupcakes for Benito's birthday. Happy to have you and Wain join us."

"We'd love to!" Key exclaimed, scribbling her signature. "What can I bring? Drinks, maybe?"

"The guys love regular old soda."

"Perfect. We'll clean up and be back here in about an hour."

★ ★ ★

Molly gave Key and Wain a big smile as they approached. "Hi, Miss Key? And this is Wain? Thank you for letting me crash the worksite for a little while." As open and friendly as her husband, she was short and cute, with wide blue eyes, shiny lip gloss, sunglasses perched on dark-blond hair arranged in a messy bun (Key could never get her hair to have that effortlessly chic look), and green-polished fingernails and toenails. She wore white leather flip-flops and a yellow-flowered sundress that hid whatever early pregnancy might be showing.

"We're happy to have you! Happy birthday, Benito," Key called. Wain set the six-pack of soda on the box next to a plate of beautifully frosted chocolate cupcakes.

"Thank you. Gracias."

Out of the blue, Wain said, "I can say happy birthday in Spanish."

"Really? Let's hear it, bud." DP popped open a can of soda and handed it to Wain. "That guy right there is the one with the birthday today. Mr. Tan Hat." He said a few words in Spanish to Benito, who laughed and replied. They all looked at Wain.

"Feliz cumpleaños." Wain ducked his head as everyone cheered and applauded.

Benito stood and patted him on the back. "Gracias, amigo!"

"De nada."

It was a day for all kinds of surprises. Key had no idea Wain knew any Spanish.

"Where'd you learn español, son?" DP asked him.

"From my friend Rico."

Of course, Key thought. Rico was Cuban.

"Well, you made Benito's day. Have a cupcake. Or two."

As she chatted with Molly about pregnancy, nursery decor, and gender-reveal parties, Key occasionally glanced over to where Wain was perched on the edge of a lawn chair, shyly showing the three men his CartWheels collection. Benito and Miguel joked and laughed and ruffled his hair, trying to get him to say more Spanish words. DP remained hunkered beside Wain's chair, not saying much, seeming to sense that his quiet presence was exactly what Wain needed.

"Wain is so cute," Molly said to Key. "He's gonna be a lady-killer one day." She rubbed her stomach.

Key smiled to herself. *Is she aware she's doing that, or is it part of that instant maternal instinct that comes with pregnancy?* "He's adorable in every sense—a truly nice little boy. And I so appreciate DP's kindness to him today."

"That man is over the moon about our baby," Molly replied, then asked tentatively, "When I was talking to him on the phone, DP told me he'd seen Wain crying earlier? Is he okay now?"

Key nodded. "Yes ... thanks for asking! Good sad tears, if there's such a thing."

"Oh, most definitely there's such a thing. I think I spent most of my junior-high years crying good sad tears over one boy or the other." They laughed.

What a day this had turned out to be. It was about a million miles from her life in Sage Pointe, Key thought, but she felt a million miles closer to home.

Chapter 21

EXPEDITION CARTWHEELS

"Ready?" Key locked the front door and turned to see Wain leaning far out over the porch railing, studying the yard. Her only instructions had been "Wear nice clothes." He'd done well, choosing khaki shorts and a dark-blue T-shirt, which, she recalled with amusement, was exactly what Guy had been wearing the day she'd met him for breakfast.

A misty drizzle now turning to rain had settled in overnight, tapping from the gutter pipes onto concrete blocks like a watery, irregular metronome. Her lawn was already happier. "This rain will be wonderful for your flowers," she said to Wain's back.

"They're kind of drooped down." He pointed to their three rows of sad-looking pansies.

"It's called transplant shock. It takes them a couple days to perk back up. That's cool that you noticed."

"Does rain help the powder make them stronger?"

"Yes! It all takes time, but it works!" Were they discussing flowers or boys? Either way, it sounded positive. Key held her purse over her head as they hurried down the walk and out the gate to the Jeep. As she opened the door for Wain, her phone pinged with a text from DP. Going to work on deck railing in my shop today.

Despite—or maybe because of—the rain, Key felt a surge of optimism; she and Wain were both looking forward to what she hoped would be a fun-filled day. "Buckle up, please, buddy." She heard a muttered "oh yeah" and then a click. At the end of the driveway, pausing to check for traffic, which, as usual, was nonexistent on Pike Road, Key reflected that Gayle's chickens must be getting close to laying eggs by now; tomorrow she vowed she and Wain would deliver the egg cartons she'd been saving for Gayle, and see if Ell was back home.

"Let's see," Key said teasingly as they headed north, "we need groceries, we're going to buy you some new clothes and shoes, the Jeep needs gas, and now that she's back from her cruise, we are going to have lunch with my friend Miss Iris. Did I miss anything?"

"Black Diamond!" Wain did a joyful little jump under his seat belt.

"Expedition CartWheels! Yes! Most important thing!" She glanced at him in the rearview mirror. "If we can't find Black Diamond, do you have a second choice?"

She'd read online about the scarcity of certain cars; and Wain's first choice was, of course, the hardest to find—out of stock online everywhere she had searched. How had she lived on the same planet, ignorant of a phenomenon like CartWheels? It was an ongoing explosion in the world of kid- *and* adult-sized toy-car collectors. It reminded her of the troll-doll craze when she was in fourth grade. Her mother couldn't understand why it mattered to Key that she got the five-inch naked doll with teal hair and a little comb in its hand. For Key, it had been the joy of having the troll her friends coveted, but she doubted that prestige entered Wain's mind; he just loved his cars.

"Second choice?" Wain thought for a moment. "Um, I don't know. I really, really want Black Diamond. It's *so* cool. My mama was gonna get it for me for my birthday." That sad fact was always a part of their conversations about Black Diamond. "Plus, Rico doesn't have it either."

Key laughed. Maybe she had underestimated the power of prestige, even in seven-year-olds. "Describe it to me. Why is it called Black

Diamond? Is it black?" She knew the answers, but she loved the enthusiasm that emerged in any conversation involving CartWheels.

"No. It's white, with like these really cool stripes. And a diamond on the hood."

"White like snow." She'd seen pictures of it online. Black Diamond was alpine themed, painted a glittery winter white, with retro ski-shaped racing stripes and an ultracool black diamond graphic on the hood. It had been on the market for about a year. It didn't have a trunk that glowed, like FireFlyer; or bright-yellow lightning-shaped doors like SunBolt, the most recent release. There was no telling why this one was the holy grail of CartWheels. Why did the most coveted troll doll have teal hair?

During her research, Key had learned that new cars came out only three times a year, garnering huge anticipation, the clever names and designs guarded like Area 51. Considering their quality, the cars were surprisingly affordable, but since the company allowed no outside trademarking of any kind, they were making money hand over fist selling CartWheels accessories (or "merch," as she'd learned it was called nowadays). Only licensed outlets could sell the cars. *Kudos to John Cart and his team for their brilliant marketing strategy*, she thought. The next new car reveal would be in October. She and Wain would be in line.

Key had found three licensed stores in Porterville that might possibly have Black Diamond. She'd considered calling ahead, but she felt Wain should have the conversations, interact with others who understood his passion for the cars. Part of Expedition CartWheels should be the joy of the hunt.

But it was a wild-goose chase. A snipe shoot. A jackalope hunt, as Key's father used to say when he couldn't put his hands on what he needed. The rain was falling much harder in Porterville, and as they got soaked dashing to and from the first two stores, Wain's hope and excitement slowly deflated. She'd been afraid of this. With all that he had lost, she had so wanted him to have just one dream come true.

On the way back to the Jeep after being told for the second time that they had almost no chance of finding any CartWheels at all, much less Black Diamond, Key glanced down. A discolored penny lay in a puddle in front of them.

"Hey!" She stopped Wain. "Check it out." She pointed with the toe of her sneaker.

"It's a penny," Wain said in a *so what* tone.

"Yes! A penny! Pick it up!" Wain was mystified, but he picked it up and offered it to her.

"No, that's yours," Key told him. "Hang onto it! For good luck! Have you ever heard that saying? About finding pennies on the ground?"

"No," Wain said, obediently wrapping his fist around it. He never questioned her instructions.

"Well, keep it in your pocket, honey! Come on, I'll tell you in a minute. We're getting soaked out here!"

As they dove into the dryness of the Jeep, Key's phone chimed. A text from Iris: Our A/C went out. Miserable! Waiting for repair guy. Too muggy for you to come here! I'll come to your place tomorrow if you're going to be home?

Key texted back—Bummer! Sure, come for lunch, call you later—then turned around in the seat. Wain was slouched down with his backpack on his lap, staring pensively out the watery window. Her heart went out to him.

"Do you want to hear about finding pennies?" she asked with a smile.

"Okay." He sighed heavily.

"Say exactly what I say, okay?" When he nodded, Key said, "Find a penny, pick it up, and all the day you'll have good luck." She waited for a beat, then added, "Say that back to me."

"Find a penny, pick it up, and all the day you'll have good luck," Wain repeated dutifully but dully, like a little automaton.

Key stayed upbeat. "Perfect! You have a really good memory, you know that? Okay. We've got one more store to try. It's called Imagine That." As she typed the address into her phone, she realized with surprise that it was downtown, almost across the street from Java U, her old coffee haunt. She didn't remember ever seeing it before, but that had been in a different life, one devoid of seven-year-old boys. Now, in this new world the two of them suddenly inhabited together, all of Wain's hopes had become centered on this one tiny point on the CartWheels globe.

"Buckled up?" *Click.*

As they started out of the parking lot, Wain asked, "Why is it good luck? The penny, I mean."

"It's an old, old saying, but I like to think of it this way: If I find a penny, it creates a bright spot in my day. Maybe the bright spot leads to a bright attitude, and that bright attitude leads to good things! Let's see what happens."

The penny was already working, or maybe the rain was keeping people home; either way Key was grateful to find a parking spot right in front of the store. Imagine That was a narrow storefront sandwiched between a drugstore and a barbershop. As the old-time etched glass door sounded a chime to announce their entry, Key held her breath and took a cursory glance around. The entire space was simply one broad red-and-black-checkered aisle with neatly arranged displays on shelves that lined both walls. Model trains, remote-control cars, dollhouse kits and dinosaur skeletons, rock tumblers and ant farms ... and best of all, right in front stood an enchanting three-dimensional cardboard display set up to resemble a mountain road with switchbacks. Eight tiny cars encased in hard plastic packaging made their way up to the peak, where a neatly handwritten sign read "Limit One Per Customer." CartWheels! Key could have cried with relief.

"Welcome. Wow! Cool backpack, bud." The clerk, a thin twenty-something girl with short choppy pink hair, dark-brown eyes, and a nose ring leaned over the counter for a better look. On the front of her orange T-shirt was the store name written in white lowercase letters, with gears replacing dots above the *i*'s in *imagine*. "Got some cars in there?"

"Hi. Yeah." Wain gave her a tiny smile and a quick flap of his hand, then made an anxious, excited beeline to the CartWheels display. He examined it hastily and called happily over his shoulder, "*Okay, so,* they don't have Black Diamond, and I have all the others except PipStreak, but they have the newest one! SunBolt!" Tugging a cheerfully packaged car from its slot, he inspected it inches from his nose, twisting and turning it in his small hands. Key had to stifle a giggle. All he needed was an eye loupe, like watch repairmen wore.

"Yes, sir! We just got those in," the clerk replied. "I gotta say, it's y'all's lucky day. We weren't supposed to get more SunBolts till next week, and as it is, we only got three! We sold out the first round in like a couple hours. A line out the door and down the sidewalk. And, um, not to be a downer, but you're gonna find that Black Diamond is, like, *crazy* hard to get."

"We're definitely finding that out," Key told her. "Is it possible to put our name on a waiting list?" She'd signed Wain up at the other stores too.

"Yes, ma'am." The girl moved her Java U coffee cup and tugged a tattered spiral notebook from under a stack of papers, flipping quickly through the pages to a list of names. "There's twenty-seven people ahead of you, so we're most likely talking months."

"We'll give it a shot." While Key wrote down their information, Wain set SunBolt on the counter.

"It really is your lucky day," the clerk told him again. "Y'all must be livin' right. Is this it for today?"

"I think I'll look around," Key answered. "Your logo T-shirt is so cool. Do you have them in kids' sizes?"

"Yes, ma'am, on the racks straight back, to your right." The clerk turned to Wain. "Want to show me your CartWheels collection while your grandma shops?" He nodded eagerly. She looked at Key. "Is that okay, Grandma?"

"Of course!" She felt no need to break the conversational flow by correcting the girl. While the clerk and Wain discussed the various merits of each car, Key browsed through the shirts. She found one with the store logo in Wain's size in hunter green and a dark-blue one featuring a cartoonlike dinosaur skeleton, then she stopped to examine a set of small binoculars. Perfect for future hikes and wildlife viewing from their new deck. She'd get those too.

The girl was doing most of the talking and had Wain's full attention. *Naturally*, Key thought with a grin, *they're speaking fluent CartWheel, Wain's language of choice.* She glanced out the window; just down the block she could see the edge of Java U. All those coffees with Iris, discussing topics that had now diffused into her own past like Pansy's ashes. What if, back then, she had been able to visualize the future, see herself as a widow, standing just down the street in this tiny store, with a little boy who was now talking to a pink-haired girl about toy cars? Would she have believed it? She laughed to herself. Definitely not. Even now, there were times when she felt as though her newfound life was happening to someone else.

"Want to put SunBolt in your backpack?" The girl handed Wain a small bag containing the tiny car. He tucked it into the secret compartment and zipped it up.

"You've been a huge help," Key told the girl as she handed her a credit card. "What's your name?"

"Evie," she replied with a smile.

"Well, I'm Key, and this is Wain. Thanks, Evie, for making our Expedition CartWheels a success. You'll be the first store we visit from now on. Wain, what do you say?"

"Thank you." Wain ducked his head.

"My pleasure. Thank *you*! I'll keep you posted on Black Diamond. But don't hold your breath." The store phone began to ring.

"I know," Wain said at the same time Key said, "We understand."

Key and Evie laughed, but Wain instantly flinched away from Key. "Sorry! I'm sorry for interrupting."

Callahan never lurked far from the surface. "Hey," Key said softly, over the ringing of the phone, "It's fine! You didn't interrupt." Evie had turned away to answer; she waved cheerily as they chimed the door. Key heard her say, "If you hurry. We've got two left."

It had stopped raining. Wain pulled the penny from his pocket. "The penny worked," he told her as they strolled down the sidewalk to a nearby sandwich shop.

She loved the still-rare occasions when he talked to her without prompting. "It did! It was a reminder to stay positive, keep going, don't give up. And you're okay with SunBolt? Expedition CartWheels was a success? You're not disappointed that it's not Black Diamond?"

He glanced up at her and smiled. "No, SunBolt is really good."

She patted his backpack. It *was* good.

Chapter 22

EPIPHANY

ey found herself making coffee even earlier than usual, jolted awake once again by a troubling dream where a faceless Callahan had appeared out of nowhere and grabbed for Wain as he played near the woods with, of all things, a chicken. Why was it Callahan? *Was* it Callahan? As she stood barefoot in her tank top and baggy drawstring pajama pants, waiting for the water to heat for the French press, Key felt an inexplicable uneasiness. Incarcerated or not, Callahan still seemed to be stalking Wain. At least in her dreams.

Carrying her full cup and the carafe out to the dark front porch, Key settled sideways onto the length of the swing, reveling in the freshness of North Carolina's early-morning air, cool but still humid from all the rain they'd had yesterday. There was no moon, but the stars were especially bright out here, far from any light pollution. Sipping her coffee, Key let her mind drift (a rare indulgence these days), smiling at the enthusiastic chirping surrounding her. The birds were waking up; she suspected that they saw it as their duty to sing the sun into position every morning.

All things considered, she reflected gratefully, life was feeling a little less bumpy. Today DP's crew would be back at work, and Iris was coming for lunch and would meet Wain for the first time. Key gave a little almost-out-loud sigh. It was difficult to predict how their time together would go, but as always, she was willing to give Iris the benefit of the doubt.

She and Wain had had lots of fun shopping the previous day. At Target she bought playclothes and shoes for him, most of which she'd let him choose for himself; and in the toy aisle, she felt like Santa Claus as she watched him wander up and down, examining everything, asking her twice, "Can I really get *five* toys?"

"Yes," she'd said, "You need more toys! I can't have you playing with the knives in my kitchen drawer!"

He stared at her with the expression she'd come to define as his *is she crazy* look. "I'm not allowed to play with knives," he replied seriously.

"It's a joke, Wain," she told him, laughing and ruffling his hair. "I'm teasing you."

He chose a soccer ball, a couple of mysterious masked action figures, a Nerf gun ("Rico has one of these!") and, of all things, a large, charmingly homely stuffed green dog. When she asked why the dog, he simply replied that he liked it. Key learned that Wain had never played a board game, so she added several of those and three puzzles as well.

Even with all his new things, Wain was most overjoyed with the addition of tiny little SunBolt to his collection, unzipping the secret compartment now and then to pull the brightly packaged car out of his backpack, turning it over and over in his hands. "I want to wait until we get home to take it out of the plastic case," he told Key solemnly as they'd driven back to Pike House much later that afternoon, with bags piled three deep in the back and strawberry-banana milkshakes from Toppers Ice Cream in the cup holders.

Home. His use of the word filled up the Jeep, warm as cocoa. "Why is that?" Key asked.

"Because I want to cut it with scissors, so I can keep this part right here." He held up the car in the plastic bubble. All the colorful cardboard graphics were below the car, enabling the package to slot into the spaces on the CartWheels display. "It makes, like, a card thing."

Key glanced in the rearview mirror. "Oh, I see! Like a collector's card? Like baseball cards? There's always a surprise with CartWheels! Coolest cars ever."

"Yeah, Rico has them from all his cars. I didn't know you could do that, so when I was little, I tore them open. But I'm gonna start saving them now." There was a short silence. "I wish I could show my mom."

"Oh, Wain, me too." Key waited, but he simply sipped his milkshake and turned on his tablet (Key had given him an old one of hers), the engine noises and tinny voices from his game wafting faintly toward the front of the Jeep. Naturally, he gravitated to any games that didn't require reading; it was another choice that, at this point, she'd let him make.

Once they got back to Pike House, before Wain cut out the collector card from the packaging, Key had snapped two pictures of him sitting sideways on a kitchen chair, proudly holding SunBolt. She told him they'd print it out later and send it to Lyric, writing whatever Wain wanted to say. Someday soon, she hoped, he'd be able to write to his mom himself. And though it seemed less and less likely as the days came and went, she still held out hope that Lyric would write back.

They'd write to Mrs. Titus as well. Yesterday there had been a postcard in the mail from her. The Ferris wheel at night on Navy Pier. In all capital letters, in black marker she had written,

DEAR WAIN, HELLO FROM THE WINDY CITY. I SURE HOPE YOU ARE DOING GOOD AND ENJOYING YOUR TIME WITH KEY. I RODE THIS WITH THE GRANDBABIES! WE WERE WAY UP HIGH BY THE LAKE! LOVE, MRS. T.

Since Wain had been asleep before Key thought to check the mail, she left the postcard leaning against the pitcher of flowers on the table, where he would see it this morning. She wondered if Mayetta had written in all capitals in the hopes that Wain might recognize the letters. It would be so like her to think of that.

She also wondered if Wain would at some point ask her to read it to him, but she wasn't holding her breath. He had never asked her what something said. In fact, just yesterday she'd seen him veer anxiously away when the server at the sandwich shop set a children's menu in front of him. "I like hot dogs and fries," he'd told Key, preempting the need to read it.

It was beyond puzzling. Four-year-old Wain had known his letters. Why not now? Key could only conclude that in Callahan's house, reading had become synonymous with punishment; and in the only way he knew how, Wain had locked himself away from that monster.

She sighed. He'd be going to school in a couple months, and she wanted him to have a firm head start from where he now was, but she wouldn't rush it. Time, as she well knew, was a wonderful healer, and inside that time, she'd keep actively working to help him find confidence and a more solid footing, especially with reading.

And in so many other areas, we've made progress! She smiled. Wain was already a very different child than the shuttered, tentative little boy who had shown her Mudflap Girl's legs on their first hike. They'd go for another hike soon, she thought idly; Wain had enjoyed it and she could show him how to use his new binoculars. He might enjoy scanning the woods for wildlife.

Key set her coffee cup on the swing and pulled her knees up, wrapping her arms around her legs, rocking gently, mulling through nonthreatening activities that might incorporate reading without making it the focus. The sun's earliest rays had colored a thin line of cirrus near the horizon, and light was now crawling up the fence, onto the pansies and Ell's rock, now casting shadows through the porch railing onto her bent knees, warming them through the thin pajama fabric. She envisioned the light traveling past the construction site, beyond the oaks, down the path, and illuminating … bent knees in the woods. The woods! Mudflap Girl! An idea flashed into her mind and exploded instantly into a fully formed plan, as though it had been there all along and this morning's sun had finally erased the shadows concealing it. Key shot upright, jolting the swing, tipping her coffee cup, and spilling the remnants through the slats onto the outdoor rug below. "Oh my word," she whispered, oblivious to the mess. "Yes!" She could hardly wait for the next hike.

Chapter 23
PLAYING DEFENSE

ris arrived at eleven, greeting Key with, "Hello! Long time no see. I forgot how far it is out here on these two-lane roads," as though she'd navigated through sagebrush and tumbleweeds on rutted wagon tracks. She handed Key a plastic bottle of green tea and several pieces of junk mail. "Here's mail from your old house. The Clements asked me to deliver it to you."

As always, Iris was immaculately put together, in pressed lime-green slacks, an untucked short-sleeved white blouse with embroidery on the collar (only slightly wrinkled from her satin seat-belt cover), and yellow kitten-heel sandals that showcased her manicured shell-pink toenails. Her dark-blond hair was freshly cut in a bob and tucked behind her ears.

Key gave her a quick hug. She had, if not exactly dressed to Iris's level, put on a pair of light-gray cotton shorts, a wide-striped gray-and-black knit tank top, and her favorite flat black sandals. Her hair was in the usual loose braid. Key didn't dislike the reflection that looked back at her these days; her happiness shone from within. "Welcome, Iris! You got your hair cut! It's so stylish!"

"For two hundred and fifty dollars, it better be! Well, with tip. Tristan at Stylize did it. I showed him an article with the most flattering haircuts for women over age sixty, and we thought this one was the best fit for the shape of my face." Iris tilted her head, regarding Key's braid. "I can see if he can fit you in. He'd do it for me. Longer hair makes us appear older."

"There's a place in Troy I plan to try, but thanks," Key replied, suppressing a laugh. "Please come in! It's a little loud at the moment— nail guns on the roof where they're connecting the deck to the house—but the builders will be breaking for lunch. We can eat in the kitchen. Soon we'll be able to have meals on the new deck! I'll show you everything later." She led Iris through the living room and into the kitchen.

"Where's your young charge?" Iris asked, accepting a glass of tea. "Thank you."

Key pointed down the hall, then poured tea for herself and took the chair opposite Iris. "Wain's in his bedroom playing with his cars. He got a new one yesterday, and it's been a big hit. This gives us time for a quick chat. I want to hear all about your cruise!"

"We had a fabulous time. Highly recommend if you ever get the chance," Iris answered succinctly, spinning around the long wooden bowl Key had purchased from SouthPaws. "This dough bowl is the real deal. I don't remember seeing it."

"It's from a place just outside of Troy called SouthPaws. It's a wonderful store, Iris, you'd love it! The nicest couple owns it."

"The ladies might enjoy a change of scenery if they don't mind the drive." The *ladies* were the ladies in the neighborhood coffee club. Iris pulled a plastic bag from her purse and set it on the table. "I brought a gift for your cousin's son. I'll give this to him when he comes out."

"For Wain? Oh! How nice …" Key's voice trailed off as she saw what peeked out of the bag. *Books.*

She was suddenly cautious in a way that she hadn't been since leaving Sage Pointe. When she'd called Iris the night before to firm up lunch plans, Key had, to her almost instant regret, shared some of Mrs. Titus's observations. Iris had commented that maybe Mrs. Titus exaggerated, or maybe Callahan *was* trying to help; maybe Wain needed a firm hand.

When will you ever learn, Key had scolded herself, feeling as though she'd betrayed Wain. She had been adamant to Iris throughout the call that she wasn't "overthinking" and that she wasn't going to force the reading issue. By the time they'd hung up, she had detected disapproval and, yes, even a shard of jealousy radiating through the phone.

Iris now held up two colorful babyish books, similar to several Key had left behind in Florida. "They're from the Baby Can Read series. Wain is, what, six? The customer-service man at the bookstore told me Wain should start at the most basic level."

"Wain is seven now." Key lowered her voice. "Iris, I appreciate your thinking of him. But he truly has very difficult issues when it comes to reading. When Mrs. Titus told—"

Iris flipped her hand dismissively. "Psh. Goodness, Key." She ticked off her manicured fingers, "Number one, you've never had children. Number two, your conclusions are based on what a *maid* told you? And number three, as far as other issues, look at this one: *Paco Helps Mama*. I chose it because there's a positive mother figure, which can't hurt."

Oh, for heaven's sake. Key stood and returned to the counter where she'd been chopping ingredients for salsa. It took effort to keep her voice level. "Iris, I do know—positively—that Mrs. Titus would not make up stories. Now is not the time to focus on whether Wain can read or even recognize letters. Like I said last night, my one goal at this point is to allow his fear and pain to subside, and that especially includes reading. I don't want these baby books to coincide with his first impression of you." Key's last, firm sentence seemed to make a tiny dent in Iris's air of surety.

"Well. All right, whatever," Iris replied airily, rolling her eyes and stuffing the bag back into her purse. "Obviously a sore topic. No doubt in my mind he could use a child psychologist. I'll get you a name."

Scooping up minced mango, Key added it to a bowl containing red onion, jalapeño, bell pepper, and cilantro, then squeezed half a lime over the mix. *It's like standing on the tracks as a familiar freight train barrels toward me*, she thought, illogically disappointed that once again Iris was trying to wrest control of Key's decisions. But why was she surprised? What had she thought would happen? As she sprinkled sea salt onto her salsa and stirred it in, she made a silent vow that Wain would not be left alone with Iris, not for one second.

"Well, hello there. You must be Wain." Iris's voice was cool, detached.

Key turned. Wain stood uncertainly at the kitchen doorway, his eyes focused on her, right bare foot on top of the left, backpack looped easily over one shoulder. He'd chosen to wear his new Imagine That T-shirt and a pair of navy-blue gym shorts. Key had combed his hair, which by now was long enough that it curled around his ears. He looked adorable.

"Hey, buddy!" She beamed at him. Wain crossed the room to stand beside her. Putting her arms around him, backpack and all, Key said brightly, "Wain, this is my friend Miss Iris from Porterville, where we were yesterday. She's going to have lunch with us."

"Hi." Wain fidgeted with a strap.

"Goodness. You do resemble your daddy," Iris remarked. "I met him not long ago." When Wain didn't reply, she rummaged in her purse and added, "I've brought you a couple—"

Key broke in. "You know what? I changed my mind. Let's eat out on the front porch. Wain, hustle out and take the potted plants off the table and set them on the floor. I'll fix up a tray. You can carry this out there too." She quickly snapped a lid on the bowl of salsa, handed it to Wain, and gave his backpack a gentle push, feeling Iris's skeptical eyes assessing her every move. After she heard the bang of the screen door, Key turned to Iris and said firmly, "Please do not mention the books or reading again. The way to Wain's heart is the cars in his backpack. Ask him about them."

For the second time, Iris irritably pushed the bag with the books back into her purse. "He certainly does resemble the man who came to my door. Just think, if I had claimed ignorance and sent him away, none of this would have happened!"

Mystified, Key asked, "Why would you have done that? Guy was *looking* for me."

"Seriously? Key, your whole life has been turned upside down! That man has inflicted *his* duties to his son onto *you*. He's manipulated you into taking in his child—*his* responsibility!"

Key shook her head. "It's not like that. I haven't been manipulated, and I have hope that at some point Guy will genuinely show an interest in his son. Most of all, Wain's presence here is absolutely not a negative in any way. And for what it's worth, Iris, my life is not nearly as upside down or traumatic as his has been." Key picked up the tray with the taco fixings and headed for the front door. "Again, please do not mention reading or anything else we've discussed."

How was she going to control the subject matter through an entire meal? Iris would toy at the edges of the conversation and pounce like a hungry cat on a mouse at the most opportune moment. As she pushed open the screen door with her shoulder, she stopped short, nearly causing a collision with Iris, who was right on her heels.

Chapter 24

LUNCH COMPANIONS

"Hey, Miss Key!"

Oh glory! "Ell!" Key could have kissed her. Just the distraction they needed. "Hello! Welcome back! Is your mom with you?"

Ell wrapped her arms around the porch pillar and leaned back as far as she could. "Naw—I mean no, ma'am, she had to stay with Granny Jewel, and besides, Dibsy has a runny nose. Mama thinks it's her molars. I already met Wain." She grinned at him. "Didn't I?"

Wain nodded. He stood beside the porch swing with a forgotten potted plant held in both hands, his fascinated eyes never leaving Ell, whose stick-thin legs stuck out of a pair of red-and-white plaid shorts. She had on a clean white tank top with a simple yellow daisy graphic and her two short ponytails stuck out over her ears. She still wore the oversized high-top tennis shoes.

Stepping onto the porch, Key gave the little girl a hug and made the introductions. "Iris, this is my friend Ell Morgan, who lives down the road. She's nine. I met her and her mother, Gayle, and her baby sister, Dibsy, the day before I went to Florida to get Wain. Ell, this is my friend Miss Iris."

"But you didn't tell me you were bringing a *kid* back with you!" Ell burst out, before Iris could reply. "I would have been so *excited!* I like your CartWheels backpack, by the way," she said to Wain.

"Thanks." Wain's face lit up.

Ell crossed to where he was standing. "Can I see which ones you have?"

"Uh-huh." Wain plopped the pot on the floor and slung his backpack onto the porch swing, ready to unzip it. "I got SunBolt yesterday!"

Iris cleared her throat. "Hello, young lady. I imagine your full name is Ellen?"

Ell nodded. "Yes, ma'am, but Miss Key knows I like to be called Ell."

Iris set down the dishes she'd been carrying. "Yes, well, *Ellen,* it might be best if you come back another time. We were about to have lunch."

"Whoops! Sorry!" Ell, embarrassed, turned quickly to go back down the stairs.

"No!" Key protested, putting her hand out to stop Ell. "Wain, you can show Ell your cars later, after we eat. Ell, would you like to join us for lunch? We have plenty of food—fish and beef tacos, and all kinds of fixings, and ice-cream sandwiches and strawberries for dessert."

Ell's face lit up. "Oh yes, ma'am! I love tacos! Well, not the fish kind, but the other kind. We *never* get to eat out! But I better ask my mama."

"Here." Key pulled her phone from her back pocket and scrolled through her contacts. "Give your mom a call. Tell her it's fine with me!"

It was fine with Gayle too. Key took the phone from Ell, who had explained Wain's presence in a few scattered words, and over Dibsy's wailing in the background she assured Gayle that Ell had not wrangled the invitation. She sent Iris back in to get another plate and juice box and put the two children to work setting the table while she arranged the taco fixings. It was warm, but the ceiling fan and a light breeze kept it pleasant enough in the shade of the porch. The nail guns and saws had ceased, which meant DP, Miguel, and Benito were taking a break.

Key knew that in Iris's opinion (shared with Key many times over the years as Iris glared at laid-back young mothers at Java U), children were not a valid source of meaningful dialogue, even though Iris had two of her own, long since flown the coop. But Ell's sunny presence evaporated Key's concerns about how the lunch conversation with Iris would play out. Sitting next to Wain, the little girl needed no urging to tell them all about her trip, life with Granny Jewel, Dibsy's attempts at walking, her older brother Cav mowing yards to save money for a cell phone, Gayle's penchant for makeup tutorials on YouTube, and her daddy's archery practice out behind the shed. To Key's great relief, Ell didn't mention her father's time in jail.

"So, Ell. What brings you over here today?" Key asked, during a lull. "Because you must have read my mind! I was planning to come by to introduce you to Wain and drop off some egg cartons. Will you be able to take them home with you?"

"Oh yeah!" Ell jumped from her chair and dashed down the porch steps and out the gate, returning with a plastic bag that obviously contained a carton of eggs. "That's why I came! While I was gone, our chickens started laying eggs! My mama sent these. They were in my bike basket."

"Thank you! Are you the egg collector?" Key asked, taking the bag from her and opening the carton. "These are lovely, Ell!"

"Yeah, I had to wash them too, because it's *so* gross how the eggs come out of their butts," Ell said matter-of-factly, wrinkling her nose and immediately biting into her taco.

Iris clicked her tongue disapprovingly, but Wain giggled, a sound that up until that moment, Key had never heard. It hit her like refreshing rain, a life-giving shower after a long, dry drought. She wanted to shout for joy, hug him, hug Ell. Instead, Key laughed and replied, "True! Farming can be a messy business. It's good for us all to appreciate where our food comes from."

"One of the eggs in there is kinda bluish," Ell told her. "See? I picked it out for you. And Mama says you don't have to put them in the fridge if you don't want. Because they're fresh."

Iris, who had been uncharacteristically quiet, interjected, her voice rigid. "No. Your mother is wrong, Ellen. You washed them. *Washed* eggs belong in the refrigerator. If they aren't washed, they will indeed stay fresh for a couple weeks without refrigeration."

Ell looked surprised. "Oh. Okay, I'll tell my mama," she replied. "Then maybe I won't have to wash them!"

Iris had already turned her attention back to Key, eyes narrowed, using her index finger to draw an invisible back-and-forth line between Key and Ell. "How, exactly, did you two meet? I don't recall hearing that you'd met *any* neighbors." Before Key could answer, Ell spoke up.

"I stole Miss Key's flowers. In a pot." Wain's eyes widened as Ell sucked loudly on her straw.

"I thought we agreed it was a trade. Remember?" Key said.

"Mama says I can't call it a trade. She says that's a, um, youthism."

"Euphemism, although youthism works too," Key answered with a laugh, remembering Gayle's excellently garbled vocabulary. "Wain, why don't you take Ell over to your flower patch and show her what's near the fence?"

"The rock, you mean?" Wain jumped up, nearly knocking over his cup; he caught it just in time, but Key didn't miss the fearful look he shot her way as he carefully set it and his plate on the table. It saddened her, but she understood. No matter how much patience she showed, three years with Callahan wouldn't be erased in just a matter of weeks.

"Yep, the rock!" she answered cheerfully, ruffling his hair. She turned to Ell. "We found the perfect spot for it, over by Wain's pansies."

While Wain proudly escorted Ell to the pansy garden, then admired her bike outside the gate, Key gave Iris the highlight reel of her visit with Ell and Gayle (she too skipped Lonny's incarceration), knowing full well that it cemented Iris's view that she'd gone completely off the rails.

"No surprise here." Iris rolled her eyes. "I believe I warned you about a certain *type* of neighbor long ago."

Thank goodness Ell and Wain weren't within earshot. "A *type*?" Key repeated indignantly. It was draining, parrying conversations this way. "They're *people*, Iris. Good, kind people. Her mother brought her back here to make things right. In my mind, that takes a special kind of honest gutsiness."

Iris, true to form, was unfazed. "It's all very ... *ugh*. Well, never mind." She shifted in her chair and changed the subject. "Did I tell you about the graveyard tour we took in New Orleans?"

When Iris stopped midconversation to return a text, Key sent Wain and Ell around back with ice-cream sandwiches for the crew. Radiating importance on their return, they passed on a message of "thanks and gracias," then sat on the steps together, eating their desserts. Key was elated at how easily they had meshed.

Moments later, from where she was sitting, Key saw Ell tap Wain gently on the head four times with her spoon. Suddenly, to Key's astonishment, he erupted in boisterous, uncontrolled laughter, falling over on his side. Ell sat grinning at him. "No, that's really how he counts!" she told Wain. "Like if we're playing Monopoly. Mama is like, 'CAVender James! That is enough!'"

Key's eyes filled with tears. "Amazing," she said quietly to Iris, who was watching the children curiously. "He's been so much happier the past few days, but this is the first time I've ever heard him *really* laugh!"

Wain sat back up, still shaking, and began laughing all over again. "Excuse us?" Iris called. "What's funny over there? Care to share?"

Ell glanced back at them. "Oh, it's my brother, Cav," she said nonchalantly. "He counts like this." Again, Ell used her spoon to tap Wain's head. "One, toot, three, fart." And once again, Wain dissolved into helpless little-boy guffaws.

"Oh my." Iris cleared her throat and said to Key, "What a little *philistine*! Honestly. You're going to allow Wain to be around this?"

Key burst out laughing; she couldn't help herself. "Well, Iris, you asked! If she can get him to laugh, a little bit of kid humor is the best therapy ever. I can imagine how our new board games are going to go. Especially if we roll a four."

"Crass." Iris breathed, her lips a thin line. "Just *crass*."

Key stood up. "Let's walk around back. I'm dying to show you the new deck! You can meet DP and his crew. Watch your step in those sandals. It's still messy from yesterday's rain, but they've got boards down."

DP waved, then strode over to the patch of grass where they'd stopped. "Hey, y'all. Sorry about the mud. Might want to stay right there. Thanks for the ice cream, Miss Key. Nice surprise."

After Key made the introductions, DP proudly pointed out each feature of the construction to Iris, who murmured "mm-hmm" now and then but remained resolutely unenthusiastic.

Key spoke up. "I'll have a deck-warming party once it's all done! You're both invited. Bring Clive and Molly."

Iris sniffed. "Doubt I'd ever get Clive out here. We're all still mystified at Key's impulsive decision to live in this, this ... *holler*."

DP's eyebrows rose, but he didn't miss a beat. "No mystery to me," he said courteously, observing Iris as though truly seeing her for the first time. Key bit her lip to hide a smile. "She's found a real peaceful spot for her and her little guy. Oh, Miss Key, Wain told me he'd found a penny a couple days ago and that it brought him good luck because he got a new car."

"Wain actually told you that?" Key exclaimed.

"With help from Lonny Morgan's little girl," DP said with a laugh. "Matter of fact, I told them my daddy wrote a song about finding pennies. It's real catchy. I'll have to sing it for you." He hummed a few bars.

"You sing?" Key asked, delighted.

"Yes, ma'am. Daddy and I play in a band with a couple of his friends in bars and places around here, summer festivals, that kind of thing. Banjo for him and guitar for me, mostly country and bluegrass. I can let you know where our next gig is at. If it's a kid-friendly venue, y'all should come. Molly's usually there with Mama. Nice to meet you, Miss Iris."

They returned to the house, grateful for the air-conditioned coolness and another glass of tea. "A decent sauvignon blanc would be better, but not with that drive ahead of me," Iris said, then added archly, "There was a time when all I had to do was walk down the block for a visit. Nothing is the same."

And it will never be the same again, Key said silently, rising to refill their drinks and glance out the window to check on Wain and Ell. She had to admit she was stung by Iris's brusque attitude toward her new life here, especially her indifference to Wain. Again, though, why was she surprised? Iris hadn't changed. But for Key, it was as though blinders had fallen off. While she hadn't defended herself, she most certainly *would* protect Wain. She wasn't placing blame; was it Iris's fault that Key had never said "Enough!" when Iris plowed unchecked into her personal space?

Even so, Key was determined to salvage what she could, let the visit end on a civil note. "How are your children these days?" she asked. Key genuinely liked Iris's daughter, Francie, a quiet and friendly nurse who had remained in Connecticut when her parents had migrated south. Their son, Gavin, on the other hand, had escaped after high school to Alaska; and to this day, as far as Key knew, he worked there on a salmon fishing crew. He rarely checked in.

Iris tilted her head and gave a little sniff. "The big news is that Francie has a boyfriend. I haven't met him yet." Francie was thirty-four and didn't have much of a social life.

"A boyfriend! Tell me about him. Have you seen a picture?" Key listened as Iris described what sounded like a very nice man, then said, "Please tell Francie hello from me. Have you heard from Gavin?"

"Nothing lately," Iris said cryptically. She began typing on her phone.

Key's phone pinged. Gayle. Miss Key, will you send Ellen home by 3:30? I sincerely hope she's minded her manners. Tell her I'm still at Granny Js. Hope to meet your little guy soon.

She texted back. Sure will. Thank you for the eggs! I'm sending the money and the cartons I've saved. So happy to see Ell—she's been wonderful company.

Wain and Ell opened the front door, red faced and panting. They had been out by the shed shooting Nerf bullets into a bucket.

As she handed them granola bars and cups of ice water, Key relayed Gayle's message to Ell. "Why don't you both cool down for a bit?" she suggested. "Maybe play Go Fish here at the kitchen table. The game's on the dresser in Wain's room."

"Yeah! Want to?" Ell asked Wain.

He squinted at Ell and shifted his feet, unsure. "I don't know how to play that."

"I can teach you! Come on! It's *super* easy."

It was. Ell was an enthusiastic teacher, and Wain caught on instantly. Though they were out of view, as Key and Iris chatted, she could hear bits of their lively conversation as they played. Suddenly she heard chairs scraping back, and both children appeared in the living room, waiting politely for a break in the conversation.

"What's up, kids?" Key queried, after a moment.

"Miss Key, what day of the week was Wain born on?" Ell asked. "Will you look it up on your phone? I was born on a Friday, and that means I'm loving and giving, but he doesn't know."

"Just a sec." Laughing, Key looked up Wain's birth date. "Wain, you were born on a Thursday. Thursday's child has far to go." *This is true.* She could tell he had no idea what they were talking about.

Before she could explain, Iris chimed in. "*I'm* a Monday's child. My mother always told me I was the perfect Monday's child."

"Ferret face!" Ell exclaimed, pointing at Iris.

Iris was shocked. "*Excuse* me?"

Key too was taken aback. "Ell, what did you call Miss Iris?"

Ell cocked her head. "You never heard that before?" she asked. "It's, like, a old-person poem Granny Jewel taught me. She was born on a Monday too. It starts out 'Monday's child's a ferret face.' And then Tuesday is, like, graceful or something. I can't remember all of it, except Friday."

"It's not *ferret face!*" Iris replied severely, shooting Ell her most withering look. "It's *fair of face*. It means beautiful."

Ell shrugged. "Mm … are you sure? Because Granny Jewel says ferret face."

"Well, you heard *Granny Jewel* wrong, Ellen," Iris snapped. "And apparently no one has taken two minutes to teach you manners of any kind."

"Iris …" Key, helpless with laughter, couldn't get the words out.

"I want to be called *Ell*. I was just saying what Gr—"

"We know, we *know*," Iris countered. "Your granny obviously never taught you the most basic real-life lesson, though, that children should be seen and not heard."

Ell was not one bit fazed. "Oh, she says that. I kinda drive her crazy."

"Ell," Key finally gasped, "I think your half hour is up. Come out to the kitchen; I need to pay your mom for the eggs."

Ell followed her out. "Can I come back sometime soon to play with Wain?"

"Anytime, darlin'. Just be sure to text first so we know to expect you." Key handed the little girl a five-dollar bill. "Egg money for your mom. Wain, let's walk Ell to the gate." He left his backpack on the table. Iris kept her eyes on her phone and didn't reply when Ell called cheerily, "Bye, Miss Iris!"

Key put the egg cartons in Ell's bike basket, then gave her a hug. "It's been a pleasure, Ell! Thank you for teaching Wain the game! Be careful riding home and tell your mama hi for me."

"Thank you for the tacos and especially the ice cream." Ell threw her arms around Wain. "Bye! We can explore when I come back! I like your cars and your green dog!"

Key was overjoyed to see he hugged Ell back. "Okay. Bye." He waved as she rode off.

"She's a good friend already, isn't she?" she asked as they returned to the house.

"Yeah. She's funny!" Wain giggled again. They had their choice of laughs from this day, that was for sure.

"I'm glad you two finally met! I've never thought to ask, but can you ride a bike, Wain?"

"Uh-huh, I learned when I was five. I used to have one, but I left it in the driveway, so Cal broke it apart and threw it away."

Apparently no memory Wain had was free from that hideous man. Key put her arm around him. "I'm sorry. I know just the place where we can look for a bike."

"Yay! Can I ride with Ell?"

"Absolutely. There are all kinds of bike adventures waiting for you around here!"

Iris left soon after, informing Key that she'd text the name of a child psychologist she knew. Key felt a twinge of regret at how the day had unfolded. *But let's face it*, she thought, *Iris sets herself up*. She couldn't help grinning just a little.

"Hey, why are these in here?" Wain asked later, as they sat at the kitchen table eating leftover tacos. He pulled the two Baby Can Read books out of his backpack and held them up, looking more confused than upset.

Tamping down the fury that hit like water from a fire hose, Key took the books from him. "Let's give those to Dibsy, Ell's little sister." She paused. "Miss Iris must have put them in there when we walked Ell to the gate. I'm sorry, buddy. She didn't have the right to get into your personal things." She needed to consider how to handle this but handle it she would.

"It's okay." Wain unzipped the secret compartment. "See? My cars are all still here."

"Hey, Wain. Look at me a second," Key said gently. She saw a hint of fear as his eyes met hers. "Don't worry, I'm not upset at you at all, but I want you to understand that even though Miss Iris is an adult and you're a kid, she needs to respect your things *and* your privacy. Does that make sense?"

"Yeah. My mama used to tell me that when I touched Cal's things, and then I got put in time-out in the closet." Wain chewed a bite of his taco and slowly rolled SunBolt back and forth.

"In the *closet*?" Key closed her eyes for a moment, imperceptibly shaking her head. *It never ends.*

Wain exchanged SunBolt for ShamRocker. "Uh-huh. The closet by the back door, under the shelf. I had to scrunch up to fit."

"Did your mama put you there?" Key asked quietly.

"No ..." He let the word trail off. He was reluctant to say, she could tell.

"Did she know you were in there?" He nodded, still rolling his car on the table, not looking at her. "Did she get you out?" He shook his head. "How long did you have to stay in there?" She couldn't believe her voice was so matter of fact.

He shrugged, staring at ShamRocker. "Kinda a long time. Sometimes I was scared they forgot me, but I could hear them talking and watching TV."

It was imperative that she stay calm; the anger boiling inside her would scare him if she showed it. Key placed her hand lightly on his forearm. "Wain, I am so sorry that happened. I promise you, that will never, ever happen here. Do you understand that? It's right to respect other people's things but locking you in a closet and ruining your bike was very, very wrong. And it was wrong of Miss Iris to get into your backpack."

"Okay." He laid his cheek on her hand and let out an enormous sigh, as though his honesty and her words had pierced a bubble of fear.

I may not have all the answers as to how to handle Iris, Key mused, *but I will fight to the death for Edie's little boy.* She pulled him into her arms, feeling a rush of warmth in the room, as though Edie was there with her, hugging her grandson too.

Chapter 25
THE ALPHABET WOODS

Before Wain woke up the next morning, a text arrived from Iris with the name of a child psychologist, with a second text immediately following, admonishing Key that Dr. Kent was expecting her call. *Perfect timing.* She tapped Iris's number before any second thoughts could interfere in her resolve.

"Iris," Key began after they'd said hello, her heart hammering so loudly that she was sure her friend would hear it through the phone. "We need to talk."

"Don't worry, Key, Dr. Kent is the best there is. I've filled him in on the particulars. He's got openings next week."

Key took a deep breath. "We can discuss that, certainly, but first I need an explanation as to why you felt it was okay to put the books in Wain's backpack yesterday, after I specifically told you I didn't want him to have them."

There was a beat of silence. "You what? Oh *please*, Key," Iris said with a sharp, disbelieving laugh. "*This* is why you called? Talk about making a mountain out of a molehill."

"I'm not making a mountain out of a molehill," Key replied steadily, determined to hold her ground. "It was a boundary I asked you to respect, and you didn't take me seriously. I meant it! Those books hold terrible memories. Wain is—"

Iris didn't let her finish. Key hurriedly took her phone off speaker to keep the screaming voice inside the little rectangle she held in her hand.

"*Seriously?*" Iris exclaimed furiously. "You want to talk about *boundaries?*" What followed was a geyser of pent-up, explosive accusations flying from every direction: Key was an ungrateful, fair-weather friend who had used and discarded Iris. Key's arrogance made her unable to accept that Iris had far more experience raising children. Key had not considered Iris's feelings *at all* when she'd moved to *York*. "I'm obviously consigned to playing second—no! THIRD!—fiddle to a … a … *house* and a distant relative's kid that until just a short while ago, you didn't even know existed! And instantly, that kid and his long-gone father are far more important to you than our friendship. Don't worry, Key," Iris concluded frostily. "You won't have to deal with the *boundaries* of my concern for you *or* your cousin's kid, ever again. That's what I get for trying to be a friend." She didn't wait for Key to speak before the phone went dead.

A little shaky but strangely uplifted, Key placed her phone deliberately on the table and went to the window just in time to catch a glimpse of a doe and fawn disappearing into the safety of the trees, as though Pike House itself was giving her a reminder of just why she'd moved. *Protect yourself … and now that little one.* She sighed. In no way was she sorry she'd made the call, and while the outcome wasn't surprising, she *was* deeply sorry it had ended so painfully, their friendship blown to smithereens because she would no longer allow Iris to call the shots. *But is that a true friendship?*

Key's mother had had a framed embroidery hanging in her kitchen for as long as she could remember: a tiny sailboat tossed high on the waves of the wide-open sea, and above it the words "You cannot control the wind, but you can adjust your sails." She had adjusted her sails and was on a new course. Maybe there was a chance for a new, real friendship if the storm ever blew itself out, but only if Iris could accept the person Key was becoming.

She spent the next few days unpacking the boxes that had sat untouched since she'd moved, usually with Wain right next to her pulling items out, full of questions and observations. *More like Guy every day*, she thought. Though she and DP would be reconfiguring the interior of Pike House, and it made little sense to do much decorating, the memory of the sterile blankness at Callahan's had propelled her to set out a few homey items here and there for Wain's sake. Stories about her little terrier elicited his most enthusiastic responses; and Wain's favorite picture of Pansy in her motorcycle goggles now sat on his bedside table. With every use of the dog's name, Key mused, Callahan's wounding version of the word receded a little further into the past. The stories reminded her too, oddly, of the best parts of Jeff. He had loved Pansy as much as she did.

She and Wain had written letters to Mrs. Titus and Lyric. Once he knew Key wasn't going to make him read or write anything, Wain had relaxed. He wanted his mama to know that he'd gotten SunBolt, that he had a Nerf gun, and that he was helping Key in the kitchen. He especially loved making pancakes and cookies. Key would read the recipes to him and sometimes, not always, she'd point with her finger and say, "That's a *C*. That means one cup," and then move on to whatever they needed to do next. Wain rarely followed where she was pointing, but she didn't sense that it made him uncomfortable. He was too enthralled with cracking eggs, stirring batters, and running the stand mixer.

Key hadn't seen Gayle since Wain's arrival, but Ell rode her bike over one afternoon, and true to her promise, she and Wain went "exploring," which meant they'd skipped down to the massive gray rock that sat in the shade between two of the giant oaks. Ell's imagination was endless, and Wain enthusiastically went along with every made-up adventure. In one afternoon, they told Key, the rock had been a pirate ship, a fort, and a volcano. If Key had conjured up the perfect antidote to Wain's sadness, she couldn't have done better than Ell.

They had a tire swing now too. Once Key realized that the oak tree second from the right had the perfect branch, she asked DP if he could find her a tire. He'd pulled a large one out of the back of his pickup the very next day and refused to let her pay for it. She'd expected to install it herself, a simple tire hanging from a rope like she'd seen at Gayle's house, but DP, Benito, and Miguel dragged a ladder to the tree, rolled the tire down, and made a perfect horizontal tire swing using three chains.

"Strong enough for an entire tribe of kiddos," DP told them during the lunch Key and Wain had brought for the crew as a thank-you.

Tomorrow morning, she and Wain were going on their second hike. She had been working on her idea from the morning on the porch, and it was time to put it in motion.

"Want to bake chocolate-chip cookies?" she asked Wain that afternoon, already sure of the answer. "We'll pack a few for our hike and give some to the crew."

"Yay!" Wain thumped his backpack onto the table and went to the pantry to retrieve the step stool they'd gotten at Troy Hardware. "Can I eat the dough?"

Key put her hands on her hips. "Now what do you think I'm going to say to that?"

"You're going to say yes." He said it confidently, as though there was no alternative.

Key pulled one of her mother's old aprons over his head and tied it. "Exactly! What good is making cookies if you can't eat dough? We need two of Ell's eggs from the basket and two sticks of butter from the fridge." He got them for her. "And the one-cup measuring cup."

He searched in the drawer. "Is that the biggest one in the set? The green one?"

"Yes, it says 1 C. And we will need one teaspoon of baking soda. It will say TSP." This was harder. All the spoons were on a ring, but he wasn't sure which one she meant. Key tapped the raised letters. "It's this one, right here. TSP."

They measured everything together. She always added a little extra salt and a lot more vanilla, and the entire package of chocolate chips. Wain ate his dough in blissful silence while she dropped spoonfuls onto the cookie sheet, thankful in a way she'd never dreamed for the comfortable companionship of Guy's little boy. And nothing set the world right on its axis like the smell of baking chocolate-chip cookies.

"Can I take cookies out to the guys?" Wain asked, clattering his spoon in the sink.

"Let's do that tomorrow; they already left for the day." She thought for a minute, then dove right in. "Wain, would you like to learn how to use my camera?"

"Your big camera? Can I hold it *by myself*?" he asked disbelievingly.

"Yes! My red one. I know you'll learn fast and take good care of it." She meant it. He rarely had to be told twice how to do anything.

It was cloudy and humid when they set out the next morning, but no rain was due until late afternoon. Wain left the workers a container of cookies on the cardboard-box table under the awning, then they strolled breezily down the path that led through the tall grass to the edge of the woods.

It had already been over three weeks. It was hard to believe that in the short time he'd been here, this increasingly confident little boy had emerged from the one who'd sat shivering in the woods with her. Some nights she went to bed wondering what exactly she'd accomplished, but by allowing Wain to expand his horizons, by simply being there alongside him, she knew she'd checked off the most important items on that day's to-do list.

"Remember our first hike here?" Key asked as they entered the leafy canopy. "When we played I Spy?"

"Yeah." He said nothing more, but she'd come to understand there could be a lot in his one-word answers.

Key pointed down the path. "Let's go farther than we did last time. We'll look for birds and wildlife. There's a sandy place by the creek where it might be fun for you to build a dam with rocks. And someone told me there's a pond called Dogleg Pond! But we won't walk that far today."

"What's a dam?" Wain asked curiously.

"I'll show you." They tromped on. As they went deeper, Key realized the entire area was probably only about two or three square miles. Mistic Meadows Horse Barn most likely bordered the south edge of the woods. She had never officially met the ladies who owned it but had waved at them several times from the front yard as they drove by. At some point, she thought, she would check into the possibility of riding lessons for both her *and* Wain.

As she showed him how the camera worked, Key was again impressed with how quickly he caught on. "Look everywhere—up, down, sky, ground," she told him. He carefully photographed fungus on a dead log and a beetle that scuttled away, leaving only a blurry image when they played it back. Key pointed out two bluebirds, a cardinal, and a squirrel; and at the same time, they both saw a small green snake slither into the grass from the side of the path. In these close quarters, Wain's binoculars weren't as much fun as the camera, but they used them to stare into a hole high up in a hickory tree, where Key hoped an owl might be hiding.

"Ready for a break?" she asked Wain, after about an hour, taking the camera from him. "We can sit on these stumps. Someone cut those trees down a long time ago. Maybe for firewood."

As Wain munched his third cookie, backpack on his lap, Key leaned down and grasped a thin two-foot-long stick lying next to her stump. She took a deep breath. "Let's play another version of I Spy, but this time using the camera. Want to try?" *Please let this work.*

"Okay." Wain finished his cookie and tilted his backpack, letting crumbs trickle to the ground. He didn't sound particularly nervous *or* excited, which in Key's limited experience was a positive.

She stood up and said brightly, "I think you'll like it. So here's your challenge. Do you see any tree branches or tree roots that have this shape?" She sketched an upside-down *Y* in the dirt at her feet, then took Wain's hand and tugged him over to stand beside her so that he'd see the same upside-down orientation. She held her breath and closed her eyes for two seconds, unconsciously clenching the stick while he quietly studied her drawing.

Rotating slowly, Wain lifted his head and surveyed the vegetation nearby. "Over there!" He dropped his backpack on the stump and dashed excitedly to a spindly, bent-over poplar tree, then pointed to a branch hanging down that intersected into a perfect upside-down *Y*.

Key willed her heart to slow down and handed him the camera. "Will you take a picture of that?" she asked, hoping she was successfully hiding the joyful relief she felt. "You might have to zoom in a little bit." She leaned over to see what was on the viewfinder screen. He had it in his sights. "Good job."

When he'd taken the picture, she had him compare her drawing to his picture on the camera. Though his only comment about the match was "Whoa! Cool!" she could tell he was already fully immersed in the game.

"Okay, let's do another one." Key put her elbows together and spread her hands apart, pointing upward. "Find anything in the woods that matches this shape."

He didn't hesitate, pointing enthusiastically to two pine trees growing at angles from one another. "There!" He took another picture. "That's *kinda* the same as your last one. Except it opens up the other way."

"You're right," Key said, laughing. "I'll think of something else." "Okay, how about you find something that looks like this?" She made an X with her forearms.

Wain didn't even hesitate. "That's like an X."

Key wanted to burst into operatic song, toll the church bells. Instead, she sat back down on her stump, stretching her legs out, and nodded matter-of-factly. "It *is* an X! Do you see it anywhere?"

"Yeah, I see two of them." Wain pointed. "Up there and right down here."

"Take a picture of the best one, buddy. Your choice."

"That one." He took a picture of tree roots, then checked it, looking at Key with a huge grin on his face. "Look! It's an X made of wood."

"It sure is, a perfect X. You should be so proud of yourself! I'm so proud of you!" Intuitively, Key knew it was enough. "Okay, turn off the camera like I showed you, and let's get going. We still have a dam to build!"

"That was fun," Wain said happily, launching himself a few inches off the ground in an awkward little skip. (Apparently Key wasn't the only one who noticed that Ell skipped everywhere.) "Can we take I Spy pictures again?"

"Now what do you think I'm going to say to that?" It was quickly becoming his favorite back-and-forth conversation with her.

"You're going to say ... YES!" He trekked backward, grinning at her, emphasizing "yes" with a fist in the air.

Key raised a fist back at him, laughing. "I am most definitely going to say yes! I'll have you find lots more branches or roots to match my drawings. These woods are full of them."

They found the creek a quarter mile farther, where Wain immediately removed his shoes, set them on top of his backpack, and waded in. As she showed him how to stack rocks to create a dam, accompanied by the music of the birds and the trickling water, Key thought of Jukey and his hunting dogs exploring these same trails, scaring up and retrieving game for Mr. Grimes and his friends. SouthPaws would be their next adventure, she promised herself. She owed Jukey and Mary a massive thank-you. If it wasn't for them and their crazy, noisy bird, Wain might not be here at all.

Back at Pike House, she downloaded the pictures onto her tablet and showed them to Wain; and once again, without hesitation or any prompting from Key, he identified the *X*. Once again, she hid her excitement, not wanting him to feel self-conscious. After Wain went to bed, she rotated the *Y* picture to its proper orientation and printed it, along with *V* and *X*, on photo paper.

From the bookshelf in her office, Key pulled out a three-ring binder she'd prepared. Flipping through twenty-six sturdy pages made of card stock, she taped one picture each on pages 22, 24, and 25. *That takes care of V, X, and Y*, she thought, smiling. *Next time we'll tackle L, J, I, and O.* She laughed to herself. A literal game of *I* Spy.

Would it work? After today's unqualified success, she felt she had reason to hope. Wain's enthusiasm had been tremendously encouraging. In any case, simply being outdoors, exploring the woods together was a win-win; she believed that wholeheartedly. She heard her father's voice: *Can't win if you don't begin.* Those had been his favorite words when she'd felt doubt about attempting something new.

She locked her hands behind her head and grinned up at the ceiling. *Yes.* X might be near the end of the alphabet, but it was a good— no—a *great* beginning.

Chapter 26

MEETING PETEY

Friday morning, Key found a space for the Jeep at SouthPaws only because another car was backing out just as they arrived. Dozens of vehicles were jammed into the parking lot and tilted into the ditches alongside the road.

"What's this place?" Wain jumped out of the Jeep, put his arms through his backpack straps, and gave it a little jostle to adjust it.

"It's called an antique store. They sell mostly old things." It was already steamy. "Hold on one sec." Key trotted back to the Jeep and grabbed a light-blue baseball cap, pulling her hair through the loop in the back. "Ahh. Much better."

"Do they have bikes here?" Wain asked. He'd been talking all morning about where he and Ell would ride once he had a bicycle.

As they crunched across the gravel, Key took a quick disappointing survey. "You know, honey, I hoped they might, but I don't see any, at least not out here. We'll check. If they don't, we'll go to the hardware store." Maybe it wasn't a good time to come here; she hadn't expected SouthPaws to be this busy. Still, they'd go in and say hello, meet the bird, check on the bikes.

People were everywhere. As they strolled to the door, Key saw Mary at the counter of the colorful produce stand, chatting easily with each customer as they lined up with festive baskets of baked goods, jewel-toned fresh fruits and vegetables, and jars of jellies and pickles. She waved, but Mary was far too busy to notice.

"I want you to meet Mr. and Mrs. King, the owners of this store," Key told Wain. "That's Mrs. King right over there. They're so nice. Someone else lives here too, someone I think you'll enjoy meeting."

"Do they have a boy?"

Key thought a moment. "I'll put it this way. His name is Petey, but he's not *exactly* a boy. Not the kind you're thinking about." She laughed at Wain's perplexed expression. "You'll see."

They stood aside as three people exited. The door jangled as they entered, but to Key's surprise, no bird noises replied. Behind the counter, Jukey was carefully wrapping a large multicolored glass bowl in brown paper, conversing with a young couple. He glanced up briefly and greeted Key and Wain with a genial, "How do. Welcome," but with no sign that he recognized Key. She felt a pang of disappointment. The Kings would not have time to chat today as they had the day she'd consigned her items.

"Look at that orange bird!" Wain pointed, suddenly very excited.

Petey hung upside down on his swing, to the delight of the two stylishly dressed teenage girls standing beside his cage, faces close to the wire, encouraging him to talk. "Hello! Hello! Petey!" they said, over and over, phone cameras at the ready. At the top of the cage, two nibbled-on clothespins held a worn white cardboard sign with a hand-drawn picture of a brightly colored bird. It hadn't been there the day Key met him.

This Is Petey

Please Tell Him Hello

Please Do Not Tap On Cage

"That's Petey! That's who I wanted you to meet," Key replied, so intent on watching Wain's reaction that she forgot she needed to read him the sign.

Wain approached the cage and slipped in next to the girls, then tapped lightly on the wire. "Hi, Petey!" The bird fixed him with a beady eye and kept swinging, stubbornly silent. Wain tapped again.

"Hey! The sign says *not* to tap on the cage," said one of the girls, scowling at Wain. "Geez. Can't you read?"

"Oh!" Wain ducked his head and quickly backed up. Key, mortified that she'd overlooked something so obvious, could tell he was terribly embarrassed. Maybe it wasn't the nicest way for the girl to have said it, but teenage girls weren't always known for their subtlety; and anyway, Key couldn't blame her. The sign *did* say that. She glanced over to where Jukey had been standing. He had finished with the young couple and was now unlocking a nearby cabinet for the next customer.

Key put her arm around Wain's stiff shoulders. His small hands were wrapped tightly around his backpack straps, and he wouldn't look at her; the girl's arch comment, Key suspected, had taken him right back to Callahan's sneering, nasty face. "I'm sorry I didn't read that sign to you, buddy! I completely blanked! Let's go look around and come back to Petey in a bit."

In the children's section, Key realized quickly that the toys were mostly vintage, geared toward collectors. She hadn't seen a bicycle anywhere. Wain's first visit to SouthPaws was definitely not going as planned.

On their way back to the main aisle, a wood-framed oil painting hanging crookedly on the rough-hewn board divider caught Key's eye. About the size of a sheet of printer paper, it depicted a dark-haired boy with his arm around a shaggy brown dog. The pair sat under a leafy tree, facing away, so only their backs could be seen as they gazed across fat green hills to a distant garden where a bent, crone-like old woman in a straw hat and a shapeless brown dress hoed a garden full of unrecognizable oversize plants. Charmed by the scene and amused at the woman's disproportionately large bare feet, Key read the signature. Violet Robbins, bless her, had painted love right onto the canvas.

She took it off the nail and dusted the frame, then showed it to Wain. "Check this out. What do you think of this picture?"

Wain was still subdued, but he gave it a thorough inspection, then asked innocently, "Is that me and you and Pansy?"

Key leaned against the wall, laughing helplessly. "Yes! I think it is." She'd never go barefoot again, but even considering the high cost to her vanity, at fifteen dollars it was the bargain of the century, worth everything to hear Wain say Pansy's name as naturally as he just had. "Would you like this for your bedroom? We need to find some special things to hang on your walls."

"Okay. I can carry it." He took it from her.

She dusted her hands together, still amused. "Want to go back and see Petey?"

"Will those girls still be there?" Wain asked anxiously.

Key ruffled his hair. "No problem if they are. We both know the sign says not to tap on the cage, right? But you can talk to him and tell him hello. I was here one time when he was making the same sound as the jangly bells on the door. He was so loud!"

"What else did that sign say?" Wain asked casually.

He just asked me to read something to him. She shook her head; once again she had been caught off guard by a moment when his brain had relaxed and unlocked a tiny bit more. She stole a glance at Wain, who was holding the picture up in front of him, gazing at it. *What is with this place?* she asked herself as they made their way back to Petey's cage. *It's as though truth emerges sideways and shines from the honest, dusty antiques.*

She matched his casual tone. "I'll read it to you."

"Okay." He seemed to have lost his worry somewhere in the picture's green hills. Or maybe the crone's giant feet had simply stomped it out of existence.

To Key's private relief, the girls were gone, and Petey had no other visitors. Jukey, now showing a sweaty, disheveled couple the contents of the cabinet, didn't notice as she and Wain passed. All around them people perused the various displays; judging by their accents, most were out-of-staters. Key wondered again how, on all their antique forays over the years, she and her friends could possibly have missed a place as popular as SouthPaws. Now that Iris had seen Key's dough bowl and the pump, however, that was bound to change.

Back at the cage, Wain watched intently as Key read the sign aloud, pointing to each word. After she finished, she spelled out, "*H-E-L-L-O.* This word right here is *Hello.*"

"Hello! Hello!" Petey hopped from his branch to the side of the cage, hanging on the wire. "Hush! Hello! Hush birdie!"

Wain turned to Key, his mouth a wide O. "He said it! Hello!" Handing the picture to Key, he moved closer, bobbing his head in reply to the bird. "Hello, Petey, hello!" He laughed out loud as Petey answered again and again.

"Well now. You all got him to talk! He's been uncharacteristically quiet today. Almost too many people around." Jukey spoke to their backs.

Key turned around. "Hello, Jukey!"

Surprised, he exclaimed, "My land! Key North! Who moved into Mr. Grimes's house! I could say I didn't recognize you in the baseball hat, but tell the truth, I never looked. We're going full speed today. How've you been? And who's this CartWheels fan right here who got Petey to spill the beans?"

Trust Jukey to know the toy trends. Key put her arm around Wain. "This is my little cousin, Wain Banfield. Wain, this is Mr. King."

"No Mr. King here, never was," Jukey replied, smiling. "Always Jukey to everyone, young and old." He held out his hand and Wain shook it. "Pleased to meet you, Wain. You visiting with Key North here?"

Wain shyly shook his head.

"Wain is living with me now," Key told Jukey. "He moved in not long after I came by and visited with you and Mary."

"That right?" Jukey gave her the same insightful gaze she remembered from their previous talk. A man approached, asking for assistance. "Be right there. Give me just a couple minutes, sir." To Key he said, "Would you like to come back on a Tuesday or Wednesday? It won't be nearly so busy, and I've got a check for you in the safe. Maybe Wain here might like to visit with Petey. Feed him some apples."

"Yay! Can we?" Wain asked, bouncing on the balls of his feet.

"A check?" Key asked, perplexed. "Oh, of course, my consigned items! We'd love to come by. And we need to pay for this." She held up the picture. "One more thing, Jukey, do you have any bicycles?"

"No, I'm sorry, no bikes. We don't have space inside, and I can't leave them to rust outside. Come on over, and I'll ring you up. Be right there, sir," he said again to the man, who was waiting patiently, leaning against a post scrolling through his phone.

"No problem," the man replied politely.

"Be sure to say hello to Mary on your way out!" Jukey told Key, pulling out sheets of brown wrapping paper from underneath the counter as he talked. "She won't let me trade places with her—she loves the outdoor part—but I have one of our boys coming to spell her soon." He laid the picture on the paper, then put on a pair of glasses and took a closer look, checking the signature. "Violet Robbins? My land. Where'd you find this? Mary must have hung it up. This painter's got some issues with proportions."

"It's got a skewed Grandma Moses feel," Key agreed, laughing with him. "We love it, especially the boy and the dog. Wain thinks the woman looks like me. Don't say it!" she added as Jukey began chortling loudly.

Outside, Key filled a basket with produce; and since the pies had sold out while they were in the store, she chose a package of four enormous frosted cinnamon rolls they'd share with the work crew. Mary greeted them warmly when they reached the counter, and they chatted as she tallied their purchases on a small electronic device. "How long are you staying with Key?" she asked Wain.

He was stymied. "Um, kinda a long time I think," he said uncertainly, then added, "Jukey said I get to come back next week and feed Petey some apples."

Key put her arm around him. "Wain's living with me now," she told Mary, whose eyes widened in much the same way as Jukey's had. "And I love having him!"

"I know a story when I hear one," Mary replied, smiling at Wain. "I second Jukey's invitation. You come back and see us next week, Wain. Petey will be very happy to see you and your apples."

Chapter 27

x.o.

In the Jeep, with the wrapped painting stowed safely beside Wain, Key checked her phone, then typed, We will be there!

"Guess what, buddy!" She twisted in the seat to look at Wain. "We're going to DP's Fourth of July outdoor concert next Saturday at a place called Brookings Farm! There'll be fireworks too! We'll take food and have a picnic."

It was obvious from Wain's confused expression that he didn't fully grasp the idea of a concert, but he asked hopefully, "Can Ell come?"

"That's a great idea! We'll invite the whole family. I'll call Gayle later." As they left the parking lot, Key added, "Buckled up? Do you remember what I said we were going to do next?"

Click. "A bike?" Wain's tone was reserved.

"Exactly! We'll get lunch and then go to Troy Hardware. I promised we were going to get you a bike, didn't I?" she asked.

"Yeah. But it's okay if they don't have them in my size. Sometimes you have to wait." Behind those words, Key suspected, was a string of broken promises.

At Chix on Broadway, they chose a table on a patio under triangular beige canvas shades. While they waited for their food, Key pulled a pen from her purse and drew an *X* on a napkin. "Remember this one?"

Wain glanced at it. "Yeah. *X*." He didn't sound at all stressed.

She put a circle beside the *X*. "How about this one?" They hadn't searched for O yet, but she decided to take a chance.

"That's O." Wain still didn't seem uncomfortable. So far, so good.

"Try saying each letter," Key encouraged him. She didn't look at him as she put the pen back in her purse and picked up her drink, hoping he'd match her nonchalance.

Wain said it confidently. "*X. O.*"

"Great!" Key put her hand up for a celebratory high five. "You just read those! Do you know what XO stands for?"

"No." Ignoring her upraised hand, he shrank away from the napkin, leaning against the back of the booth, both hands gripping the edge of the table, his eyes instantly distrustful.

Key's heart sank. What had just happened? Where did that question take him? She *had* to pull him back from whatever precipice he was standing on. Leaning across the table, she touched his rigid fingers. "Wain, if I write XO to you, that means hugs and kisses and love, to you from me," she said lightly. She picked up the pen and underlined each letter as she spoke, then handed him the napkin. "XO. Here's your letter from me!"

Wain took the napkin, stared at it for a moment, then laid it down next to his cup. "Okay," was all he said. But in that simple reply, Key sensed, gratefully, that he believed her.

It was more than enough for one day. Relief washed over his face as she exclaimed, "Hey, look! That brown dog walking by looks like the one in the picture we found at SouthPaws!" As they ate their cheeseburgers and enthusiastically discussed his upcoming bike rides around Pike House, Key noticed Wain glancing now and then at the napkin and XO. She hoped he was absorbing the meaning of those two simple letters. *That, after all, is reading.*

At the hardware store, George showed Wain three bicycles; and after much deliberation, he chose a royal-blue one with red trim, a blue-and-red seat, and fat tires. Key helped him find a Spider-Man helmet, lights for the wheel spokes, and a pair of kid-sized silver-framed sunglasses. At the register, George unpackaged the helmet, then snipped the tag off the sunglasses so Wain could put them on right away.

Wain's beaming face telegraphed his gratitude as he said to Key, "Rico had lights on his bike too, except he had a Captain America helmet." He took off the helmet and slid his sunglasses to the top of his head. An ultracool mini-Guy stared proudly at her. "I'm gonna wear these like Rico does. Like this."

She laughed. "Very cool! Look over here." She held her phone up and snapped a picture.

After they'd fit the bike into the back of the Jeep, Key stopped at the drive-up at Chix to get an iced latte. They made their way to a large empty paved lot, where she showed Wain how to buckle his helmet, then she sat inside the open back of the Jeep, feet on the bumper, savoring her drink and Wain's joy as he rode endless laps. On a whim, she texted Guy the picture she'd taken of Wain in his sunglasses. Your mini-me. He got a new bike today. He's over the moon. She sent another picture of Wain on the bike.

More than once, as Wain rode toward her, he lifted a hand to wave, then quickly grabbed the handlebars again. Each time, she enthusiastically waved back, warmed to the core that he wanted her to share his joy and deeply grateful that she could give him yet another Callahan-free memory. She hoped it would last the rest of his life.

As heartwarming as it was to see him swoop and swerve and gain confidence in every lap, Key felt a sudden wave of sorrow for the battered, fearful little boy who so recently had been on the outside looking in at Rico's untroubled, carefree life, admiring his friend's things with no hope of having any of them himself, yet showing (as far as she could tell) no hint of envy. Sadly, those were years Wain (or Guy, for that matter) would never get back.

She leaned her chin on her fist. There was no magic number with grief, no certain day in the future when Wain would wake up and dust his hands together and say, "Well, thank goodness that's done." She couldn't change the past, and she would be doing Wain no favors by seeing him as a perennial victim; but running parallel with that thought was Wain's need to acknowledge the abuse he'd endured, understanding without question that he was not to blame. He needed the freedom to feel every emotion; and that would happen only if he trusted her wholeheartedly. Key considered their brief lunchtime conversation. Had she pushed too hard with the *XO*? No, she didn't think so. Wain seemed to have dealt with whatever he had feared, and let it go.

In the days following, Key was at a loss to remember what Wain had done before he got his bike. Even in the North Carolina summer heat, he rode all over the property, his sturdy legs pumping, obeying Key's instructions to avoid the construction site and the road. She was in awe (and a little envious) at what his lungs could handle as he pedaled effortlessly up the path past the rocks and the giant oaks to the house. Ell came over to ride with him, bringing another carton of (unwashed, Key noted) eggs. She and Wain spent most of the afternoon on their bikes and the tire swing, coming in only for drinks and snacks.

Over the weekend, Wain rode his bike to the edge of the woods and left it there while he and Key took two short hikes. Except for *X* and *O*, he had not specifically identified any other letters, but he loved the hunts and being trusted with the camera, eagerly searching for branches or roots that matched the upside-down or sideways letter shapes Key drew for him. *C* was a little tricky, but she had drawn it like an arch, and Wain succeeded in finding a bent-over branch. She did the same with *U*, except she drew it sideways, like a backward *C*. Again, he found the shape. He'd discovered *O* in a round hole in a tree trunk but didn't seem to connect that it matched what she'd written on the napkin. On Sunday evening, after Wain went to bed, Key rotated, printed, and added eight more pictures to her notebook. She leafed through the pages. *C, H, I, J, L, O, T, U, V, X, Y.* Eleven letters down, fifteen to go. Their Alphabet Woods book was nearly halfway full.

Chapter 28
HOSPITALITY

Key and Wain. Late June

Key had hoped to bring Wain's bike along with them to SouthPaws on Tuesday, but the forecast had for once been exactly right, and they woke that morning to a steady rain that promised to hang around for the day.

Before they left, Key retrieved their six most perfect chocolate-chip cookies from the freezer (she couldn't believe she was going to give Mary anything they'd baked, but those were going to be from Wain), a bag of gourmet coffee she'd gotten at Chix on Broadway, and a collection of her five best-selling cards tied with a green gingham ribbon. She arranged everything in a gift bag, then wrote a heartfelt note inside another card, one of her first designs. It had stayed very popular, featuring a small red heart in the center of the front, with "Thank you" written in beautiful black calligraphy flowing out from underneath it to the bottom of the card. Inside, above an identical heart, in the same calligraphy going up, were the words "From the top too."

She tucked the card into the gift bag. "Ready, buddy?"

"Ready!" Wain jumped down from his step stool and held up a small plastic bag. Key had given him apple sections and a table knife, and he'd sliced them up into smaller portions for Petey. "I'm gonna put these in my backpack."

"Good job. Petey will love those."

"Will he sit on my finger?"

"That's up to Jukey and Mary. Be sure to ask permission." On a bulletin board at the store, Key had seen pictures of children holding Petey, but she didn't want to promise anything. She pushed the chairs in and gathered up her things. "Did you brush your teeth?"

"Not yet." Wain took off down the hall, sliding his backpack on as he ran.

On this wet day, the parking lot was as empty as it had been overfilled the previous Friday. Key parked in a spot close to the building and they hurried inside, once again jangling the door.

To Wain's great satisfaction, Petey immediately jangled back, making them both laugh. Since Ell's hilarious first visit with him, Wain had been laughing more often, but it was still rare, and Key never tired of hearing it.

Jukey looked up from where he'd been arranging vintage tools on a shelf near the front. "Well, how do, Key North and Wain! You all are true adventurers, braving this rain. Petey, we've got company."

"Morning, Jukey! I would have had a very disappointed little boy if we hadn't." Key set the bag on the counter. This is for you and Mary."

"My land, for what? Thank you!" Jukey wiped his hands on a rag, opened the door behind him, and glanced around. "Mary's out on the patio. She'll be in soon," he said over his shoulder. "I've got something for you too." He twisted the handle on the door of a tall ancient safe, opened it, and flipped through a box of envelopes. Handing her one, he said, "Sold quite a few of your things over the past month."

"Thank you! I've got more boxes in my shed. When life settles down, we'll bring them over."

"Appears you've had reason to be busy since we first met. We've had changes too; we just lost old Badger." At Key's blank look, he added, "My last hunting dog. Man never had a better friend."

"Oh yes! Oh, I'm so sorry, Jukey," Key said sympathetically, remembering the ancient sleeping retriever she'd seen on her first visit. "I truly do understand how you feel."

"Dog lovers do. Thank you." He gestured at Wain and said quietly, "I don't recall you mentioning having a little boy." It was as much a question as a statement.

"No, I didn't. My life has done a one-eighty since then! If you and Mary have time, I'd love to tell you how something you said that day contributed to Wain moving in with me."

Jukey tilted his head, looking at her curiously. "Really? Something we said?"

From over by the cage, Wain spoke up. He had taken off his backpack. "I cut up some apples for Petey! Can I give them to him?"

"Did you hear that, Petey?" Jukey said to the bird, then nodded at Wain. "If you don't mind the feel of his little claws on your finger, he'll sit there all day and nibble fruit. Ever held a bird?"

"No, sir," Wain replied, his voice sounding as eager as Key had ever heard him. *He would have crawled into the cage himself if he could fit,* she thought, amused.

From the corner, Jukey rolled a rickety office chair nearer to the cage. Patting the duct-tape-patched seat, he instructed, "Sit right here, get yourself a couple pieces of apple, hold your finger inside the cage opening like so, and say 'hop on.'"

"Hop on, Petey," Wain said tentatively, and the bird fluttered onto his finger. "Whoa! It tickles!"

Jukey squatted by the chair, cupping his hand under Wain's. "Hold still, you'll soon get used to his crazy, grabby little claws. It's okay if he moves up your arm to your shoulder. Now give him that apple to nibble, and he'll be all set."

Key snapped two pictures with her phone. In the second one, with Petey on his shoulder close to his face, Wain's face radiated pure happiness, his shining eyes as brilliant as the bird's feathers. Jukey, too, took a picture. "The young pirate Wain with his sidekick Petey! That'll be on our bulletin board back there."

"Key North! Good morning!" Mary entered with her usual welcoming smile.

Jukey groaned as he pressed his palms on his knees and stood up. "When am I going to learn I can't hunker down like that! Hold him as long as you want to, sonny."

After Petey had eaten his fill of apples and was jangling and talking so loudly that they were having trouble conversing, Jukey returned him to the cage, and Wain went to wash his hands.

"I've got some pie and coffee waiting, juice for Wain," Mary said. "We thought you might enjoy seeing what's behind our store."

"Behind your store?" Key asked curiously. She wouldn't turn down a slice of Mary's pie, but what did that have to do with what was behind the store?

"Mary's been baking this morning with her ladies," Jukey said. "Nothing like fresh pie on a rainy day when adventurers and bird minders stop by. You go on back. I'll be there in five." Jukey handed Mary the bag. "Key North brought us a gift."

"For us?" Mary asked, surprised. "Why?"

"You truly can have no idea ...." Key was suddenly close to tears. Finally, she could relay to them how they'd helped change the course of her life. "The day I stopped by here with my consignment items has taken on almost a mystical quality, because the conversation we had helped me realize that I *could* do what I knew I *should* do." She smiled at them. "Does that make any sense?"

"No," Jukey and Mary said at the same time, bewildered but laughing.

"We'll chat over pie. Do you like pie, Wain?" Mary asked, leading them to the door.

"Um, I don't know." Wain seemed confused.

"Wain, have you ever *had* homemade pie?" Key asked, highly doubting that the crumbs of a freshly baked pie had ever sullied the sterile counter space in Callahan's house.

"No." He was back to his distrustful self. New situations brought his fears to the surface.

Key ruffled his hair. "Great! Now I've got no chance! You'll be starting at the top, having your first piece here!"

Mary laughed. "Thank you, Key." She held the door open.

Key let out a tiny gasp as she stepped onto a tiled floor in a wide glass-enclosed breezeway that led from the back of the store to an antique stained-glass door set in a brick wall about fifteen feet away. To their right, between the store and the brick was a patio with a painted concrete floor, sheltered from the rain by a high roof set on large hand-hewn beams. Several plants and trees in oversized brightly colored pots accented the space; and on one of the dark wicker chairs arranged around an authentically rustic coffee table, a yellow cat lay curled up asleep. Out the breezeway windows to their left, perfectly manicured shrubs ringed a lush lawn.

Key turned slowly, taking it all in. "Mary! This is gorgeous!"

Mary smiled. "Thank you, Key," she said again. "Go ahead and open that stained-glass door, honey," she told Wain.

"Oh ..." Key's voice trailed off as they stepped into the house. It was stunning. Polished wood floors pointed her to the far end where a gleaming kitchen with two huge ovens and ten feet of countertop, with at least a dozen pies cooling, took up an entire corner. Five spotless globe lights illuminated a gigantic island. In the living-room area, a gray sectional sofa faced an electric fireplace with an enormous television above it. Tall windows on the far wall to the left of the kitchen framed the hills and woods beyond. The simplicity of the design and the effortless homeyness made it all the more entrancing.

"Whoa," Wain said, something he'd picked up from Ell. It amused Key every time he said it.

"Mary!" Key exclaimed again. "This is absolutely *amazing*. Like something you'd see in an architectural magazine! I'm blown away!"

"Thank you, Key. Yes, quite a bit different from the front to the back, isn't it? We love both worlds equally—dusty and dirty, shiny and new. She pointed at the floor. "Right here, we used to have a little house, raised our family in it. We tore it down several years ago and rebuilt. Come in and sit down. It's peach and berry pies today. And I've got fresh coffee."

As they settled onto the stools around the kitchen island, Jukey came in from the breezeway. "Did you get the tour, Key North?"

"Yes! Jukey, this is the nicest house I've ever been in, and definitely the best smelling!"

"The nicest house for me too," Wain added.

"Thank you," Jukey said, patting Wain's back as he passed. "We're real pleased with it."

"I'd love to hear how it all came to be," Key said, accepting the plate and mug Mary handed her. "Thank you!" She took a small bite. It was perfect, with a crust that melted in her mouth and delectable peach slices dusted with just enough cinnamon and nutmeg. "This is absolutely delicious."

Rain fell rhythmically on the roof as they ate. Jukey and Mary took turns telling Key and Wain how they'd saved for years, searching for just the right piece of land, then ultimately realized that they were never going to find any place they loved as much as where they already were.

"We just had to think outside the box, let the dimensions of our lot tell us what kind of house would fit," Mary said, pointing outside. "Jukey and I designed it, but we needed help building it." She refilled the cups. "And that's when we called Dawson."

"Dawson Plummer?" Key asked. "The dad or the son?"

"You know Dawson?" Jukey forked another piece of pie into his mouth. He still hadn't sat down.

"His son, DP, is doing the remodel at my house." Key finished her pie. Would it be rude to lick the plate Kitty-hound-dog-style? She took a sip of coffee instead.

"Good man," Jukey said, nodding approvingly. "Dawson II did this place, with a lot of help from DP. You know they're both in a band? Dawson the daddy is the original singer-songwriter." He thought a moment. "O'Brien. That's the band's name."

"*Orion*, honey," Mary corrected, laughing. "Like the hunter constellation. You say O'Brien every time!"

"Ahh! Orion!" Jukey tapped his head with the handle of his fork. "I never remember! I think of them as Irish."

"Are they Irish?" Key asked, weirdly imagining DP and his father skipping Riverdance-style across the stage.

"I have no idea," Jukey replied, rolling his eyes and cracking them all up. "But Dawson and that band have been popular around these parts for decades. They have a concert next Saturday. Our family's going."

"DP told us about it! We plan to go too. He's told Wain about a song they sing about finding a penny."

"'The Good Luck Song,'" Mary said. "One of our favorites."

"Yours, honey. Mine is the 'Fishing Line' song."

"Jukey *loves* to fish!" Mary said to Key.

They had such an easy rapport, their love and respect for one another evident in every sentence. *Such fortunate children they've raised,* Key thought, observing the pictures scattered about.

"How's the work coming at your place?" Jukey asked Key, cutting himself another slice of pie, this time berry.

"Wonderful!" Key replied. "I'm very happy with DP and his crew."

"Miguel and Benito." Wain spoke up for the first time. He'd taken just one or two bites of peach pie, then sat quietly drinking his juice.

"Are you not hungry, honey?" Mary asked, when she noticed his unfinished pie, then said understandingly, "Or maybe you'd rather have some cookies?"

"Um, yes please." Wain ducked his head, embarrassed.

Mary handed him two oatmeal cookies she'd extracted from a jar on the counter. "There you go, little mister. And here's more juice."

"Thank you," Wain said tentatively. He gave Mary a relieved smile.

Key hid her surprise. To date, Wain had eaten everything she herself had cooked. Slightly embarrassed, and for the first time just a little irritated with Wain, she handed his plate to Mary, mouthing, "Sorry!"

"Oh, no problem!" Mary replied, just as understandingly as she'd spoken to Wain moments before. "Little boys and their taste buds are real familiar to me. Two out of my three didn't like 90 percent of any foods when they were younger, and now they are all gourmet cooks and sushi connoisseurs." She laughed and took Wain's plate to the sink.

Lesson learned, Key thought ruefully, remembering Lyric's words: "He eats what's put in front of him; Cal sees to that." Today marked another milestone in Wain's growing independence, and if it hadn't been for Mary, Key would have missed it; she would in fact have approached Wain's refusal to eat the pie exactly as Callahan had done. She sighed. Wain might need to learn the actual alphabet, but she was right there with him trying to master the ABC's of child-rearing. She couldn't ask for better role models than the two right here.

"Would you like to go out on the patio, son?" Jukey asked Wain, as if he'd read Key's thoughts. "You can meet Clem, our cat; and there's a wide-open space for those CartWheels. I want to see your collection. You can't believe how many people come in hoping I've come across them in my junking. Surprised folks haven't asked to buy them right off your back!"

Wain slid off his barstool, still holding a cookie. "I got SunBolt the other day."

"Did you now! That the newest one?" Jukey asked, genuinely interested.

"Uh-huh. I wanted Black Diamond, but we couldn't find it. I've got ShamRocker, Martial Star, CopperTop ..." Their voices faded as they walked outdoors.

"He's such a cute little boy," Mary said to Key.

"He's an absolute jewel of a kid." Key took her dishes to the sink. "I have almost no family left, so Wain is a very unexpected, wonderful gift. It's been a big adjustment for both of us, but I truly love having him with me." She gestured to a bookcase filled with photographs of handsome couples. "You mentioned you have three boys?"

"Yes. Kurtis, our oldest, is my stepson, though after Jukey and I got married, I raised him as my own. We had two more sons together, Christian and Jonah. All married, no grandchildren yet, but Jukey never misses an opportunity to remind them we're not getting any younger! We are so fortunate that they all live close by."

"Wain is all set." Jukey came back to the kitchen and picked up his fork. "He's got a real solid collection there. I know some grown men who would cry with envy. So how, Key North, did Mary and I come to play a part in your mystical memories by consigning your things?"

"It wasn't the consignment," Key replied with a laugh. "It was a conversation we had about Petey." They listened, mesmerized, as she recounted her story, starting with Jeff's death and ending with the gift bag she'd packed for them that morning.

Twice the shop door chime sounded and Jukey left, saying, "Hold that thought." He wasn't gone more than five minutes at a time. Wain returned from the patio and Mary settled him on the living-room sofa with a monster-truck demolition-derby video, and Key lowered her voice.

When Key finished, the smashing noises emanating from the television sounded like a final crescendo. Mary's eyes filled with tears that spilled over and slid down her lovely face.

"So on the very day you asked for a definite sign," Jukey remarked slowly, handing Mary a section of paper towel, "you ended up at SouthPaws. I do remember saying that with a name like yours, you were for sure someone's true north. And we told you how we adopted Petey ... and that story helped you decide to take Wain in. Appears I was right."

"Yes," Key said quietly, "but of course, at that point, neither his father nor I had *any* idea what Wain was going through. How terribly rough his life was." *And Guy still doesn't*, she thought with a pang.

"Thank you so much for telling us, Key." Mary dabbed her eyes.

"A miracle." Jukey rubbed his neck. "And I don't say that lightly."

"Yes, that's what I meant when I said it was almost mystical," Key replied. "Because it all happened so ... so serendipitously. Wain and I are just getting started on this journey, but he's far happier than he was just a few short weeks ago. And honestly, so am I." The shop door chimed again, and Key stood up. "We need to let you get on with your day. Thank you so much for the pie and the visit! I just wanted you to know—you've been *my* true north, in so many ways."

Mary gave her a long hug. "You are doing a wonderful, wonderful thing, Key," she said. "You bring Wain back anytime. I've got a niece who has a little boy about his age, Reynold. Maybe they could meet and play together sometime."

"Oh, that would be wonderful!" Key exclaimed. She and Mary traded phone numbers.

Jukey hugged her too. "This has been an unforgettable day, Key North. I'm very humbled by your story. Words mean things. Bye, young man!" he called as he hurried from the room to answer the chime. There was no answer.

Key went to check. Deep in the cushions, his backpack still clutched in his arms, Wain was fast asleep. "It's your house that did it," she said to Mary. "It's so full of peace."

It was still raining hard, and as she hurriedly buckled a groggy Wain into the back seat of the Jeep and climbed in behind the steering wheel, her phone pinged. A text from Guy, the longest so far.

Hey, Key! Thank you for the pictures. Wain looks great. Happy. Cool bike. Guardianship paperwork is coming via priority mail soon for you to sign, as we discussed. I'm leaving tomorrow morning for Dubai for the next five months. Maybe at Christmas I could visit you and Wain, or you both could come to Houston? Jessica and I broke up. Hard decision but I know for the best.

Before she could reply, three small dots appeared in a conversation bubble. Guy was still typing. A second text appeared.

Lyric is still locked up, but at some point, her boyfriend bonded out. Go figure. What a pair, huh? Thanks again, Key, for everything. I'll be in touch.

She read the second text twice, her racing heart falling to her toes.

Chapter 29

DOWNPOUR

"What happened? What?" Wain asked when he heard Key gasp. He knelt on the seat and stared through the rivulets of rain sliding down the Jeep window. "What's out there? I can't see anything. I'm really thirsty." He plopped back down, picked up the water bottle Key kept in the car for him, and took a long drink. "I liked those people, but I didn't really like pie. Can we come back and bring Ell? It was so fun feeding Petey the apples. Petey really likes me. I'm gonna tell Ell when she comes over again."

Trust Wain to be the chattiest he'd ever been, right at this moment. Key couldn't call Guy to explain why she had concerns about Callahan's release, not with Wain here in the car; and besides, the rain was so loud on the roof that she'd have trouble hearing.

She turned around. "No, it's nothing outside." She held up her phone. "I got a text that surprised me, that's all. I'll answer it, and then we'll head home." She started typing quickly:

Guy, I'll call you in about fifteen minutes, but is there any way you can find out if Gary Callahan has to stay in Florida now that he's out on bail? It's—

Her phone rang, interrupting her typing and making her jump; on the screen was an unknown Florida number. Couldn't be Mayetta;

she had that number. Possibly Rico's mom? What was her name? Key closed her eyes and thought hard. *Sasha*. Curious, she tapped the green button and put the phone up to her ear. "Hello?"

The rain made it nearly impossible to hear the robotic voice that intoned, "Will you accept a call from Angela Tremain at the Ann DeLavein Correctional Facility for Women in Brookings, Florida? Please press three to accept or press star to decline." Key sat up straight in the driver's seat, hitting her left elbow hard against the door handle.

"Will I ... Oh!" Hurriedly she pressed "three," then increased the volume and put the phone back up to her ear. "Hello?"

"Hello. *Hello*?" Lyric's voice was as irritable as Key remembered.

Key didn't want to say Lyric's name in front of Wain. "Hi, um, yes, hi, this is Key."

"Put Wain on."

The abruptness shocked her. "Ah, hold on one second? Sorry! We are in a parked car in a very loud rainstorm."

There was an exasperated sigh. "Maybe you forgot where *I* am? I don't have a lot of time, you know? Just put *my kid* on the phone."

It didn't exactly sound promising, but maybe Lyric finally wanted to connect again with Wain. Maybe the time away from Callahan had done some good. What else could she possibly want? Hoping Wain's mother would brighten her tone when she talked to her son, Key said briskly, "Please wait. I'm going to move to a place where we can hear better." Reluctant to go inside or bother Jukey and Mary again, she switched on the windshield wipers and inspected their surroundings, then turned to face Wain, who was nonchalantly chewing the last huge bite of a granola bar he'd fished out of his snack basket.

"Buddy, we need to take this call but it's impossible to hear with the rain pounding the Jeep. Let's go sit on those red chairs under the overhang near the front door. Quick." Key jumped out, opened the back door, and they raced over. "Sit right there." Wain sat down quickly, crumbs around his mouth, his eyes anxious and questioning. Key knelt beside him. "Wain, this is your mom on the phone." As long as she lived, she would never forget the spectrum of emotions that passed across his face in a split second, but the clearest, if she had to describe it, was a cautious joy.

"My mom?" He reached for the phone.

"I'll hold it up," Key told him. "You can talk." She scooted a chair close to Wain's and put it on speaker. "Here's Wain." She held the phone close to his face. "Say hi to your mom, honey."

"Mom?"

"Hey, baby." There was no emotion in the voice.

"Mom? Mama, are you coming home? Are you coming to get me?" He scooted forward, clutching the arms of the chair, very close to tears.

"Ha! Don't we all wish! Listen, baby, I have a *very* important question for you. Did you take your backpack from Cal's house?"

"What?" Wain asked, looking confused.

"You *heard* me," Lyric snapped. "I don't see it in the pictures you've sent! Did you take your backpack out of Cal's house?"

Wain's voice was timid but hopeful. "Um, well, Mrs. Titus did. She found it. Guess what, Mama, I got SunBolt! We couldn't find Black—"

"Are you *kidding* me?" Lyric's voice exploded into the space around them. "You had *no* right to go in there and take that! What else did you steal? Cal needs that backpack. *Now*." Wain's head drooped, then he lifted it up as a loving, upbeat voice said, "To put the Black Diamond in, baby! We gave you the one black car—I don't remember the name—but we didn't get a chance to add Black Diamond. We've gotta get that to you. Put your great-aunt back on the line, and I'll tell her how."

"Mama? Can I talk to you some more? Are you coming to get me?" There were tears in Wain's trembling voice but not in his eyes.

Cold flat was back. "Ugh! Stop being a baby. I'm not coming, at least not right now. You're gonna have to get used to that. Now put *her* back on the line."

Key was blindsided by the ugliness of the conversation. The Lyric she'd met was hardly warm and fuzzy, but this was beyond anything she could have predicted. She hurriedly took her phone off speaker and put it to her ear. With effort, she held her voice steady. "This is Key."

Lyric started in again. "You need to return that backpack to Cal. That's his property! His money paid for those cars. *His* money! Mayetta had no right to go into his house without permission!"

Wain had bent sideways onto the arm of the chair and buried his head in the crook of his elbow. Key put her hand on his back and said calmly, "I won't be doing that, Lyric. The backpack and cars belong to Wain. All we did was—"

"So you were there too?" Lyric's voice rose as she spat out, "With Mayetta? *Stealing* Cal's stuff?"

"Lyric, on the day I visited with you, we simply packed up Wain's clothes, his CartWheels backpack, and a few books. We didn't take a single additional item. Oh, his beach towel. But that's it."

"No, correction, you *stole* the backpack. And Cal wants it back. With *all* the paperwork inside. And the cars. He's not allowed to leave Florida to come get it, so write this address down and mail Cal that backpack. And the papers! Now. Today." There was a pause, then she read out an address.

"I think we've talked long enough," Key replied coldly, taking no notice of the address, relieved her voice didn't betray how rattled she was. Without waiting for Lyric to answer, she tapped the screen to end the call, then stood up, took a deep breath, and quickly walked several steps away from the chairs, watching the rain fall in sheets from the edge of the overhang. *What in the world was that all about?*

Two women holding handbags over their heads hurried toward the front door, nodding at Key as she made her way back to Wain. He sat exactly as she'd left him. What was going through his mind?

Putting her hands under Wain's arms, she boosted him up. "Come on, buddy, let's get to the Jeep." He didn't resist as she propelled him along and half lifted him onto the back seat, buckling his seat belt for him. If she had taken parenting classes every day for fifteen years, they couldn't have prepared her for this.

She started the engine, then took a moment to gather her wits, committing as much of the call as she could to memory. What papers was Lyric talking about? It had to be the foreclosure documents Mrs. Titus had shown her, the ones Wain had pulled out when he'd first unzipped his backpack. And why the laser focus on Wain's backpack? One thing was for sure: Key was going to examine that CartWheels backpack inside and out once Wain went to bed. The papers too. Lyric had been upset enough to call. There had to be a reason.

Through the window, she saw Jukey at the counter, conversing with the women, handing one of them an envelope. How had everything changed so quickly? Her heartfelt conversation with the Kings, Wain's bright, delighted eyes against Petey's iridescent feathers, the stunning peaceful house and delicious pie—was that just minutes ago? She and Wain had been dumped from a first-class cruise into a raging storm they never saw coming. For the first time since her move, Key felt slightly uneasy about Pike House's remote location. Lyric had said Callahan wasn't supposed to leave Florida, but if he was absolutely bent on getting the backpack, would he abide by his bail stipulations?

Think, Key. Think! As the Jeep's air-conditioning kicked in and the mugginess dissipated, the fresh coolness cleared her mind as well. The backpack mystery would have to wait; her priority had to be Wain.

She didn't allow herself to second-guess her next action. It was time to put another not-quite-resolved plan into motion. Picking up her phone, she went online to check a Porterville posting she'd been following for over two weeks, heaving a huge sigh of relief and a prayer of thanks when she realized she wasn't too late. Next, she typed a quick text, waited for a reply, then spoke out loud. "Hey, buddy." No answer. "Wain?"

"What?" he said dully. She would have preferred him to be sobbing instead of this listless, heartbroken silence.

"Are you ready for our next adventure?"

"What adventure?"

"Honey, look at me." He lifted his pain-filled eyes to hers. "I can't help your mama, Wain, but today you're going to help me set a prisoner free."

Chapter 30
FARO

Inside the Jeep, the drive to Porterville was as heavy as the forty-five miles of low-hanging gray clouds that accompanied them. Wain remained silent, clutching his backpack and staring out the window, while Key, her mind in overdrive, forced herself to pay attention to the road.

What words did she have that could possibly mitigate Lyric's devastating, contemptuous rejection? She couldn't say, "Your mama's just having a bad day. But remember, she loves you." Lyric's silence up until now, then what she'd said and done today were the furthest thing from love. Key also couldn't say, "Your father loves you." Guy didn't even *know* Wain. She herself would continue to show Wain unconditional love, though she knew he didn't recognize it yet for what it was. So they were on the way to Porterville to employ a new option: she would *find* him love.

The downpour had lessened considerably, but it was still drizzling when Key pulled up in front of a long low brick building on the outskirts of town. Across the street was a police station. She briefly, illogically considered barging in to report a possible bail jumper from Florida. She could imagine how that conversation would go. "No, officer, I don't know that he left Florida. But just in case, will you please guard the entire border of the state to keep a horrible man with a Mudflap Girl tattoo and whose smug face I can barely describe out of North Carolina?" *That* would go over well.

Before they left the Jeep, Key rewrote the text she'd started to Guy that had been interrupted by Lyric's call. Everything with Wain is going well, but before you leave, we must talk, either this evening or tomorrow. Wondering too if you can tell me anything about Gary Callahan? Text me with a good time to talk! Thanks, Guy!

She opened the back door, and as Wain jumped down, she pulled him to her, hugging him tightly, immensely relieved to feel him hug her in return. She grabbed his hand. "Ready to make a run for it?"

Inside, as Key rubbed the water off her arms, she was encouraged to see Wain was looking around curiously, already intrigued. He'd briefly covered his ears against the noise that had greeted them, then attached his hands to his backpack straps like an adventurer ready for the next challenge.

"Hello!" Key said loudly to the stout gray-haired woman at the front desk and a teenage girl who sat slouched, legs extended, on an old-fashioned hardwood office chair, staring at her phone. "I'm Key North? I've been talking to someone named Ingrid about Faro."

The gray-haired woman regarded her with sparkling brown eyes. "Oh my! Hi, there! I'm Ingrid. I'm so glad you've made the decision! Wonderful news on this dreary, wet day! Okay, everything's in order, just need to print your approved application." Key was fairly sure she had detected a *finally!* in Ingrid's words as the woman balanced a pair of glasses on the tip of her nose and ran her fingers expertly over a keyboard. With a flourish, she tapped once more, then stood up, while across the room a printer kicked out the paperwork for the next phase of Key's ever-expanding world.

"Would you like to visit before making a final decision?" Ingrid asked.

"That might be best," Key replied, her heart pounding. What if this was all wrong?

"Come with me." Ingrid emerged from behind the desk. She had a pronounced limp, with one shoe sole thicker than the other.

Clipping her glasses onto the neck of her T-shirt and picking up a small notebook, she gestured *I'm going with them* to the girl, who acknowledged it with a brief nod and a flip of her hand. "Teenage volunteers," Ingrid said by way of explanation, with a slight eye roll. "And who do we have here? Faro's new best friend?" She smiled down at Wain.

He had no idea what she meant. "Wain," he answered simply, staying right next to Key, his hands still tightly gripping the straps.

Ingrid waved a key fob to unlock a heavy metal door, then opened it and led them in. The noise exploded. "He's in number twelve!" she yelled over the din, limping awkwardly backward so Key could read her lips. "We'll get him out, then go to the room in the back. Normally we'd take him outside, but with the rain, we'll have to stay indoors."

Key put Wain in front of her as they made their way down the aisle. He pressed close to the wall, hands again over his ears, staring wide-eyed at each kennel's occupant. Some hurled themselves hard against the gates, yelping frantically, others cowered in the back, frightened, and a few bared their teeth in a way that made her glad for the sturdy barriers. Not one of them had asked for this cacophony of loss; and her heart broke for all of them, especially the ones who lay quietly depressed, paying no attention as their trio passed by. It was why Key had searched online when she'd started thinking in this direction. She knew it would have been impossible to choose otherwise.

"Here we are!" Ingrid hollered. "I'll put him on a leash, and we'll go through that door right there."

Key and Wain peered into the kennel. A very fuzzy medium-sized jet-black dog with a bubble-gum-colored tongue sat panting, gazing earnestly back at them. His handsome bearded face was offset by a shock of fur that stood straight up like a sheaf of wheat between floppy triangular ears. He exuded a sweet dignity, as though he'd held himself apart, had not absorbed the frenetic energy of his counterparts along the walkway. He tipped his head slightly as Key met his intelligent, engaging brown eyes; she felt as if he could read her mind and was keenly aware that she'd hesitated for nearly two weeks. *Where, oh where have you two been? I've been waiting.* He was perfect. She loved him instantly. She would not tear up. She would not.

"Whose dogs are these? Why are there so many?" Wain yelled, as Ingrid slipped a leash around Faro's neck and led him out.

"Let's talk once we're out of here!" Key yelled back.

In the visiting room, with the door shut, the relative silence washed over them like a wave. Ingrid took no notice of any of it, loud or quiet; she slipped the leash off Faro's neck, and he wandered placidly away, sniffing interestedly. Wain stayed right by Key, never taking his eyes off Faro.

Ingrid consulted her notebook. "Faro is a mixed breed, we think possibly some Airedale terrier or schnauzer, and maybe black Lab, but we don't know for sure. He's very healthy, two and a half years old, weighs forty-seven pounds, and is of course neutered and up to date on all vaccinations. He was relinquished by a family with four young children who moved from the area and unfortunately just did not have space for him. So per your request, Faro is a dog absolutely accustomed to kids." Ingrid tugged on her earlobe, thinking out loud. "Hmm. What else? He's housebroken and really, just a wonderful dog, with a calm energy. He's a favorite with our volunteers."

"He's even cuter in person!" Key exclaimed, feeling a twinge of sadness for the children in Faro's former family. "Do you know how he got his name?"

Ingrid chuckled. "You'll get a kick out of this. It is actually *Pharaoh,* you know, like the kings in Egypt, because of that crazy fur on his head. But when they brought him in, one of our teenagers wrote down Faro."

"Oh, I see it!" Key laughed with her. "We'll keep it Faro, but now I'll never be able to unsee an ancient Egyptian king. Does he bark a lot? Is he a good watchdog?"

"I don't know about a watchdog per se; he's not much of a barker," Ingrid replied. "He's been very close to being adopted a couple times, but they ultimately chose puppies, and that's what's kept him here."

Faro approached Wain, pressing his face into the little boy's knees, then stood motionless, waiting. Wain put his hand on Faro's bent head, petting the crazy topknot, then knelt beside him and put his arms around his neck.

"Well, would you look at that!" Ingrid exclaimed, smiling broadly.

Beaming, Key squatted down beside them. "Wain, would you like to take Faro home with us?"

When he checked her face to ensure he'd heard correctly, she saw the same unmistakable joy from earlier, at the start of his phone call before Lyric had shattered it. "For real? To keep? You mean like my *own* real dog?"

"Yep." Key grinned at him. "Meet your new best friend. You can tell he loves you already! Will you help me take care of him? I'll show you what we need to do."

"I'll take care of him! Can he sleep with me?"

"Absolutely. We'll have to stop and get some supplies." Key was as excited as Wain.

Wain jumped up, his backpack bouncing. "Come on, Faro. Come on, boy!" he said ecstatically. "You get to come with us!" Until that moment, Key realized, he truly had no idea why they were there.

"I think we've decided," she told Ingrid with a wide smile. Lyric's voice was finally far, far away.

Chapter 31

MAGNIFYING GLASS

They stopped at a pet store for supplies, where Key helped Wain make a green bone-shaped ID tag for Faro. Dinner was fast-food chicken eaten outside. (Key read Wain the sign, pointing to each word: Furry Friends Welcome on the Patio!) Their freshest family member, sporting a new collar and leash, sat calmly beside Wain's chair, happily accepting tidbits of chicken and lapping water from a paper bowl the server set on the ground.

At the restaurant, Key got a quick reply from Guy. Is 5:30 a.m. your time too early? I can talk then. I'll be at the airport.

5:30 is perfect. I'm an early riser, and Wain will still be asleep. She was glad she had the hour-long drive to Troy to consider how she'd approach their conversation.

As it turned out, she had no time to contemplate much of anything. Faro lay quietly on the seat, but Wain was almost garrulous. The element of surprise and the instant bond between boy and dog had done wonders in erasing the pain Lyric had caused. "I *always* wanted a dog! Do you think Faro will chase my bike? You know what, if I was, like, *blind*, you know? Like I couldn't *see*? He could lead me around! I'm gonna shut my eyes and try that! Can I show him to Ell tomorrow? Will he eat apples, like Petey? I'm gonna teach him to shake hands!"

Key could hardly keep up, laughingly answering one observation or question after the other. The outcome was worth every evening hour she'd spent searching online for just the right dog, talking with Ingrid while Wain played outside, and filling out adoption paperwork.

After a full sniff around his new home and the front yard, along with a quick meal and a long thirsty drink, Faro jumped up onto the sectional between Key and Wain and slept as only a freed prisoner does. While they nibbled popcorn and watched a kids' cooking competition, Wain's hand never left the dog's head. Once again, Key thought, as Wain nodded off midshow, her life had changed in mere moments; and in choosing Faro, she sensed she'd hit a grand-slam home run.

After tucking Wain in and showing Faro his cushion beside Wain's bed, Key sat down at the desk in the extra bedroom that doubled as an office and took a moment to think. She'd give Wain half an hour or so to fully fall asleep; in the meantime, there was the paperwork Lyric had mentioned. Over the past weeks, Key had been so focused on getting their new life in order that she had completely forgotten about it, but now her curiosity was ignited. She found the folded papers easily, stuffed midway into her too-fat to-do file.

She carefully peeled off the wide tape that held the edges together and unfolded the papers. To her surprise, a flash card enclosed between the sheets fell out. Key picked it up. Two black letters filled the front: an uppercase *S* and a lowercase *s*. On the back was a picture of a purple-and-yellow snake, with the word *snake* in lowercase underneath it; and below that, handwritten in indelible blue marker in perfect, almost architectural print were the words:

RETARD GAMES

S IS FOR SPIT

She heard Wain's words: *he spit on me.*

Her mouth dropped open. *Unbelievable.* "Who *does* this?" she whispered. Between Mrs. Titus's insights, the minimal stories Wain had told, Lyric's vague references to Callahan's "helping," and now this, a picture was emerging. Gary Callahan was far worse than a bully. He'd intentionally bastardized innocuous, normal childhood experiences like reading and eating in order to inflict terror upon a little boy's psyche. He had put insidious, time-consuming effort into tormenting Wain for no reason other than cruelty. And he was out on bail. Key had never been this angry. *If you come anywhere near him, I will destroy you, Gary Callahan.*

Setting the card aside, Key examined every letter of both sheets of the foreclosure paperwork but could find nothing unusual about any part of it. None of it was unfamiliar—she'd been married to a banker, after all—but she went online anyway and searched generic foreclosure documents, comparing them. Again, no significant differences. So most likely, Lyric was after the flash card. But why?

Pulling out her notebook, Key scribbled bullet-point thoughts:

- Wain left his backpack on the table the evening of May 16, expecting Black Diamond for his birthday.
- Backpack was there when Mrs. Titus left Callahan's eve of 5/16.
- Wain went to school w/o backpack.
- Instead of Black Diamond, the disappointing black car was put into the backpack. (Key couldn't remember the car's name.)
- Lyric & Callahan were arrested the next morning, May 17. (Wain's b-day? Significant???)
- In approx 12-hour time frame, before arrests, Lyric or Callahan (or both of them??) put new car & folded foreclosure papers containing the flash card into the backpack.
- Backpack buried (hidden?) deep in obscure drawer.
- Judging by Lyric's phone call today, whoever hid it did not plan for anyone (not even Mrs. Titus) to find it.
- Once Callahan was out on bail, he went looking for the backpack & didn't find it.
- When Callahan didn't find it, he contacted Lyric; she called Wain.
- Did Callahan look for it on his own, or did Lyric tell him where to look?

There were far more questions than answers, but that summed up what she knew. Key set her notebook aside and examined the flash card again. Nothing. Feeling a little foolish, she opened the desk's center drawer and scrabbled around until she found a powerful magnifying glass left over from her long-abandoned foray into antique stamp collecting. Pulling the desk lamp down, she bent forward, holding the magnifying glass an inch from the face of the card. As far as she could tell, nothing unusual on the *S*'s. She flipped it over, slowly working her way over a cheery purple snake with yellow diamonds marching down its back and friendly eyes sparkling from a smiling heart-shaped face. Its colorful cuteness made Callahan's use of the card all the more malevolent. She inched along the blades of two-tone green grass, crawled up an orange flower, and scrutinized a little red-and-black ladybug. Something on the snake's back? The ladybug? The word *snake*?

Wait. Go back. An adrenaline tornado swirled through her body, jolting her forward as she leaned farther over the desk and put her eye even closer to the glass in her best Sherlock Holmes manner, scrutinizing one spot. "*Aha!*" she said softly. "I *knew* it!"

Marching up a blade of grass, written in a superfine-tipped marker exactly matching the green of the grass, was an almost invisible, impossibly tiny version of that same perfect, architectural "*S IS FOR SPIT*" handwriting. Squinting, Key read a sequence of letters and numbers, saying slowly in a soft voice, "SitG@591856207842758." *A password, of course.* She picked up her pen and painstakingly copied the entire series, double-checking each character, then picked up her camera and snapped pictures of both sides of the card. No matter how hard she tried, though, she couldn't get the green printing to show up in a photo. It was that well hidden.

She ejected the camera's tiny SIM card and placed it into an envelope along with the flash card and the paperwork. After digging around in the center drawer again, this time to find a never-used key, she locked the envelope and its contents in the bottom-left desk drawer, then added the little key to the ring she kept in her purse. Her pounding heart was still not beating normally. She *had* to check Wain's backpack.

As she pushed the door to his bedroom open, Key could tell by his even breathing that Wain was deeply asleep, curled on his left side, facing her, covered only by the sheet. Faro lay at the foot of Wain's bed, head on his paws, watchful eyes trained on her, stubby tail thumping, but he didn't move. Obviously, a dog bed wasn't his first choice. Laughing quietly, Key reached over to pat him. "Good boy, Faro," she mouthed, then holding her breath, she slid the sheet off Wain's shoulders. He had both arms clasped around his backpack; in the dimness she could see just the first two letters of the logo, *CA*. Grimacing, she tugged lightly on one of the straps, then a little more. *CART.* When Wain sighed softly and relaxed his arms, Key decided to go for it. Gritting her teeth, willing him to stay asleep, she whisked the backpack up in one quick move, then froze in place and held her breath, her teeth clenched. If Wain woke up and saw her hovering over him in the dark, trying to abscond with his backpack, every bit of trust she'd earned would come unraveled, especially given their discussion about respecting others' belongings. She watched for a few seconds longer, resisting the urge to smooth his hair, and he peacefully slept on. Holding the backpack in one hand, she gently tucked the sheet back over his shoulders with the other. His exhausting, emotional day was working in her favor.

Welcome to Pike House, sweet pup, she telegraphed to Faro with a wry laugh, as she left the room. *I'm not sure what you've gotten yourself into.*

Back at her desk, Key unzipped the backpack's secret compartment and removed the cars from their mesh pockets, inspecting them one by one under the magnifying glass. It took nearly an hour. Nothing out of the ordinary. Except for FireFlyer's light-up trunk and wing doors, CartWheels were straightforward toy cars. From what she'd read online, it was the sturdiness, exceptionally detailed art and workmanship, and the limited-release numbers that made them such sought-after collector's items.

Setting the cars aside, Key went to the backpack itself. She pulled and prodded, examining each letter on the logo, admiring again the imaginative *e*'s shaped like wheels. She ran her fingers along the edges, turned it inside out, felt for cuts or gluing or restitching, checked all the way to the bottom of each mesh pocket. Nothing. Exasperated, she leaned back, interlacing her fingers and stretching her arms above her head. What, besides a password, were Lyric and Callahan so determined to get their hands on? She was missing something big, but it was after midnight, and her brain was running on empty. She would reinvestigate with fresh eyes tomorrow.

She replaced the cars and closed both zippers. As she gently laid the backpack under the sheet beside her sleeping little boy, she realized she had not compiled the list of topics she wanted to discuss with Guy the next morning. She'd have to wing it. She was asleep on her feet.

Chapter 32

CONFRONTATION

After a short night full of crazy dreams featuring snakes, cars, dogs, and birds, Key was on the porch swing by five the next morning, coffee and notebook in hand, jotting a list of discussion topics by the light of the lamp in the window. This was the exact place she'd been sitting with her ciabatta BLT when she'd first spoken with Guy just several short weeks (and a lifetime!) ago. She hadn't dwelt overlong on whether they should have had today's talk much sooner, but if Guy questioned her timing, she'd already formulated her reply.

Her phone rang right at 5:30. "Guy!"

It was only 4:30 his time, but Guy sounded upbeat. "Hey, Key! I've got sixty minutes that are all yours. How are you? How's everything going with Wain?"

"I've got so much to tell you, but overall, things are wonderful. Are you excited to finally be on your way?" She took a careful sip of coffee and positioned her notebook and pen on her lap.

"You know, I am. Having the particulars in order after so long is a big relief ... but, Key, is everything going okay? Is Wain all right?"

She put her phone on speaker, turning the volume down. "He's amazing! We do need to go over some things, but, Guy, first I just want to say how much I love having Wain with me. I see characteristics of both you and your mom in him." She cleared her throat. "So maybe because he's yours and Edie's, getting to know him from ground zero hasn't been as much of a challenge as it could have been. I've had a head start in decoding his DNA."

Guy's relief showed in his laughter. "Oh boy. In other words, you're in for a wild ride. I don't remember much about being seven, but I think that's the year I broke my wrist falling off a merry-go-round *and* got sixteen stitches in my leg after getting snagged on a barbwire fence. Seriously, that's great to hear, Key! I wasn't sure how to take your text. I was afraid it might not be working out."

Key sat a little straighter, adjusting her coffee cup to stay upright against the movement of the swing. "Like I said, it's working out far better than I could ever have hoped, but it *has* been a bit of a wild ride, ever since day one. Once I got to Florida, I realized Wain's situation was nothing like what you thought it was."

Guy was instantly cautious; she could hear the frown in his voice. "Wain's *situation*? What do you mean?"

Key gave him a short synopsis of her visit at the jail with Lyric. "Bottom line, Guy, she was just emotionless when it came to Wain. Cold, even. Maybe it was the fact that she's in jail, but she did *not* come across as the caring mother you described to me. Do you remember the housekeeper Wain was staying with, Mayetta Titus? While I was there, Mayetta shared some observations with me that were extremely concerning—about Gary Callahan. Well, and Lyric too."

"What do you mean by *concerning*?" Guy replied tensely.

Key picked up her notebook. "The truth is, Guy, according to Mayetta—and actually Wain himself—your little boy suffered some serious abuse at the hands of Gary Callahan. And I suspect Wain's mother, at the very least, sat back and allowed it to happen. Mayetta Titus is the one person in the world who gave Wain any sort of protection and comfort."

There was a short silence. "What kind of abuse?" Just four icy, clipped words, but Guy's fury vibrated through the phone.

"Physical, mental, emotional. Callahan is a calculating, malevolent bully who, from what I can gather, seems to have been extremely resentful that Wain was included in the Lyric package."

Guy was obviously up, pacing around. "I can't sit still and listen to this. Tell me everything you know, Key. Everything."

She chose her next words carefully. "During the years they lived with Gary Callahan, I doubt Wain lived a day without fear. Callahan, and I believe Lyric to a lesser degree, inflicted ongoing psychological trauma by punishing him for ... well ... basically for being a kid! For instance, if he ate something without asking, or made a mess, or stepped out of line in even the tiniest ways, he was physically punished. He was called names, had very few toys or possessions, and was at the very least ignored and marginalized from their lives. It all added up to a heartbreaking loneliness for a very vulnerable little boy. One of the repercussions is that Wain has lost his ability to read, doesn't even recognize letters. I believe absolutely that this is directly tied to the abuse."

There was a short intense silence. "Unbelievable," Guy finally replied, in a dangerously calm, icy voice. "This is unbelievable. I'm seriously going to hunt that bastard down and kill him. I'm going to *kill* him."

Not the best words to use in an airport. Key stood and stepped to the front door, peering through the screen. The coast was clear. She sat back down, this time in the wicker chair, speaking softly. "Guy, I understand, believe me, but *please* keep your cool. I need to go over everything with you, and we don't have a lot of time. So please, sit down and listen. Okay?" It was imperative that Guy understood how much Wain had improved since moving in with her.

"Okay," Guy said tersely, his voice slightly cracking. "But you have to believe me, Key. I had *no* idea. I thought Wain was like this bright happy kid and that Angie—I mean, ugh, *Lyric*—was a great mom ...."

And you never checked to make sure. The truth floated unsaid between them.

"Guy, this has been a terrible shock, I know," Key replied. "And Wain still has issues, of course, but he's safe now. Every day removes him just a bit further from that fear, and his resilience is astounding! You *have* to have seen the happiness in his face in the pictures I've sent."

"Yeah." Guy sighed heavily. "Yeah, the pictures have made me really happy. I bet I've looked at them a hundred times, and the one with the sunglasses is my screen saver now. To be honest, Key, since Wain moved in with you, I've become far more aware of how bitterly disappointed my mother would be in me, in what I've allowed to happen over the past several years. I do want that to change." Key didn't reply, and after a brief pause, Guy asked bluntly, "Key, why didn't you share this information about Lyric and Callahan with me before now?"

She took a deep breath. *Here we go.* "I'm going to ask you a question to answer that question."

"Okay?" he sounded wary.

"Think back to our conversation the day you came to North Carolina and asked me to take Wain. How much did you truly know or want to know about him?" There was another, much longer silence.

"I had no idea he was being *abused*," Guy finally replied, sounding defensive. "There's no way I would ever have let Wain endure something like that if I'd known."

"Oh, I know that, Guy!" Key answered kindly. "I've never once thought otherwise." She heard him take a deep breath. Was he crying? It broke her heart. *So much unnecessary loss.* She continued. "Let's say that right off the bat, I *had* told you what Mayetta told me. You would have shown up to help correct the situation. Am I right?"

"Of course I would have!" he replied angrily.

Regretting that she was adding salt to his wounds but wanting to make her point crystal clear, Key said, "You were very specific that you had no plans to go to Florida because you didn't want to show up for just a few minutes in his life and then leave."

Another silence. Out in her yard and beyond, daytime spilled light behind a still-cloudy sky. Birds were waking up. High overhead, the hum of a jet faded in and out, and a truck rumbled past, towing a horse trailer toward Mistic Meadows.

"I did say that," Guy admitted at last, sounding as though he was in pain. "But, Key, he's still my *son*. It's far more complex than I ever imagined. I would have appreciated being involved."

Key felt her cheeks go warm. It was the closest he'd come to criticizing her. She gave herself a moment, added coffee to her cup, and looked again at her notes. "I understand. But, Guy, what *you* must understand is that Wain's trust in adults is fragile at best. The last thing he needed after losing his mother *and* Mrs. Titus, not to mention moving in with an old lady he'd never met, was his estranged father's entrance and then immediate exit. In other words, more chaos for his young mind to process. Because let's face it, Guy, you *are* a stranger to your son. Even now, I rarely hear from you." Key felt as though she'd just torn the bandage off a gaping wound.

Another tense, quiet spell. "There's not a thing you just said that I can argue with." Guy's anger had vanished like a vapor. "I wish I could tell you why I haven't called, but I can't."

There was no use wasting time trying to figure out Guy's thought processes. "Please, let's leave all that in the past and start from here. We both want the best for Wain," Key replied, more encouraged than she'd been since meeting Guy for breakfast. "Your little boy and I need you to be involved to whatever extent you can be."

"We *will* start fresh from here. You have my word," Guy said, still subdued, then he asked, "Does Wain know his mom's in jail?"

"Oh yes. Wain understands his mom isn't coming back for a long time. Mayetta, bless her heart, explained it to him in what I'm sure was the nicest possible way. I'm sorry, Guy, that it's been such a distressing conversation. You know I want the best for you too."

"I know, Key, I know. I've put so much on your plate, and you've handled it like—well, like my mother would have. I'm sorry too, for so many things." She heard another prolonged sigh. "What happens now?"

She hoped he could hear the smile in her voice. "One day at a time." Guy listened closely as she gave details about their life at Pike

House, the hikes, the camera lessons and letter searches (Guy loved that story), Wain's penchant for cooking, and his friendship with Ell. "And yesterday Wain and I drove to the pound and brought home a sweet two-year-old dog named Faro," Key finished. "Wain is already crazy about him."

"That's so cool. We always had dogs, growing up." Guy sounded wistful. "It's great to hear all the good news, Key. But I'm still trying to get my head around all this information. So you truly think Wain's improving?" He seemed to need extra reassurance.

"Absolutely. He's your son, Guy, and I see so much of you in him. You were always tough in the best way, so smart and driven, so quick to catch on to anything that caught your interest. That side of Wain is emerging. He still misses his mother terribly though."

"Key … I am so grateful. Pretty sure my mom is too." Guy cleared his throat, then added, simply, "Thank you."

She blinked back tears. "You are so welcome. Thank *you* for coming to me in the first place. It's been wonderfully healing for me too." She looked down at the final item on her list. "Oh! One more thing. Guy, very off topic but—have you ever heard of CartWheels?"

"You can't live in Texas and be unaware," Guy said, dryly. "They're based in San Antonio."

"Really? I was way out of that loop before I met Wain. Well, anyway, your son is a huge CartWheels fan. We found the latest car for him, SunBolt, but Black Diamond is his holy grail, and that one has been very elusive. No luck so far."

He sounded distracted. "Black Diamond, huh? I mean, I know CartWheels makes toy cars, but I don't know the particulars."

Key heard keyboard tapping. "Do you need to go?"

"No, no, Key, I have time. I'm just pulling up some info to share with you." More tapping. "I should have done this long ago, but yesterday your text made me curious enough that I asked Ameera, an attorney in our uh … Citrine's legal department, to dig up what she could about Gary Callahan. Interesting what she discovered."

Key sat forward. "What did you find out?"

"Derek Garth Calhoun, a.k.a. Gary Callahan."

She gasped. "No way!"

"He's from San Francisco. Embezzled nearly a million dollars from a graphic-arts company where he was an artist slash CFO," Guy chuckled darkly. "Talk about the fox in the henhouse. Tailor-made for forging, eh? Anyway, he's from a prominent family in the Bay Area. They quietly repaid the company he ripped off, and voilà, no arrest, no charges filed. Golden boy landed on his feet and headed for Brookings, Florida, where the Sojourner Hotel is owned by a relative of the Calhoun family. They hired him as general manager, with, I have to believe, some ignorance about his past. I don't know that for sure though. They obviously went along with the name change. Maybe they thought he wouldn't rob family."

Key rolled her eyes. "Bad decision! If he wasn't arrested in San Francisco, why change his name?"

"I'm gonna go with self-preservation," Guy replied. "Anyone could have put the word out there about the sins of Derek Garth Calhoun, regardless of charges filed."

"Good point. Any online search might show something." Key set her phone on the arm of the wicker chair and stood up and stretched, walking to the door to check the living room again. Still no sign of activity.

"And now he's out on bail. I don't have time to worry about any of the embezzlement crap," Guy said roughly, "except that I'm happy it's put them in the hands of the law. But what he did to Wain ..."

She picked up her phone and sat back down. "I know. I feel the same way." There was another brief silence, and then Key heard a click.

"Key, I've got a call I absolutely have to deal with before I board. What you've told me about Callahan and Lyric has made me the angriest I've ever been, but I know now that Wain is *truly* safe and thriving, and that makes me the happiest I can remember being in a long, long time. I feel like a huge weight is off my back. Dubai is nine hours ahead of you, and I'll be doing more traveling, but texts to this number will work anytime. And let's plan for Christmas. I'll be back then for at least a couple weeks. And no matter what, Wain will never go back to Lyric. I'll make sure of it."

"You have no idea how happy that makes me, Guy!"

"Tell Wain hello for me, maybe give him a hug?" He seemed reluctant to end the call.

"Of course!" she exclaimed. "We'll set up some video calls. And I'll keep sending the pictures. He really is thriving."

"Thanks to you. I'll be in touch. I promise. Thanks again, Key."

"Bye, Guy! Safe travels." She settled back on the swing and gave herself a little push. It was overcast this morning, but only in the sky. Despite her vague uneasiness about Callahan's bail, despite the questions that Lyric's call had raised, Key too felt as though a load had been lifted. Guy truly cared about his little boy. *Feel that, Edie? That sunshine breaking through?* She could have danced across the dewy lawn.

Chapter 33

MUDDLED

"Who were you talking to?"

Key jerked up from the swing, dumping the remains of her coffee as Faro dashed down the steps and galloped joyfully around the front yard, pausing here and there to thoughtfully water the flowers. "Argh!" Again! She needed to either get a brown rug or start using a cup with a lid.

"Wain! Faro! Good morning! You two are like stealth bombers!" She laughed and gave Wain a hug. Where'd you come from?" It was 6:20 a.m.

"I woke up, and Faro was gone. I saw him at the door, so I opened it and heard you talking on the phone."

"Wain, please run into the house and get my tablet. It's on my nightstand." When he brought it back, she said, "Sit here by me, buddy. I want to show you something." Wain sat, leaning slightly on her arm, watching as Key scrolled through her pictures. "I've been waiting until we talked about your dad to show you these. This man in the picture with me, and in this next one, is your father, Guy, my cousin." She handed Wain the tablet. "You can see he looks like you! That's who I was talking to. I've known him for a long time, since he was younger than you are. He was checking in to see how we're doing."

"Oh." Wain pointed. "That's your Jeep!"

"It is. I took that the day your dad came to North Carolina to ask if I'd have you move in with me." She explained Guy's upcoming trip, the video-call idea, and Guy's desire to come at Christmas. "How do you feel about that?"

Wain examined the pictures. "Is he nice?"

"Very nice. He said to tell you hi and he's happy you got Faro, and here's a hug from him! We can write him letters if you want, the same way we did for your mom and Mrs. Titus."

"Yeah, okay." Wain seemed to take it all in stride. Scrolling down through Key's more recent pictures, he said excitedly, "Hey, here's the ones I took!" He showed Key. "There's that wooden tree root *X*. And look! *O* in the tree trunk!"

"Do you see any other letters?" she asked casually. She had rotated and cropped all the pictures he'd taken so that the letters were configured correctly. She held her breath.

He pointed. "That's shaped like a *C*. Like on my backpack." He handed her the tablet and jumped up. "Whoa! I forgot my backpack in my room."

"Wain," she said, laughing, hugging him before he bolted off, "that *is C*! You are amazing! I'll mop up this coffee, then how about some breakfast for us and for Faro?"

"I can feed him! Here, boy! Here, Faro!" He tried to whistle, failing miserably, and Key stifled a laugh as she held the door for them.

"Want to take Faro on a short hike this morning before DP and the guys get here? They are going to love meeting him!"

"Can I show him to Ell too?"

"Absolutely! I'll text her mom. If it's okay, we'll drive over to get Ell after our hike."

While Wain was in the house, Key went around back to check the construction work. The roof was now finished, the beautiful dark-gray-stained pine ceiling had been installed, and they'd begun building a wide bench at the kitchen end that would double as seating for one side of the table. Once the mud dried a little, they could keep laying pavers too. She needed to find a cushion, she thought happily, and deck furniture, and a new rug for the porch that hid coffee stains.

After a leisurely pancake-and-sausage breakfast, they set out. "We're like the Three Musketeers," Key said to Wain, then almost regretted it when he asked what a musketeer was and followed up with enough questions to underscore her ignorance about antique guns.

Faro needed no leash; it was as though he'd waited his whole life to be included in a pack. He ranged a short way ahead, constantly doubling back, and always returned when she whistled. Wain ran eagerly behind him, mud splattering over his shoes and legs, his backpack bouncing. He'd hurriedly tucked two dog biscuits in the secret compartment with the cars before they left, and Key hoped they wouldn't be pummeled to crumbs by snack time.

It remained cloudy but quickly grew warm. Drops of water from low-hanging leaves clung to Key's hair, her legs were soaked from the grass, and her shoes were already heavy with red claylike mud. Yes, she resolved as she swiped the perspiration off her nose with the sleeve of her damp T-shirt, today would be a *very* short hike, but they were here, and she wanted to add at least a couple pictures to the binder. She'd forgotten to check, but she knew for sure they hadn't so far found *W* or *N*. Wain had done so well with recognizing his previously photographed *X, O,* and *C* on the tablet this morning that she decided to take a chance.

"This is a good place to stop," she called, plopping down on a soaking-wet log. *In for a penny, in for a pound,* Key thought. Why should their shorts stay dry when everything else was waterlogged? Faro sat on the ground at the end of the log close to Wain, panting happily, his nose inches from the backpack.

"Wain, do you know how to spell your name?" Key asked him casually, handing him the camera. They would either fall into the abyss or they would cross the bridge.

He didn't miss a beat. "*W-A-I-N.*"

"Awesome. So if I drew this,"—with her stick, she scratched out a perfect *W* in the mud—"can you find that shape in the tree branches or roots?"

Wain turned on the camera, then took a long look at *W*. He got up and took a few steps, then came back and stared at the *W* from the other way. "That's a *M*," he said as confidently as if he'd said, "That's the color blue," or "That's SunBolt."

She willed herself not to jump up cheering. "It is," she said calmly. "From one direction it's a *W* and from the other it's an *M*. Can you find either one?"

Ambling toward the path, Wain studied tree configurations, roots, branches, and fallen logs. Finally, at the intersection of several tree roots, he took a picture.

"Wow!" she exclaimed when he showed her. "That's a *W*, and if you rotate the picture, it's an *M*. These are both hard to find, so great job!"

"Can we do one more?" Wain asked. Again, Key simply wrote the letter correctly, and after traipsing around for several minutes, he found two trees with a log leaning diagonally between them for his *N*. *This is how I'd define "momentous breakthrough,"* Key thought happily. Except for the letter *X* on the first day, today marked the first time Wain had searched the woods for correctly oriented and identified letters. She sensed with relief that he wasn't equating the terrifying symbols on the flash cards with what he'd been photographing with her camera. This patient, accommodating patch of forest was providing a traumatized boy with a soothing new version of the alphabet. Exactly what she'd hoped.

Key set the camera next to her on the log, then dug in her bag for the packages of cheese crackers she'd thrown in that morning. "Let's have a snack to celebrate *W* and *N*, and then we should head back."

Wain unzipped his backpack and fed Faro the dog biscuits. "Whoa!" he exclaimed as Faro crunched enthusiastically. "Why is PyroTire in *that* space?"

Yikes. Key froze, biting her lip and sliding her eyes sideways.

"And why is CopperTop here? That's not where it goes! It goes here, but SplishFlash is there! *All* of them are wrong except ShamRocker!"

Irritated and mystified, Wain pulled six of the cars out of their mesh pockets and rearranged them.

The sun had finally broken through. Nibbling her cracker and gazing through treetops at roughly outlined blue patches, Key sorted her thoughts. Somewhere above those stratus clouds (thank you, Edie), Guy was winging his way to Dubai, now knowing far more about his son's life, but still oblivious to the backpack mystery. She sighed. She had purposely not told him about Lyric's unsettling call. Because how could it possibly make sense to Guy, when at this point none of it made sense to her? Sometime soon, Key vowed, she would share the entire mystery with him, but before she did, she wanted to collect more facts and hopefully resolve it herself.

She had new information as well: Guy's surprising prescient decision to research Callahan had been more helpful than he knew. A background in graphic arts perfectly explained Callahan's precise handwriting *and* the use of a green ink that exactly matched the blade of grass on the *S* card.

Take that, Derek Garth Calhoun, she thought triumphantly. *Not only do I know your real name, but also your password.* She just didn't know what files it unlocked.

After restoring order in the CartWheel chaos Key had created, Wain held a cracker in one hand and rolled PyroTire over the wet bumpy bark with the other. Faro had finished his exploring and flopped down in the soggy grass, directly in a sunbeam. A flock of Canada geese flew over, honking madly; and from far beyond the woods a faint train whistle drifted over them like a lonely birdcall.

Yesterday's events and the emotional conversation with Guy had drained her. Key's brain, like the day, felt sluggish and steamy. How should she explain to Wain the reason his cars were mixed up? What was he capable of understanding? *I need to simply be honest*, she mused; and Mayetta's perceptive advice floated into her thoughts. *Respect them when they're little, they'll respect you when they're big.*

Of course. Wain absolutely deserved her respect. And of all the mysteries Key had to choose from, his was one she could solve right now. She put her hand on his back. "Wain," she said easily, "I can explain why your cars were in the wrong slots."

"Okay?" He made it a question, still bumping PyroTire across the log.

"I need your full attention, so do you mind putting your car back and zipping everything up?" She waited till he was done, then said, "It's actually tied in with your mom's phone call yesterday."

As if he sensed a tenseness, Faro stood and stretched, then put his chin on the little boy's leg, waggling closer as Wain put his hand out and rubbed it slowly on the dog's warm black back.

"Oh," was all Wain said, giving Faro a final long stroke, then he reached for his backpack.

"I wondered," Key continued gently, "if you have any questions about that call. Because that had to have been very hard for you."

Clutching his backpack to his chest, Wain fixed his blue-green eyes on hers, dark hair flopping over his damp forehead. There was something different there, though, a determined defiance intermingled with his fear. "Do I have to send my cars and backpack to Cal, like my mom said?"

Key shook her head vigorously. "Nope. Not the backpack, not the cars. *Never.*"

He visibly relaxed. "Okay. My mom was really mad." Wain traced the letters on the backpack, something Key had noticed he did when he needed comfort.

"She sure was," Key agreed. She put her arm around him.

Wain kicked at the leaves under his shoes. "She gets mad, and then she's nice again."

Very perceptive, kiddo. "I know. You can still write her letters if you want. You don't have to be mad back. I'll help you."

"Can I tell her about Faro?" Wain asked hopefully. "Because he's like the coolest dog ever. Aren't you, boy?"

"Definitely you should tell her about Faro!" Key lifted each of her shoes in turn and used a stick to scrape energetically at the clingy mud while she talked. "So here's the thing. I need to be honest with you, Wain. I just can't figure out why your mom even *wants* us to send

Cal your backpack! So last night while you were asleep, I took it and examined all your cars. I didn't find a single thing. I put the cars back, but guess what? I didn't know you kept them in their own special slots." Her mud-scraping stick broke in two, and she tossed it into the wet leaves, then rubbed her shoes on the grass. "From now on, I'll ask you to show them to me, okay? I'm sorry."

"That's okay," Wain said immediately. "I don't care if you look at my cars! I show them to everyone! Like Jukey, Ell, Benito ..." He leaned against her, eating his last cracker and scratching absentmindedly at a mosquito bite on his knee.

Ask him, said a little voice in her mind. *Ask the expert.*

"Hey, buddy," Key said, turning sideways suddenly so he could see her face, knocking him a little off-balance. "By any chance, do you know if there's anything special about any of the cars? I mean, I know FireFlyer's trunk lights up—"

"No, it *glows* in the *dark*."

She laughed. "Oops. I stand corrected. Glows in the dark. Does any other car have something cool or unusual about it?"

"Not really. Well ... um, maybe." Wain opened his backpack to reveal the now correctly arranged cars. Key watched intently as he touched them one by one, scrunching up his grubby face in concentration. He seemed to be auditioning them, coming to a reluctant conclusion as he stopped at one car. "Just what that girl with the pink hair showed me at the store," he finally said. "But it's not very cool."

A chilly prickle of goose bumps started at Key's neck and inched slowly down her arms. The woods were suddenly very quiet. "Evie?" she managed to say. "The clerk at Imagine That? What did she show you?"

"Okay. *So*, look at this." Wain freed a car from its pocket and expertly flipped it around. "If you press on this one black headlight goggle exactly right here, then pull the middle, this thing pops out between the fins." He showed her a small silver square, then pushed the middle of the car back together, pressed a different button, and the square disappeared. "That's all it does! It's so boring! It doesn't light up or *anything*."

SplishFlash. A flash drive.

Isn't there supposed to be dramatic organ music when moments like this occur? Should I not be shouting, "Eureka!" and dancing like a crazed Rumpelstiltskin on top of this log? Instead, Key stood and briskly brushed the bark and dirt off the rear of her very damp shorts. Keeping her voice casual, she said, "Hmm, very interesting! Do you mind if I check out SplishFlash at home?"

"Sure." Wain shrugged, raising his eyebrows and tilting his head in a suavely seven-year-old "be my guest" kind of way. Key never took her eyes off SplishFlash as he slid the car into its mesh pocket and zipped it up. Beside them, Faro panted, hot breath on her bare knees.

Key laughed aloud. "Ready to head back?" she said to her boys.

Chapter 34

TO-DO LIST

On their hike back, her head spinning from what she'd just discovered, Key had to stop herself from walking nearly on top of Wain, wanting to cling to his backpack like a baby possum. He had no idea he'd become a guardian of secrets.

"Mornin', Miss Key! Hey, little man," DP said, grinning broadly as they approached the house. "Looks like y'all been wrestling mud turtles." He reached out his hand to Faro, who approached him cautiously. "Who've we got here? Where'd you get the crazy-haired dog, son?" DP squatted down and held out his hand, clicking his tongue. "C'mere boy. Aren't you a dandy." He scratched Faro's ears, laughing at the damp, flopped-over topknot.

"It's Faro. I got him yesterday. He's my very own dog." Wain could hardly contain himself.

"Aw, congrats, little man! Boy's best friend. Molly and I have a shepherd mix, Greta. Dogs are family."

"Morning, DP! We've been on a hike, but I'm questioning that decision." Key lifted a muddy shoe. "Like hiking with weights on my feet." She checked to make sure Wain's backpack hadn't flown off his back. "We got Faro from the shelter in Porterville. He already fits right in."

"You don't let the grass grow under your feet, do you?" DP laughed and stood up. "Got any other cute little dark-haired adoptees around here, muddy or otherwise, that I haven't met yet?" He gestured to the deck. "What do you think?"

"It's going to be the perfect space. I love it! I love the bench."

"Glad to hear it. Your idea, Miss Key. We're just building it."

"*Just*," she replied with a laugh.

They shed their muddy shoes at the front porch steps and finally went inside. It was only nine thirty in the morning, but Key felt that if she sat down for five minutes, she would sleep all day.

SplishFlash was immediately locked in the desk drawer with the other items; it was easily Wain's least favorite car, so he'd handed it over with only a little hesitation. Key recalled his description of the collector's cards attached to each car. That had to be how Lyric or Callahan had discovered that SplishFlash was far more than simply a cute little '57 Chevy-style car with fins and goggle headlights.

She could hardly wait to plug it into her computer, but that was not going to happen anytime soon. The house was long overdue for a deep clean, she had ignored the laundry for days, there were a dozen emails she hadn't answered, bills to be paid, and they would soon be eating crackers and water if she didn't go grocery shopping. Not to mention, weeds were popping up everywhere. Her newly hectic schedule would level out in time, Key was sure, but she had never been this far behind. How did parents of large families do it? Having children was a monumental undertaking, and she had incorporated only one!

She was also hours from a deadline for ten card ideas in the "General Sentiments" category, CORE's abstract line, where they gave the creative talent free rein. Normally she'd take days mulling over ideas, but this month's submissions would be culled from ideas she'd previously scribbled into her CORE IDEAS notebook and rejected. She'd deal with that later.

After lunch, they left Faro at Pike House while they went to pick up Ell, who clambered into the Jeep next to Wain, carrying a small wooden box. "Hey, Miss Key! Mama said she'll come and get me once Daddy comes back with the car, like around four o'clock." She rattled the box. "I brought a penny game," she said to Wain. "It's like, really, really fun."

Wain could hardly contain himself. "We got something *so* supercool to show you!" He had told Key he wanted to surprise Ell.

When Faro met them at the door, Ell's delight at meeting him was as naturally heartwarming as her other visits had been. "You got a *dog*? A dog! Hey, sweet pupper!" She knelt and hugged Faro while Wain told her about their visit to the shelter.

"You could get one too! They have so many in there! They just give them to you! You walk in, and they're like, 'Oh, hey, it's you. Here's your dog.' And you get to take it."

Key burst out laughing. *Yes, that simple.*

Wain, Ell, and Faro spent most of the day outside in the shade of the backyard oaks, on the big rock and the tire swing. As she swept purposefully through the house restoring order, Key couldn't hear much, but she surmised that at one point, Faro was a dragon. That's exactly what she needed: a watch dragon patrolling the property. *Stop it*, she told herself. She was blowing this way out of proportion. She had no proof whatsoever that Callahan planned to come around; and besides, as far as she could tell, no one could approach Pike House from any direction without being exposed.

When the trio did come back, muddy all over again, Key gave them towels and had them hose themselves off, then set them up with a movie and snacks. Exhausted, she picked up her phone from the kitchen table and tapped a number, then walked out to the porch swing. Faro, still wet from playing in the water, flopped down with a doggy groan at her feet.

"Hello?" A familiar voice, warm and sweet as sunlight filtering through honeycomb, filled her ear.

"Mayetta? Hi, it's Key North! Wain's cousin?"

"Key! Mercy! Hello! My phone gets poor service here at Tasha's, but let me walk outside. It seems to work better out there." Key heard Mrs. Titus say something unintelligible, then the open-and-close sound of a sliding door. "That's better. Is everything okay? How's my little Wain doing?"

"Wonderful!" Key replied. She detailed the highlights of the past weeks to a delighted Mrs. Titus. After they'd caught up for a few minutes, Key said, "Mayetta, I wanted to let you know something I heard."

"Mr. Cal, he's out," Mrs. Titus said simply.

"Yes!" Key answered with a surprised laugh. Mrs. Titus always seemed to be one step ahead of her. "How did you know?"

"Remember I told you my boy Isaac helps me out now and then. Well, he came to Brookings not long ago for a few days, fixed my car, did some handywork and whatnot. We were talking yesterday, and he mentioned that while he was there, Mr. Cal had come by to see if I was home. Left when Isaac told him I was gone to Tasha's. Mr. Cal didn't tell Isaac what he wanted, and he hasn't called me."

No doubt Callahan was looking for the backpack. Key decided it would be best not to mention it. "How long will you be in Chicago?" she asked.

"I'm here for the summer, not going back until late August, after school starts."

Hopefully, everything would have blown over by that time, but Key made a note to check in with Mrs. Titus later in the summer. "Oh! One more thing! Mayetta, would you describe Callahan's and Lyric's cars?"

"Yes, I can see them clear as day. Mr. Cal has a dark-blue BMW, like a sedan, and Miss Lyric drives a big white SUV, a Lincoln I think. But wait a minute." She clicked her tongue. "Come to think of it, though, Key, I looked in the garage for Wain's backpack, and I definitely remember only Miss Lyric's car was there. Mr. Cal's might have been at the hotel, though, sometimes they rode home together."

Key scribbled it all down. "Thank you so much, Mayetta, for everything." She was the grandma everyone coveted, Key thought as she hung up. In a lopsided way, Wain was a very fortunate boy. Mrs. Titus's loving-kindness at such a vulnerable time in his life would remain a part of him forever.

After drying Faro with an old towel and letting him back into the house with Wain and Ell, Key stretched out on the swing to answer emails and indulge in Words with Friends.

Right at four, Gayle drove up, stylish in blue-jean leggings and a stretchy sleeveless yellow pullover, hair in a messy bun, with full makeup, blue eye shadow, and all. This time Key was ready with glasses of ice and two cans of cranberry-lime-flavored sparkling water. When she asked if Ell could stay fifteen minutes longer to finish the movie, Gayle folded herself gracefully into the rocker, put her phone on the porch railing, and sighed tiredly.

"Oh, please twist my arm, give me a reason to sit down! Dibsy is a full-on Tasmanian devil these days! Thank you, Miss Key. It's good to see you again. Busyness just gets in the way of visiting, doesn't it?" She took a sip, then looked at the can. "Never tasted this before."

"How's everything going with you?" Key asked her, happy to have a chance to catch up. "I'm so glad you all are coming to the concert on Saturday. Are you bringing Granny Jewel?"

Gayle nodded, expertly tucking an escaped hair back into her bun. "She wouldn't miss it. She loves them guys that are singing that evening. Lonny was hoping Larry and Pee would take her, but they are gonna be out of town for the Fourth, so you get the full Granny Jewel immersement experience." She took another tentative sip.

"She sounds like a true character." *One of many in the Morgan clan,* Key thought, hiding a smile.

Gayle laughed and replied, "Oh, I married into a family of characters, then produced a few of my own. But Granny Jewel is more work than Dibsy and Ell combined. My life these days consists of old ladies with opinions versus babies with no sense careening all over the house and nine-year-olds who blurt out any thought that comes to mind, not to mention a teenage boy who lives in an alternate universe. No one understands him because, you know, we were *never* teenagers ourselves. I have to run around holding my tongue all day long."

"It sounds like you're the reason it all runs smoothly. I can barely manage one small boy!" Key replied, laughing. "And, Gayle, thank you so much for your helpful advice about the, um, the jail situation. It was Wain's mother who I went to visit."

"I gathered as much from some things Ell has said. Wain mentioned it to her."

Key raised her eyebrows. This was news. "Oh really? I didn't know he had, but I'm not surprised. Ell's been the perfect antidote to his previous situation. She's a gift."

"I'm glad you see it that way. Ell is a handful, but she's one of those pure-hearted people who deep down feels others' emotions and defends the underdog. I don't know nothing more about Wain's circumstances, but I can imagine. His mama's locked up," Gayle said pensively. "That must be very hard on her. Does she call him regular?"

"She doesn't seem to want anything to do with him." At Gayle's disbelieving look, Key nodded. "I will never understand it. I'm still trying to figure it out. Fortunately, I think his father is genuinely going to try harder to be involved."

"Poor little boy." Gayle rocked her chair. "I didn't know any of that. And there's no explanation. It's unnatural when a mama pushes away her own."

Their conversation ended suddenly when Ell and Wain catapulted onto the porch behind Faro. "Mama! Wain got a dog!"

After chatting a few minutes longer, Gayle stood to leave, making Key laugh again when she said, "Better get back. Lonny's mowing, and Cav is watching Dibsy. Or more likely she is watching him." She gave Wain a perfumy hug. "It's a pleasure to meet you, darlin', finally!" They drove away with Ell in the front seat listing all the reasons they should drive into Porterville right that minute and pick up a free dog.

Deciphering would have to wait. So would Ell's penny game, which sat forgotten on the entry table by the front door. After much-needed showers, an early dinner of grilled cheese sandwiches, roasted green beans, and ice cream, and a full bowl of dog food served to a famished Faro, all three were asleep before dark.

Chapter 35

CONSTERNATION

SplishFlash was burning a hole in her desk drawer. Key sat at the kitchen table with her feet up on a second chair, adding bite marks to a scarred pen and sketching out her one new idea, inspired by Wain: On the front of the card were two little white envelopes with red-and-blue borders, one angled jauntily on top of the other, with squiggly lines for the addresses. Under those, she wrote "Did you get my letters?" Inside the card, the envelopes were open, with a bright-red *X* and *O* spilling out. She thought of and discarded several sentiments for the inside; as on the napkin she'd given Wain at lunch, *X* and *O* said it all. Flipping through the previous scribbles on the pages in her CORE notebook, she found nine more that would work in a pinch, then on a whim added a note to Dorothy: "How about doing a line of cards in braille? Might be something to consider!" Not everyone had the option to read in the traditional sense.

It was fully light outside, but the sun wasn't yet over the horizon. Faro wandered from his spot at the end of Wain's bed to the front door, so she let him out, hoping his roommate would sleep for at least another hour, then refilled her coffee cup, grabbed her keys from her purse, and made a beeline for her office, where, to her illogical relief, she saw the drawer was undisturbed.

After letting Faro back in, she settled in the chair and pulled out the envelope containing the flash card and her handwritten copy. Picking up SplishFlash, she followed the steps Wain had shown her, and the drive popped out. *Ingenious.* You would never, ever know it was there. *Moment of truth*, she thought, and inserted it into the USB on her desktop computer, whispering, "Okay, little car, tell me your secrets."

Immediately a passcode box popped up. Heart pounding, her voice barely a whisper, Key moved her cursor to the box, then pointed with the tip of her pen to each of the twenty individual characters she'd copied, double-checking each one as she typed. "Uppercase *S*, lowercase *i*, lowercase *t* ..." until *SitG@591856207842758* filled the box. Then she pressed "enter."

INCORRECT PASSWORD. TRY AGAIN.

Her heart fell. "*What?* No, no, no!" She banged her closed fist on the desk, exhaling softly through gritted teeth. She was positive she had copied everything correctly, but perhaps her handwritten copy was wrong, maybe she had miswritten a letter or number, ignored a capital letter? She glanced at the clock; she didn't have much time. If Wain woke up and saw her in her raggedy, old summer pajamas, hair askew in a crazy bun, playing Sherlock Holmes with a magnifying glass and his little CartWheels car locked in place in a USB port like a tethered, helpless lab rat, he might just take off running down Pike Road and never come back.

"Come on, *come on*, SplishFlash!" Using the magnifying glass and flash card this time, she scrutinized the impeccable minuscule green writing, typing everything exactly as shown. Nothing. The files may as well have been on Mars for all she was able to access them. Maybe she should call the jail and ask Lyric for help. That would go over well.

Think, Key. Go the easiest route. She would assume the numbers were correct. That left the letters. What might SitG stand for? A place? A name? Situation. Sitcom. Sitter. Sitka? She heard rustling, then Wain talking sleepily to Faro. Bitterly disappointed, she hurriedly ejected SplishFlash, returned everything to the drawer, and locked it. She'd been stymied, but she was more determined than ever. She would simply have to sit back and let the SitG enigma marinate to fruition in her mind.

Chapter 36

THE MORGANS

Key and Wain. Early July

P wants 2 no if u & Wain wld like 2 say hello 2 the band b4 they play? Emoji music note, waving boy, American flag, guitar. & 2 remind u no dogs aloud! Emoji dog, pink heart, crying face. Taken aback, Key had to read it twice before she laughed delightedly and added the number and a name to her contacts. DP must have shared her information.

Thanks, Molly! We'd love to! Yes, we plan to leave Faro at home.

She showed the text to Wain. He didn't flinch or look away, she noticed happily. Probably the emoji had caught his eye. "This is from DP's wife, Molly. I know it's disappointing, but Faro has to stay home. That's actually a good thing. Fireworks are often terrifying for dogs."

"Why are they scared?" Wain asked, leaning down to fiddle with the stars-and-stripes bandanna around Faro's neck.

Key leaned against the counter and shrugged. "You know, I'm not sure, honey. Pansy slept right through the noise, but I had a neighbor who always turned her TV volume way up so her dog wouldn't hear the fireworks. She had a special shirt for him and even gave him calming medicine, but when he heard fireworks, he shivered and shook and went kinda crazy. I don't know how Faro reacts to loud popping noises, but he'll be safe here at the house."

"You wouldn't be scared, would you, boy?" Wain scrubbed his hands all over Faro's wiggling back. Key wondered if on some level he sympathized with the fearful dogs.

"Take your snacks to the porch and let Faro play outside for a bit." She added two dog biscuits to a plate containing a chocolate doughnut and a banana and gave Wain an affectionate swat. "Now, don't you eat the biscuits! Faro is the lucky one! *You* have to eat the doughnut!" She was discovering what type of humor made him laugh.

"Eww!" He sauntered off, still smiling, Faro racing ahead.

Ping. Gr8, c u then! Happy 4th! One smiley face, four flags.

It would take me twice as long to text that way, Key thought in amusement. Was it faster to spell "great" like that? Maybe. But for now, she'd stick to the plain alphabet found upside down and sideways in tree branches. Much simpler.

The day so far had been uncomfortably hot. Even the loose, airy fabric of Key's sleeveless white cotton dress felt constricting. She wondered if she'd regret her choice to wear sandals, but for the first time in months, she'd painted her toenails, sitting on the living-room sofa with her feet angled on the edge of the coffee table. The dark-pink polish made her feel a bit more festive. Ten minutes to let them dry was a luxury anymore; long gone were the days when she'd spent hours at the spa.

She still didn't trust herself when it came to styling a little boy, but did it matter? When they'd gone to Troy earlier in the day for groceries, Wain had found a T-shirt on a sale rack outside the store featuring a red-white-and-blue dog. It was a little too big, but he had picked it out himself and tentatively asked if she would buy it for him. It was the first time he'd worked up the nerve to request something without her offering beforehand: another milestone. His pride in his new shirt exactly matched her gratitude for his growing confidence.

Late in the afternoon, after coating herself and an impatient Wain with another layer of sunscreen, Key loaded the Jeep with two chairs, a blanket, the cooler containing their picnic dinner, a bag of essentials, and a folding wagon she'd gotten recently. It had already become invaluable in carting items from the house to the Jeep and vice versa. She'd made enough outdoor trips already that she planned to ask DP about building a garage close to the house, with a covered breezeway, an idea she'd been mulling since she'd seen the one Jukey and Mary had designed.

She and Wain were early enough that they easily found the Morgans. It was hard to miss Ell, who dashed excitedly to meet them in red shorts with white stars and a blue-and-white-striped shirt. On her head was a wide band with springy red, white, and blue stars that lit up and bounced with every move. "My mama got all this except the headband at the Shepherd thrift store!" she said proudly, twirling with arms extended.

"Whoa, cool," Wain said admiringly. He tugged on his shirt. "Look at my flag dog!"

It had been years since Key had attended an outdoor concert, but the atmosphere felt familiar and energizing. Along a path on the west side the food trucks and bar tents were doing a brisk business; and all around her was the buzz of conversation accented by bursts of laughter. Adults stood chatting with drinks in hand and eyes on toddlers, teenagers with phones glued to their hands congregated like a flock of penguins, and children galloped every which way, miraculously (Key thought) somehow avoiding calamitous collisions. With Wain and Ell pushing, she tugged the wagon to an open spot beside the Morgans and laid down a blanket, then unfolded their chairs.

"Granny Jewel," Gayle said, leading Key three chairs down, "this is Miss Key from up the road."

Key took a second to adjust her thoughts. *This* was Ell's Granny Jewel? Not at all who she'd imagined. Not tiny. Not a white hair to be seen. No cane that Key could see. But yes, Velcro-strap shoes. *One out of four.* Key saw the walker behind the chair. *Okay, two out of four.*

Granny Jewel's tightly permed hair was dyed a stubborn light-brown and cut short above her ears, from which dangled gold stars on chains of varying lengths. Oversized tortoise-shell sunglasses covered most of her upper face, but when she smiled, Key saw the same small gap Ell had between her two front teeth. Several gold chains cascaded down her formidable chest, and only her thumbs didn't have rings. Dressed as patriotically as her granddaughter, in a red-white-and-navy block-print top and stretch pants made to look like blue jeans rolled at the hem, the woman exuded a matriarchal strength that would be a match for any man.

"I'm so pleased to finally meet you," Granny Jewel said, taking Key's extended hand, not to shake, but to grasp it tightly. "Feel like we know you already, Key! Ell's been overjoyed to have a friend right down the road."

"The feeling is mutual! It's wonderful to finally meet you too, Mrs. Morgan!"

Granny Jewel let go of Key's hand and waved as though a gnat were in front of her face. "Oh, I stopped being Mrs. Morgan two husbands back. Granny Jewel is just fine."

Gayle introduced Wain and Key to the rest of the group. Lonny, Gayle's husband, was as tall and lanky as she was, with wavy sandy-blond hair, a square handsome face, and Ell's blazing iris-blue eyes. He wore jeans and a T-shirt with a Troy Brewing beer logo.

"Lonny," he said simply, shaking Key's hand. "Y'all been doing a lot of work up there at Mr. Grimes's place. Saw it when I delivered block, talked to DP awhile. It's gonna look real nice. This here is Cavender. We call him Cav."

Finally. The famous Cav, a smaller version of his father, but with Gayle's brown eyes. Already, several young, giggly teenage girls had gathered nearby, Key noted in amusement. "Hey. Nice to meet you, Miss Key," he said, shaking her hand. To Wain he merely said, "Hey, little buddy, how's it going," then, "Hey, y'all, I'm gonna go over there with them," and melted, new phone proudly tucked in his back pocket, into the teenage crowd.

Granny Jewel watched Cav leave. "Better enjoy that little boy now," she boomed to Key, pointing at Wain, "because in a blink of an eye they are *too* cool for school."

"Nobody says that anymore, Granny Jewel!" Ell exclaimed. She held a struggling Dibsy, who was much bigger than Key thought she should be in the short time since she'd seen her.

"Big for your britches, ain't you? When did that saying end, missy? What's the new, approved lingo? Turned on and tuned out? Something in emojicon?" Granny Jewel tipped her head back and fixed Ell with an appraising stare. There was no bite in her bark.

Unfazed, Ell set Dibsy down, took two juice boxes out of a cooler, and handed one to Wain. Then she put her arm affectionately around Granny Jewel's shoulder and said to Key, "She says, like, *old-time* words. She calls the remote the clicker."

Granny Jewel snorted. "I need the clicker, to watch my stories." To Key she said, "*Bold and Beautiful* is my favorite these days. Oh, that Brooke! Do you watch?"

"Not since my college days in the student center between classes," Key replied with a laugh. She plopped down into an empty chair next to the old woman. "Easily over thirty years."

"Probably not much has changed since then," Granny Jewel observed. "I enjoy *General Hospital* too. Real thick plot going on nowadays. Intrigue and mayhem." She said the last three words with relish and caught Key up on the latest goings-on. Apparently, in the world of soap operas, nothing *had* changed.

"Cool *dungarees*, Granny Jewel." Ell reappeared for a moment and patted her leg, then scampered off to capture Dibsy with Wain in tow.

"Fiddlesticks!" Granny Jewel called after her, then slapped her hand on the arm of her chair, saying to Key, "That child will never walk if she can catapult. Cracker-brained as a baby goat but good hearted as all get-out. Wouldn't you know, as genetics would have it, she's me reincarnated. Scares me spitless." It was obvious the old woman was bursting with pride over the similarities, and that her dialogue with her older granddaughter was a well-traveled, comfortable path. No wonder Iris's prim disapproval hadn't fazed Ell.

Obviously used to the exchanges between his mother and daughter, Lonny paid no attention, simply opened a cooler and took out a beer, making small talk with Key while Gayle lifted Dibsy from Ell's arms and set her on a blanket. The baby immediately toddled off again, this time with Gayle in pursuit. As Key watched it all unfold, Wain suddenly seemed like the easiest child on earth.

Around them, empty spaces gradually filled with locals, happy to be with family and friends at this event, on this day. Granny Jewel held court like royalty with an endless stream of people who came over to greet her. It was understandable that Gayle might feel overwhelmed by her status as a newcomer and Granny Jewel's caretaker, but there was an inclusive easiness in their family's conversation; they took for granted that these were their people and their people loved them. Forgiveness, loyalty, acceptance. *It's all so … normal*, Key thought.

And in her neck of the woods, things were … well, maybe not quite normal, but very much looking up, even though Key still had the elusive passcode letters *SitG* simmering in her mind, rolling around like a rock in a river, waiting to land on the solution.

After they'd eaten dinner and visited for an hour, Key pushed up out of her chair. "Excuse us for a few minutes. Wain and I want to go say hello to DP and his family before the music starts. Anyone want to go with us?"

Ell jumped up. "Me!"

"We'll hang out here," Gayle answered. "It's a slice of heaven to just sit." Lonny had sauntered off after Dibsy and was now holding her, chatting with two men.

At the stage, Key briefly met DP's father, Dawson II, an easy-going balding man whose face told the story of many hours outdoors. "I've been real busy, but one of these days soon I'll come see what my son is doing over at your place," he said with a wide smile. "And you must be Wain. Heard a lot of good things about you, son."

"And this is my mama, Olive," DP said after Key had hugged Molly. His mother fit the quintessential picture of a Southern woman— reserved, graceful, well dressed, polite, seemingly unbothered by the heat. Key had long since come to terms with the fact that she herself would never achieve that kind of presence, but she always admired women like Olive.

"Are you gonna sing the penny song?" Ell asked DP. "The one you told me and Wain you wrote?"

"Not me, him." DP pointed at his father. "He's the songwriter. But, yes, we are gonna sing it!" He picked up a piece of paper from the edge of the stage and handed it to Wain. "Right here's our list." He pointed. "Check it out, little man. Gonna be our last song."

Ell read it over Wain's shoulder, but he simply looked down and away from the paper, saying nothing. Eyebrows raised, DP cocked his head questioningly at Key. She quickly shook her head and bent to Wain's level, pointing at the paper he held. "Wain, the penny song is called 'The Good Luck Song' and—" Startled, Key pointed to the second-to-last song. "What's this one?" she asked DP.

DP glanced down. "Oh, Daddy wrote that song in like ten minutes one day when he was *super*-ticked off at a guy. It's a fun one. Dancing music." He hunkered down by Wain and took the list from him. "Hey, buddy, I gotta get going, but I want you to listen *real* close to the words of 'The Good Luck Song,' you hear?" When Wain nodded, DP gave him a quick pat on the shoulder and walked backward toward the stage with one finger up, saying to Key, "Y'all listen close to the words."

"We sure will! DP, what is—"

"Ready son?" Dawson II called from where the band had gathered. With a wave, DP jumped onto the stage.

"Come on, let's run!" Wain and Ell tore off as Key watched in disbelief. How did they have the energy in this wilting heat? She tipped her head back and lifted the hair off her neck, welcoming the breeze that offered just a bit of respite. Miles above her, in the Carolina blue sky, cirrus clouds floated, a cottony white river adjusting its course with every tiny gust of wind. *Hey, Edie. SitG. You want to help me out, here?*

Chapter 37
THE GOOD LUCK SONG

"Hey, Key North!" Over to her right, two people in a large group waved at her.

"Jukey! Mary! Hello!" Delighted to find them in the crowd, Key wove her way through the maze of blankets, chairs, and people to where they stood, surrounded by at least ten other people, three of whom, judging by their familiar-looking handsome faces, were their grown sons. "I was hoping I'd run into you!"

"Don't worry, we don't expect you to remember all these names," Mary joked, after they'd introduced Key to everyone. "Where's Wain?"

"He and Ell ran back to where we're sitting. He'll be sorry to miss you! We're here with the Morgans."

"The famous Ell?" Jukey asked. "Our family got a big kick out of the 'ferret face' story."

"Oh! I just remembered," Mary said, after they'd chatted awhile. "My niece Serena said she'd love to meet you in Troy next week, maybe at the pool, bring Reynold to play with Wain?"

"Oh yes, we'd love that! Please give her my number! She can call me anytime." The music had started. Key stood and waved at the group. "I better get back. Enjoy the concert! It was so good to meet you all."

No wonder the band, Orion, was so popular, Key thought, as the music began. DP's father was a talented lyricist whose heartfelt songs touched his listeners where they lived. Judging by the singing around her, most of the spectators were locals who had heard the songs many times before, and in front of the stage the crowd grew: shag dancers of all ages and sizes, boho ladies in flowing flowery skirts, aging hippie rockers of both genders sporting gray ponytails, parents holding their small children, teenagers with complex moves Key appreciated but had no desire to try. Once Wain hung his backpack on his chair, Ell got him to dance, and they gyrated crazily in the grass by Key's chair, Ell's headband star lights twinkling and jouncing.

The evening flew by. "Two more songs to go," Dawson II boomed from the stage. Key sat up straight, homed in like a laser to his every word. "We all know someone like this! Ready to dance them right out of your life?" Most of the crowd had stood, cheering, raising their drinks.

"Oh yeah!" exclaimed Granny Jewel from her seat, suddenly seeming decades younger. "Let's rock!" She clapped her hands lightly and tapped her white Velcro-strap shoes and sang every word.

All along life's highway
People share their time with you.
Some come for the party,
Some bring the love that sees you through.

But some are down and dirty,
Only want to get there fast.
They'll take what's yours and leave you,
Beware! Snake in the grass.

It don't matter what your job is.
It don't matter rich or poor.
And if someone tells you different,
Kick them out your door!

Cause they are down and dirty,
Only want to get there fast.
They'll take what's yours and leave you,
Beware! Snake in the grass.

Beware the glib pretender.
Look past the pretty face.
Trust until you can't, then,
Leave them in their place.

Cause pretenders are down and dirty,
Just want to get there fast.
They'll take what's yours and leave you,
Beware! Snake in the grass.

Over the cheering crowd, Dawson II spoke again. "Our last song—"
Boos interrupted him.

"'Fishing Line!'" someone called out.

"'Universe!'"

"'Brick by Brick!'"

"'Good Luck Song!'"

Dawson II held up his hand. "Y'all know we'd play all night if we could, but this night ain't over. We got fireworks to come. This ballad is for all y'all that struggle now and then, with whatever hardship might be present in your life, young or old. Join in on the chorus, and let's sing this night to a close." He tuned his banjo a bit and turned to the band. "'Good Luck Song.' Ready guys?" Facing the crowd, he said again, "Y'all join us on the chorus."

Cheering. It was another of those moments Key would never forget. Wain had finally plopped down in the chair next to her, red faced and panting. "I'm *so* hot!"

She popped the tab and handed him a cold Biggars Root Beer from the six-pack they'd bought together that morning. "Okay, buddy, this is the last song, the one DP wants us to hear."

Wain took a long drink and nodded, sitting forward, legs dangling, his too-big patriotic-dog T-shirt covered in grass stains, mayonnaise spots, chocolate drips, and spilled juice.

I saw a penny on the ground, passed it without blinking.
Mama gave my arm a shake, "Boy, what are you thinking?
Don't you know the saying? If you don't, it's time you do.
Now pick that penny up. I've got some words to say to you.
Oh, find a penny, pick it up, and all the day you'll have good luck.
Find a penny, let it lay, and you'll have bad luck all the day."

I picked that penny up and looked at Honest Abe.
He smiled at me as if to say, Thanks, son, for the save.
It wasn't but a minute, when to my great surprise,
A dollar bill lay on the ground, right before my eyes.
I gave a shout of laughter and picked that greenback up,
And Mama said to me, "See, now? There's that penny luck."

I grew up and went to school, tried to learn my ABC's.
The teacher got impatient, and the kids made fun of me.
They called me names, like stupid head and Mama's boy and ninny.
Until the day by the school-bus stop, I found a shiny penny.
Honest Abe just looked at me and said, "Hang in there, son.
You think your life is ending but in truth, it's just begun."
So I studied hard and learned to read and write; and at the end,
Mama was so proud of her valedictorian.

Now I was a man, and it was such a troubled day.
Mama went on to heaven, and I cried there by her grave.
I knelt and placed the flowers on the dirt they'd piled high,
When something tarnished, old, and gray, caught my blurry eyes.
Abe looked at me, "Good find, young man, I understand your sorrow.
But mark my words, you'll soon find great joy in your tomorrows."
I put Abe in my pocket, and he's in there to this day.
A reminder of my mama and the words she used to say.

Well, every penny tells a story, and mine didn't end right there,
I went to Carolina to breathe the mountain air.
Hiked along the Blue Ridge, pitched my tent and played guitar,
Sat beside the campfire, gazed up at the stars.
I thought of Mama, Honest Abe, the years that had gone by,
When suddenly I heard a voice, "I'm camping next door. Hi."
A brave and feisty woman, a shining golden girl.
I knew at once I wanted her to join my lonely world.
We chatted late into the night, the hours quickly passing.
She said her name was Penny. And I heard Abe and Mama laughing.
Oh, find a penny, pick it up, all the day you'll have good luck.
Find a penny, let it lay, and you'll have bad luck all the day.

"Thanks, y'all! Thank you! Come see us at Troy Brewing in a couple weeks!" With a final wave, the band left the stage. As the sun surrendered to the night sky, the crowd's applause was deafening; and no one clapped harder, no one had better reason to cheer, than Key North.

Chapter 38
SITG

fter the fireworks, Wain fell asleep within minutes of fastening his seat belt, and it was well past eleven when they arrived back at Pike House. Faro met them at the front door, whining and wagging, then bounded back and forth ecstatically as Key first tucked Wain into bed, then unloaded the Jeep.

Until Faro's arrival, Key hadn't realized how much she'd missed the uninhibited, uncomplicated joy Pansy used to bring. *No one issues a "welcome home" like a dog waiting.* She sat on the porch steps and gave the dog a long pet. "You were a great find, pup. Let's take a walk down the drive. I forgot to get the mail out of the box yesterday."

High above her, wearing his three-star belt, constellation Orion hunted gauzy clouds filtering across an almost full moon, while the last of the fireflies, tiny slow-flashing fairy lights, floated in the shadows of the azaleas along the fence. It was as though nature had decided to one-up the fireworks and succeeded. Once they were back in the yard, Faro embarked on a long sniffing expedition. *Probably a rabbit ... maybe a possum,* Key thought. She'd let him explore for a bit. Dropping the mail on the green table, she kicked off her sandals and sank down onto the porch swing, barely swaying, humming a stanza from "The Good Luck Song." To her surprise, she felt no rush to get indoors. SplishFlash could wait until tomorrow. Closing her eyes, she let her mind fully relax for the first time in days.

Finally—after a nudge from a wet nose stopped Key from fully falling asleep on the swing—she followed Faro through the front door and padded toward her bedroom carrying the mail, which consisted of a grocery flyer and a white envelope lying upside down on top of it. Curious, Key flipped it over, then stared at it in shock, the hair standing up on her neck. It was addressed to Wain from the Ann DeLavein Correctional Facility for Women. Heart hammering, and now fully awake, Key sliced the envelope open with a kitchen knife and extracted one page with just a few handwritten lines.

DEAR BABY,

CAL WILL COME GET THE BACKPACK SO YOU DON'T HAVE TO WORRY ABOUT SENDING IT. HE WILL BE SUPER HAPPY TO SEE YOU. NOT SURE WHEN, BUT SOON! LOOK FOR HIM!!! MAMA

"No!" Key slapped her hand over her mouth; the word had come out as a disbelieving cry, much more loudly than she'd intended. Once again, their peaceful world had been violently invaded by Wain's mother's words.

She carried the paper into the office and sat down hard in her chair, still severely rattled, and took a closer look. There was no date on the letter itself, but the postmark on the envelope read two days prior. This innocuous, syrupy note certainly wouldn't have raised any red flags with the jail censors. If they even had censors. *Of course,* she mused, *Lyric knows full well that Wain can't read it and that I would never read it to him.* Which meant only one thing: the words were intended solely for her own eyes. Key pulled out her camera and the previously stashed SIM card and went through her photography routine with both the letter and the envelope, then sat back, considering her new information. Lyric had revealed far more than what her written words relayed. Another significant piece of the puzzle had fallen into place.

Well, I'll never be able to sleep now, so let's see what SplishFlash has to say. Inserting the little car's drive into a port on her laptop, Key waited confidently for the passcode request.

Was it a coincidence that when she'd read DP's song list to Wain, the second-to-last song was "Snake in the Grass"? Was it a coincidence that, on that list, the song's name had been shortened to S.I.T.G.? Was it a coincidence that, as the lyrics floated out to meet the cheering crowd and the high cirrus clouds, Key saw the reverse side of the S card with its cheery purple-and-yellow snake in tall green grass, smiling guilelessly at her? The flash-card picture itself had held the answer all along.

She typed her first try.

SnakeintheGrass@591856207842758

INCORRECT PASSWORD. TRY AGAIN.

Holding her breath, she tried again.

SNAKEintheGRASS@591856207842758

We did it, Edie. It felt *almost* anticlimactic as she opened the file.

In the main file were two folders with additional individual files inside each of those—thankfully with all other information accessible, including passwords. Key was heartsick as she clicked through it, but as horrifying as the new information was, Lyric's letter had already given her a hint as to what she'd find.

After Key copied everything onto a new flash drive, she pressed her forehead into her open palms and allowed herself a few moments to absorb the magnitude of her new knowledge. Then she wiped her eyes, straightened her shoulders, and opened her notebook to her list of bullet points. Fresh questions regarding scenarios she'd never considered were already simmering in her mind. She'd need to formulate the perfect plan. A plan to outsmart *two* snakes in the grass.

Chapter 39

BRAINSTORM

Faro leapt into the back seat with Wain, whining excitedly. He was overjoyed to be included on their Sunday drive.

"Move over a little, Faro! Whoa! Eww! He just licked my *mouth*!" Wain scooted sideways to accommodate the dog and laughed as Faro pushed against him. "He wants to be so close to me."

"Because he loves you! And I don't blame him!" Key checked the contents of her purse for the fiftieth time, wondering briefly if she had recently contracted a full-blown case of OCD, then put the Jeep in reverse. "You're already his best friend. Are you buckled up?"

"Yep. See?" Wain showed her the seat belt across his chest. "Jukey and Mary are gonna love Faro! Will he chase their cat, Clem?"

Another question Key had neglected to ask Ingrid at the shelter. "Good point. I don't know how he behaves around cats, honey. Did you bring the leash?"

He rustled in his backpack. "Yeah, it's right here. And I put his collar on like you said. You still have SplishFlash, right?"

"I do." Key glanced both ways, then pulled out onto Pike Road. "To be honest, Wain, I'm going to need it for a while."

Long heavy sigh from the back seat. "Okay."

Key changed the subject. "Mary told me they have a place where their boys used to ride bikes, behind their house. With little hills and things, like an obstacle course. You get to try that out!" She checked the rearview mirror, angling her head to see around Wain's bike tire sticking up in the back. *Get a grip, Key. No one is following you.*

Mary had not hesitated when Key called her at eight that morning. "You come right on over," she said. "We've got no plans except church, and that's done by ten thirty."

Jukey met them out in front of SouthPaws with a big smile, still dressed in his Sunday best. "My land, Key North, you must have signed up for the supersized adventure package when you moved into Mr. Grimes's place. Never a dull moment. Now who's *this*?" Jukey rubbed Faro's head.

"Faro! He's my dog. We got him from a lady at like a dog zoo kind of place." Wain buckled his bike helmet on, then shrugged into his backpack.

Key smiled. "Shelter in Porterville. Hold still a second, Wain." She pulled the leash from his backpack and connected it to Faro's collar, then with Jukey's help unloaded the bike.

"Dog zoo. Not a bad description. They do good work there. Let's go around back." Jukey led Key and Wain out of the yard, down a slope to a tree-free slice of land with grass-covered, mogul-like humps crisscrossed with worn dirt trails. "Our boys made this course years ago for their bikes. Even cut down the trees. They called it their motocross track. Might be a little overgrown, but you can still see the path there. There's a ramp of some kind further down."

"Cool!" Wain didn't wait for more instructions, just jumped on his bike and pedaled off, leaving a very unhappy Faro with Key.

"You go ahead to the patio, Key North," Jukey said. "I'll wait for Wain to do a full loop, tell me if there are any obstacles that need fixing."

On the patio, Mary had glasses of iced tea waiting. At the sight of Faro, who as it turned out showed no interest in the cat whatsoever, Clem uncurled himself and stalked indignantly out into the shrubbery. While Jukey got Wain situated and then changed his clothes, the two women chatted about the concert, and Key admired all over again the relaxed, simple beauty of the space the Kings had created. "But they didn't play 'Fishing Line,'" Mary said. "Jukey and the boys were disappointed; they love that song."

"It was one of the best evenings I've had in years," Key replied. "I hope they play another venue like that. They are the perfect outdoor band."

"He's all set up, and I'm back in normal duds." Jukey poured himself a glass of tea and sank into a chair, extending his long legs onto an ottoman. "Takes me back to the fun our boys had on that track. And their stamina!" He shook his head. "Even being around that kind of energy wears me out. I promised Wain we'd say hello to Petey before you leave."

"In case Wain doesn't want to ride too long in this heat, I've got another video for him to watch," Mary told Key. "From what you said in your call, I assume you don't want him to hear this conversation."

"No, he has no idea we're here for anything but to ride his bike and show you his new dog. Speaking of, sit, Faro." Key tugged on the leash. Faro whined but flopped down obediently by her chair.

Jukey laughed. "Typical teenager. He's not happy being stuck with the old folks. So, Key North, I understand a whole peculiar new chapter is being written in your book. What's the latest?"

Key leaned her head back on the chair cushion and blew out a long breath, staring at the ceiling fan rotating above her. "Where to begin? I'm so glad we got to talk last Friday because I can pick up the story from there." She pulled the manila envelope out of her purse and held it up. "I don't want Wain to see what I've got in here."

"I've got eyes on him from where I'm sitting," Jukey said, pointing two fingers to his own eyes and then out toward the track. "Just riding the course, typical kid who doesn't feel the heat. Looks like he's having the time of his life. I'll let you know if he heads this way."

Key spilled the envelope's contents onto the coffee table and picked up SplishFlash. "Thanks to Wain and a girl named Evie at a hobby store in Porterville, I now know that this CartWheels car of Wain's is actually a flash drive." She pushed the goggle headlight and popped out the drive.

Mary said, "Ohh!" in understanding, but Jukey didn't react.

"It's a memory stick, Jukey," Key explained, holding it up. Still no answer. She tried again. "You plug this silver part into a port on your computer, and you can save files on it. And, come to find out, this CartWheels car, called SplishFlash, has files on it. Wain's been carrying it around all this time."

Jukey's eyes grew big. "That right!" he exclaimed. "How'd you find that out?"

Key gave the Kings a full rundown, starting with Lyric's phone call that rainy day outside SouthPaws and ending with a description of the devastating information she'd discovered the previous evening. After she finished, the ensuing silence seemed to amplify her words, making them harder to absorb. The ceiling fan emitted a tiny rhythmic squeak. A nearby mockingbird sang its entire repertoire.

Mary put her hand to her cheek. "Oh! That poor little boy. His grandma Edie is for sure an angel watching over him. So much to get through my head. It's terrible. And it makes me so very angry."

"Crazy as an afternoon dream," Jukey put in, examining Lyric's letter once more. He removed his eyeglasses and lifted his chin, slowly scratching his neck.

Key returned the items to the manila envelope. "Yes. Crazy and terrible. I've had to fight to keep rational, but for my plan to work, I have to."

"Your plan?" Jukey asked.

"Are you going to call the police?" Mary asked at the same time.

Key hesitated, then shook her head. "I hope you don't think I'm crazy, but I have my reasons not to call the police, most of all because of the trauma it would cause Wain. He would have to be involved, and I worry what that would do to him; he's lost so much already. I'm after a couple of snakes in the grass, and I think I can catch them. There is one thing I need one snake to tell me, and if I'm wrong, if that snake doesn't say exactly what I expect, I promise I'll call the police."

She pulled her notebook from her purse and took a few more minutes to explain.

Jukey considered her words, absently stroking Clem, who had jumped onto his lap after making a wide circle around Faro. "And you don't think there's a risk?"

"I honestly don't think so," Key answered. "I wouldn't consider going this route if I thought there was. Everything changed once I read Lyric's letter and saw the files. But I have a few more questions for you before I decide for sure."

"Key, it's like a crazy, crooked maze, and you're still in the middle!" Mary exclaimed. She rose and refilled their glasses, ice cubes splashing from the pitcher. "From what you've said, there definitely must be more to the story. Of *course* we'll do what we can to help you find the answer."

"Mary *loves* a good mystery," Jukey said, winking at his wife. "Hours of true-crime podcasts while baking pies. She sees the shape of a body in every bag of garbage by the road. All I can do to get her to keep driving."

It was a relief to join their laughter. Key held up the envelope. "Jukey, would you be willing to keep this in your safe? I've got copies at home, but I'd like the originals in a place nobody would think to look."

Jukey set Clem gently onto the ottoman and stood up. "Absolutely, Key North. Let's do it right now."

When they returned, Wain was on the patio, gulping thirstily from a bottle of water. He stopped when he saw Key. "That is *so* fun!" he said, then tipped the bottle again.

"It's like the old days, having a little boy around again." Mary slid the door open, and Clem dashed between her legs into the house. "Wain, how about you and Faro come inside where it's cool. I've got a video and cookies, even dog treats, left over from sweet old Badger." She shook her finger at Key and Jukey before she closed the door. "Don't you two *dare* say a word till I get back!"

Once Mary returned, Key stated, "Jukey, you once told me you spent time hunting in the woods behind my house. Would it be possible for someone to park a car on the far side of the railroad tracks and hike through the trees to the house without the car being seen?"

"No. Impossible," Jukey replied immediately. "They'd have to park in plain sight, then hoof it a quarter mile across open pastures to the berm where the railroad tracks are. Anything out of the ordinary sticks out like a sore thumb. A car parked alongside the road would raise eyebrows, no question."

Key nodded. "Good. That's what I thought. I'm trying to figure out any way that Callahan might try to access my house, try to take Wain's backpack without me knowing."

"Well, it definitely wouldn't be a stealth move from that direction." Jukey clinked the ice in his cup, pondering. "Your house is remote, but it's on that little hill, in plain sight. There's only one way to get to it, and that's directly south from Troy, on Pike Road. I'd say you'll need to be on the lookout for slow drivers, someone looking for your house number. And obviously since it's a dead end, they'll have to turn around and come back."

"But Key can't stand staring out the window for the foreseeable future looking for slow-moving traffic," Mary teased.

"True!" Key said, laughing. "On the bright side, I'd most likely recognize the car. Mayetta gave me descriptions of their vehicles."

"Doubt he'd drive them," Jukey replied. "If he's jumping bail, he'd probably borrow a car. Maybe rent."

"True," Key said again. "Florida plates, though, right?"

"On a rental? Not necessarily. But I don't think you have to worry about that. Let's brainstorm, Key North." He leaned forward, gesturing toward her notebook. "You've built the bones of a real solid plan. It just needs fleshing out."

Chapter 40

BAIT

Key and Wain. Mid-July

Key dried her hands on a tea towel and swiped to answer her ringing phone, then listened to the message and pressed three. "Hello, Lyric. Thanks for returning my call."

"What do you want?" Lyric's voice was as sour as usual.

Okay, there were to be no social niceties. "I got your letter," Key replied. To quell her nervousness, she took the flyswatter off the nail in the broom closet and crept slowly toward the window, stalking a bluebottle fly trying furiously to escape. Calliphora vomitoria, *you are buzzing your last.* (It was such a random thing to remember from a tenth-grade biology class, but one of Key's friends had nicknamed their school cafeteria after the fly's Latin name, and it seemed oddly appropriate to her current conversation.)

"You mean *Wain* got my letter," Lyric snapped. "So?"

How could she possibly have thought this woman was attractive? Key kept her voice friendly. "Has Mr. Callahan left to come up here yet?"

She glanced out the window as the fly escaped to live another minute. Down at the second oak, the tire swing shot out from behind the tree's broad trunk, then disappeared, forward and back, Wain and Ell tipping crazily, shouting and laughing. Faro, panting heavily from whatever foray he'd completed, lay in the coolness of a patch of dirt, ears alert, his tongue pink against the dark fur. She had a view of heaven while talking to hell.

"Not yet," Lyric answered brusquely. "Cal has to get some things worked out."

Key thought for a moment. The less she said, the less she'd give away, but it was time to ramp it up a notch. She gave a coy little laugh. "I'm going to be honest, Lyric, I looked all through Wain's backpack because I thought maybe something secret was in it!" When Lyric didn't answer, Key continued, "It's beyond me why you'd want to bother with a backpack and some toy cars. Why would you take it away from the little boy who loves it so much and is never without it?"

"You can buy him new cars then. Because you know what? It's none of your *freaking* business! It belongs to Cal! Was there paperwork in there?" Key thought she detected a note of relief in Lyric's rude reply. *She thinks SplishFlash's secrets are still intact.*

"Paperwork?" Key settled onto a chair, every bit Wain's clueless aged relative.

"Yes! Paperwork! Cal has some very important issues to take care of, and it was all on that paperwork."

"Hold on. Let me check the boxes we brought back."

Key heard an exasperated "Ugh!" from the other end. She put her feet up on another chair, played two moves on Words with Friends, and took a satisfying drink of iced tea, then went back to the call and said in a triumphant tone, "I found it. It was in a box with some of Wain's things. Oh dear, foreclosure papers."

"Good," Lyric said, this time absolutely sounding relieved. "Is there anything else with the papers?"

"Well, I don't know. The papers are folded and stuck together with tape. Should I open them? I'd need to find some scissors."

"No! Leave it exactly like that. That's what Cal needs."

"Well, if that's all he needs, why take the backpack?" Key was enjoying every minute. Old people could get away with anything.

"It's *none* of your business, is it?" Lyric said again, furiously. "Just have it ready for Cal!"

"Okay, fine. So should I call Mr. Callahan to arrange getting these things to him, or——?" Key asked.

"You'll actually give them to us?" Lyric asked in disbelief.

"Well, that's what you've been asking for, isn't it? Why do you think I called you, Lyric? There is just one condition, and this is from Wain's father. Naturally, I called Guy after I got your letter, and he gave me instructions." In truth, she hadn't had any contact with Guy since his phone call from the airport, but he had alluded to what she planned to say next.

She heard another "Ugh!" then, "Typical Guy. Always out of the picture. What does *he* want?"

She pulled her notebook toward her. "Let me see, ah, here's his note. Guy says he's aware that you and Cal were abusive to Wain. He wants full custody of Wain from now on. You are not to fight that or even try to see Wain before he turns eighteen, not when you get out, not down the road. Guy will see to all the legalities."

Key stood to check on the children. Wain and Ell were off the tire swing now, chatting animatedly to Miguel and Benito, who had come to work despite the Monday holiday and were now having lunch under the awning. The men didn't look like they needed rescuing quite yet. The fly attacked the window again.

"Guy said that? What a five-star *hypocrite*." Lyric's voice was filled with disdain. "Yeah, I admit maybe Cal and I didn't want Wain there 24-7, but we weren't *abusive*. He exaggerates all the time. He got disciplined, nothing worse."

Key could feel the heat rising in her cheeks. *Spare me the lies.* It was getting difficult to continue the pleasant-grandma act. "Please, I don't want to get in the middle of it. It's what Wain's father has stipulated. Callahan is to bring your handwritten, notarized statement, and I am to give him the backpack and the papers." She grabbed the flyswatter again and waited; Lyric was obviously weighing her options.

"What*ever*. Fine. I'll get it done," Lyric snapped. "But Cal's not supposed to leave Florida. It would be better to meet him somewhere in between, like Savannah." There was a rustling noise. "Yeah, yeah, hold *on* a second," Key heard her say irritably to someone. "I'm almost finished."

Yes! Silently thanking the impatient inmate next in line for the phone, Key said, "It sounds like you need to hang up. But one last thing, Lyric, I'm not comfortable driving long distances at my age, so Mr. Callahan must come all the way here, to my house. Please give him my address and phone number." She added an anxious note to her voice. "But how will I separate Wain from his backpack? What am I going to tell him?"

"Oh my gosh, tell him freaking *anything*. Tell him it's lost. Tell him it got *stolen*." There was a click, and Lyric was gone.

With an effortlessly quiet swish, Key swatted the clueless bluebottle, picked it up with a paper towel, and threw it away. She scrubbed the window clean. *Goodbye, Miss Calliphora Vomitoria.*

Chapter 41
WEEDING

Key and Wain. Mid-July

"Hey, DP!" It was before eight in the morning, and Key was sweating despite the cooling bandanna she'd pulled out of the refrigerator earlier. *If nothing else,* she'd thought as she tied the knot, *it is very dapper, even if the rest of me is a grubby, perspiring mess.*

DP shut his truck door and waved. "Hey, Miss Key! You're out early!"

She crossed the yard to the fence, Faro at her heels. "You too! I'm trying to beat both the heat and the weeds! Would you like some coffee?" She pulled off her gloves and used them to brush the grass and dirt from her knees.

"No, thanks, got a big cup in the truck." DP reached over the fence and rubbed Faro's head. "Hey, pup."

Key pushed several escaped hairs back from her eyes and redid her ponytail. Next time she'd tie the bandanna around her head. "DP, we loved the music the other night! Your father is a very talented songwriter."

"He sure is. It's his passion. Did you catch the words of 'The Good Luck Song'? Daddy's always struggled to read."

Key nodded. "I did! It makes his songwriting even more inspiring. Does he read now?"

"He does, yes, but his dyslexia still shows up, especially when he's tired. He used some creative license in the song. Daddy wasn't anywhere close to class valedictorian, but he's made a very successful life despite that. Am I right in thinking Wain might have problems reading?"

"Yes, but in his case I'm almost 100 percent sure his issues are associated with trauma. I haven't actually discussed his inability to read with him; I'm approaching it in a bit of a sideways fashion at the moment. I do have a lot of hope that he's overcoming his fear."

DP raised his eyebrows. "Wow, trauma, huh? Makes more sense now … it kinda knocked me sideways when I handed him the song list to read. From his face, you'd think I'd just belted him. Felt for him. I hope he's doing okay?" He looked around. "Where is the little guy?"

"Still asleep." Key waved a glove. "And he seems to be fine! He bounced right back. In fact, he and Ell danced like dervishes under a full moon."

DP laughed. "I'm glad to hear it. I'll let my daddy know how much it meant to you." He started to leave, then turned back. "Oh, one more thing: we should be done with everything out back before the end of July. Daddy's got a three-week job for us, then we can start inside your house. I hate to say this, but I've discovered some repair issues that may mean you'll have to move out for a while."

Dismayed, Key stared at him. "Really? What issues?"

"I don't wanna say for positive until we get under there, but for one the whole place needs rewiring, and I suspect all the pipes need replacing. Just some observations we've made digging around out there. All for the good, believe me. This house is as sturdy as they come, very structurally sound, but wires wear out, and old pipes rust. We can cross that bridge when we come to it, but I thought you might like a heads-up."

Why was she surprised? The plumber who'd fixed her leaky kitchen faucet had told her that very thing not long after she'd moved in. "Okay, DP. Thanks. Oh! One *more* thing." They laughed. "We don't have to discuss this now either, but as long as we're making a mess, let's make it huge. I'd really like a garage and a breezeway to the house, like the addition to Jukey and Mary's store. Would you be able to fit that into your time frame?"

He tipped his finger. "Funny you should say that! Got ideas about it already. I've always thought a garage made sense right there." He pointed to the area between the house and the shed. "I'll sketch something out later."

"Exactly where I thought it should be! Thanks, DP." She would deal with a possible move another day. She had a list of tasks that needed her full attention; weeding in the relative coolness was number one.

When she looked up again, Wain was sitting on the porch swing with his backpack and a juice box. "Hey, buddy!" Key called. Wain waved back, pushing with one foot to make the swing go. Sitting there so casually, with a drink he'd gotten all on his own, it was like he'd lived there forever. It warmed her to the core. "I'm going to be weeding for a while longer. You can make yourself a bowl of cereal if you're hungry, bring it out onto the porch if you want. Also, Faro's water dish is almost empty, so please fill it and give him breakfast."

"Okay! Come on, boy!" The screen door slapped shut as Wain and Faro went inside.

Smiling a little sadly, Key shook her head. Given what she now knew about Lyric and Callahan, even the simplest conversations she had with Wain took on new meaning. It seemed impossible that Edie's beautiful, good-hearted grandson had ever been a part of that dark world. *What does living with that kind of ugliness do to a child?* Key yanked at an especially recalcitrant weed, and the leaves snapped off, leaving the root underground. *Oh, no, you don't.* Grabbing her garden trowel, she dug and chopped until every inch of root was destroyed. Okay. Maybe she was a little bit perturbed.

After a shower, Key felt much better. She had Wain help her fold towels and tidy up the living room, then they played a game of Memory, which was another activity she'd found he loved. He made eighteen matches to her ten, then joyfully helped her put the game back in the box. "Maybe next time *you'll* get to win," he told her soliticously.

She laughed. "Maybe. But I doubt it. You're *way* too sharp. I need to make a phone call, then we'll make a lunch and go to the woods where it's shady and cool."

"Yay! A picnic? Can Faro come? Are we taking pictures?"

"Now what do you think I'm going to say to that?" She gave him a quick hug. "Of course, to all the above. Go let Faro out, then maybe you'd like to play on the tablet?" She needed a few minutes alone.

★ ★ ★

"Citrine Oil, how may I help you?" a sweet young Texas drawl answered the number Key dialed.

"Hi! I'm looking for someone in your legal department. I can't remember her name exactly, but I think it's something like Mira."

Chapter 42

TRACKS

ith Faro bounding ahead and circling back, Key and Wain set off on their well-traversed path, but this time they turned right after five minutes; and just as Jukey had described, they found themselves almost immediately on a narrow, semiovergrown trail. Though her conversation with Lyric had changed Key's uneasiness from "spooked" to "highly alert" and though she now fully expected Callahan to come directly to her door, she wanted to verify for herself that (should Callahan decide to take the sneaky route) any nefarious vehicle parked on the other side of the railroad tracks would be exposed. She laughed wryly. Never in a million years would she have seen herself in a position to use the word "nefarious" associated with her own life.

Key had promised Wain that they'd have their picnic at the creek where they'd made the dam, so eventually they'd return to the main trail. For now, though, they were on the hunt: he for his letter *E* and she for peace of mind.

Wain hadn't recognized the correctly oriented *E* she drew on the ground at the start of their hike; or if he did, he hadn't said anything. "If you forget, I can draw it again," she told him. He'd stared at it, nodded, then took off after Faro.

They were near the west edge of the woods when Wain stopped short. "Whoa. What's that?" He pointed to a rise ahead of them, beyond which there were no trees.

"Railroad tracks! Jukey told me they aren't used anymore, so we can chug up there and check out what's on the other side."

"Cool! Come on, Faro!" Wain raced easily up the incline, turning around to wave when they got to the top. *He doesn't chug*, Key thought, grinning.

Once she'd scaled the berm, she stood on a railroad tie, shading her eyes as she took in the view. It really wasn't much of a rise, but for the first time, she was on elevation high enough to see what lay past the woods. Except for clumps of two or three trees dotted here and there, the land was wide open: fenced pastures and cotton fields filled the entire space between the tracks and a country road. Three older farmhouses with outbuildings and barns, surrounded by more fields, lined the other side of the road. She breathed a sigh of relief and nodded. It was exactly as Jukey had described. No car could park anywhere without attracting attention.

Maybe at some point it wouldn't be as unpopulated. To the northwest, in a large open space she calculated was a few miles south of Troy, giant construction equipment raised dust zephyrs, the distant grumble of their motors drifting across the silent summer landscape. Under the baby-blue sky, all was serene, the aroma of honeysuckle and wisteria mingling incongruously with the faint but acrid smell of warm creosote wafting from the aged railroad ties. It took her right back to her childhood in Illinois, when she and her friends had laid pennies on the tracks for the passing trains to flatten. But there it had been cornfields, not cotton.

Holding his arms straight out, Wain staggered along one track, using it as a balance beam, then he jumped off and began hopping, tie to tie, on one foot, then the other. Key snapped pictures, smiling at more memories. She'd done the same at his age. Finally, she said, "Ready to go, buddy?" They were in no danger from a train, but she wasn't sure they weren't trespassing; and besides, the sun was urging her back into the shade.

"Just about, but I need the camera." Jerkily, Wain made his way to her along the narrow track and jumped off.

"Really?" Key handed it to him. "Here you go."

Wain put the strap around his neck. On their last hike, in his excitement at finding and photographing N, he'd tripped on a root and dropped the camera; Key could still see his fear as he hurriedly picked it up and said, "Sorry! I'm sorry! I'm really sorry!"

It was such a tiny thing, but only to her. Though she had never so much as raised her voice to Wain, Key knew he still stepped carefully through his day, trying hard to avoid saying or doing anything he feared might trip the wire, trigger her anger. It was all about her own consistency. If he didn't believe she'd allow him to make mistakes, he would never fully trust her. "No harm done," she'd told him. "It was an accident. We'll just make sure it's secure from now on."

Standing on a railroad tie a little to the left of center, Wain raised the camera to a slight angle and studied the screen, made a couple small adjustments in his position, then snapped a photo. He pressed the button to review his shot, then without comment shrugged out of the strap and handed the camera carefully but nonchalantly back to Key, saying, "E." He waited expectantly, arms crossed, while she examined the feedback.

She let out a little gasp. "Wain! This is amazing!" A railroad-track E, with the rail for the spine and ties for the three horizontal lines. She would forever associate the smell of creosote with the letter E. "How did you see that? I didn't! You're awesome!"

"I saw it, just now where I was standing, so I took the picture. Come on, Faro!" They raced full tilt down the grassy slope. Was there a little Guy-like swagger in that run? Smiling, Key heard Granny Jewel say, "Too cool for school."

Back at the main trail, they had a drink, sharing their water with Faro, who had inherited a portable canvas bowl of Pansy's that Wain proudly carried hooked to the outside of his backpack. "He can drink the creek water too," Key told Wain. "We'll be there soon."

Along the way, Key drew more letters while Wain carried the camera and eagerly hunted. In the dirt, crisscrossing roots formed A.

Two horizontal branches extending like arms from a forlorn dead tree shaped a perfect *F.*

At the creek, they sat on their favorite log and ate the lunch Key had packed. Between bites, Wain and Faro played in the water while Key snapped more pictures. *Guy will love these,* she thought. He'd texted that morning, telling her he was settling in, still slightly jet lagged but traveling again the next day, and to please give Wain a hug from him. It was impossible to keep up with Guy's schedule; talking with him would have to wait.

"Would you like to keep going?" she asked Wain. "We've got a little more time." She shoved a stubbornly hovering vision of her obese to-do file to the back of her mind along with its latest addition: a note she'd scribbled on the blank side of a piece of junk mail, "Find rental???"

"I want to see what that white-and-black thing is up there." Wain pointed through the trees to a white square about fifty yards ahead.

"Looks like a sign of some kind," Key told him. "Let's check it out."

While Key packed up the lunch leftovers, Wain wrestled socks and shoes onto his wet feet, then raced Faro to a statuesque pine parked squarely where the path forked. Nailed to it about six feet up was a rectangular sign, white paint peeling, with a black circle in the center.

"It's two *R*'s in a *X* in a *O*," Wain said when Key caught up, "with a arrow pointing that way."

"Do you know what that means?" Key asked.

"Umm, not for sure." Chewing on his thumbnail, he tilted his head, gazing at the sign, frowning slightly.

From where they stood, they couldn't see anything but path and trees. "If you followed the direction the arrow is pointing, what might you find?" Key asked helpfully. "Remember what's over there?"

"The railroad tracks?"

"You win the explorer award!" She ruffled his hair. "R R means railroad tracks. Someone made that sign out of wood, quite a long time ago." With a wide smile, she handed him the camera. "Great job, Mr. Reader! Better take a picture of your two *R*'s in an *X* in an *O*."

Chapter 43

SETUP

Key and Wain. Mid-July

Four days had passed since their hike to the railroad tracks, four long days where as far as Key could tell, no strange cars had driven by, at least not slowly. No strangers lurked in the woods, no nefarious (oh, she loved that word) persons knocked on her door. Lyric had not called to say whether Callahan had left, which meant that every minute was heavy with anticipation and dread. The longer it went, the less Key had hope that he'd bring the letter at all.

To calm her jitters, Key had determinedly focused on the everyday, reducing her to-do file by eleven tasks, enjoying a long-overdue hair appointment while Wain played at Ell's one morning, mowing the lawn, and searching online for possible rentals. She and Wain had gone on another hike where he'd easily found *K* in tree branches and *S* on a twisty vine, but they'd hunted quite a bit longer to finally discover *Z* at their feet. Thank goodness for tree roots.

She'd taken Wain, Ell, and Faro for ice cream and to Troy Municipal Park; and yesterday she and Wain had met Mary's niece, Serena, and her eight-year-old son, Reynold, at the public pool in Troy. It was the first time Key had taken Wain swimming; she wasn't sure what memories it might evoke, but she was relieved when he excitedly jumped right in. He and Reynold hit it off immediately, and Serena was funny and easy to talk to. Wain was a competent swimmer (she would give Lyric that), but when he was in the water, Key reverted instantly to her teenage lifeguard days, never taking her eyes off her subjects. All in all, it had been a much-needed change of scenery, one that she couldn't help but compare with a grin to the lazy summer days she had spent lounging beside their backyard pool at Sage Pointe.

Key had just started heating water for a pot of coffee and settled with her laptop at the table, anticipating a few uninterrupted minutes of perusing deck decor ideas, when her phone rang. For the past few days, every "unknown number" call she'd answered (and she'd answered them all) had been spam, a scam, or a bot, so when she answered this time with an impatient "hello," she was stunned to finally hear the words she'd almost stopped expecting.

"This is Gary Callahan. Looks like, uh, I should be there in about an hour." His voice, less menacing than she'd expected, sounded on edge. Finally, the man had emerged from the shadows. It felt surreal.

"Do you have directions for how to get here?" Key asked, surprised at how normal her own voice sounded. "It's very rural, four miles outside of Troy."

"I'll find it."

She glanced at the kitchen clock. "Okay, Mr. Callahan, I'll see you at about six thirty." *Get it together, Key, because here we go.* Her hand shook as she ended the call and tapped a text. He's on his way. Don't forget the envelope!

Her phone pinged thirty seconds later. Jukey must have been standing by the safe. Already got it. Be there in 15. Locking up.

"Wain?" Key checked his bedroom, then the sofa, then the porch, where she found him lying comfortably on the swing, his head on a fat pillow, backpack on his extended legs, the tablet perched on top of that. Below him, Faro sprawled on the rug, dozing. Much to Wain's disappointment, Faro refused to sit on the swing.

"Hey, buddy," Key said, taking a seat on the edge of the wicker chair. Wain swiped at something, then looked at her questioningly. She smiled. At that moment, in that look, she could see teenager Wain waiting in the wings. "Listen, Jukey and Mary are on their way here, and Mary is going to take you home with her. Something has come up that I need to take care of, and Jukey is going to help me. We need a little time to figure it out."

He didn't request details, simply closed the tablet and sat up straight, causing Faro to jump up too. "Can I take Faro and my bike?"

"Faro is going, and you can ask Mary about the bike; there's enough light left to ride for a bit. Here's the thing, though. I need your backpack for the time you're with Mary. Would you be willing to leave it here?"

Wain hesitated, trying not to look anxious, then asked hopefully, "Are you going to put a new car in it?"

"Not today." She hadn't thought about that, but she wished she had. Naturally he'd be worried; the last time he'd been asked to leave his backpack behind, it had disappeared, and his life had been blown to smithereens. She scooted the wicker chair closer to the swing, putting her hand on his leg. "Wain, you can trust me. It will be here when you get home. So will I! Everything will be just the same."

He heaved a sigh. "Okay."

Key gave him a quick hug, closing her eyes in relief. "Honey, I know what it took for you to say that. Just leave it on the living-room couch." As he and Faro went indoors, she pulled a folded piece of paper out of her pocket and once again reviewed the bullet points and questions she'd written earlier.

Mary arrived in her white SUV, did a three-point turn, and parked facing out toward Pike Road. Jukey emerged from the passenger seat carrying Key's manila envelope and a long slim leather bag, which he immediately laid down out of sight under some shrubbery.

She knew Callahan was at least half an hour away, but Key couldn't load Wain and Faro (and the bike) fast enough. As Mary turned onto Pike Road, Key waved, then raised her eyebrows and regarded Jukey apprehensively. "Are we ready for this?"

He handed Key the envelope and retrieved his bag. "Haven't had this much fun since Jonah and I scared off two scrawny shirtless losers trying to abscond with a coil of copper wire when we were building our place. They had no idea we were sitting right there in the store, following their every sneaky, cowardly move. I'll never forget their faces when we charged out, yelling at them, waving our flashlights and shotguns." Jukey smiled at the memory. "I doubt we scared them straight, but we scared them *good*." He hoisted the bag to his shoulder. "Yes, sir, that was an enjoyable evening."

She felt better already. "And you could also say you scared them shirtless," she said, deadpan. They shared a hearty laugh. "Did you call the police?"

"Nope," Jukey replied happily. "All we wanted to do was chase them off, and we accomplished that. No one has ever tried to rob us again."

"Well, I couldn't ask for a better partner in noncrime." Key led him inside, which seemed eerily quiet without the noise and motion that had already become such a part of Pike House. It wasn't long before they heard tires on the gravel.

Callahan *had* driven the blue BMW. Through the living-room window, Key watched as he executed a three-point turn exactly as Mary had done half an hour earlier. There was no one in the passenger seat. *Ready for a clean getaway*, she thought. She moved toward the front door.

"Is 'clean getaway' still something they say?" Key asked Jukey, nervously patting her sweaty palms on her capris.

He laughed. "You're asking me? Chasing off copper thieves is my limit. I'm not up on the latest police lingo." He settled himself comfortably into the corner of Key's blue sectional. "Do they still say 'lingo'?"

Before the man on her porch could knock, Key opened the door. "Hello, Mr. Callahan." She *almost* felt sorry for him. This was going to be … well, not fun, exactly. More like satisfying. The satisfaction of words that needed to be said and a mystery finally untangled.

Chapter 44
SHAPE SHIFTER

She'd surprised him. Startled, Callahan stepped back, his right hand still raised to knock. A dark-brown leather messenger bag hung from his shoulder, and he carried a large white envelope in his left hand.

"Key North?" he asked.

She put him at about forty, six feet tall, not as bulky as she'd envisioned. Expensively cut, thinning dark-blond hair parted on the side, the same sunglasses Key had seen in his picture with Lyric, light-blue polo shirt untucked, khaki shorts, manicured feet in broad-strapped leather flip-flops. She held the door open. "Yes. Please, come in."

He shook his head and held up the envelope. "No need. We can do this right here. I've got Lyric's letter. Notarized as you requested. Do you have the backpack?"

"It's in the house. Please come in, Mr. Callahan." She moved farther aside to allow him to enter.

"I prefer to wait out here."

"Fine. Hold on." Key shut the door and leaned around the doorway into the living room, gesturing a *"come on"* motion to Jukey. "Your turn," she said quietly.

"I was hoping I'd get at least a supporting-actor role." He strode to the front door, opening it quickly, raising his shotgun. "Come on in, son."

"What the hell!" Key heard Callahan exclaim, then a loud commotion and the sound of someone scrambling backward, trying to keep his balance. "I *knew* this was too easy!"

Jukey's voice was level. "Get *in* here. Settle down, we aren't gonna hurt you. Just need to talk." Key wouldn't have been surprised to see him dragging Callahan through the door by the shirt collar, but he simply held the gun at torso level as he followed their angry visitor into the living room.

"Are you *kidding* me?" Callahan strode in, his hands raised halfway to his shoulders, still holding the envelope.

"Sit." Jukey gestured with the shotgun. "Right there in that white chair."

"Whatever, Wyatt Earp. This is *unbelievable*." Gripping the strap of the messenger bag still hanging from his shoulder, Callahan sank hard into the recliner, his mouth a thin enraged line in a face gone pale under his tan. Jukey casually returned to his seat on the sectional and laid the shotgun across his knees, placing his hands on top of it and fixing the man across from him with a relaxed, unreadable stare. Callahan pointedly ignored him, glaring instead through his sunglasses at Key, who perched on the edge of the other end of the couch. She forced herself to sit back, laced her hands together to hide the shakiness, and put them around her knee.

"Are you people *insane*?" Callahan burst out, waving a hand toward Jukey's gun. "Do you think for one second that I didn't tell *three* people, one of whom is a *cop*, exactly where I was going?"

To Key, he didn't appear particularly nervous, just furious. Maybe his privileged upbringing made him feel invincible.

"All right," Key said, once Callahan had lapsed into silence. "Introductions first. This is Jukey, a friend of mine who's here to keep things civil. And as you know, I'm Key North, Wain's cousin and guardian. Would you like a drink?"

Callahan snorted. "No. Let's get this over with. I have no idea what your deal is, but Lyric and I have 100 percent done as you asked. Look for yourself."

As Key stood to take the envelope, she noted the ostentatious emerald-and-gold ring on his right hand. Lifting the flap, she pulled out a single sheet of paper, feeling the bumps of the notary stamp. She read the handwritten letter, then slid it back into the envelope. "Yes. That's what I asked for. And now, Mr. Callahan, I want to have a conversation. Then you can be on your way."

Jukey shifted slightly, indicating with his chin. "Put the bag flat on the floor, son. Take off your sunglasses. The sun's doing its shining outside, and I think Key North should be able to see your eyes. Much better," he added as Callahan grudgingly complied.

With his sunglasses off, Callahan's steely-blue eyes shone almost hypnotically from his tanned even-featured face. A nasty onetime neighbor of Key's had owned a beautiful but vicious dog with electric-blue eyes exactly like the ones she was facing now. *Beware of dog. Proceed with caution*, she reminded herself, because although she couldn't stand the man, Key had to admit that she could see why Lyric had fallen for him. Those eyes would be the first feature anyone would notice, and the reason for some women's last use of common sense. Derek Garth Calhoun's startling good looks had no doubt contributed to his ability to con his way through life.

Key cleared her throat and reached behind a throw pillow, pulling out Wain's backpack. Just holding it gave her resolve and clarity. "Mr. Callahan, I didn't want Wain to see you, naturally, but I know if his CartWheels backpack could talk, it would have endless horrendous stories to tell." Key saw a wariness flit across Callahan's face. Lyric had to have told him that Key knew *something*, but he didn't know how much.

She continued, "You forced him to live in fear, you ... you *reveled* in making him feel completely worthless, locked him in a closet, called him 'retard' and 'baggage' and I'm sure much worse. You starved him of nice things, food, happy childhood memories, but most of all, you starved him of love. His mother's love?" She purposely made her last three words a question.

It was difficult to stop speaking, to allow what she'd said to hang suspended while her oversized wall clock methodically ticked off seconds of oppressive silence. Jukey kept his hands resting on the shotgun and his eyes on Callahan. Key held the backpack in her lap, legs crossed, and waited.

Callahan wiped his hand down over his mouth with his fist. "His mother's love," he finally replied, sarcastically, rolling his eyes and nodding in an exaggerated way. "Riiiight. You've obviously got it *all* figured out. Yep. I starved him of his mother's love."

Key raised her eyebrows. "Are you saying you *didn't* abuse Wain? You may as well be honest because I already know what you did. Mrs. Titus and Wain have both shared stories with me."

Callahan shrugged, then blew out a long breath, scratching his neck and shifting uncomfortably in the recliner, glancing now and again at Jukey's gun. He seemed far more off-balance than he'd been just moments before. "Well, uh, there's a lot I don't remember. It's ... complicated. I'm, ah ... an angry drunk."

Give me a break. Key fixed her eyes on Callahan. "Oh, okay. So you're saying alcohol is to blame. Maybe you believe that lie, but it's no excuse—not to me, not to Jukey here, not to Mrs. Titus—and *especially* not to the little boy who lived in fear of you every single minute of every single day he was in your home. The simple fact is, it doesn't matter whether you were drunk or sober. Your actions toward Wain were the actions of a monster. And he's paying the price." She set the backpack where Callahan couldn't help but see it and stood up. She'd let him stew for a minute. "We're going to be here awhile. Does anyone want coffee?"

Jukey nodded. "Love some, Key North, with a little cream if you don't mind."

"None for me," Callahan said shortly. He watched as Key fetched two cups and gave one to Jukey. She could tell the man's mind was racing, trying to figure out just why they had him sitting there.

Key sat down again and unfolded the paper with her notes. "I have questions that need answers, Mr. Callahan. Why don't we start with the morning of Wain's birthday? Tell me about that day."

Callahan seemed taken aback. "What's to tell? Lyric and I got arrested."

"For what?" Key asked.

"Embezzlement, mostly." Callahan jiggled one foot as he talked. "A few other things. Identity theft. Misuse of company funds."

Finally, she could ask him the question she'd asked herself a hundred times since SplishFlash spilled its secrets. "But why Wain's birthday?" she persisted. "Why were you arrested *that* day?"

"Uh, you're aware you don't get to choose when you're arrested, right?" Callahan's tone had become more cautious, as though he was analyzing her words.

She shrugged. "I believe there's more to that story, but okay, we'll come back to it." Key had lost most of her nervousness; in any case, she refused to give this man the satisfaction of eliciting even one hint of uncontrolled emotion from her. "Instead, let's discuss the flash cards. You know ... the Retard Games."

Callahan's head involuntarily jerked backward, his mouth falling open in shock. "The ... how did you ... wow, he really spilled his guts to you, didn't he? Or was that Mayetta?"

"Tell me what, for instance, your *K* flash card stood for?" Key leaned against the sofa cushion, crossed her arms, and waited.

"Tell her what *K* stood for," Jukey said quietly, when Callahan's mouth remained stubbornly shut.

Callahan looked at his hands, rubbed the ring. "Kick," he replied reluctantly, just loud enough for them to hear.

"*P*?" Key asked.

"Uh, push," Callahan muttered, nervously jiggling his legs.

More likely "punch," Key thought coldly. In her mind's eye she saw Wain with her red camera, eagerly searching the woods. They hadn't gotten to *P* yet, but when they did, she'd draw it lying flat on its back exactly as she'd choose to see Callahan at this moment, knocked out cold by her fists pushing, punching, pummeling, and pounding *his* face.

She shook her head and refocused. "*B*?" she asked, drumming her fingers on the sofa arm.

"Seriously?" Callahan retorted. "Are we going through the whole alphabet here?"

"Answer, son. If Key North wants to cover all twenty-six, we will go from *A* to *Z*." Jukey's voice was dangerously calm.

Callahan closed his eyes and shook his head. "*B* ... was for burn," then he added hastily, "but I never actually *burned* him. And if anyone tells you different, they are *flat-out* lying. I just hovered my cigar over his skin."

Such a saintly snake in the grass. "*S*?" Key asked.

With every letter, Callahan's bravado disintegrated just a little more. He shook his head and grimaced. "Spit. Only did *that* a couple times."

Only. At least she knew he was telling the truth about that one. "*D*?"

"Uh, dunk. Like, hold him under, in the pool." Callahan almost involuntarily held his hand out, palm down, level with the chair arm, as though Wain's head was under it.

Key picked up the backpack again. "I think we all get the ugly, sickening picture, and unfortunately I'm sure we're just scratching the surface." She leaned forward, trying not to picture Wain's suffering at the hands of this man, fighting to keep her voice modulated, but she knew her eyes were blazing. "I still need to know *why* though. Did Wain's presence in your house offend you somehow? Did you hate having to provide for him? Was he chronically disobedient? Were you embarrassed that he couldn't read? Were you jealous of his relationship with his mother? Did he leave his bike in your driveway on purpose so you could *break it up and throw it away*? *Why* would you choose to inflict pain and torment and unending fear relentlessly, brutally onto a vulnerable, helpless little boy? A child who did absolutely nothing wrong except have the terrible misfortune of having a mother who chose you!"

She didn't expect an answer, but before their eyes, Callahan seemed to deflate, as if Key's furious words had zapped the cocky belligerence right out of him.

"I can only say that in almost every situation, I had had too much to drink." He repeated his previous excuse almost inaudibly, slowly shaking his head. "And for what it's worth, I had pretty much quit doing anything to him the last few months. Regardless, Wain *didn't* deserve it."

From his corner, Jukey gave a disbelieving snort. "Well, if that isn't the all-time kicker. You apparently *do* know right from wrong. That makes your actions ten times worse."

As Callahan continued staring at his hands, Key sipped her coffee and studied him, startled that he seemed genuinely uncomfortable in the face of their accusations. He was weak. A typical bully, preying on the helpless. Of course, it was just as likely that she and Jukey were watching a master manipulator at work. Maybe he was simply acting the part and saying what he knew she wanted to hear. Well, it was a waste of her time to try and discern the man's motives. They needed to move on, and Jukey's piercing words were the perfect way to end that piece of the conversation.

She tilted her head. Back to the question he still hadn't fully answered. "Again, I'm curious, Mr. Callahan, how did it happen that you were arrested *that* morning? May 17, Wain's birthday?"

Callahan lifted his chin and fixed his eyes on her. Unflinchingly, Key stared back. She could see the wheels turning in his head. *How much does this old lady know?* He shifted slightly in his chair and took a deep breath. He seemed to have come to a decision.

"Because I arranged for the police to arrest us that morning," Callahan said slowly and deliberately, now sitting still as a statue, his wintry eyes never leaving her face. "I'm the one who turned us in … and I did it to save Wain's life."

Chapter 45

SECRETS

Key and Jukey exchanged glances, and he gave her a slight nod that said, *You were right.*

"To save Wain's life?" Key repeated. "Would you explain that?"

Callahan again became more combative. "How do I know you and Lyric haven't set me up?" he challenged. "That you won't go straight to her with this?"

Key shook her head and gave a slight laugh. "Believe me, we are *not* fans of Lyric's." *Or yours.* "We're here only for Wain's sake."

Callahan sighed, then after a moment slowly lifted his right hand and rubbed his thumb across his fingers in the universal symbol meaning *cash*. The emerald in his ring flashed, reflecting the light from the lamp beside his chair. "It was all about money, of course. What is it *ever* all about with Lyric? About two years ago, she took out a quarter-million-dollar insurance policy on Wain, with the sole intent of cashing it in at some point."

The room crackled with the intensity of his unsaid meaning. Jukey sat stone-still, with the rifle across his lap, never taking his eyes off Callahan. Key was very grateful for his presence.

"By 'cashing it in,' you mean Wain had to die," Key stated bluntly, cringing as she said the shattering words aloud. Callahan needed to know she wasn't going to skirt the truth. Here she was once again, she thought in wonder, stating hideous pieces of information as matter-of-factly as if she were ordering food from a menu. It boggled the mind.

"Yes." Callahan nodded, crossing one ankle over his knee, again jiggling his foot nervously. His face had lost color. "It took me a long, long time to believe she was truly serious about it, but yeah, naturally, in order for her to cash in on the policy, Wain, uh, had to die." He pointed to his own chest. "And his death was supposed to be *my* job. In Lyric's twisted mind, she'd taken all the risks, even getting arrested twice for other lesser thefts, writing bad checks and so on. So in her mind, I owed her. But *murder*? Seriously? *No way*. I refused, over and over, thinking of course she'd come to her senses, realize how absolutely insane it was. For the last several months, we fought about it constantly, and by the time Wain's birthday rolled around, Lyric flat-out informed me that if I wouldn't do it, she would. She ultimately made a plan that during a pool party with just the three of us on the evening of his seventh birthday, Wain would 'accidentally' drown." He shook his head. "She's deranged."

As opposed to your plain-and-simple abusive, bullying evilness, Key thought. Wain had barely escaped the unspeakable, terrifying darkness that had surrounded him. "So you decided to …?"

Callahan shrugged, compressing his lips. "I had to do something. She wouldn't let up. And I couldn't leave her, break up with her, you know? If she was alone with Wain, he had no chance. Do you have any idea what it's like to realize your girlfriend is willing to kill her own kid? It terrified me. I bit the bullet, went to my great-uncle, who owns the Sojourner, and confessed to him about the embezzlement, requested that he have us arrested. He was—"

Key interrupted. "What's your great-uncle's name?"

"Carl Drexel. Why?"

"Just wondering." Key set down her cup of now-cold coffee and jotted the uncle's name on her paper, then asked, "Why not just turn

Lyric in for embezzlement? Get *her* arrested. That would have saved Wain. Why turn yourself in too?"

"Not an option. Lyric had incontrovertible proof of my involvement in the hotel theft, so I *had* to get out in front of her with the truth of my part. Seriously, though, by then, confessing to my uncle was the least of my worries. Wain's life was on the line; and, frankly, mine too. Her threat was that once Wain drowned 'accidentally,'"—Callahan made quote marks with his fingers—"if I turned her in or even broke up with her, she'd implicate *me* in being involved in Wain's death. Given my, uh, history with him, no one would have doubted her. I know Mayetta has witnessed some, um, incidents between Wain and me. It would have been my word against Lyric and Mayetta."

"History? Incidents?" Jukey put in scornfully. "Why the euphemisms? Why not just say Mayetta saw you *abuse* Wain on multiple occasions?"

Callahan pretended not to hear, but he shifted awkwardly in his chair, rubbing his neck, then laced his hands together and cracked his knuckles. He appeared shell shocked. This was obviously not what he'd been expecting when he'd stepped onto Key's porch.

"Give us a timeline," Key demanded. "I want to hear how it all unfolded." She had a pretty good idea, but she wanted to hear his version.

Resigned, Callahan replied in a flat voice, "On May 16, I had a long talk with Uncle Carl. I told him I was sick of the lying and thieving and hoped he'd give me a chance to make it right. But it was so urgent that I told him a lie: I said that Lyric and I had planned to take Wain and leave the country on May 18 on the *Knotty Cal*—that's my boat—taking all the money she—we—had embezzled. It wasn't hard to persuade Uncle Carl to have the cops arrest us at my place early in the morning of May 17. He was all for that scenario, of course—he didn't want a public arrest at his hotel. Bad for business to see the GM and the accounts manager in cuffs," he added, as though they needed an explanation. "But you have to believe me, I mainly did it to save Wain's life. I may be a lot of things, but I'm *not* a murderer."

Jukey spoke up again. "Fine line between child abuse and murder in my mind, Mr. Callahan."

"Why not just tell your uncle the truth?" Key asked. "That Lyric was going to drown Wain and try to pin it on you?"

Callahan looked down and rubbed his fingers over his lips, as if attempting to keep his words from spilling out. "Well, uh, I couldn't tell him *how* she was blackmailing me, that she had evidence that ..." He cleared his throat. "That ... I had a history ... that I had hurt Wain."

"So you don't want your family to know you're a child abuser." Jukey, direct as ever, got right to the point. "Is that what you're saying?"

"Well ... yes."

Jukey shook his head. "Truth to cover lies, lies to cover truth. This is the most convoluted story of low-down cowardice, maliciousness, and greed I have ever had the misfortune to hear."

"The main issue is true. I didn't want Wain to die," Callahan said again, chewing on his lower lip, still jiggling his foot. He picked up his sunglasses and unfolded them, then set them back on the table.

"Did your uncle really have you both arrested, or was it just Lyric?" Key asked.

Callahan laughed humorlessly. He had perfectly straight white teeth. *Probably veneers.* "Oh no, they're pressing full charges against both of us, but Lyric's two priors and Uncle Carl's influence were the reason she didn't make bail. Uncle Carl insisted I sit in jail for four days; talked my parents out of helping me. And there are conditions."

"Conditions?" Key asked. It spoke volumes that the man in front of her was forty years old and still relying on his parents to unsnarl his messes.

"Oh yeah. Reimbursement, every penny. He's not messing around. I get the book thrown at me if I don't repay it. The problem is, only Lyric knows how to access that money, and she says she absolutely won't do it until she's out too. My instructions are to bring the backpack to Florida, get her out on bail, and then she'll repay the money."

Not once had Callahan referenced SplishFlash, but he had to know about it, Key thought. Why else would he be there?

She held the backpack up again. "Why is Lyric so keen for you to get your hands on this? And why would you risk jumping bail to come all the way to North Carolina to get it?"

"Why do you even care?" he answered angrily, returning Jukey to alert status. "Didn't we have a deal? Lyric's letter for Wain's backpack?" He lifted his right hand and one by one bent the fingers on his left, enunciating each point slowly, as if they were slow witted. "Lyric told me she needs the backpack, the whole thing with cars *and* paperwork. I am to bring it back to Florida. I am to get her bailed out. Then she'll access the accounts from wherever she's hidden them, and repay Uncle Carl. That keeps me out of jail. That's *all* I know."

Key unzipped both zippers and pulled out tiny SplishFlash, which she'd returned to the backpack earlier. Without popping out the flash drive, she put the car on her palm and held it up for Callahan to see. "So what you're saying is, your *freedom* is contained in Wain's tiny little car right here?" She allowed herself just a little touch of triumphant smugness ... until she saw the confusion on his face.

Callahan looked at her like she was crazy. "My freedom? In that car?" It was obvious he had absolutely no idea what she was talking about.

Key thought quickly. "Do you recognize this particular car?" she asked.

"Nope. But I never paid much attention to them." He shrugged, then said brusquely, "For the hundredth time, I'm supposed to bring her the backpack. I'm just doing what I'm told, so I can get out of this mess."

Chapter 46

THANKS

Momentarily confused, Key glanced down at her notes. She'd been positive Callahan was aware of SplishFlash's significance, but he seemed genuinely clueless. She stood and tucked SplishFlash into her pocket. "I'm going to get us all something to drink," she stated, "and then I need to hear the whole story of the morning you and Lyric were arrested."

Callahan rolled his eyes and heaved an unenthusiastic sigh. "Of course you do. I don't know where Lyric got the idea you were a clueless old lady."

Key distributed cans of sparkling water and sat back down. "Okay. First question. Who put the backpack in the kitchen drawer?"

"Lyric. I didn't see her do it. The whole morning was insane. Wain went to school without his backpack, super-excited because he thought he was getting the car he really wanted. In reality, Lyric had posted his cars on an online auction site several days prior, and a few of them had sold the night before, for a shockingly good profit. She was going to ship them that day from work." He paused, turning the can around in his hands. "When she listed those cars a few days before his birthday, that was the end of it for me. I realized for sure how serious it had gotten. That Lyric would make sure Wain wasn't around to miss them. He almost caught her looking at her auctions on her phone one evening, which she thought was hilarious. He couldn't read, but he'd have definitely recognized those cars."

So Lyric planned to sell the cars. First SplishFlash, now this. Apparently there were no depths to which Wain's mother would not sink. Key stole a look at Jukey. He had laid his shotgun on the floor and sat holding his drink, one leg crossed over the other, appraising Callahan's words as carefully as if he were jury foreman in the snake-in-the-grass trial taking place in her living room. They were just missing a codefendant.

"Anyway," Callahan went on without prompting (Was he relieved to talk about it? It seemed that way to Key.), "that morning Lyric walks out to wave at Wain, always great at putting that loving-mom face forward when necessary, and she finds some, uh, foreclosure papers taped to our front door. Another issue we had going on." He grimaced. "So she rips them off the door and brings them in. I go upstairs to put on a shirt, and while I'm up there, the cops come. When I come down, two cops are in the kitchen, the papers are off the table, the backpack was nowhere in sight, and we were arrested." He shrugged and took a long swallow from his drink. "I didn't know where the backpack was—to be honest, I never gave it a second thought, until I visited Lyric in jail, which was a couple weeks after I'd bailed out—I'd gone straight from jail to the house for a few things, then to Tampa, moved onto my boat. And she went *ballistic* when I didn't find it in the drawer. Told me that if Wain had it, I *had* to get it back. So I'm here. That's it. That's all I know."

So he'd been living in Tampa. That explained why Mayetta hadn't seen his car in the garage.

"Just one more thing." Key picked up the manila envelope Jukey had brought back from the safe at SouthPaws and pulled out the *S* card. She pointed at the words "RETARD GAMES," then at "S IS FOR SPIT," and asked, "Whose writing is this?"

Callahan's jaw dropped. "You've *got* to be kidding me. How did you …? I took the box of cards with me when I packed up and went to my boat! I tore every one of them up and threw them away in the garbage at the marina!"

"The writing?" Key insisted, flapping the card.

Callahan was still reeling. "I have *no* idea where that came from. It's Lyric's writing. Those cards were her idea. I just ... used them." He was either a terrific actor, or he really didn't know the password was hidden on the card she held. She was inclined to believe him; he was so truly mystified that the ironic, ugly truth of his words "*I just used them*" didn't seem to register. But judging by Jukey's grim face, Key knew he'd caught it.

She knew, though, that Callahan wasn't lying about whose writing it was. It was what had almost knocked Key to her knees on the night of the Fourth of July. Lyric's handwriting on the letter from the jail perfectly matched the beautiful print on the flash card, proving that Wain's mother was not the passive bystander Key had initially thought. Lyric was actively involved, a sadistic instigator in her son's torment. SplishFlash's files and Callahan's own words had confirmed the rest. Now Key possessed every piece of information Callahan needed, which meant she was very happily going to cut Lyric's bargaining chip out of the picture.

But she didn't trust Callahan either. Both he and Lyric were snakes in the grass.

She glanced out the window at the dogwood rustling in the breeze, throwing confetti shadows onto the fence; it was past dusk. Time to wrap it up. *Hold it together, Key.*

She sat a little straighter. "Mr. Callahan, I'm a daily witness to the fallout from the terrors you inflicted on Wain, and there are no words strong enough to express my disgust at your revolting, despicable actions. There was a time when I gladly would have turned you in myself for what you've done to Wain; in fact, a part of me still feels that way. I would have called the police immediately, from this house, if you hadn't told me exactly what you did today, because I would have suspected you were complicit in a murder plot. I honestly don't know how you live with the shame of what you've done." She cleared her throat, fighting for control, then continued. "Whatever your convoluted motives were for confessing to the embezzlement, I do believe that saving Wain's life was the primary one. It was a choice that came at some cost to you, and it literally means Wain is alive because your confession separated him from Lyric. The letter you've brought me today will remove him from his so-called mother for good. For these two things, I do genuinely thank you." Her voice caught in her throat.

Callahan nodded slightly, not looking at her. *Was* he ashamed of himself? She would probably never know.

"I'm going to tell Wain's father everything, explain why I've made the decisions I have, why I'm not turning you in," Key went on. "Guy will be deeply grateful for what you've done *for* Wain, but he also already knows what you've done *to* Wain. You don't want to cross paths with him. You might want to change your name again, Derek Garth Calhoun."

For the third time (Or was it fourth? She'd lost track.), she'd ambushed him. Callahan blanched, thrown completely off-balance, then he said, almost to himself, "My mug shot."

Key let him believe that's where she'd learned his real name. "What I'm still not sure of is the truth of the rest of it. For all I know, you're planning to bail Lyric out, take off with the money, get on your boat, and sail away. I don't know whether to believe that your relatives truly plan to press charges against you, as you say."

"That's because you don't know my Uncle Carl," Callahan said grimly.

"Do you have your phone with you?" Key asked.

"It's in my bag." Callahan reached down.

"Stop right there. Stop. I'll get it." Jukey jumped up and seized the messenger bag, rummaged through it, and said to Key, "Laptop computer, charging cords, and this." He held up the phone. "Do you want me to give it to him?"

Callahan snorted. "Oh please. You were expecting what? A snub-nose revolver?"

Key ignored him. "No, I'll take it, Jukey, thanks. Passcode?" she asked Callahan.

"Aren't we cloak and dagger … 070681," he added quickly as Jukey picked up the shotgun.

Key scrolled through his contacts, found Carl Drexel, and sent his information to her own phone. "Mr. Callahan, you have my word that tomorrow I'll call your Uncle Carl myself to tell him how to access the money. I believe I owe you this." At his disbelieving look, she nodded, raising her eyebrows. "Yes, I have that information." She took a sip of her drink, savoring the moment. "And just for the record, regardless of what I promised Lyric, you're not taking Wain's backpack *or* the cars." *Maybe I am a bit of a SitG,* she admitted silently, *but only in the best possible way.*

Callahan shook his head, nervously turning his ring around and around. "Lyric will go crazy. She'll turn me in."

"For what?" Key asked. "She has no bargaining chip. Leave her where she is. You yourself told your uncle about the embezzlement, and I know how to access the files to repay him."

"She will find something, anything she can throw at me." Callahan seemed a little desperate, even fearful. *I had that relationship all wrong,* Key thought. *Whatever it was, whoever is wearing the pants, they deserve each other.* A few moments passed. Finally, Callahan said resignedly, "Fine. I'll tell my uncle to expect your call." He picked up his sunglasses, then set them down again, as if a thought had occurred to him. "If you want more evidence against Lyric, I've got a screenshot of a text of her asking me about the *D* card. I kept it because I was terrified she'd blame me for Wain's death."

"The *D* card?" Key asked curiously.

"*D* was for dunk, but also drown. That was her code. Occasionally she'd text me to ask if Wain finally read the *D* card. Just a reminder that I hadn't done my job."

With every sentence, it got uglier. *On some unconscious level,* Key thought, *Wain had to have been as mistrustful and afraid of his mother as he was of Callahan.*

Key handed Callahan his phone. "Text the screenshot to me."

When her phone pinged, she saw he'd sent exactly what he'd described. About a month before Wain's birthday, Lyric had texted Callahan to ask if Wain had read the *D* card (ending with a smiley emoji), and Callahan had replied, your insane no way NOT GONNA HAPPEN.

"Are we done here? Any more PI moments on your list?" Callahan put his hands on the arms of the chair and scooted forward. He seemed to have regained a bit of bravado.

"We're done," Key said.

They all stood, and an awkward silence ensued.

"Do you want to tell him what I've got stashed?" Jukey asked Key, as Callahan bent to retrieve his sunglasses and bag.

With effort, she kept the questioning look off her face. What was he talking about? "You go ahead, Jukey."

"I have copies of the evidence, should anything untoward ever happen to Key North or Wain ... or Mayetta Titus ... or even this backpack here. And think about the path you're on, son. It's not too late to change."

Callahan rolled his eyes. "Yeah. Well, no offense, Wyatt Earp, but I don't take advice from men who hold me hostage with shotguns. And for the record, I never plan to see any of you ever again."

Jukey paused from zipping his shotgun into its leather case and stared frigidly at Callahan. "And for the record, I'm not in the habit of allowing child abusers to walk free without a visit from the butt end of my Wyatt Earp shotgun here. So maybe you need to start counting your blessings."

As Callahan retreated quickly from Jukey toward the front door, Key finally saw the black widow spider on the back of his calf, but Mudflap Girl was hidden by his collar. Strange how life worked. In the woods that day, Wain's reference to that tattoo's legs had been the inspiration for their alphabet hunts.

She followed him out. "Derek," she called from the porch, causing him to turn as he unlocked his car. "Take *very* seriously what I said about Wain's father. Don't let your paths cross."

Chapter 47
SUNLIGHT

Key and Wain. Mid-July

ey had grown up in a prairie town surrounded by cornfields, with parents who weren't comfortable travelers. They preferred picnics at the lake near their home to any ocean beach and chose homegrown festivals over distant theme parks. The summer she was ten, though, they drove north and spent a rare four days at Wisconsin Dells. One afternoon, their trio joined a group tour at a cave, going deep into the hillside. Although it was well lit, and the stalactites and stalagmites were fascinating, Key could hardly wait to leave the chilly underground for the sunshiny warmth waiting outside. Her relief when they exited the cave remained her starkest memory from an otherwise fun-filled vacation.

The memory of that relief flooded over her when she'd hung up after her conversation with Callahan's temperamental, pugnacious great-uncle, who confirmed that Callahan had indeed confessed on May 16. Mr. Drexel and his attorney had been expecting her call, he told her; his great-nephew had given them a heads-up after he left Pike House, and was due to arrive at his office later that day. Once

Key provided the account numbers and passwords for the missing money, Mr. Drexel asked if he could send her a reward as a token of his deep gratitude. Key declined, but gave him an address in Chicago. If Mayetta hadn't found the backpack, she told him, they wouldn't be having this conversation.

For at least the fortieth time, as she and Wain drove to the bank that afternoon, Key mulled over the convoluted mess in which Lyric and Callahan had ensnared themselves. No wonder Lyric was insistent on making bail! Her organized files on SplishFlash were as precise as her handwriting: several bullet points listing reasons Callahan could be blackmailed or blamed for Wain's death in the pool, the quarter-million-dollar insurance policy on Wain with the agent's contact information, the phone number of a local crematorium, and a reservation confirmation for two at a hotel in Nassau in early June— once, Key surmised sardonically, Wain's funeral had taken place and his grieving mother could leave her job with the embezzled money, wait for an insurance payout, and seek solace with a margarita or five on the beach. Most monstrous and damning of all was Wain's obituary, already written, the cause of his death: drowning, and the date of death: his seventh birthday.

Callahan had been equally ensnared. He couldn't reveal Lyric's manipulative blackmail tactics or her murderous plans without admitting to his willing role in routinely abusing and traumatizing a helpless little boy. He'd have to stick with his explanation of wanting to turn over a new leaf. Maybe he would.

During Key's conversation with the Kings on their patio, Jukey and Mary had been invaluable in helping her compartmentalize the unknowns, the facts, the possibilities, and the maybes, as though the three of them were solving an enormous logic problem; and improbable as it seemed, they kept coming back to just one solution: Callahan had turned himself and Lyric in. They'd also agreed that if, on the evening he came to her home, Callahan had not admitted to this very action, Key would have called the police then and there, using the SplishFlash files as evidence that he and Lyric had been planning Wain's murder.

She was grateful, though, that it all had turned out as it did. If she had given the files to the police, as was her first instinct the night she'd opened SplishFlash, Callahan, as awful a man as he was, may have been unfairly blamed for plotting a murder. Wain would have been dragged into the center of yet another extremely traumatizing situation. His backpack and cars would have become evidence. Guy would have been called back from Dubai. Mayetta, too, would have been forced to be involved. With all that Wain had gone through, Key simply couldn't see her way clear to opening that can of destructive worms. Guy was coming for Christmas, and she would lay it all out for him, agree to do whatever he felt best; in the meantime, Lyric wasn't going anywhere. Carl Drexel had assured Key of that.

In the face of Wain's difficulties, Key knew she'd continually struggle to find full peace with her decision to let an abusive, bullying man simply go free. But running stubbornly parallel with that thought, like sunshine creating the shadow of a train, was the starkest, unlikeliest of truths: Derek Garth Calhoun (a.k.a. Gary Callahan) *had* saved Wain's life.

★★★

"Why'd we have to put SplishFlash in that weird drawer?" Wain asked as they walked out of the bank.

Key smiled down at him. "It's called a safety-deposit box, and remember how I told you that SplishFlash has important information stored on it? That's why I can't give it back to you. I want to show it to your dad when he comes to visit."

"Oh yeah. I'm really glad it wasn't FireFlyer or SunBolt." Wain patted his backpack.

She opened the back door of the Jeep, and he climbed in, hurriedly buckling his seat belt, then raising his fist in the air. "Yessss!" It had become a game where he tried to get it done faster than she remembered to ask if he had. This time, he'd beaten her to the click. "Are we gonna go for ice cream? Can we take a treat home to Faro?"

From the driver's seat, Key glanced over her shoulder and grinned at him. "Now what do you think I'm going to say to that?"

Chapter 48

MACK

Key and Wain. Late July

"DP! These are perfect!" Key exclaimed, leaning both hands on the kitchen table to better examine the hand-sketched house plans DP had laid out. "It's even better than I hoped! I'd show them to Wain, but he's spending the day at the pool with Ell and her mom."

It was as though DP had waved a magic wand. Pike House's interior would be transformed, with an open-space kitchen/dining/living room, a second bathroom added, and the bedroom currently housing her desk remodeled into a dedicated home office, with a picture window providing light and an expansive view of the front yard.

DP beamed as he patted an ecstatic Faro, who believed every visitor was there for him. "Just ideas for now, but I wanted to give you a rundown on what I'm thinking, get your input. This here's the breezeway, and we'll pour concrete for extra parking between the shed and the garage." He pointed to a tiny circle. "Be sure to show this to Wain—that right there is a basketball hoop! Might want to bone up on your HORSE game. Take a day or so to check everything over—get back to me with changes or additions …. Have you found a rental?"

"Yes! Granny Jewel knows a couple who plan to hit the road in their new RV. They need a house sitter for a few months, so it's a win-win. They'll be back by the new year."

"Here in Troy?" DP asked.

"Yes, about six blocks from the elementary school, on Veronica View."

"Sounds perfect. Since you all won't be living here, the wiring, pipes, and remodel will easily be done by December. Then you and little man can move back in, and we'll start on the garage."

"Do you have a minute to see what I've done out back?" Key asked. As they stepped through the kitchen door onto the new deck, she added, "I'm so glad you convinced me to screen the entire deck. Being able to close it off with these window panels during the winter makes it a year-round space."

"Not to mention, you won't have to deal with the pollen," DP observed. "I tell everyone they'll thank me come springtime for talking them into the more expensive option when their deck furniture isn't all dusty pea green for five weeks." He was exactly right. Pollen in the North Carolina springtime, Key had long since learned, was like nothing she'd ever experienced, a silent incessant sprinkling of almost iridescent green dust that settled everywhere for weeks on end.

To their right sat a long farm table between the built-in bench and three unmatched chairs she'd found at SouthPaws, and to the left was her brand-new, just-unwrapped outdoor seating; the navy-blue cushions contrasted perfectly with the pine floor's warm honey tones. She'd strung fairy lights across the length of the deck but would wait to add more finishing touches until after the remodel was fully complete.

From the deck door, three wide brick steps joined a rock path that led to the spacious open-air patio, with a stone fireplace on one side and an L-shaped arbor bordering two others. Already her backyard was the best space Key had ever owned, peaceful and invigorating all at the same time.

DP nodded his approval. "You've made everything look real nice, Miss Key! Homey and inviting. Molly and my parents are gonna love it."

"Thank you again, DP." Key adjusted two flowers in the pitcher on the table and looked around, bursting with satisfaction. "Wain loves it, especially the access to the backyard. I think our front porch is a little lonely." They laughed.

"There's space for a hanging bed right over there. Let me know," DP replied, grinning. "Wain will end up out here one way or another, I guarantee. My brother and I slept on our screened porch many a night as kids." He pointed outside. "This will grow even more beautiful once the new plants become a natural part of the landscape. Knowing something you've built is being used and enjoyed is the most satisfying piece of our job."

"Miguel and Benito will both be at the deck-warming party with their families."

"They told me. They're really looking forward to it. Gonna be a fun time. How many are coming?"

"Around twenty, I think. Oh, will you bring your guitar? And lawn chairs?" Key didn't have seating for the fireplace patio yet.

"Planning on it."

★★★

Key was in the front yard watering a newly transplanted clematis when she heard the crunch of car tires on the gravel drive. She tugged off her garden gloves, watching quizzically as a late-model silver SUV parked next to the fence and a man she'd never seen before emerged from the driver's side. He looked about her age, just under six feet tall, trim and handsome, standing very straight, with a full head of dark-brown hair going silver, deep-set brown eyes, a goatee, and an engaging smile. He was dressed simply, in jeans and a white Henley T-shirt and brown leather chukka boots.

He pulled off his sunglasses and put them in the car, then to Key's utter shock, he awkwardly held his phone up and away from his face and snapped a grimacing selfie. He tapped the phone, stared at it for a moment, made a face, said, "Oh well," and tapped again. Once he'd finished, he looked over the fence at Key and smiled. "Hi," he said in a deep friendly voice. "Are you Key North?"

What was *that* about? "Yes, I'm Key." She opened the gate, holding Faro's collar. "Are you here about the catering?" She had ordered dinner for her deck-warming party from Chix on Broadway.

"Catering? I have an open package of dill-pickle-flavored sunflower seeds and a half-full bottle of water in the car if you're in a pinch."

"Never mind, obviously not," she replied, laughing. *Who is this?*

"You don't have your phone with you, do you?" he asked.

"Yes, I do." Key patted the overalls pocket over her chest with her free hand. No phone. She'd left it in the kitchen after talking with DP.

"I'll wait out here while you get it." The man leaned casually on his car, arms folded, ankles crossed, still smiling a little, as though he was thoroughly enjoying himself.

"What's this about?" she asked. He wasn't the least bit threatening, but it was all very odd.

"Suggest you check your phone."

"Come, Faro." Key shut the gate, then went inside and retrieved her phone. "*What?*" she said to the empty kitchen, staring in consternation at a new message from Guy. It was an unflattering photo of the man in her driveway. Judging by her own loblolly pines in the background, it was obviously the selfie the stranger had taken moments before. Under the photo Guy had texted, He's better looking and generally happier than this. But he's legit. Please talk to him.

??? This man is in my driveway right now! she texted back.

I'm aware. I'm taking you at your word. Getting involved to the extent that I can. Talk to him. Catch up with you later.

Key went back to the gate. Her guest was now bending over the fence, petting a sanguine, tail-wagging Faro; a watchdog their canine adoptee was not.

"Nice pup," the man said, straightening up. "I'm a fan of calm dogs. That's quite the hairdo between his ears."

"That's Faro." She opened the gate again as she held up her phone. "So you're a friend of Guy's?"

"Yes, I am. Maxwell Simons. Mack. Guy is a very good friend. Coworker too." He gave Faro a final pat, then reached into his vehicle and retrieved a business card and a small paper bag with twine handles. He handed the card to Key. "That's the first selfie I've ever taken. It's shockingly bad. Or maybe I just like to think I'm better looking than that." He held out his hand.

Laughing, Key shook it. He had very nice hands. "Nice to meet you, Mack. Sorry I'm so grubby. You're with Citrine Oil? Would you like to come in?"

"I would, if you have time to talk?"

"I do. Just let me turn off the hose faucet." Key glanced at the business card, which had three lines: his name, a phone number, and an email. Tucking it into her pocket, she twisted the faucet handle, then led him through the house to the deck, Faro at their heels. "Have a seat. You're my first official deck visitor." She suddenly wished she was wearing something other than her ratty overall shorts and a now-sleeveless T-shirt she'd attacked that morning with a pair of scissors when the sleeves wouldn't stay rolled up. She'd kicked off her wellies at the door and was barefoot.

"Wow. This is a terrific space," Mack set his phone and the paper bag on a side table and walked to the railing, taking in the patio, the meadow, and the woods beyond. "A dreamworld for a kid. Well, for anyone. Impressive craftsmanship too." He dodged Faro, who was lapping sloppily from a nearby bucket of water and went to check out the other end of the deck.

"I have a wonderful builder. I'll be right back." Inside, Key scrubbed the stains off her hands and slipped into flip-flops, quickly checking her hair in the hallway mirror. She smoothed it into place, then shrugged, a little annoyed at herself. Who was she trying to impress? After loading glasses and beverages onto a tray, she rejoined Mack, who still stood, hands in his pockets, jingling coins. "We can sit over here. I have sparkling water or beer."

"Beer's perfect. Thanks," Mack said, taking a bottle and settling into one of Key's new easy chairs. "Where's Wain?"

Key set the tray on the coffee table and took a seat across from Mack, patting Faro's head. "Sit, buddy. Wain's swimming with friends. They'll be home by three."

Mack checked his watch. "About an hour. Okay."

"Did you work with Guy at the Houston facility?" Key asked.

Mack answered her question with a question. "Do you remember making a call to Citrine Oil awhile back?"

Startled, Key thought quickly. What now? How could Mack possibly know she'd made that call? She had hoped the attorney could find out how Callahan and Lyric's embezzlement from the Sojourner had been discovered, but the call had gone nowhere. "Yes," she answered, pouring sparkling water into her glass. "I called your legal department looking for an attorney who had researched some information for Guy, but they told me no one with that name worked there."

Mack nodded. "Ameera."

"Yes, that was it!" She gave him a dubious look. "I said Mira. That's not *that* far off."

"No, it's not. Ameera works for Guy. It's just that Ameera doesn't work for Citrine Oil."

"Really," she said matter-of-factly, leaning back and crossing her arms. She should have known the craziness wasn't over. Mack was watching her closely as she added, "That's a bit confusing."

"Yes, it is. Guy has not been at liberty to tell you the full extent of his job, but when we became aware you'd called—"

Key raised her eyebrows and shook her head. "I never gave my name."

"Your number showed up on a list we audit." Mack brushed a few drips of condensation off his jeans and took another swig.

The bubbles in Key's glass raced each other to the top, mirroring the rise of a tiny niggling question that in her recent frantically busy life, she hadn't allowed to surface. "Okay," she said slowly, "but how would they know my number is connected to Guy?"

"We have a list of Guy's contacts. It was an easy match, and calls at Citrine are recorded."

"We?"

"The audit team contacted me. I checked with Guy, asked him why you'd be calling Citrine, asking for Ameera. He said he'd been caught off guard early one morning during a particularly distressing conversation about Wain, and that he'd inadvertently mentioned Ameera's name to you, never expecting you'd pay such close attention, much less follow up in any way with Citrine. It was a mistake on his part, and we're fortunate it was you he was talking to."

"This conversation is like trying to lasso a basketball!" Key exclaimed, thumping her glass down a little harder than she'd intended. She leaned forward. "So *exactly* what are you telling me?"

Mack smiled. "I can give you limited but hopefully helpful information. Guy *is* employed by Citrine; he *does* have a position in their purchasing department; he writes software for them. All true, but for the past several years his work has also included a parallel primary job. Suffice it to say that what Guy does is vital—and his bona-fide knowledge of the oil business is a critical component. He's a very valuable asset to the *private* firm we both work for."

Key stared at him. "You're kidding." But she knew he wasn't. Silt was finally settling in a cloudy, muddled pond.

"No. You understand, it's imperative that this conversation stays here, between us."

Her head was spinning. "I understand. And it will. But I need to let this soak in."

"Take your time. First and foremost, Guy is extremely relieved that you'll finally know the truth behind many of his choices and the main reason why he can't have Wain with him. As a family member and Wain's guardian, you're entitled to know." He took another long drink.

A gentle breeze joined them on the deck, lifting the corners of the napkins on the tray and ruffling the leaves on the potted ficus Key had placed behind the sofa. As she watched two impossibly acrobatic bluebirds flit back and forth from her new arbor to the branches of the nearest oak, she began to replay the few conversations she'd had with Guy, examining his sentences through this new lens.

Mack was watching her. He exuded calm. Key said, "I was just thinking how difficult it must have been for Guy to let me think he was *that* callous when it came to Wain."

"Yes. It's been very hard. Once you became Wain's guardian, Guy was required to wait for us to okay your limited knowledge of our business, which, as I said, is private, not a government entity. And *even* then, he couldn't tell you on the phone or email or virtual anything. Hence, my visit today. You've passed with flying colors, by the way." Mack tipped his bottle out as if toasting her and bobbed his head.

Key tilted her cup back at him. "Well, that's good to know. Hopefully, no one withered away from boredom while researching me. Seriously, Mack, you have no idea how much this has lightened my heart!"

"Glad to hear it," Mack replied. "Feel free to ask questions. I may or may not answer."

Oh, she had questions. "Is Guy really in Dubai?"

"Oh yes. He's based there."

"And he speaks Arabic?"

"Fluently."

"Was Jessica, the girlfriend, real?" she asked, knowing she was probably being ridiculous but still feeling a little off-balance. Why would Guy make *that* up?

Mack leaned forward and placed his empty bottle on the tray. "Jessica is real. Guy has his normal life. We all do. He's been honest with you; it's more about what he *couldn't* tell you."

None of it sounded normal to Key. "His normal life just hasn't included Wain." She didn't intend for her words to sound harsh, but they probably did. However important Guy's line of work, he had not carved out time for his son. She knew she would be able to process that, but could Wain?

Mack cleared his throat, then after a moment replied, "That is true, unfortunately. In Guy's defense, much of his absence, especially in the first year and a half, was due to training. He was gone for months at a time." His intense brown eyes met Key's. "He wants that to change."

"I know. We've talked about it. Wain's had a hard time, and Guy is paying an emotional price too."

"Yes, he is. I'm truly sorry about that." As they continued their conversation, Mack toyed with the little brown bag he'd brought in with him, picking it up and setting it down several times. Key found him very easy to talk to; they discussed Key's move, Guy, Wain, family, and the deaths of their respective spouses. Mack's wife, he told her, had succumbed to melanoma several years earlier. "I mostly work and hang out with a gaggle of little kids," he said, grinning. "I've got five grandchildren, and for some reason, they all think I'm the greatest. Being a grandfather is very humbling. I have a flight out early tomorrow morning, got a birthday party tomorrow night for my granddaughter who's turning eight, but if it's all right with you, I'll check in from time to time."

"Of course!" Key exclaimed. "Any means of staying in closer contact with Guy is a bonus." Impulsively, she added, "Would you like to stay for dinner? I'm making pork chops in the slow cooker."

He didn't even hesitate. "I would have started hinting if you hadn't asked. Love to. It smelled delicious in there."

Key laughed. *He's so nice.* Once Wain got home, she'd have him show Mack his CartWheels, so she could change into something with uncrooked sleeves.

Faro suddenly raised his head, then galloped to the door, whining eagerly, jumping aside just in time to avoid getting hit when it flew open. Wain and Ell tumbled through, still in their swimsuits—hair askew, cheeks pink from the sun, mouths stained with orange. Wain held his backpack and wore his CartWheels towel draped around his neck. He immediately bent and put his arms around Faro.

"Miss Key! Miss Key? There's a weird car in your ... oh!" Ell exclaimed, surprised. She stopped short as Key and Mack stood up.

Key gave both children a quick hug. "Hi, kids! I spy something orange on those lips! How was swimming?"

Ell shrugged. "Eh. Broken straw."

"Broken straw?" Key braced herself for the latest Cav-inspired Ell-ism.

Ell put a hand on her hip. "Didn't suck!"

"Didn't suck!" Wain echoed, laughing helplessly, and Key and Mack joined him.

"I should have guessed," Key said. "By the looks of things, you two obviously had fun!"

"It was *so* fun. Wain dived. I taught him. Didn't you?" Ell draped her arm around Wain's shoulders and gazed at him like a proud mother. Her proprietary pride in any new accomplishment on Wain's part was always humorously touching.

"Wow! You *dived*?" Key asked Wain.

He gave her a big grin and nodded.

"High five!" she held out her hand and both children slapped it. "That's awesome! I can't wait to see! Kids, this is Mr. Simons. He stopped by for a visit."

Mack was still laughing. "Just Mack is fine. I'll have to remember the broken straw. Grandkids will love it." He raised his eyebrows and addressed Wain. "Whew! I've seen the pictures, but in person you are a mini-Guy with longer hair." Key wondered if Wain would ever get tired of hearing that. He'd just have to get used to it; she sensed there was a lot more to come.

A horn honked, and Ell made a face. "My mama's in the car with Dibsy. She just wanted to make sure you were home. Bye, Wain! Tell Miss Key all about diving in the deep end!" She raced out the deck screen door and around the house, waving to acknowledge she'd heard Key calling after her, passing on her thanks to Gayle.

In the sudden wash of silence that only Ell's sudden absence could create, Mack held out his hand to Wain. "I'm Mack to all my friends, and I think we're gonna be friends."

"Mack is a good friend of your dad's," Key added.

"Hi." Wain shook hands, still shy. He set the towel and backpack on the coffee table.

Mack sat back down. "It's great to finally meet you, Wain." He handed Wain the small paper bag. This is for you, a gift from your dad. He said to tell you he'd be here if he could."

"From *my real dad*? Thanks." Wain opened the bag and took a peek inside, his blue-green eyes widening as though he couldn't believe what he was seeing, then he pulled out a small colorful package containing a glittering, snowy-white CartWheel. "Black Diamond! My *dad* got me Black Diamond!" he exclaimed joyfully, clutching it to his chest. His ecstatic face said it all.

Chapter 49

DECK PARTY

Key and Wain. Early August

"It's a wonderful party and a really lovely space, Key." Mary appeared from the kitchen onto Key's new deck, holding a glass of white wine. "Perfect for a big group. Reynold was so excited to come."

They stepped out the screen door and paused on the brick steps. Behind them, laughter and conversation mingled with the sound of clattering dishes as the catering crew from Chix on Broadway cleaned up, moving quickly back and forth through the house to their food truck in the driveway. Their last job would be to line up the gift bags on the deck table.

"Wain would have been so disappointed if he hadn't! Thanks for bringing him; I'm sorry Serena couldn't make it." Key smoothed her dress and put her hands on her hips, surveying the outdoor patio. "Do you know, Mary, except for Iris and Clive, every person here is someone I've met since moving to this house just ten weeks ago! How is that possible?"

Had she successfully masked her shock when she answered a knock at her front door and saw Iris and Clive standing there? Key wasn't sure. Since that acrimonious phone call, she had not heard a single word from Iris, but remembering her long-ago promise to invite the Lompocs to her deck warming, Key had (with some trepidation) dialed Iris's number. When Iris didn't pick up, Key stubbornly sent a text, also unanswered. No doubt she'd been blocked. Well, she could be stubborn too. As a last resort, she sent a paper invitation via the US Postal Service, and now here they were, with absolutely no warning. Though civil, Iris had remained cool to Key, but Clive was his usual genial self, and Key suspected he had been the one who'd gotten the mail and opened the invitation; she had no doubt he was the reason behind their attendance. *It is what it is*, she told herself, too busy to spend much time with them but glad she'd found the courage to rise above the angry words Iris had hurled at her. *And it will be what it will be. But it **won't** be what it was.* As the evening went on, Iris had at least relaxed a little. She and Clive had taken their drinks and joined Gayle, Dibsy, Molly, and Benito's wife, Soledad, all of them drawn in by the sidesplitting nonstop banter between Granny Jewel and Jukey, who had known one another all their lives. The stories were flying back and forth, with bursts of laughter escaping from where the group had congregated under an awning Key had put up. If anyone could show Iris the value of life out here, Key thought, it would be Jukey and Granny Jewel.

Just off the patio, Lonny and DP stood conversing with the older Dawsons; judging by his gestures, Key guessed DP was describing the construction project. Alongside the arbor, Benito, Miguel, Cav, and Miguel's wife, Ana, were finishing what was obviously a very close game of cornhole. Wain, Ell, Reynold, Benito's son, Aldo, and Miguel's daughter, Dolly, had started a game of freeze tag down by the rock with Faro in the thick of it, trying in vain to herd his group of charges.

"You and Wain have had the full-immersion baptism by fire, a lifetime compacted into ten weeks," Mary commented. "Jukey is still on cloud nine from his part in the Callahan drama, but he regrets that he didn't grab the man and shake the living daylights out of him, rattle his teeth, maybe throw him off the porch."

Key laughed. "Understandable. I think I did enough shaking for all of us that night. I've never been so nervous. I'm so grateful for both of you!"

Mary nodded. "We were more than happy to help. People sure can mess up the one life they're given, can't they? No word from Wain's mama or Callahan?"

"Not a peep. I don't expect it! Lyric will remain in jail for the foreseeable future; no word yet on what's going to happen. I'll let Guy keep tabs on that."

"I hope she's there for a long, long time," Mary replied fervently, then added with a laugh, "You know, what with Jukey and the gun and all, we agreed it's best to let some time go by before we even tell our kids what happened. Then it's bound to become legend."

Key laughed too. "My lips are sealed. But Jukey is already a legend, isn't he?"

"Oh, he is that. This will add to the lore. And Wain's daddy? Is he coming around to the idea of spending time with his little boy?"

It was difficult to let Mary think more poorly of Guy than was necessary, but that could not be helped. "Oh yes. Guy had his first video chat with Wain last night. It was pretty emotional; Guy was so regretful, and Wain is naturally shy, but it'll get easier as they get better acquainted. The real connection occurred when Wain showed Guy his car collection." *CartWheels, bless those little cars.* "But in Wain's eyes, Guy has already hit hero status. Black Diamond is the new favorite car by a mile, and a big part of that is because of who gave it to him."

"He showed me the car, told me it was from his daddy. It's like a miracle that they can talk face-to-face. Some of what Jukey calls 'electronic voodoo' isn't all bad. How's Wain's reading going?"

Key smiled. "That's another work in progress, more high hopes. He's very proud of himself because he recognizes all the uppercase letters now. Along with doctor and dentist appointments next week, we have a visit scheduled with his new school. They've been very encouraging."

She had finally showed Wain the "Alphabet Woods" notebook he'd unknowingly helped her create, with pictures of the twenty-one letters he'd so far photographed in the woods. He'd immediately asked to hunt for the remaining five so they could finish the book together: B, D, G, P, and Q. These shapes might be their biggest challenge yet, but they were up for it. They were going for another hike tomorrow.

"Maybe living in town for the first half of the school year will be a positive thing," Mary observed.

"I think so!" Key answered. "And much easier if he needs remedial classes or tutoring for a while." They stepped onto the path. "Time to mingle."

Mary headed down to join Jukey, but Key's phone pinged from the pocket of her dress. She pulled it out and glanced at it, delighted to see the name at the top.

How's the party going?

She quickly texted back. It's been perfect. Wish you could have come!

I got short notice from the host. Not knowing me till two days ago is no excuse. =) I booked a fly-fishing trip to NC in Oct! Bringing my granddaughter. Maybe you and Wain can join us? I'll call you later.

Since his visit, Mack had phoned both nights after Wain went to bed, and they'd talked for hours. Her new deck would always be the setting where her life had taken yet another serendipitous turn. Key was content, though, that at this point there was some distance and Mack's work between them. She needed time to become acquainted with her new life: with Wain, Guy, *and* this new version of herself.

After she'd made the rounds visiting with each of her guests and finishing with the children, Key took Wain's hand and strolled to the outdoor fireplace. "Hey, everyone, please grab a drink and have a seat," she called. She waited, still lightly holding Wain's sweaty little hand while everyone toted their chairs over to the outdoor patio space and settled in, then cleared her throat, smiling affectionately at the familiar faces beaming back at her. "Dawson and DP have a song for us, but first I just want to say thank you all for coming. I hope this is the first of many get-togethers! This home is the *first* place Wain and I have lived together, and in the short time we've been here, each of you has contributed to making it the *best* place we've ever lived. The future looks as bright as this beautiful sunset! Thank you all from the bottom of my heart." She thought of the card she'd designed and added, "From the top too."

To her great surprise, when she sat down, Wain dragged his chair over beside hers, leaning into her as she put her arm around him.

DP and his father stood and retrieved their instruments from behind the fireplace, and while they tuned them up, Dawson II said, "Key has asked us to play a song for you all, but especially for Jukey. We understand it's your favorite, sir, and we didn't get to it on the Fourth of July. It's mine too, and I just got news this week that ... well, hold on a sec." He turned to DP. "Want to say anything, son, or am I speaking out of turn? I'm busting to tell!"

DP stepped forward, a huge smile across his face. "We still got blue confetti all over our lawn! Molly and I just found out we are gonna have a fishing partner for his PawPaw here!" Over clapping and congratulations, Dawson II called, "Here you go, Jukey! 'Fishing Line.'"

> *When I was just a little boy, eight and turning nine,*
> *My grandpa brought a gift to me, a box tied up with twine.*
> *"Open it," he said, a happy twinkle in his eye.*
> *"I've brought you love and happiness, and the secret code to life."*
>
> *Oh, I opened up the box and saw nothing but some string.*
> *What could he be thinking? This was such a boring thing.*
> *"It's just a piece of fishing line." I was a disappointed boy.*
> *"Yes, fishing line," he said to me, "the quiet key to joy."*
>
> *It's a beat-up metal tackle box; it's slippery feet on river rocks;*
> *It's digging worms in the chilly dawn; it's evenings at the pasture pond;*
> *It's sandwiches that Grandma made; it's naps at high noon in the shade;*
> *It's companionship and solitude, conversation and interlude;*

It's stick with what's familiar; it's explore the great unknown;
It's hanging out with buddies; it's standing on your own;
It's the lake at sunrise, red and gold; it's growing up and growing old;
It's dare or truth and lies this big; it's sing the blues; it's dance a jig;

It's stand back, son; it's take a bow; it's give it time; it's do it now;
It's dry runs, hot spells, try again; it's victory, but you don't know when;
It's thinking hard, or going blank; it's deposits at the riverbank;
It's hiking to the mountain brook; it's tie a fly, bait a hook;

It's sunlit rocks on the riverbed, hope hanging by a gossamer thread;
It's the deepest understanding of a love you can't define.
It's flying and it's landing—all tied up in fishing line.
It's escape and it's the daily grind—all tied up in fishing line.
It's Mother Nature, Father Time—all tied up in fishing line.

Oh, you'll forget the heartbreak and the sorrow you've been through.
The rocking of the vessel will bring sweet peace to you.
The breeze will blow away your pain; the sun will warm your soul.
Your life becomes the clearest when you hold a fishing pole.
You might catch or tell a whopper, but, son, it's not a lie.
That every gift of life, you'll find, is all tied up in fishing line.

Their voices blended perfectly, meandering toward the four majestic oaks, the path, the woods, and upward to the evening sky, mingling with a luminous wash of orangey-pink cirrus clouds that lay stubbornly still above the horizon, unwilling to leave just yet. When the song ended, there was a silence, as though the words had reached deep enough into their souls that nothing remained to be said.

You'll forget the heartbreak and the sorrow you've been through. Yes, she and Wain *would* go fly-fishing with Mack and his granddaughter. If Key got tired of casting, she would stow away her fly rod and pick up her camera.

From his place beside Key, Wain raced off to join his friends, obviously not the slightest bit worried she'd be upset that he'd clumsily tipped over his chair in the process. She set it right, then leaned back, admiring the sublime sky, unsurprised by the sudden tears that sprang to her eyes. *Beautiful Edie,* she telegraphed to the clouds, *do you see him? He's the best gift I've ever gotten ... but oh, how I wish he could have known you.*

Behind her, Key heard Miguel's daughter, Dolly, ask Wain, "Who's that lady in the blue-flowered dress?"

"Oh, that's Key," Wain said her name as easily as if she were a CartWheel. "She takes care of me 'cause my dad's gone right now. She's *kinda* like my cousin, but she's more *really* like my grandma."

Acknowledgments

ll my life, my mind had said to me, "You can't draw." So when I reluctantly signed up for an art class, in the process of getting my bachelor's degree at age forty something, I was dreading the pathetic results I'd create. The first day, we were given the book *Drawing on the Right Side of the Brain* by Betty Edwards and shown a way to draw a Beetle Bailey cartoon—I know, this dates me! To my amazement, I drew it perfectly! It changed my entire outlook. The method this book teaches allows the brain to circumvent negative thoughts, and this is where I got the general idea for Key's innovative forays into the woods with Wain. Thank you, Betty Edwards, and thank you to my art-class teacher!

Wain's character is very, *very* loosely based on a young man I met nearly twenty years ago at an adult literacy center, where I worked with him as he struggled to simply recognize the letters of the alphabet. His backstory provided the seed of inspiration for this book. Dear friend, even though you gave up after several sessions and never (to my knowledge) came back, I so hope you found a way to learn to read. I hope you were able to put those demons to rest. Thank you for sharing your story with me.

In early 2022, I asked the editors at Warren Publishing in Rock Hill, South Carolina, to read the first draft of *The Alphabet Woods*, and that was where it all began. My heartfelt thanks to Amy Ashby, Melissa Long, Mindy Kuhn (cover design), and everyone else at Warren for their encouragement, guidance, enthusiasm, and great communication. I am also very grateful to developmental editor Erika Nein and copy editor Melisa Graham for their skills and insights on my storytelling and character development; and thank you to Marketing Director Lacey Cope for her assistance with marketing. Every one of these ladies worked hard alongside me to help Key's story unfold the way it did.

Thank you to the warm and welcoming wonderful state of North Carolina.

Thank you to a huge contingent of relatives and friends for your listening ears, and to all who have been so enthusiastic over the past year! Your belief in the end result kept me energized and focused.

Thank you to those who willingly read *The Alphabet Woods* in its most raw, inelegant stages and shared encouragement and very helpful thoughts, especially my three daughters, Lindsay, Danica, and Courtney.

Thank you to our grandchildren, whose emerging personalities, lively conversations, and hilarious observations helped me develop Wain and Ell.

And last, so much love and gratitude to my husband and best friend, Ken, who read the book all the way through three times and spent dozens of hours just listening to me, treating the characters as friends, discussing the plot, expanding on my ideas, providing feedback, and feeling emotion in the right places. He patiently held down the fort while I was hanging out with Key and Wain, typing them into existence word by word. I could not ask for a better True North.

CPSIA information can be obtained
at www.ICGtesting.com
Printed in the USA
LVHW041312170523
747145LV00029B/558